Heather Phillips grew up and lives in Hampshire with her husband, Ian, and two grown-up children. She has always had a story or two going around in her head and decided at last to try writing one down, hence this book was born. It just goes to show you never know what you can do until you try. Heather loves gardening, which is rapidly taking second place in her affections to writing. She has two cats, Bertie and Coco, who have 'helped' enormously in the writing of this book.

For Ian, Abby and Sam. With love.

Heather Phillips

A MOZART KIND OF MORNING

AUSTIN MACAULEY PUBLISHERS™

LONDON * CAMBRIDGE * NEW YORK * SHARJAH

A CIP catalogue record for this title is available from the British Library.

ISBN 9781398468962 (Paperback)
ISBN 9781398468979 (Hardback)
ISBN 9781398468986 (ePub e-book)

www.austinmacauley.com

First Published 2023
Austin Macauley Publishers Ltd®
1 Canada Square
Canary Wharf
London
E14 5AA

I would like to thank the team at Austin Macauley Publishers for their assistance in bringing this book to publication. Also, thanks to my parents, Audrey and Peter Jackson, for taking me on holiday to France and dragging me round numerous chateaux of the Loire Valley, giving me bucket loads of inspiration, my daughter, Abby, for being a willing volunteer in reading the first draft and giving me copious feedback (with illustrations!) and my husband, Ian, and son, Sam, for putting up with me while I squirrelled myself away writing each evening. I couldn't have done it without you all.

The love of gardening is a seed once sown that never dies.
Gertrude Jekyll

Table of Contents

Prologue

The room was dark and quiet apart from the laboured breathing of the waif-like form in the bed. You could be forgiven for thinking she was elderly from her pale papery skin and sunken cheeks, but cancer had taken its ugly toll, waging war with her body until she could fight no more. Her husband sat by the bed; his heart shattered into a million pieces.

'Listen to me,' she breathed. 'I want you to find happiness when I'm gone. Live life.' She closed her eyes, summoning the energy to continue. 'Make sure our son lives his dreams. Find him a love like we had,' she gasped, her breaths increasingly shallow. The end was near now, and she knew it. 'I want you to be free to love again. You have so much goodness in your heart, share that with someone.' She smiled weakly at him, her heart breaking to see his distress. She tried to squeeze the hand she held but she was so tired. She felt a hot tear escape the corner of her eye and run down the side of her face into her hair. 'I will always be near, my love, watching over you both.'

It was an hour later that her breathing finally stopped and she slipped peacefully from his life. How could he even think of a life without her? She was his life. They were life and breath to each other and had been since the day they met. Now he felt utterly bereft.

Chapter 1

Box hedges, Jo decided, were a wonderful addition to a garden until you were the person designated to trim them twice a year. Especially when you worked here. Standing up and rubbing the small of her back for the third time that morning, she looked out across the parterre before her. Sixteen large square-shaped beds, each delineated and criss-crossed with low hedging of different varieties, all waited their second trim of the year. They lay in the shadow of the grandiose chateau, where she worked as a gardener. Its blue slate turrets, white walls and dark windows watching over the garden. It was one of the most famous chateaux in the Loire Valley.

Across the garden, diagonally in the far corner, more of her colleagues were busy digging the faded annuals out from the spaces between the hedges and planting bulbs ready for the spring display. The next team would soon follow to plant winter bedding over the top. A seamless continuum of colour for the endless visitors to enjoy. Although it was now autumn and the busy summer months were over, tourists still roamed the famous gardens and marvelled at their beauty and order. She was glad this was only the autumn trim, just a tidy-up for the winter, not as time-consuming and messy as the late spring cut-back.

She was not alone in her task, working on the bed in the opposite corner from her was Serge. His tall gangly body and dark head bobbing up and down as he moved along, snipping off shoots that had seemingly sprung out at weird angles during the summer growth. She was relieved to be far enough away from him to avoid having to make polite conversation. There was something about him that made her feel uneasy, an awkwardness in his behaviour towards her that made her think he was always somehow watching her. Just looking at him made her shiver.

Jo casually glanced at her watch. Five to eleven! Holy moly! She was going to be late. Dropping her tools and gloves into the trundle trolley that held all her useful bits and pieces and quickly fastening down the lid, she made a dash for a door in the side of the chateau. Speed walking rather than running, it would not do at all to look sweaty and out of breath.

'Darling, we were about to send out a search party!' exclaimed Miles taking a lace-edged handkerchief out of his top pocket and twirling it gaily in the air. He pirouetted in his embroidered frock coat and wig. 'Our public awaits! Depeche-toi!'

'Sorry, I lost track of time,' she replied, somewhat muffled by the dress that was being dropped over her head by the other performers. 'Quick, wig!' she squeaked as her dress was zipped up from behind. These costumes were far too tight! The powdered wig was plopped on her head and Jo hurried over to the mirror to tuck away strands of dark hair that poked out from underneath. Finally satisfied with her appearance, she and the other performers swept their way along the corridor smiling to the visitors who then followed in their wake to the main salon of the chateau, where a larger crowd of visitors waited expectantly for the morning concert.

Music had been part of Jo's life for as long as she could remember. One of her earliest memories had been sitting on her father's lap pressing piano keys with her short chubby fingers as he performed for her mother. Sometimes her mother would whisk her up into the air and dance around the room with her in time to the music, the room spinning around them as they twirled. It was a happy childhood memory that Jo kept tucked away in her heart.

Now she was the performer, sitting at the harpsichord in the opulent salon, playing some of the finest pieces of Renaissance and Baroque music ever written. On occasion, she would close her eyes whilst playing and imagine that the rustlings of the tourists were in fact the rustlings of court ladies and gentlemen, dressed in their finest silks, gossiping about the latest intrigues of the day.

She and her fellow musicians had put together a playlist which lasted about half an hour and tracked the history of the chateau around them. Normally a piano player, she had been persuaded to take up the harpsichord to become part of the group that gave concerts twice a day throughout the summer months to the tourists.

The crowd hushed and the concert began, each of the musicians dressed in Renaissance costume to give a more authentic performance. However good they looked, on a hot summer day when the chateau salon was bursting with tourists, it was stifling to be sat for even half an hour in a full costume and wig, the latter of which could be horribly itchy sometimes. Still, this was their last week of performances and, apart from a couple of Christmas concerts, she would be done with dressing up for the year. Playing in the concerts earned her extra money too, all of which came in useful for paying the bills which seemed endless when one had an elderly relative in a care home to look after. Now the concerts were finishing, she would have to eke out her gardening salary carefully. Perhaps she could get an evening job in one of the cafes nearby to help make ends meet.

As she mused on these thoughts, they reached the part of the programme where she and Miles sang a duet. She felt she was not a particularly strong singer, but her voice was soft and melodious and as no one else had been willing, she had stepped forward. He was a born performer and revelled in attention whether playing his violin and singing in a concert or leading groups of Japanese tourists around the interior of the chateau as a guide. As the music began, she opened her mouth to sing.

Thomas and Henri had arrived early at the chateau that morning. They were due to meet Alain for lunch at one but had decided that for old times' sakes they would have a wonder around, even though they had both been several times before. Henri had noted on entry that they did concerts now and as a former professional pianist, he was keen to hear what was on offer.

'Thomas, we must make sure we visit the salon at eleven. We'll still have time to do the rest of the main staterooms before we see Alain.'

'Ok Dad, but don't tire yourself out doing the house,' Thomas replied looking at his father with concern. 'Remember that Alain said he was going to show us around the garden after lunch to see the changes they have made. I'm sure that will involve quite a lot of walking.'

'Nonsense! I'm as fit as a fiddle,' he retorted. 'I may be slightly greying at the edges, but I'm not dead yet!' He chuckled to himself. He loved that his son looked out for him but wished he would worry less. This trip was supposed to be a holiday as well as a research trip for Thomas and he for one was going to drink in every moment of pleasure possible. It had been a few years since he had come home to his country of birth, and he was thoroughly enjoying it. He had to secretly admit though that he was not as young and fit as he had once been and, by the end of the day, was glad to fall into his bed but he was not going to tell Thomas that!

They trundled their way around the chateau commenting to each other on new things that had been put on display or how the furniture had been rearranged in a particular room since they had been there last. The main tourist crowds for the season had gone. All the hordes of impatient children were once again in school and most of the visitors were adults or university aged teens, wandering around with their colourful backpacks in pairs or small groups.

At five to eleven, Henri and Thomas made their way to the main salon. Glad to see that a few chairs had been put out, Henri took a seat while Thomas stood, leaving the rest of the chairs for the more elderly visitors. They waited expectantly for the concert to begin.

The musicians were good, very good actually, and the music appropriate for the different periods of the chateau, Henri thought to himself critically. However, it wasn't until two of them started singing a duet that his ears particularly pricked up. The male singer had a strong tenor voice but was rather flamboyant for Henri to think him exceptional. The female voice was beautiful, truly sublime like liquid sunshine on a beautiful spring morning. He closed his eyes and thought of Mary, her voice had been similarly melodious, it was one of the things that had first attracted him to her, that, and her eyes. She had had the bluest eyes that he had ever seen, like cornflowers.

For him, it had been love at first sight. She had taken more persuading that he was the love of her life and he had spent the best part of two years pursuing her until she finally agreed to marry him. Now, as he listened, he could see her face, young and full of life, he could feel the touch of her soft lips as they brushed against his, smell the perfume she always wore. It was as if she had returned and was singing to him once more.

Opening his eyes, Henri could not quite see the performer from where he sat as a large elderly lady had taken the seat in front of him. He leaned a little to one side and saw her then, seated at the harpsichord. He could tell from the way she sang, occasionally shutting her eyes, that she felt the words she was singing, that music came from her heart and not just her mouth. Pretty too, he mused, and he wondered what colour her hair was under the wig. He glanced behind him to see if Thomas had noticed her. It seemed he had. His face wore a look of pure enchantment. Henri knew what that look meant. Thomas used to look like that when his mother had sung to him as a little boy. He wondered if his son was thinking of that time too. Oh, how he longed to live those days again.

What was it about music that could take him back in time so, to bring to the fore all the treasured memories of long ago, when happiness seemed to fill his world? Why was life so cruel, snatching away the one thing you loved most? He could feel his eyes welling with tears. He felt in his pocket for his handkerchief and surreptitiously dabbed them away. Really, Thomas would think him a sentimental old fool.

The duet ended and a spontaneous round of applause erupted. The two performers took their bows before the finale of the concert was played, ending with more applause and bows. As the performers cleared their music and disappeared through the far door of the salon in a flurry of silks, Henri turned to his son.

'Well, that was definitely worth waiting for, don't you think?'

'Mm?' It was as if he had to drag his attention back into the room from being elsewhere. 'I noticed you get your hanky out, Dad,' he smiled. 'You are an old sentimentalist. I know you were thinking about Mum.' With this, he put his arm around his dad's shoulder. 'Come on, let's go and see the other rooms before finding Alain for lunch.'

Jo grabbed herself a quick sandwich for lunch, eating it as she sat on her trundle trolley trimming the low hedges, sandwich in one hand, clippers in the other. Getting to the hedges that crisscrossed the centre of the bed was slightly trickier as there were only certain places you could put your feet. She remembered when she had first worked here, losing her balance one spring, and landing in a very unsightly heap amongst the tulips, ruining the neat symmetry of the planting. She had been supremely careful after that.

The concert had gone well that morning despite being a little late starting. She decided that she would have to set an alarm on her phone, so she was not late for the next one at three-thirty that afternoon. Meanwhile, she had a lot of hedges to get through. Alain, the Head Gardner, would not be pleased if these were not all finished by the end of the week.

She liked Alain and his wife Marie. They had been so welcoming when she had arrived seven years ago and despite the fact that Jo now lived in her Grand-mere's house, they were always inviting her around for meals. Their only daughter was grown up and currently lived in Nice with her husband, so she suspected they were suffering from empty nest syndrome. In fact, all the young gardeners at the chateau were welcome at Alain and Marie's house, some even lodging with them until they found their own accommodation. Marie had tried her hand at matchmaking between some the team, inviting different pairs of youngsters to tea together and watching to see if the sparks flew. She was determined that everyone should be partnered off with the right person and be as happy as she and Alain were. She had even tried pairing Jo up with Serge once. Jo shuddered at the memory; it had been the most awkward evening of her life. Marie had meant well but Jo had had enough on her plate at the time and a romantic entanglement, especially with Serge, was the last thing she needed.

Alain was a good boss to work for. He had high standards and expected the same of his staff, although he earned their respect rather than demanded it. He counted on everyone to pull their weight and get stuck in to get jobs done on time but also took into consideration where people excelled and generally let them work in areas where they would be most happy. For instance, Maurice, the wispy haired old man who had seemingly been on the gardening team since the first brick of the chateau had been laid, loved the nursery where he could coax any plant to flower and talked to his seedlings daily. She had learnt so much from him during her time here. It was also why she had been given the task of trimming the box. She had a good mathematical eye for a straight line; the skill of topiary came naturally to her. It gave her an immense feeling of satisfaction when it was finished. She loved order and neatness; it made her feel good.

Jo loved all aspects of gardening. It was her twin passion with music. There was something truly magical about planting a seed and seeing it grow into a beautiful flower or picking a juicy ripe tomato in July having sown a tiny seed in March. She felt at home in a garden. Gardens helped quiet her soul and bring peace to her inner self. No matter what was going on in her life she felt that nature was always listening, as if Mother Nature herself was an actual being never far away, who understood her feelings without her ever having to explain them. Plants seemed to sooth her worries away. She wondered if any of the other gardeners felt like that. She was sure Maurice did. Some thought him slightly strange, talking to the seedlings in his care, and generally avoided him. But she understood that to him, each tiny plant was like one of his children, to be given the best start in life, love, and encouragement to grow until they were set free to be planted on in the wider gardens of the chateau.

Jo looked up from her labours and saw Alain slowly coming across the garden towards her. He seemed to be deeply engrossed in conversation with two men, gesturing with his hands as he talked, pointing out plants and beds they passed. The two men nodded in understanding and occasionally laughed at a humorous remark. She stuffed the remaining corner of her sandwich into her mouth. Strictly speaking, staff were supposed to eat in the designated staff canteen area, but with two concerts a day taking an hour or so out of her gardening time, Jo rarely had time for a leisurely lunch, preferring to eat on the go whenever she could, as long as there weren't too many people around to notice. She swallowed the half-chewed mouthful somewhat painfully and stood up as they approached.

'Henri, Thomas, I'd like you to meet one of our highly valued gardeners. This is Jo Stanton. She is part of the team that looks after our famous parterre that I've been telling you about.'

Jo smiled as she removed her gloves and greeted the two men. The first was older, probably about the same age as Alain but slightly shorter. He had the kind of build that indicated a comfortable life and slightly too many good dinners. His careworn face spoke of kindness, and he had eyes that twinkled as he smiled and shook Jo's hand. There was something instantly likeable about him. The other was taller, younger and more athletically built, with soft brown hair that appeared sun bleached at the ends, but it was his eyes that Jo noticed first. Blue, like pieces of a clear summer sky fallen to earth. He held her gaze momentarily as they shook hands and Jo felt as if he had somehow looked into her very soul. The corners of his mouth twitched into a smile, and she felt the heat rise to her face. She looked back at the older man who was considering her slightly curiously.

'Pardon me, but you look familiar,' he said. Jo saw light come into his eyes in understanding. 'Do you perchance play the harpsichord, young lady?'

'I do, yes, were you at the concert this morning? If so, I hope you enjoyed it.'

'It was marvellous!' he exclaimed. 'Alain, what are you doing keeping this young lady out here in the cold doing this manual work?' He waved his hand about indicating the flower beds before him. 'This is no work for a pianist's hands, she should be inside keeping her voice warm and her hands soft.' He winked at her conspiratorially.

She laughed. 'Ah but this is my day job, we musicians still have to pay the bills, you see.'

Alain turned to his friend, 'We really couldn't do without her, Henri, she is one of the hardest working team members we have. Besides, we do let all of our gardeners wear gloves. We take care of our staff here, don't we, Jo?'

'Of course, and I love gardening. How could anyone not love being part of this?' She spread her hands wide to indicate the beauty that surrounded her, each bed like a miniature tapestry where the design stayed the same but the infill of multicoloured stitches constantly changed. 'Music and gardening, it's what makes me tick.' She smiled at Alain putting her gloves back on.

'Well, I must show you the new orchard we've planted,' said Alain, addressing his two friends. 'It has been a very exciting project, and we have many rare heritage varieties sourced from all over France and some from Britain too. It is a bit of a trek, Henri, are you sure you're up for it? I can easily take Thomas and leave you here with Jo. I'm sure she'll look after you.'

'That sounds like a very pleasant idea to me,' he twinkled at Jo. 'You don't mind, my dear, do you, keeping an old man company?'

'Not at all, it will be a pleasure,' Jo smiled. 'If my boss will let me, we'll move one of the benches over there so you can sit a bit nearer, and we can chat as I work,' she said, looking at Alain, 'I can't be caught slacking now!'

In the event, it was Thomas who helped her move one of the long benches from around the edge of the garden nearer to the bed she was working on. Normally they did not allow the benches to be moved but it wasn't busy, and Alain had thought it a good idea too. Henri sat down and stretched his legs out before him. It was sunny despite the chill in the air.

'Ah, this is the life!' he sighed as Alain and Thomas took their leave, promising to be back soon. 'So, my dear, your French is perfect, but do I detect an English accent hiding under there?' Henri queried, looking at Jo.

'Yes, I grew up in England, but my mother was French. I spent much of my time back and forth between the two countries as I was growing up. I live here permanently now, in the village down the road from here. It's only a short cycle ride for me to get into work each day.'

He laughed softly. 'Ah. For me, it is the other way round. I was born in France, not far from here actually, but I fell in love with a beautiful English girl.' He paused as if conjuring up her image in his mind. 'She had elderly parents to care for so naturally I moved to England when we were married, and we cared for them together until they eventually passed on.' He looked at her thoughtfully. 'Do you think you will ever return to England sometime in the future?'

'Maybe. Maybe one day,' she replied. Maybe one day she would go back, deal with everything that she had left behind there. She had to face it one day but for now she was here, safe, shutting away the past. Why change that? She looked away from him and back to the work in hand. 'So did your wife not come with you today?'

'Sadly, my dear, I lost my poor Mary several years ago,' he said, suddenly downcast.

'Oh, I'm so sorry to hear that,' she said, coming to sit next to him on the bench. 'It's so painful losing ones we love, isn't it? Life can be unbearably cruel sometimes.' They sat for a while, each lost in their thoughts and memories.

'So how do you know Alain?' she asked, hoping to brighten the conversation. A smile came over his face.

'Ah, Alain and I were at school together. We became friends because we shared the same sense of humour as well as a few girlfriends back then!' he chuckled. 'Eventually we went our separate ways. Alain took up horticulture and I had my music, but we always kept in touch. He was my best man when I was married, and he is Thomas' godfather. Although we do not see each other very often now. He is a good man.'

'Yes, he is,' she agreed. 'Everybody here likes Alain and Marie. They are so welcoming, and he is a very good boss. People who come to work here usually stay on for some time.'

'And how long have you been here young lady?'

'Nearly seven years now. I love it here. Sometimes it's a bit frantic in the spring when you've got lots to do and tourists milling about here there and everywhere, getting in the way. But then again, I work at a tourist attraction and visitors coming to the chateau pays my wages, so I shouldn't really complain. You said you had your music earlier, is that what you did for a living?'

'Yes, I am a pianist, although I am retired now, too many young folk out there who are much better than I ever was. I say *I am* rather than *I was* because you can never give music up, can you? Even though they stop paying you for performances and you stop earning a living at it, it is always in your soul, isn't it? It's always a part of your life, a way of expressing your feelings sometimes, it never leaves you.' He looked at her intently, 'I saw you playing earlier so I don't need to ask if you feel that way about it too.'

She laughed gently. 'You are so right.' It was refreshing to find someone who felt about music the way she did.

'Did you ever think of taking up music as a career?' he asked.

'Not really,' she lied. She did not want to think of that time. Choices had had to be made and dreams left behind in the face of reality. 'I've heard it's very competitive to get into the good academies and I don't think I'm really a competitive type of person. Besides, I love gardening equally as much as music.

It's an immensely satisfying job even if sometimes you have to wait months to see the fruits of your labours. I still enjoy my music when I can, but with perhaps less pressure than if I were a fulltime musician.'

'Hmm, perhaps you're right,' he pondered.

They sat in silence each enjoying the afternoon sunshine and drinking in the garden around them. After a while, to stop the silence becoming awkward, she asked,

'What part of England do you live in? Do you have a garden?'

At this, he reached into the top pocket of his coat and brought out his mobile phone.

'Let me show you,' he said, sounding excited. 'I live in a wonderful old house in a small village in Oxfordshire. It belonged to my wife's parents, we shared it with them when we married, and Thomas grew up there. I couldn't imagine living anywhere else now. It's a bit higgledy-piggledy with the extension, but it has character. As for the garden, well that's another story.'

She wondered what he meant by that and dutifully leaned over to look at the pictures he brought up on the screen. The main house seemed to be constructed of red brick and beams, Tudor by the look of it and the diamond pained windows that looked blankly out on to a gravelled driveway. The main front door had a covered porch, over the top of which scrambled an enormous honeysuckle in serious need of pruning. On the right-hand end of the house, a narrow two-storey 1930's extension had been added at right angles to the main building. A garage at the bottom and windows at the top. He swiped left on the screen to show the house from a different angle. Here she could see the extension from the side. The upper floor seemed to be entirely made of the typical elongated windows of the period and a long, curved balcony ran the length of it, one end of which had a spiralled metal staircase that disappeared down behind a high brick wall.

'Wow,' she marvelled. 'That's a beautiful house you have Henri. It's an unusual combination of styles to put together.'

'Yes, and the story behind that is that my wife's great grandfather was an artist. He was the one who bought the house in the first place, apparently because he fell in love with the garden, but being an old house there was not enough light inside for him to paint. So, he added the extension sometime in the thirties and used the top floor as his studio, hence all the windows along the side. He had a motor car which he kept in the garage underneath so he must have been doing alright for himself. He was quite a modern thinking man and so used the latest styles in construction. I don't suppose you'd get away with doing that these days with all the planning laws we have now. It's quite…how would you say…quirky isn't it? Mary and I added the balcony after her parents died. You know, it's a wonderful vantage point for seeing the garden below. If you stand at this end,' and here he indicated the end where the staircase descended, 'you can see the whole garden set out before you. Look, I have a few pictures of the garden here.' He showed her the screen, swiping left every so often.

From what Jo could see the garden had not been looked after as well as the house. There seemed to be an orchard area, a very small single storey cottage and then a main open area with paths and what had been flower beds around the edge. Obviously at some point it had been well tended as she could recognise the occasional plant amongst the weeds, but it had been left to run amok recently. Some of the pictures showed areas that looked as though they had not been touched in well over a decade.

'Gosh, Henri. Fabulously big garden but you need to get somebody in to help you with that.'

As soon as she had said it, she realised she'd walked right into his trap.

'Yes, my dear. It's strange you should say that, I've been looking for a gardener recently.' He looked at her, eyes twinkling with mischief. 'How would you like to come back to England and restore it for me? Breathe some new life back into it?'

She opened her mouth to reply but he cut her off before she could say anything.

'Let me tell you what I can offer you before you decide. Last year, Thomas and I renovated the gardener's cottage, we were going to use it as a holiday let but I think this is a much better use for it. It is not very big, but it would give you your own place to live, rent free, while you worked on the garden. I would pay you, let us say fifty percent more that you get here. You could have complete control over renovating the garden, within reason of course, be your own boss. Tools and equipment provided.' He looked at her hopefully and added, 'I also have a baby grand piano which you would be welcome to come and play any time you like. Tempted?'

She thought for a moment. If ever she was to leave here and work elsewhere, it would be for a project like this. She had often dreamed of maybe starting up her own business one day, tending gardens for people who could not manage them themselves, but right now it was impossible.

'Oh Henri, I am really tempted and it's a truly kind offer. But I can't.' She watched as the hopeful excitement faded from his eyes. 'You see, I have to look after my Grand-mere and I can't leave her, I'm all she's got.'

She felt that after such an amazing offer she owed him an explanation of sorts. 'She had a stroke about seven years ago and became largely paralysed down her left side. I was living in England at the time. The neighbours didn't find her for two days until they noticed she hadn't gone to church on Sunday as she usually did. By the time they got her to hospital, most of the damage was permanent, and she was in a pretty bad way. That's when I came to live here permanently. After she came out of hospital, she couldn't manage at home on her own, and I had to work to pay the bills, so now she lives in the nursing home about 2 miles from here. I go to see her nearly every day, but I can't leave her. I'm so sorry.'

'My dear,' he looked at her kindly and took her hand in his, 'there is no need to apologise. I was merely being a hopeful old man. You are making the right choice. Family must always come first.'

'Thank you,' she said as she squeezed his hand and got up to carry on with her work. She looked up to see Alain coming back along the path from the orchards with Thomas and nodded in their direction. 'Looks like they've finished touring the orchards.'

Henri followed her gaze.

As they stood to greet the returning pair, the opening chords of Beethoven's 5th symphony emanated loudly from Jo's trolley. Henri looked at her and raised his eyebrows in surprise.

'Oh, excuse me, I need to get that. It's the ringtone for the care home,' she explained apologetically, dashing to the trolley to unearth the phone she always had with her. Normally staff taking personal calls in work time was distinctly frowned upon but once she had explained the situation with her grandmother to Alain, they had agreed that she was free to answer calls in case of emergencies. The same went for staff who had children at school. Family was important and sometimes emergencies happened, that was life. She had set a special ring tone for the care home as she knew that if they rang during the day, it would be important.

The three men watched on as they saw Jo's face turn ashen. Her head dropped and she rubbed her temples with her hand. This did not look like good news. It wasn't. Jo turned to Alain, tears already prickling behind her eyes.

'It's Grand-mere, they think she's had another stroke. The doctor is on his way, and they say I need to get there fast because it doesn't look good.' A tear splashed down her cheek and she felt in her pockets for a tissue to wipe it away. 'Alain, can you give me a lift, I don't think I'll be able to see straight on my bike?'

'I would gladly but Marie dropped me off this morning and she's gone to visit her mother, so I don't have the car today.'

'I'll take you, that is, if you can show me the way.'

They all turned to look at Thomas, momentarily silent. Well, this was no time to look a gift horse in the mouth.

Chapter 2

'I've parked in the staff car park.' Thomas looked sheepishly at Alain and shrugged. 'Well, we are kind of family. Dad, you stay here with Alain. Make sure your phone is on. I'll keep you posted.' He turned to Jo. 'Anything you need to collect before we go?'

She shook her head. 'I don't think so. Oh no! The concert this afternoon!' she wailed.

'Don't worry, I will get a message through, perhaps Henri can fill in for you!' Alain reassured her. 'Just go. Don't worry about a thing here, we'll take care of everything. Go!'

'Thank you!' she called back. Thomas was already setting off across the garden for the car park and she had to run to catch up with him. 'This is very kind of you. I'm most grateful,' she gasped. Gosh he walked fast.

He smiled at her. 'Not a problem, glad to help.'

They walked on in silence, until they reached the car park.

'This is me here.' He indicated a sleek black Land Rover Discovery. Jo almost made the mistake of getting in the wrong side of the car. That would have been embarrassing, she thought. It had been a long time since she had been in an English car. Seeing the very swish interior and cream leather seats, she hoped her trousers and boots were not too dirty. He started the engine and backed out of the space.

'Turn left out of here and then immediately right at the traffic lights then straight on for about 2 kilometres,' she instructed. The tears had dried and all she felt now was a kind of urgent panic to get to her grandmother as fast as possible. Thomas did not hang about, flooring the accelerator as soon as they had taken the right turn. Jo held on to the sides of the seat, her shoulders tense with anxiety.

'Is your Grand-mere very old?' he asked, trying to put her at her ease.

'She was seventy-six last birthday.' Jo remembered the cake she had made and taken in for her grandmother and the residents to share. That had only been about six weeks ago. She had wheeled her grandmother out into the little garden at the back of the nursing home and parked her in the shade as it had been a lovely warm and sunny day. Jo had lent her sunglasses and the nurses had joked about her grandmother looking like a movie star. Jo had crocheted a blanket for her knees for when the weather turned and given her some of her favourite lavender hand cream. It had been such a happy, carefree afternoon. 'Turn left here and the entrance is just up here on the right.' They turned into a sweeping gravel driveway with a rough car park area at one side. Thomas stopped the car and Jo jumped out. She turned to speak to him. 'Thank you once again, you've been so kind. I hope you can find your way back ok.'

'Don't worry, I'll park up and stay in case you need a lift later.'

'Oh, please don't. I don't want to inconvenience you anymore, you've your father to look after.'

'He'll be fine. Now go on in and see to your grandmother.'

She did not have time to argue anymore. She shut the car door and rushed inside hoping that he really would not wait for her, or he could be a here for a long time.

On the other side of the lobby, which was set out with comfy armchairs, was the main desk. There, one of the nurses she had seen many times before was waiting for her, a kind faced girl called Helene who looked up and came to greet her as she walked in.

'Hello Jo, the doctor is with your grandmother now,' she said.

'What happened?' asked Jo, feeling the emotions rise once more. 'When I saw her yesterday, she seemed so well.'

Helene reached behind the desk for some tissues and pressed them into Jo's hand. 'Yes, and when I saw her lunch time, she was ok too, but seemed more tired than usual. She didn't really want much to eat, but that's normal for her, you know, we pop in and out encouraging her with the protein drinks all the time. Then the last time I popped in she was unresponsive, so I called Matron. We sent for the doctor straight away and then called you. It is likely having had one stroke already that she's had another one. We are waiting for the doctor to confirm that now. Matron is in there with him. I'd wait until they come out,' she said, putting her hand on Jo's arm. 'It can be a little distressing for relatives to watch their loved ones being assessed. Don't worry, it's Dr Martin, he's incredibly good.' She smiled. 'Can I get you a drink while you wait?'

'Um…no, thank you Helene.' It was hard for Jo to process. She knew that people who have had one stroke were likely to some extent to go on and have another. But her grandmother had been such a fighter after the first one and although her left side had been partially paralysed, she had fought on valiantly. She had not had the appetite of former times, but Jo and the nurses had tempted her with her favourite foods and boosted her intake with protein shakes which she sipped through a straw. She had found it hard to communicate after the first stroke Jo remembered. Her speech had been very slurred, and she seemed unable to recall the words she needed, but that had improved slightly the more she tried. Jo was startled out of her reverie by the appearance of Matron by her side.

'Hello Jo,' she said. 'Come on down to your grandmother's room. The doctor has finished assessing her now. I am afraid it is another stroke as we suspected, quite a bad one. He'll have a word with you before you see her.' Jo followed the matron down the familiar corridor, the cheerful pictures of flowers and countryside scenes that lined it a blur as they swept past.

The matron knocked softly on the door and the doctor came out shutting it quietly behind him. A tall balding man dressed in a tweed suit. He must have been in his late fifties, Jo reckoned. He looked at Jo over the half-moon glasses perched on the end of his nose. You would guess he was a doctor just by looking at him.

'Hello, you must be Josephine's granddaughter. I'm Dr Martin, I've been assessing your grandmother as you know,' he explained in a soft quiet voice. 'I'm afraid it's not good news. She has had a very serious stroke. I think it is too late to take her to the hospital, there would be nothing that they could do. Her sight has gone, and she is beginning to fade, I think she may not have very long now.'

Jo legs went all wobbly and a sensation of pins and needles ran up her arms, she felt slightly surreal, as if this wasn't really happening.

'I've given her some morphine, so she is not in any pain,' the doctor continued. 'Go in and sit with her. Talk to her so she knows you are there, she may well be able to hear you and understand what you are saying. We'll give you some time alone with her.'

'If you need us,' Matron added, 'just use the buzzer by the bed.'

Jo opened the door and slid quietly into the room. The curtains over the windows had been closed, giving privacy, but it made the room feel gloomy inside as a result. The bedside light gave out a soft golden glow which cast uneven shadows on the face of the white-haired lady in the bed next to it. Jo sat down on the chair and pulled herself close to the side of the bed taking hold of her grandmother's hand that rested on top of the counterpane. It was cool to the touch. The only sounds she could hear were the ticking of the clock on the wall and the uneven rattling breaths of her grandmother.

'Hello Grand-mere, it's me, Jo,' she whispered. The old lady's eyes flickered slightly as if in recognition and Jo squeezed her unresponsive hand hoping that she could feel it. 'I've come to see you. I love you Grand-mere,' she choked as large, fat tears welled up and ran down her face, making round, wet marks on the sheet below. Jo wiped her eyes with the back of her hand, but she could not stop the tears from flowing no more than she could stop a river flowing to the ocean.

Jo did not know how long she sat there just talking to her grandmother, telling her about the day she'd had, talking of little inconsequential things, recalling memories of times gone by. She had had to make herself talk to start with. She forced herself to sound as cheerful and as normal as she could, knowing that this would probably be the last conversation she would have with her grandmother, albeit one sided. She talked about the times when she, Jo, had been young and her grandmother had taken her to the local market for the first time, how exciting it had been with all the different sights and smells and being given different cheeses to taste from some of the stalls. She had remembered being allowed to try an olive for the first time, spitting it out into a hanky and thinking how disgusting it was, and pulling a face that had made her grandmother and the olive man roar with laughter. Strange that, she thought, how tastes change, she quite liked them now.

There was soft knock and Helene popped her head around the door.

'How are you both doing?' she asked. Although from Jo's red rimmed eyes she knew. She had seen death many times now and it was never easy. 'Cup of tea?'

'Thank you, that would be lovely,' Jo replied.

Jo sipped her tea. Strong, hot, sweet and reviving.

She could sense her grandmother was gradually slipping away, her breaths becoming more irregular and noisier. On occasion, she would take a few rapid shallow breaths followed by silence where she did not seem to breathe at all and Jo in turn held her breath willing her grandmother to breathe again. Dr Martin had been back to check on his patient while Jo had gone to freshen up a bit.

'Not long now, I think,' he had said as he'd patted her arm and left the room.

Jo had no idea what time it was, she glanced at the clock: five past eight. What time had she arrived? She sat once more holding her grandmother's hand and smoothing the hair from her cool forehead. Her grandmother had had long hair for as long as Jo could remember, usually worn tidily in a bun at the nape of her neck. Today, as she lay dying, it was loose, sprawled across the pillow in long white waves. Jo imagined what she must have looked like as a young girl, quite beautiful probably. Her hair had once been dark, so her grandmother had told her. When she had been young, her husband had loved to brush it for her, but since his death, when Jo was little, it had turned increasingly white with the years. Jo could remember her mother telling her that she took after her grandmother in looks and had resembled her so much when she was born that she had been christened Josephine after her, although that had quickly become Jo once she had started school.

Jo held her grandmother's hand in both of hers, time ebbing away. The old woman's breathing becoming shallower and shallower until finally, gently, it ceased altogether and all that could be heard was the relentless ticking of the clock on the wall.

'Goodbye Grand-mere,' she whispered as she kissed her on the forehead. 'Thank you for always being there for me. I love you.' She rested her head down on her arms on the side of the bed and wept.

After the initial wave of grief had passed, Jo rang the buzzer. Matron and Helene arrived at the same time.

'She's gone,' was all that Jo could say between the tears.

Helene silently came over and hugged her. Matron quietly stood the other side of the bed and checked for vital signs.

'Yes, my dear,' she said looking across at Jo. 'She's at peace now. Would you like to sit with her for a while longer?'

Jo looked at the face of her grandmother and sighed, she looked restful now the final struggle was over. All that Jo had needed to say had been said. Her grandmother was not here to hear her now. Jo imagined her arriving in heaven and being reunited with her grandfather at last.

'No, thank you,' she said. 'I've said my goodbyes. She's gone now.' She turned to the matron. 'So, what happens next?'

'Come into my office and I'll take you through what needs to be done,' Matron said kindly. As they moved away from the bed, she saw Helene gently lift the sheet and cover her grandmother's face. It was all so horribly final.

It was about an hour later that Jo left Matron's office. She had been given more tea, been talked through what the procedure was when someone died and given lots of leaflets that explained what she had to do as next of kin. She would read those later when she was more able to take them in. They were so kind here, she thought. She was glad that her grandmother had been surrounded by that during the last years of her life and that she been able to be there for her too, trying to make each visit a happy one. She wandered out to the entrance lobby suddenly feeling the coolness of the night air on her face. She wondered how she was going to get home, call a taxi she supposed, and then she saw him.

Sprawled in one of the armchairs and with his coat wrapped tightly around him was Thomas, fast asleep. Next to him on a small table, the remains of a packet of sandwiches and an empty coffee mug. He had waited for her. Jo felt guilty that she had not even thought about him and embarrassed that this man who she'd only met that afternoon, which suddenly seemed a complete age away, had spent the entire afternoon and evening waiting in a completely strange nursing home for a woman he hardly knew. She would have to wake him and apologise. As she moved closer, he stirred and stretched his arms out in front of him. He rubbed his face over with the palm of his hand.

'Oh, hello,' he said sleepily, looking around. 'How is your grandmother?'

Jo found she could not get the words out and instead of saying 'I'm afraid she's died,' a great sob escaped her, and she burst into tears once more. The next thing she knew was his arms surrounding her in an all-encompassing hug. She noted the pleasant aroma of his cologne as she took great wracking breaths between the sobs. The tension of the day spilling out uncontrollably. He stroked the back of her hair.

'Hey, hey, it's ok,' he whispered. 'Let it all out. I'm so sorry.' He stood with her in his arms until finally she could cry no more.'

'Gosh, I'm sorry,' she sniffled, stepping back, 'I've made your jacket all wet.' She went to wipe the wet patch away.

'Don't worry,' he smiled at her. 'I'm waterproof, or rather, the jacket is.'

She laughed through her tears; he was being unbelievably kind.

'Have you really been waiting all this time? I really didn't mean for you to wait.'

'It's ok, Dad and Alain popped by a few hours ago and kept me company for a while, they brought some supplies, and the nurses here have kept me going in hot drinks.' He indicated the remains on the table. 'Let me take you home, you look exhausted.'

She probably looked a right wreck, she thought to herself as he led her to the car. She never looked good when she cried. Her eyes went all red and her face puffy and blotchy, never delicate, and needy like heroines in movies who dabbed pearl-like tears from perfectly made-up eyes, but right now she really didn't care.

The air was crisp and cold outside. It was a starry night with a full moon that made the trees stand out like black shadows against the navy-blue velvet of the sky. She shivered and felt suddenly empty and lost inside.

Jo directed Thomas as they made their way back past the chateau, now beautifully illuminated, to the village beyond. Her grandmother's house was a small narrow affair situated to one side of a large open square. Thomas pulled up at the curb in front of the house and switched the engine off.

'Will you be alright on your own?'

'Yes, yes, I'll be fine, thank you. I've lived alone since Grand-mere had to go into the home. I'm used to it,' she shrugged and turned to face him. 'I don't know how to thank you; you have been so kind. I am sorry for crying all over you earlier. It's been a long and emotional day.' She did not know what else to say.

'Look, Dad and I will be around for a few days, we're staying with Alain actually. Perhaps we can meet up again, we will take you out for a meal, cheer you up. That is if you feel like it and you can put up with my father. Absolutely no pressure.'

She laughed. 'Your father is delightful. I enjoyed talking with him earlier, there is no 'putting up with' to be done. Yes, that would be nice. Thank you. Although I may not be the best company. I will leave a message with Alain tomorrow. I must phone him to tell him what's happened anyway. I will probably need a few days to get the funeral sorted and other paperwork done.' It was a sobering thought and they sat for a few moments, each not knowing what to say next.

'Well, thank you again, I'll be in touch,' she said as she got out of the car and felt in her pocket for her keys. He waved as she shut the door and walked across to the house.

As she closed the front door behind her, she heard him drive away, the sound of the engine fading until she could hear it no more. Jo stood in the darkness of the house, listening to the silence, a shaft of pale light casting the shadow of the window frame on the opposite wall. Never had she felt so entirely alone, like a small boat lost on the vast ocean of life with no land on the horizon and no compass to guide her home. She flung herself on to the sofa and cried herself to sleep, not for the first time in her young life.

Chapter 3

Two things woke Jo the next morning. The soft pinging of her phone telling her there was a new message, and the awful pain in her neck from where she had fallen asleep on the sofa in an awkward position. She eased herself upright, gently rubbed her neck back to its rightful place and looked at her phone screen. Alain. She should have phoned him last night. She guessed he would know by now anyway. Thomas would have told him.

So sorry to hear about your grandmother. Don't come in today. Take your time. We are all thinking of you. Marie sends her love and a big hug. Alain x

It made her think of the hug that Thomas had given her last night. How comforting it had been just to be held and to know that another human being could take the weight of your pain, even if it was just for a few moments. She thought about her grandmother. She would have to go back to the home today to collect the death certificate and the personal items that had made her room feel more like home. She also wanted to thank them properly for looking after her grandmother so well, she would miss seeing the staff there on an almost daily basis. Then there was the funeral to arrange. She had been recommended a good local funeral director by the matron last night, who had said that they would arrange for the body to be collected and that sometime today she should call in to set a date for the funeral and sort out all the details. There was so much that had to be done, but first she was in desperate need of a hot shower and something to eat, realising that she had not eaten since yesterday lunchtime. Yesterday, it seemed like a lifetime ago, not less than twenty-four hours. Weird to think that this time yesterday, she had got up as normal and gone to work looking forward to the morning concert and her day ahead. Now it felt as if her whole world had shifted sideways, and she did not quite know which way was up.

She texted Alain back to thank him and let him know that she would stay in touch regarding work and went to shower.

A hot coffee and sadly stale croissant later, she was ready to go. She would take an old, wheeled suitcase with her for the clothes and, packed inside it, a folding plastic crate for the other bits and pieces. She checked herself in the mirror before stepping out. It was not a pretty sight. Her eyes were still swollen and puffy from crying, although less red than they had been, and she looked tired. She would walk to the nursing home, she decided, and then get a taxi back later with her grandmother's stuff. A good brisk walk in the autumnal sunshine would do her the world of good and should only take her about an hour. She would have to pick up her bike that she had left at the chateau another time.

She had been walking for about half an hour and had just reached the traffic light junction where the road to the nursing home turned off, when a car pulled up next to her and stopped. The window wound down. Probably someone asking for directions she thought, until she noticed the car more clearly. Thomas stuck his head out the window.

'Need a lift?'

'Do you rescue damsels in distress every day?' she smiled. 'Or only when you're supposed to be on holiday?'

'Only the ones I like the look of.' He grinned back. 'Get in.'

She got in, putting the suitcase carefully on the backseat.

'Where to, my lady?'

'The nursing home please. Can you remember the way?'

It turned out he could.

'How are you feeling?' He glanced at her sideways and noticed how tired she looked. 'Did you get any sleep last night?'

'A bit, yes. In fact, I fell asleep on the sofa and woke up with terrible neck ache this morning. Nothing a hot shower and coffee didn't fix though. I need to clear out Grand-mere's room this morning. It all seems a bit surreal still, I can't believe she's gone.'

'Would you like some company? It might make it a bit easier, and we can load the car to take things back to your house. I won't intrude if you'd rather be alone though.'

Jo thought for a moment. Maybe it would be nice to have some company, and it would certainly save her the taxi fare home. 'Thank you, that's very kind, company would be lovely.'

Her grandmother's room was still and quiet and wore a lonely kind of emptiness as if it too mourned the loss of its occupant. The bed had been freshly made with crisp new sheets and the curtains drawn back to let the autumnal sunshine in. It was strange for Jo to see her grandmother's things, knowing she was not there anymore. They seemed sad and redundant somehow. She put the suitcase on the bed and unzipped it to take the plastic crate out.

'I'll sort her clothes if you wouldn't mind putting all the bits and pieces on the dressing table and on the top there in the crate.' She indicated a chest of drawers in the corner of the room. There were only a couple of photographs, a few ornaments, and the mantle clock, which hadn't ever worked but that her grandmother had insisted taking with her.

'Ok. Will do,' he said.

They worked in silence for a while, but it was not an awkward one. Her grandmother did not have many clothes at the home, just a few items of underwear and some blouses and skirts. Jo had always taken her washing home and brought her fresh clothes regularly so there had been no need for a full wardrobe of clothes to be kept there. It was odd picking up her slippers and seeing the familiar shape of her feet inside, as if she would be back any second to put them on. Jo put them together and stuffed them down the side of the clothes in the suitcase. At the bottom of the wardrobe, she found a small lavender bag that she had once made for her grandmother when she had been at school in England. She squeezed it and smelt to see if any of the scent remained. It didn't. Still, she might keep the bag and refill it someday. She would hang it with her favourite clothes to remind her of Grand-mere every time she wore them. Lavender had been her favourite scent; it had a kind of wholesome, old-fashioned smell to it that Jo loved too. Every garden should have lavender in it she thought; it was one of her favourite plants.

Jo found a wash bag in one of the draws and popped into the small bathroom that took up a corner of the room. There were only a few bits in there. The towels belonged to the home. She picked up her grandmother's hairbrush that lay on the shelf under the mirror. Long strands of white hair wove themselves through the bristles. She had probably used this yesterday, thought Jo. Suddenly a hot wave of grief rose in her spilling itself out through her tears and forming a painful lump in her throat. She grabbed a handful of tissues to wipe them away. She blew her nose and stuffed the hairbrush into the bag. Picking up the other items on the shelf she caught her reflection in the mirror, her eyes had already gone all red again.

Thomas popped his head around the door.

'You alright in there?' he asked, knowing full well that she was not, but trying to sound upbeat for her. He knew how raw grief could feel. 'Come here.'

Once again, she let herself be enveloped in his comforting arms and the tears flowed. How could a mere hairbrush cause so much pain? She had managed to keep herself together until then.

'It was seeing her hairbrush,' Jo sniffled into his chest. 'It made it all too real again, I think.' She took a deep breath. 'It's such a personal thing to her. I'm sorry, I'm making you all soggy again.'

'I know,' he soothed, 'but it doesn't matter. It's the little things that creep up and get you every time, isn't it? It's ok, have a good wail if you need to, I've got you.'

They stood for a while, Jo heavy with sadness, and he with his arms around her thinking of the time his mother had died and how lost he had felt then. She pulled away.

'Thank you,' she sniffed. 'I needed that.'

'Hey, no worries, anytime,' he smiled and looked around the room. 'Have you got everything you need? The crate is nearly full.'

She stuffed the washbag into the suitcase and zipped it up.

'I just need to do a final check around and then call in on Matron on the way out to pick up some paperwork and say goodbye properly. Can you take some of this out to the car while I do that?'

It had been an emotional goodbye to the staff at the home. They had become almost a second family to her. Always cheerful and calmly coping with any dramas that happened in the daily lives of the residents. She must remember to send them some flowers later, she thought, cheer up their day as they had cheered hers so often.

'So, what's next for you today?' Thomas asked on the journey back.

'I've got to call into the funeral directors this afternoon, get all of that sorted and then make an appointment with Grand-mere's notary to start all the legal stuff off.'

'Did she make a will?'

'Yes. She was always very good about doing things properly. I don't think she has much though, just the house and a few savings.'

'How about your parents Jo, can they come and give you a hand?'

She had been hoping that nobody would ask about them. 'My parents died,' she said. 'It was just me and Grand-mere. What have you done with your father today? I enjoyed chatting to him yesterday.'

It was such a blatant change of subject that Thomas felt he could not ask about her parents further, it was obviously a no-go area, and he wouldn't intrude. He had pushed his luck with her already today, he thought.

'Marie has taken him shopping into Tours. There is a great music shop there and knowing him he'll probably be there for hours trying out all the pianos. Marie will have to drag him out kicking and screaming, or just leave him there and go shopping on her own. Honestly, he'll be like a kid in a sweet shop!'

She laughed at this. Having spoken to him yesterday she could well imagine it. 'Do you play?' she asked. She looked at his profile, he had not shaved that morning and the stubbly shadow gave him a slightly rugged look. It suited him, she thought idly.

'Yes, a little. Growing up with a concert pianist for a dad how could I not? But I'm not as good as him.'

'What do you do for a living then?'

'I'm a writer, novels mostly.'

They had arrived at the house now and she did not get the opportunity to quiz him further. He helped her take her grandmother's belongings in and she offered him coffee, but he made some excuses about meeting up with Alain for lunch and that he had better be off. She thanked him again and waved goodbye as he drove off towards the chateau. When she got inside the house, her phone pinged.

Come for dinner. I'll get Thomas to pick you up at 6. Marie says she won't take no for an answer. Alain x

She texted her acceptance back. It would save her having to go food shopping she thought, and some company would be good after today.

It was a busy afternoon for Jo. The funeral directors took much longer than expected. Who knew that there was so much choice to be had in coffins these days? And the elderly undertaker had wanted her to view all the options available in the catalogue before making her final selection. She knew that her grandmother would want to be buried in the same plot as her grandfather in the cemetery just outside the village, so at least that was fairly straight forward to arrange. She would have to find a stone mason to alter the headstone. Then there were flowers, so much choice, did she want a wreath, a cross or letters spelling out her grandmother's name? She thought, 'Josephine' would look a little crowded on top of a coffin and opted for a simple cross of white roses dotted with sprigs of lavender. Then she phoned the notary to make an appointment to sort out probate and her grandmother's will. By the time she got home she was exhausted, and it was beginning to get dark. She checked her watch, she had time for a cup of tea and a quick change before being picked up for dinner.

She had just kicked off her shoes and was about to sit down when there was a knock at the door. A bit early for Thomas. Still holding her cup of tea, she opened the door. Serge! Serge, holding a large pot of apricot-coloured begonias. Her heart sank.

'Bonjour Jo.' He greeted her with an over familiar double kiss, whether she wanted it or not. She supposed it would appear very rude to ignore him. 'Can I come in? I've brought you some flowers, well a plant actually, it will last longer than flowers, but I don't need to tell you that. So sorry to hear about your grandmother. It must have been quite a shock for you.'

By the time he had finished speaking he was in, walking through the small front room to the kitchen beyond. She followed him. He put the begonias down on the kitchen table, turned to face her and came towards her arms open. The second hug she received that day was almost the polar opposite of the first. Instead of bringing her comfort she felt a sense of mild panic. She had to fight down the urge to squirm her way out of his gangly arms and instead of cologne, the faint tang of stale sweat assaulted her nostrils.

'Thank you, Serge, it's very kind of you,' she managed. He obviously did not know that, of all plants, begonias were the only ones she really disliked. She could not say why exactly. Maybe it was their slight fleshiness and texture that made her skin crawl, a bit like his hug. She was still holding her cup of tea and he eyed it expectantly.

'Would you like a cup?' she asked turning away from him to get another mug from the cupboard. She knew he would say yes. At least he would not be able to stay for very long as she had the excuse of going out soon.

'That would be nice,' he said, removing his jacket.

They chatted about their respective days for a while, as they drank their tea, Serge sat at the small table, Jo leaning against the sink at the far end of the kitchen.

'So, now you are all alone in the world, Cherie,' he sighed, getting up and coming over towards her. 'You know I'd be happy to…look after you.' Before she knew it, his arm had gone around her waist and he was whispering in her ear, 'You know how I feel about you, Cherie. I'm mad about you, we were meant to be together. I want to…' and he squeezed her tightly bending his head down to kiss her neck.

'Serge! No! Stop!' she cried, pushing him away as strongly as she could. Mild panic rising to severe. How could he even think of making advances to someone who had only just suffered a bereavement? Wasn't it obvious that he repulsed her? 'I think you should go now!' she insisted firmly, not even able to look at his face. She pushed past him into the front room towards the door, still open from when he had marched in. There, framed in the light stood Thomas.

Oh hell! Was her immediate thought. He has probably heard all of that. And by the look she saw on his face, he had.

'Everything alright here, Jo? I'm a little early, but good thing by the looks of it.'

He came to stand in the front room, hands on his hips and a serious expression on his face.

'Serge was just leaving,' she said tersely as the other man snatched up his jacket, scowled at Thomas and left.

'Merde!' he swore, banging the front door shut behind him.

'Are you ok?' Thomas rushed over and took hold of her hands. 'You're shaking!'

'I'm sorry you had to witness that,' she said pulling her hands away. 'Give me five minutes to change, I'll be right down.' She dashed up the stairs into the bathroom and locked the door behind her. She really wanted to jump in the shower and wash the feeling of Serge off her, but she did not have time. Instead, she held a cold flannel to her face making herself breathe slowly to calm herself down. This was not your fault, not your fault, she repeated to herself in her head. She looked at her reflection. 'You, Jo Stanton, are going to freshen up, slap on a bit of make up to make you feel good and go to dinner with people who are kind and good. Now, pull yourself together and forget about idiots like Serge,' she instructed herself. She would be calm now; she could do this.

Ten or so minutes later she found Thomas sitting on the sofa in the front room checking his phone.

'Ready to go?' he asked cautiously. 'I'm sure people won't mind if you'd rather stay at home.'

'No, it's fine,' she assured him. 'I think I'd like to get out of here for a while. Let me just pick up my keys and check the back door is locked.' She went into the kitchen and checked the handle of the door. It was locked. She turned and noticed the plant still on the table. She could not deal with the begonias now. In the morning she would throw them out. Picking up her keys she followed Thomas out of the house switching off the lights as she went.

'Do you want to talk about what just happened?' he asked as she locked the front door and popped her keys in her bag. 'I mean talk to the police or something?'

'No, not really. He has never done anything like that before. He's been a bit over attentive sometimes at work, but nothing like that. I'm sure he's got the message tonight though. I'll just steer clear of him.' What else could she do? An amorous advance was hardly a crime, especially in France. 'Come on, let's go. Thank you for rescuing me *again*. Wow, three times in two days!'

'I know,' he smiled. 'It's becoming a habit!'

They both laughed.

Chapter 4

The evening at Alain and Marie's house lifted her spirits immensely, it was good to see Henri again, who greeted her warmly and insisted on showing her some music he had bought in Tours 'Duets for the piano.' Maybe he and Thomas played together sometimes. The meal was a simple one, but shared amongst friends old and new, it was as good as a feast. After the initial hugs and condolences, nobody mentioned her grandmother much for which Jo was rather grateful. It was nice to feel normal again after the last couple of days; it was good to laugh at shared jokes and know that nobody minded if you looked tired and weepy because they all understood that life and death happened, and everybody went through ups and downs at times in their lives.

After they had finished their coffee, Marie and Alain got up to clear the table, Jo offered to help but was quickly shushed back into her seat. Thomas wanted to talk to Alain, and so followed him out to the kitchen where a discussion ensued between Alain and Marie about the loading of the dishwasher. Henri raised his eyebrows and smiled at Jo.

'You know, the offer of a job still stands Jo,' he said looking at her, suddenly serious. 'Think about it, reconsider.' He took a deep breath and sighed when she didn't reply.

In truth, she had thought no more about it.

'Thomas and I are going to Limoges tomorrow and then gradually making our way across to Nice for a few days, bit of a grand tour round. Thomas has some research he wants to do for another book. We will be coming back this way in about two weeks, I forget the exact date, Thomas will know. Think about it. I expect we will see you and you can give me your answer then. I think you will find a change will do you good for a while. If you find you cannot stand us, I'm sure your old job here will still be available, I can put in a good word with the boss.' He twinkled at her mischievously. 'Promise me you'll think about it seriously?'

'Think about what, Dad?' said Thomas, making Jo jump before she had time to reply.

'I've offered this young lady a job,' declared Henri proudly. 'She's promised me she's going to think about it.'

She had not actually, but that was beside the point. Perhaps she should.

'Henri, you're not poaching my staff are you, you old devil?' Alain said, coming back in to gather more plates. 'You can't have her you know, we need her here, don't we Marie?'

'Don't we what love?' Marie said, coming in from the kitchen.

'Henri's offered Jo a job in England. He's trying to steal one of my best gardeners from under my nose. Cheeky sod.'

'Oh Jo, you can't leave us!' Marie exclaimed. 'I haven't found you a husband yet!'

Jo was feeling increasingly embarrassed and despite the friendly banter, the question was a real one. As yet she hadn't been able to get a word in edgeways and it was her future they were all squabbling over.

'I think Jo can decide for herself where she wants to work and which country she'd like to live in,' Thomas said diplomatically, sitting down at the table next to Jo. 'Although we'd love to have her, the garden is a right mess.' The others all laughed at this, breaking the slight tension in the room, but Thomas was still looking at Jo quite seriously.

'Well, what can I say?' Jo said, looking between Henri and Alain. This was awkward. 'It's nice to be in demand. Alain, I am quite happy here, honestly, you couldn't be a nicer person to work for and I love the chateau gardens. Henri, I will think seriously about your exceedingly kind offer but I don't think I can decide right now. Too much has happened in the last two days and my head is still spinning from that. I don't know what else I can say to you both.'

'I've still got time to find you a husband then, while you decide,' Marie said, at which they all burst out laughing and the subject was dropped for less serious matters.

Later, Thomas drove Jo home and walked her to her front door.

'Be careful of Serge won't you. I'm sorry but I felt I had to tell Alain what happened tonight,' he confessed. 'Just so you've got another pair of eyes looking out for you.'

'Oh, did you? I suppose I ought to thank you then.' In truth, she was slightly annoyed and a little embarrassed. She did not really want everybody knowing she'd been pawed over. 'Enjoy your trip to Nice. Thank you for helping me this morning. I might see you when you get back?'

'For sure, take care of yourself.'

After seeing her safely in the door, he drove away.

Josephine Hubert was buried the following week on a cold, bleak, early November morning, the weather about as cheerful as Jo's spirits. Jo had opted for just a graveside ceremony as there was none but herself to attend and she did not want to find herself the only member of a congregation, singing hymns in a large empty church. In the event, Marie had joined her to give her moral support and the two women stood forlorn under a large black umbrella that the funeral directors had helpfully provided, the rain dripping from the spokes like extra tears.

Jo had returned to work the day after Thomas and Henri left, preferring to keep herself busy, although her evenings and weekends seemed strangely empty. With no trips to the nursing home and no one to look after or keep cheerful for, she felt low and listless.

The afternoon of the funeral she had an appointment with the notary to read her grandmothers will. She hoped it would all be straightforward.

'Ah, Miss Stanton, lovely to meet you,' greeted the middle-aged, bespectacled notaire, shaking her hand. 'I'm sorry it's under such sad circumstances.'

They sat down on either side of the leather topped desk that stood in the middle of the room.

'The terms of your grandmother's will are very straightforward actually. In the absence of any of Madame Hubert's children, as her daughter predeceased her, you inherit all her savings and the proceeds from the house sale. Congratulations, you will be quite a wealthy young woman.'

Jo sat there feeling slightly numb and confused. 'I'm sorry I don't quite understand, what house sale and what savings? I thought my grandmother didn't have very much apart from the house we lived in.'

'Ah, yes, well, it seems that your grandmother was quite a wealthy woman.' Glancing at Jo's utterly confused face, he took a deep breath and continued, 'Miss Stanton, I have been your grandmother's notaire for many years now. When your parents died, all their assets were left to your grandmother with the understanding that she would pay for your school fees and see that you were well looked after and that on her death you would inherit any remaining funds. It appears that there are substantial remaining funds.' He pushed a piece of paper across the desk and showed Jo a figure that made her head feel dizzy.

'But I have been scrimping and saving and using her meagre pension and my wages to pay for her nursing home fees, all these years, why didn't she use this?'

'It may well be that she felt the money, that came from your parents, was rightfully yours and that she couldn't use it to pay for her own needs. This will was written before she had her first stroke,' he said, checking the date at the top of the piece of paper he held. 'It is possible that after she had the stroke and you came to live here, she was unable to explain the situation to you or was simply unable to remember that it was here. We will probably never know.'

Jo felt numb.

'So, what house sale do I benefit from?' she queried, her heart sinking. She suspected that she knew already.

'Ah yes, I'm afraid that's the slightly awkward bit of all this. It is the house that you are currently living in, your grandmother's house. You would have been a minor when this will was written and still at school. The will states that her house be sold, and the monies put into a trust fund for you until you are twenty-one. As you are currently over twenty-one,' he looked at her over the top of his glasses and she nodded, 'we can dispense with the trust fund, and you will just inherit the monies from the house sale. I'm afraid that as your grandmother's will specifically mentions selling the house, you are legally obliged to sell it.'

Jo felt devastated. She loved that house. It was small and cosy and lovely. It was the house her mother had grown up in, the house her grandparents had lived in. It was her home and now as well as losing the last remaining member of her family, she was to lose it too.

She walked home from the meeting in a melancholic daze. Soon she would be homeless and, even though she had a large inheritance coming her way, she knew she did not deserve it at all. She stopped to look in the window of a dress shop. It did not bring her any joy, her heart was too heavy about having to sell the house and she wasn't much of a clothes horse anyway. Jeans and tops were her style, well you didn't need much else when you were a gardener, a few smarter tops and the odd sundress for going out with friends in the summer but that was all. A good pair of wellies and a reliable waterproof had probably been her biggest extravagances of the year clothes wise, or any wise come to that.

It was tearfully that Jo explained the events of the afternoon to Alain and Marie who had thoughtfully invited her around that evening, knowing she would be a bit down after the funeral. She did not tell them about the money, just that she had inherited a few savings and had to sell the house.

'I'm sure you'll find another nice house to buy,' comforted Marie, 'or a small flat, although I expect you'll want somewhere with a garden.'

The thought of buying another house in the village and seeing her grandmother's house with strange people coming and going from it all the time was not an appealing one.

'Yes, I suppose so,' she replied miserably.

'Or, and I can't believe I'm saying this, you could take up Henri's offer and make a fresh start,' Alain said. 'Have you thought any more about that?'

She hadn't really, but she must, they would be back soon and wanting an answer. As if reading her thoughts, Alain continued. 'They are coming back here next Thursday, just for a couple of nights before making their way home. Honestly, Jo, I don't want to lose you from the team, but it would be a fantastic challenge for you. Something to put on your C.V. Maybe even start your own business on the back of. I remember the garden when Mary was alive. Do you remember Marie, how beautiful it was? Henri showed me the pictures of it now. Looks like nothing much has been done since she died.' He paused. 'You can always come back here if it doesn't work out, stay with us until you find your own place.'

Jo thought long and hard about it as she lay in bed that night. Stay here, safe in a job she loved but a house that she would not because it would not be her grandmother's house or make a new start with people, to be honest she didn't know that well, but who she knew to be kind. She would then be taking on a garden that needed a lot of work. She was still in two minds about it as she went to work the following morning.

All the hedging on the parterre in front of the chateau had been trimmed now and was looking its best for the coming winter months, but they were still busy planting the last of the bulbs and winter bedding. Jo walked up to the nursery with the large flatbed trolley they used to collect trays of bedding plants to transport them to wherever they were needed in the garden. It was nearly lunchtime and she hoped to catch Maurice before he went to the staff canteen. She left the trolley outside and wandered through the long poly tunnel, trays of plants on raised wooden benches either side of a central narrow path, ready to be planted out. She loved the smell of all the plants in here and breathed in deeply. Jo thought she could see the plants she needed but wanted to check with Maurice to make sure. Unfortunately, it looked like he had gone to lunch already so she turned to go. She froze in her tracks when she saw who had followed her in.

Immediately she felt the panic rise. She had managed to avoid Serge since that evening. She wondered whether Alain had strategically placed him in a different part of the garden to where she had been working.

'Have you thought any more about my offer Cherie?' he drawled, coming towards her. 'It's been nearly two weeks now and I've hardly seen you. Have you been avoiding me?'

She looked behind her, the tunnel the other end was closed, and there was no way past him, she would have to think quickly. She picked up a tray of plants and held it in front of her as if she were about to carry it out to the trolley.

'I'm sorry Serge, I'm *really* busy right now. I've got to get these plants down to the parterre, they are needed right away, can we talk about this later?' She moved towards him expecting him to back out of the tunnel to let her pass. He didn't. 'Serge, let me past, please,' she begged.

'Not until you answer my question,' he insisted, still blocking the way.

'Serge, I don't think you and I are a good idea. I can take care of myself thank you and have been doing so for a long time. Why don't you find some nice girl who needs a man like you to look after her?'

'You let that English guy look after you last week,' he argued petulantly and spat in disgust. A great fat glob of saliva dribbled down the leaf of the primula it landed on and dripped onto the tray underneath. Inwardly Jo shuddered.

'He wasn't looking after me, Serge, he was being a friend, nothing more.' She was not going to tell him that he would be back this week. 'Now, let me go please, I've got to get on.'

He came towards her until all that was between them was the tray of plants she was holding. Leaning across he took hold of her head between his hands and pulled her face towards his. She could feel his unpleasantly sour breath on her skin.

'I will never let you go Jo Stanton. Never. I will wear you down until you are mine Cherie,' he pressed his lips against hers.

In shock and disgust, Jo dropped the tray of plants and lashed out at his face to push him away. 'Get away from me!' she shouted, blind panic kicking in now. Moving back as fast as she could she stumbled, and taking several of the nearby plants with her, ended up in a heap on the floor covered in bits of leaf and compost. To her immense relief, when she looked up, she saw that Serge had gone. How on earth was she going to clear up this mess?

She stood up and brushed herself down. A whole tray of plants and several others lay in a mess at her feet. Lots had fallen out of their pots, and many had lost leaves. She would have to tidy up as best she could.

Repotting the plants took a little while, especially as her hands were shaking uncontrollably. Some of them sadly were unsalvageable. She hoped Maurice had planted a few spares, he usually did, or she would have to somehow change the planting design of the beds. Jo found a dustpan and brush under one of the counters and did a final sweep round. It was not quite as good as it looked before but was tidy anyway. She would have to find Maurice and explain. She would tell him she had tripped over, which was kind of true. Nobody needed to know about Serge. Soon she would be out of here, she thought. She had made up her mind.

The following Thursday evening Jo was invited to Alain and Marie's once more to meet up with Henri and Thomas. She had been thinking about what to say to them. She knew now that she needed a fresh start, away from Serge, but she had the house to sell still, and the paperwork would take time to get sorted. She had also assured Miles that she would be there for the Christmas concerts this year for which they had all been practising hard.

Over dinner, she announced her decision to take Henri up on his kind offer.

'Oh. I am pleased, my dear!' he exclaimed, squeezing her hand. 'You won't regret it. Will she, Thomas?'

'I do hope not. You'll have to get used to my father, I expect he will be badgering you to play duets with him every evening and Barbara will be trying to fatten you up with her latest delicious culinary creation,' he murmured sipping his wine thoughtfully.

'Who is Barbara?' She had not heard mention of her before.

'She is our wonderful live-in housekeeper,' explained Henri. 'She came to us many years ago as a nurse when my wife was very ill and looked after her when I couldn't be there because of work commitments. After Mary died, I asked her to stay on. Thomas and I are no good at cooking at all and I didn't fancy starving to death.'

'Hey, speak for yourself Dad, I do a mean scrambled egg in the microwave,' Thomas protested making everyone laugh.

'Do you live with your father then?' Jo asked Thomas. She had not really twigged the 'we' and 'our' parts of the conversations before tonight. Henri jumped in.

'Yes, he does. Thomas uses the studio for his writing. Can't seem to get rid of him! Although I really haven't been trying to. He's a good boy, looking after his father in his old age.' Henri looked at Thomas and winked.

Jo didn't think that Thomas appreciated his father calling him a 'boy.'

'I'm afraid I can't come to you until the house is sold and all the probate paperwork has gone through, although the notary said it should all be straightforward and not take as long as usual.' She could feel the tears welling up at the back of her eyes again. Thinking about selling the house seemed to have that effect on her. 'I went into the estate agents yesterday to put it on the market, they sent a man around straight away to take pictures. Sorry,' she said reaching into her bag for a tissue.

'The house means a lot to you, doesn't it?' said Henri and she nodded, dabbing away the tears again. 'Life can be so cruel sometimes, giving with one hand and taking away with another. However, I am sure it won't take long to sell. It is small and pretty looking on the outside, somebody will want it for a holiday home or something I expect.' He looked across at Thomas.

'I will have to clear all the furniture out. I haven't even started on Grand-mere's clothes yet,' she sniffed.

'We can help you with that,' offered Alain. 'I am sure if you've got heavy furniture to clear, we can mobilise a team of strapping gardeners. Offer to pay them in wine and they'll all be banging on your door to help carry things!'

It was agreed in the end that they would all stay in touch and that with any luck a move date at the end of January would be possible.

Chapter 5

As it turned out Henri had been right. Jo received a phone call from the estate agent two days later to say that they had a buyer for the house. She had not even shown anyone around yet. Apparently, the buyer was someone who bought houses to do up as holiday lets. They were also willing to take the furniture as they thought it part of the 'period charm' having seen the photographs. All she had to do was clear out any personal belongings. Looking around her grandmother's house she hardly thought of the very careworn furniture as 'period charm' but if it saved her a job, who was she to argue? An added bonus was that she could move out whenever she liked, so a moving date was set for the end of January, and it was agreed that Thomas would come and get her.

Jo spent the following weeks sorting through her grandmother's clothes and belongings. Most of them went to charity shops but personal items, like photo albums and her grandmother's well-thumbed handwritten recipe book, Jo packed away in on old wooden trunk that she would take with her. She was sure it would fit in Thomas' car and between them they should be able to lift it, even when it was full. She had made a few interesting discoveries in her clear out, like a bundle of old love letters sent between her grandparents before they had married. Jo sat down and read them one evening, tears coursing down her face at the words they had used to describe their longing for each other when apart. It was sad to think that nobody wrote letters like that anymore, nobody had the time these days to sit and think of beautiful things to say to the person they loved most in the world. It was a shame she thought, if anyone wrote a letter like that to her, it would make her love them all the more.

Christmas passed peacefully. It had been strange without her grandmother, but Jo had made a wreath of evergreens and laid it on her grave. A few weeks later came the end of her work at the chateau. She was sad to go. She had not told many people she was leaving and certainly not where she was going to for fear of Serge finding out. The last thing she wanted was more trouble on that front. In the middle of January, Alain and Marie had thrown her a very low-key leaving party at their house with just a few select guests like Miles and Maurice and a couple of the girls she had worked with.

Finally, moving day arrived and with it, Thomas and a swirling blizzard of snow. He had come the previous evening and stayed overnight with Alain and Marie. Loading the car up Jo wondered if they were going to be able to get to St Malo to catch the overnight ferry to Portsmouth. It was a journey she was not looking forward to.

Shutting the door to her grandmother's house for the last time was a surreal feeling, knowing that the next person to walk through it would be the new owner who would see it as just another house in their portfolio rather than a home, well-loved and full of treasured memories. Jo popped the key into an envelope and walked across the square to the estate agents, the snow already thick enough to crump under her boots. When she got back to the car, Alain and Marie had arrived to wave them off. She felt a lump form in her throat as she hugged them and thanked them for being such good friends, she would miss them dreadfully.

'Well, take care of yourselves, drive really carefully, if the weather gets too bad turn around and come back, I've got a job going on the gardening team,' Alain joked to ease the tension. He could see that this was not easy for Jo. Marie gave her another tight hug.

'I'm going to miss you,' she said. 'I'll have to persuade Alain to take a break in the summer and we'll pop over and see you, or you can come to us when you get the chance.'

Finally, all the goodbyes had been said. Thomas and Jo got in the car. Turning the heating up full whack, Thomas looked across at Jo.

'Ready?'

'Ready.'

Jo wound down the window and waved at Alain and Marie and at her grandmother's house until they turned the corner, and she could see them no more. They drove up the road, past the turning to the nursing home and the chateau, and then off into countryside, onto the road that would take her to the next part of her life. As they drove in silence Jo felt an almost overwhelmingly heavy sense of loss, as if her heart had been torn from her body and her grandmother had died all over again. She looked out the window, her watery eyes just able to make out the snowflakes that swirled through the air like a million frozen tears mourning her departure. She wondered if she would ever come back. She thought of the early morning visit she had made to the graveside to say her final farewell, her warm breath making soft clouds that hung in the air like ghosts floating over her grandparent's grave. Closing her eyes, tears seeped from the corners and trickled slowly down the side of her face. Surreptitiously wiping them away, she took deep breaths to try and stop herself sobbing and then blew her nose on one of the many tissues she had stuffed in her pockets earlier, knowing that she'd probably feel like this.

'You alright?' asked Thomas glancing at her quickly.

'Yes. Just being sentimental. I don't seem to be able to help myself. It's hard, you know, leaving somewhere that has been a part of your life ever since you can remember, not really knowing when or if you'll ever be back. Sorry, I didn't mean to be a complete blubbery mess. I really am looking forward to working for your dad.'

'Blubber away if you want to, I don't mind.' It was the way he said it that made her laugh. 'I think being sentimental is a good thing, it means you feel deeply and care about things. Too often these days we hide our feelings away, denying what we really feel, pretending to the world that we are alright when really, we are breaking on the inside.'

'Wow! That was deep. Personal experience?'

'Sort of,' he hesitated wondering whether to tell her. 'When my mother was ill, I was at university in Edinburgh in my final year, facing some tough summer exams and although I'd been back and forth regularly to see her, I couldn't get back at the very end. I was miles away sitting my last exam on the day she died. It was awful. For a while, I felt I'd let her down and let Dad down not being there for him either. I bottled it up for a long time, over a year, feeling so angry with myself and the world in general for being such a cruel place. I was not a nice person to be around.'

'Gosh, that must have been really tough, how did you come through it?'

'Writing and love.'

She waited, hoping that he would explain.

'I got to the point where I was so broken up inside, I had to let it out somehow, so I wrote God a letter, telling him what an awful useless son I was, and asked Him why He had to take my mother from us? I told Him how Dad was broken too and just how plain angry I was at the whole damn situation and asked Him what was He going to do about it? When I'd finished, I felt different, kind of clean and new. As if in writing all my feelings down I'd poured them out from myself onto the paper. I showed the letter to Dad and Barbara. We spent the afternoon crying and hugging and talking to each other, like a little family therapy session. We promised that we'd always talk and look out for each other, Mum would have wanted that, she loved all of us so much. It was then that I really knew I wanted to be a writer. It was as if I needed to start writing to be able to live again.' He smiled at her. 'So, I kind of know how you're feeling. Grief and loss make us cry, it's good to let it out. Just don't let it get you down for too long.'

She looked at him across the car. Never in her whole life had she ever heard a man speak about feelings like that and she felt a sense of privilege that he had shared something so personal with her. It touched a nerve deep in her soul somewhere and made her think of events in her life that had brought her to this moment in time. It was hard to know what to say.

'Thank you for sharing that. It means a lot.'

'What are friends for?' He smiled. 'Besides, you are coming to live with us, you need to know how just plain crazy we can be at times!'

The snow was still falling outside the car, thick fluffy snowflakes that smashed against the glass, before being swept away by the wipers and squashed into a layer of ice at the edge of the windscreen. Traffic had slowed to a cautious crawl but was still moving. Jo was extremely glad of the warmth in the car, feeling cocooned against the cold of the icy winds outside.

'Do you think we're going to make it?' she asked.

'I hope so, we left reasonably early, so we have a bit of contingency time built in.'

They were about half-way to St Malo when the traffic on the main road slowed to a stop altogether and had been sitting there stationary for about an hour, when the blue lights flashed by in the opposite direction. A few drivers had got out of their cars, braving the cold to find the reason for the holdup. Apparently, a nasty accident further ahead. They were stuck. Unable to go back or forth with no side roads on this section all they could do was sit, wait and watch as time ticked by. It took another three quarters of an hour for the debris of several cars in the pile up to be cleared and get the traffic moving slowly once more. It was late now and obvious that they would miss the ferry.

'We'll have to rebook for the crossing tomorrow,' Thomas said. 'It should be ok at this time of the year; they can't be too busy. It's the end of January, not the height of the holiday season.'

They arrived at the ferry terminal late and tired after having stopped for a short break and some food along the way. Jo had not felt very hungry, the thought of a ferry crossing made her stomach churn, but a hot coffee had been very welcome. As it happened the ferry had not been able to sail anyway because of high winds, but the man at the desk in the ferry terminal was fairly certain that he could find them space on tomorrow's overnight crossing which should go ahead as the weather forecast looked more promising then. There were no cabins available, all the spare ones having been snapped up already by people in the same position as themselves, but they did have seats available. They booked a couple and then went to find the nearest hotel for the night. The first one they tried was, surprisingly, fully booked.

'It's because of the rugby,' explained a harassed looking receptionist. 'The friendly between England and France? We get a lot of fans that take the overnight crossing and then go to the game the next day. Because the ferry hasn't sailed, they've all booked in for the night, hoping to get across on the early hydrofoil tomorrow. It's been madness here. You could try the motel across the road, they might have something.'

After slithering through the ice across the road, they dinged the bell at the motel reception desk and a scruffy unshaven man with a cigarette drooping from his lips shuffled out from the room behind, looking for all the world as if he had only just woken up.

'Only one room left,' wheezed the man. 'It's a single, far end of the block, but you two lovebirds won't mind cosying up for the night, eh?' He winked at Thomas and held up the key as the ash from the cigarette dropped onto the counter. Thomas and Jo looked at each other trying not to laugh, Jo blushing at the man's suggestive remark.

'What do you reckon, fancy being my roomie for the night?' Thomas smiled.

She was too tired to look for anywhere else and it was late and cold. She hoped the room was cleaner than its owner.

It was clean. Clean but cold. The miniscule heater barely warm to the touch. Jo insisted that Thomas take the bed as he had to drive the next day and needed the rest. There was space on the floor for her and they found a thin extra blanket and pillow in the rickety wardrobe. She lay for a while, in the darkness trying to sleep, running the events of the day through her head. It was so cold in the room that when she lay on her back, she could see the moisture from her breath illuminated in the faint streetlight seeping through the inadequate curtains. She could not remember when she had last felt so cold. She shivered, trying to tuck the blanket around herself in a vain effort to trap some body heat.

'Look, this is no good,' Thomas said at last, sitting up and switching on the light. 'I can't bear it. You are freezing down there, I'm sure I can hear your teeth chattering. Why don't we share the bed? There's room if we snuggle up close. If we put your blanket on top of the duvet, we'll both be warmer.'

Jo could see the sense in it but the thought of 'snuggling up close' to a man like Thomas made her insides feel all weird and her face go suddenly hot with embarrassment. He sensed her hesitation.

'Look, we are both fully clothed, no funny stuff, it just makes sense if either of us are to get a wink of sleep tonight.'

'Yes, you're right I suppose. Needs must,' she agreed reluctantly.

They arranged the spare blanket on the bed and then both got in at the same time from their respective sides.

'Which side do you sleep on best, we'll probably fit better if we both turn the same way?' he said.

'Right, I think.'

They lay in the bed together in the dark, Jo hardly daring to breathe. She could feel his body weighing the mattress down behind her, his warm breath on the nape of her neck. It was strangely comforting to hear him breathing next to her and definitely warmer than the floor. Despite her reservations, she felt safe and eventually they both slept.

Jo woke first the next morning, her face cold but her body deliciously warm. Somehow, she must have rolled over in the night for she found herself nearly nose to nose with Thomas, his arm thrown over her almost pinning her to the bed, their legs somewhat entangled. She studied his face for a moment relaxed in sleep still, the faint creases of laughter lines at the corners of his eyes. With two days of dark stubble and tousled hair, he looked impossibly, boyishly, handsome. Suddenly his eyes flickered open, and he smiled.

'Good morning, Miss Stanton. Sleep well?' he murmured, rolling onto his back and releasing her from his grip.

She blushed and hoped he hadn't noticed her studying him, quickly she swung her legs over the side of the bed and got up.

'Yes, thank you. Sorry if I disturbed you in the night. I seem to have managed to roll over,' she said sitting on the side off the bed with her back to him to pull her boots on, giving her time to compose herself.

'Do you know you talk in your sleep?' he teased.

'Oh crikey! Do I? I'm sorry. What did I say?'

'I'm not really sure, you were muttering something about you shouldn't have done it. Didn't really make a lot of sense. Probably just overtiredness from yesterday.'

'Mm, must have been. Do you want the bathroom first?'

After taking it in turns to have a quick wash in decidedly lukewarm water, they checked out, the scruffy motel owner winking again at Thomas as he asked them whether they had had a pleasant night. Really, some people have a one-track mind thought Jo as they went to find something hot for breakfast. A Relais Routiers was the best nearby, full of early morning truckers but if it was popular, it must be good, she thought. They found a newly vacated table and pushed the dirty plates to one end as they sat down and picked up the slightly sticky plastic covered menus.

'I'm starving,' Thomas declared. 'Must be the cold, always makes me feel hungry, I could murder a full English right now, sadly not on the menu here. I will, however, have the rump steak and fries. How about you?'

Jo thought about the upcoming ferry crossing later. 'Just some toast and coffee for me thanks.' They ordered when the waitress came to clear the table and sat in a companionable silence eating their food when it arrived.

They spent the day killing time, pottering around a couple of the small local towns. There was not much open and little to see apart from a few small churches, which were only slightly warmer inside than out. It had stopped snowing sometime in the night, the pristine white turning to a slushy grey as it melted and was trampled underfoot, but the wind was still quite strong and icy cold. They sat in a café for a while, lingering over hot drinks in an effort to warm up, Thomas hungrily devouring another portion of steak and chips. As afternoon turned to evening, they made their way back to St Malo relieved to find that the ferry was due to sail on time.

Finding their allocated seats, Jo was already feeling queasy. Thomas said he was going to try sleeping for a bit and rested his head back in the seat, eyes closed. Jo had brought a book to read, and she tried to concentrate on the words which swam about on the page before her, rather than the churning feeling in her stomach. It was going to be a long night. As the ferry headed out to sea and away from the calmer waters of the port Jo promptly made a dash for the deck and vomited over the side. She wiped her face with a tissue, strands of dark hair that had escaped her ponytail whipping about her face in the wind. She was not a good sailor. Staggering to the side of the boat, Jo looked through the window. She could just see their seats; Thomas was blissfully asleep already by the look of it.

It started to rain about an hour into the crossing. Fat icy droplets, swirling through the dark of the night, that drenched Jo's hair and ran down the back of her neck soaking her clothes as she continued to retch over the side. She felt utterly miserable, terribly cold, and horribly sick. Unable to go inside for any length of time because of her continuous seasickness, she huddled down on the deck as the ferry tossed back and forth in the swell, willing herself not to be ill again for 5 minutes together at least. She tried to think pleasant thoughts to distract herself, imagining herself walking around the gardens of the chateau telling herself the names of the plants that lined each walkway, but it was no good. The relentless heaving of both the sea and Jo's stomach continued. After an hour or so, she did not have anything left in her stomach to be sick with, just horrible mouthfuls of bile that she spat over the side leaving her feeling exhausted and utterly weak. Dawn found her pale and drawn, slumped on the deck looking like a piece of flotsam washed up after a storm. She didn't care how she looked, she felt like death.

It was here that Thomas found her as they approached Portsmouth Harbour. He had slept through it all, woken to find her missing, and gone out on deck to look for her.

'Damn it, Jo,' he said, 'why didn't you tell me you got seasick?' He wiped the hair away from her ashen face, gently scooping her up off the deck to carry her inside.

'Put me down Thomas, I can walk, I'm ok really, just not a good sailor,' she moaned feeling her stomach heave again 'Oh, no put me down, I need to…'

Her words were lost as Thomas put her down and she clung on to the side rail retching again. Looking up, she could see the harbour coming into view. Thank goodness it would soon be over, and she would have her feet back on solid ground again. The ferry docked and Thomas kept his arm around her as they descended to the car deck. She did not complain. Her legs felt like liquid jelly.

It was about a two-hour journey to Oxbury, the small village just outside Oxford that she would call home and an immense relief to be in the car riding along, warm air blowing on her frozen feet. It had not snowed here but heavy grey skies dripped a continuous light rain. They had stopped at a service station for Thomas to get breakfast and Jo a bottle of water which was all she felt she could manage in the circumstances, taking small sips as they continued their journey. Her clothes were still wet through, and she felt chilled to the bone as she sneezed. By the time they reached Oxbury, she was feeling shivery and feverish.

Henri and Barbara stood in the doorway of the house ready to greet them as they came in.

'Jo, wonderful to see you again, looks like you've had a bit of a journey,' said Henri as he kissed her on both cheeks. 'This is Barbara. I've been telling her all about you.'

'Non-stop since he came back from France in November!' continued Barbara, laughing and giving her a friendly hug. 'Lovely to meet you dear. Oh, you are wet through, aren't you? Come into the warm. Thomas, take her coat, will you?'

'Thank you, it's lovely to meet you too.' Jo felt the room suddenly sway around her, she felt awfully fuzzy. 'Do you mind if I...'

The words 'sit down a minute' never left her lips as everything went black and she passed out; Thomas just managed to catch her before she hit the floor.

Chapter 6

Gently, Thomas carried Jo into the living room at the back of the house and rested her down on the sofa.

'Elevate her feet,' Barbara instructed. 'It might help bring her round.' She gathered up a few cushions and put them on the end of the sofa lifting Jo's legs and removing her sodden boots before resting them down on the pile of cushions.

'Jo! Jo? Can you hear me?' Thomas was kneeling down beside her rubbing her hand, a look of deep concern on his face. This was all his fault. He should have taken better care of her. He smoothed her hair from her face and rested his hand on her forehead. 'Barbara, she feels very hot.'

'I've called Dr Bob,' Henri announced, coming into the room. 'He should be here any minute. Luckily, he was in the pub, I hope he hasn't had too much to drink.'

'Let's see if we can take her coat off,' suggested Barbara. 'Thomas, you lift her up and I'll wrestle with the coat.'

Between them Barbara and Thomas managed to remove Jo's coat only to find that underneath her clothes were completely soaked.

Jo came around a few minutes later to see a bearded face and a pair of smiling brown eyes and three other faces all looking genuinely concerned peering down at her. She felt heavy and fuzzy all over.

'There we go! Back in the land of the living again,' said the man with the brown eyes. 'Hi, I'm Dr Bob. Looks like you passed out for a few minutes Jo. Do you know where you are? I'm just going to take your temperature.'

Jo looked around. 'Yes, I think so,' she said groggily as the thermometer beeped in her ear.

'Hmm 38.6. That is a bit high. What have you been doing to yourself? I think I need to give you a bit of a check over.' He turned to the others who shuffled out of the room and closed the door behind them. Dr Bob helped her sit up, listened to her chest through his stethoscope and took her pulse and blood pressure all the while getting her to tell him about the journey and the seasickness.

'Well,' he pronounced, 'you are certainly dehydrated, the fact that you haven't eaten anything for a couple of days doesn't help and that's probably the main reason you passed out, but I think on top of that you've got a touch of the flu going on. However, you are young and normally healthy?' She nodded, and winced, her head felt like a lump of lead stuck on her shoulders. 'You need plenty of fluids, paracetamol and ibuprofen to bring your temperature down and most importantly, rest. You might feel a little rough for a few days, but this will get better on its own. Ok to tell the others? I think you gave them a bit of a scare,' he smiled.

Jo thought he was nice. Young. Beautiful eyes. Maybe she should register with him if he was local.

He walked over to the door and called the others back in. They looked worried as Dr Bob explained she had the flu.

'Right,' said Barbara, taking charge after they had seen him out, she had been a nurse after all. 'We need to get you out of those wet clothes, into a nice warm bed and feed you lots of soup and copious cups of tea,' she smiled. 'Thomas, I think we'll put her in the guest bedroom, can you carry her up and I'll find something for her to wear? Henri, make some tea and find the paracetamol.'

Jo did not protest.

'I'm so sorry, to be such a nuisance,' she said to Thomas as he carried her up the stairs. 'After all the trouble you've gone through to get me here.'

He kicked the door of the bedroom open with his foot and put her down so she was sitting on a stool that belonged to an old-fashioned dressing table set against the wall. He sat down on the end of the bed opposite, took her hand and sighed.

'You have nothing to apologise for. It is me that should be apologising to you. I should have taken care of you on the ferry. I am so sorry Jo. I had no idea you were feeling so ill. I feel really rotten about it all.'

'Please don't. It's not your fault, these things happen. I'm sure I will be fighting fit soon enough, although I may not be able to start on the garden for a few days. I hope your dad won't mind.'

'He won't mind at all,' said Henri coming into the room with a tray of tea, biscuits, and paracetamol. 'We must look after you first. I don't care if you don't start on the garden for another month! We're just glad you are here, aren't we Thomas?'

'What are all you men doing in here?' Barbara bustled in with a floral nightie and dressing gown over her arm. 'Off you go now and leave poor Jo to get changed and into bed. Shoo!'

A hot shower and two paracetamols later Jo had been tucked into bed, pillows propping her up as she sipped her second cup of hot sweet tea. Henri and Thomas had returned sitting on the end of the bed, one on each side, and Barbara occupied the stool with her ample bottom. They were all chatting about the best combination of vegetables to make soup with. Jo felt suddenly at home, instantly comfortable with these people who had been so kind. She could feel her eyelids drooping, when had she last slept? It seemed like an age ago.

Jo was woken several hours later by Barbara.

'Just need to check your temperature, my love and you should try to eat something. I've got some nice soup on the hob.' She sat on the side of the bed and looked at the thermometer. 'Mm still high. I'll bring you up some ibuprofen.'

When she had gone, Jo looked around the room. It was old fashioned but in a cosy pleasant way. Soft pink floral wallpaper covered the walls and matching curtains were drawn across the windows. It looked dark outside; she had no idea what time it was. There were three doors in the room she noticed. The far one, which she had come in through, led out to the corridor and stairs, the one in the corner opposite the bed was the ensuite shower room and the one opposite that looked like it should connect to a room next door. She could hear the floorboards creak gently as if someone were in there, pacing backwards and forwards.

Barbara appeared in the doorway with a tray.

'Grubs up!' she called cheerfully.

The soup was delicious. Barbara stayed and chatted while Jo ate. She was a comfortably built woman with short, greying curly hair and a kind face, pale blue eyes rimmed with a delicate touch of makeup behind her glasses. She had a motherly air about her, had even smelt motherly, Jo thought when she had taken her temperature earlier.

The next time Jo woke was to hear her name being called softly, the voice sounded far away as if coming to her from another world. She opened her eyes, boy did she feel awful! Her limbs ached, and she was bathed in sweat, her hair plastered to her face, her mouth dry and scratchy.

'Jo are you alright?' The voice was nearer now.

'Thomas?'

She felt the mattress dip and a hand on her arm.

'I think you were having a nightmare; you were calling out.'

He switched on the small bedside light, and she could see that the door between the two rooms stood open. She swivelled her head to look at where he sat. Loosely wrapped in a towelling bathrobe, hair dishevelled, he had obviously just got out of bed. The gape in his bathrobe showed a fine sprinkling of dark hair across his chest.

'Oh gosh, I'm sorry,' she mumbled feeling the heat rise in her face. 'Sorry, did I wake you up?'

'It's ok. I wasn't really asleep,' he fibbed. 'You look awful, here, let me fetch you some water.' He went across to the bathroom room and came back with a small glass of water and a cold damp flannel. Gently he wiped her face. 'Better now?'

'Mm, thank you.'

'How are you feeling really?'

'A bit like I've run a marathon, done a hundred press ups and swallowed a cactus. What's the time?'

He laughed softly, padded into his room and came back.

'Three o'clock.'

He picked up the thermometer.

'Better check,' he whispered.

Her temperature was still high, so he gave her two more paracetamol and she swallowed them down with the glass of water. She would rattle soon she thought as she lay down.

'Do you want the light left on?'

'No, thanks.'

He switched the light off and whispered into the darkness.

'I'm just next door if you need me. I'll leave the door ajar. Sleep tight.'

Jo heard the floorboards creak as he left, and she slept soundly once more.

Three days later Jo was feeling much better, her temperature was mostly normal, and she didn't ache quite so much, although she still hadn't been let downstairs. Dr Bob had been back to check on her and declared her to be on the mend. He had stayed quite a while, sitting on the end of the bed with Barbara who had insisted on making him tea whilst they talked about France and holidays he had taken there. She had discovered that his full name was Bob Everton, but everyone called him Dr Bob and that he lived in the village with his ginger cat Eunice, named after a great aunt he'd once had, who had also been ginger. He was pleasant, easy to get along with and had made her laugh.

Jo decided that today she would shower, dress and venture downstairs. It was time she made an effort.

Unsurprisingly, she had not noticed the house on her arrival. Standing on the galleried landing outside her room she took in the curved wooden staircase that swirled down to a square entrance hall with a deep red carpet. Wooden beams and linen-fold panelling echoed its history. A piano was being played softly in one of the downstairs rooms and the aroma of baking wafted through the air. Gingerly she made her way down holding the handrail, her legs a little wobbly still. She followed the delicious smell and found herself in the kitchen. This was the bottom half of the newer extension and was wonderfully light and spacious. A large rectangular oak table sat in the middle of the room and on the far side Barbara was washing something up in the sink, humming along with the music.

'Oh! Hello dear. Should you be down yet?' Barbara said, turning on hearing her come into the kitchen. 'Have a seat, I've just made a fresh pot.'

'Thank you. I feel much better this morning, thought I'd better start making and effort. Is that Henri playing?'

'Yes, he does most days, it's in his soul you know. I always know how he's feeling depending on what he plays.' She smiled and listened. 'He's happy today, it's Mozart. You probably think I'm a bit daft.'

'No, I know exactly what you mean. Some days are dark, loud Beethoven days and others are busy Chopin days, but I agree today is definitely a Mozart kind of morning.'

They both laughed and Barbara went to call Henri for his tea.

'Ah ma petite, you are feeling better today?' Henri said coming into the kitchen with Barbara.

She nodded.

'Yes, thank you, much better.'

'Good. You look better, more colour in your cheeks, eh?'

'Thought I had better start to make an effort,' she replied.

Henri looked at his watch. 'Hm, Thomas is late today.'

Jo looked at Barbara confused.

'Elevenses dear,' she explained. 'You'll have to get used to our funny little ways, Jo. Whatever we are doing, if we are "in", we meet for elevenses every morning in the kitchen. Tea and biscuits or coffee if you prefer. It's our way of keeping in touch throughout the day. Thomas is usually up early, Henri and I at different times so we don't always see each other for breakfast. It's good to touch base.'

'Yes, and we always try to eat together in the evening too. Will you join us my dear? We would all love your company but there's no pressure, you know. If you want to go out night clubbing one evening, you are absolutely free to do so or whatever else you young people get up to these days,' Henri said, tucking into a plate of what looked like homemade cookies. He offered her one.

'I would love to join you, thank you. Don't worry, I'm not really a nightclubbing sort of girl,' she laughed.

'Are you not, Jo? Dad, are you trying to persuade Jo to take you nightclubbing?' Thomas quipped coming into the kitchen and pinching a cookie off the plate his father was still holding out to Jo.

'Do you know, if she asked me, I probably would,' said Henri. 'What do you think Barbara? I'm sure we could "shake our booty" with the best of them.'

'I don't know about you Henri, but my "booty" likes to get to bed on time these days,' she said, giving him a look over the top of her glasses. 'But really Jo, you can come and go as you please. Let me know if you don't want dinner, if I'm not in just leave me a note.'

After the tea and several delicious cookies, Jo felt a little less wobbly.

'Now you are feeling better, we must show you the gardener's cottage. I say cottage, but it's actually a very tiny bungalow, no upstairs. Come. I'll show you now.' Henri got up and fetched a key from a drawer. 'This way.'

Following Henri out the front door Jo could see a white painted building across the rectangular gravelled driveway. It lay at right angles to the main house and had sign saying 'Gardener's Cottage' next to a celadon-coloured front door. On entering, Jo could see that it was indeed small, but perfectly formed. A kitchen area with floor to ceiling cupboards one side and a sink, hob and counter the other, led through to an open plan tiny lounge. Two small sofas almost filled the space and a French door led out onto the main garden. Beyond the lounge was a reasonably spacious bedroom with a tiny bathroom in one corner. Jo could see that all the things she had brought with her had been thoughtfully taken in already and lay in a pile on the bedroom floor ready for her to make herself at home.

'This is delightful Henri. I'm sure I shall be very happy here, thank you.'

'This used to be a double garage and tool store you know, when I first lived here with Mary. We always talked about converting it into something more useful but never got around to it. Thomas and I finished this last year. You are officially the first occupant. You must let me know if you have any problems with anything, it should all be ok as everything is new. Sadly, there is no room for a piano, but I hope you will feel free to come and play mine whenever you want.' He turned to her and touched her arm. 'You must not stop playing, my dear, ever.'

Henri and Jo strolled back to the house, and she caught a glimpse of the garden through a pair of huge iron gates. Henri followed her gaze.

'We will explore the garden tomorrow, Jo. Today is for making yourself at home and I think you need to rest still. The garden is not going anywhere, and we are in no rush. Let's go in and have an early lunch, eh?'

After lunch, Jo went back to the cottage to unpack her things. Hanging her clothes in the wardrobe and stuffing the suitcase on the top she realised how little she had, and actually how little she really needed in life. There was a bookcase in the bedroom on which Jo placed her books, 3 of them her faithful old gardening manuals. She explored the kitchen and found a washer dryer in one of the cupboards and a set of four of everything she would need in terms of china and cutlery. Really all she needed was some food for breakfasts and lunches if she was eating in the main house for dinner, and she was good to go. She went back to the house to pick Barbara's brain about the best places to shop nearby.

'Locally, dear, there's the Oxbury Stores and Post Office. It's run by Mrs West and her daughter Ellen. It's a small shop but they have all the basics. Turn left out of our gate and follow the wall of the garden along until you get to the T junction with the pub opposite, turn left there and the Stores are just a short way along the street. I shouldn't say this but just so you are forewarned: Mrs West is the head of the village gossip group. If you tell her anything, guaranteed the entire village will know it within the hour. Plus, she can talk the hind leg off a donkey. I don't know how Ellen puts up with her sometimes, it's time that young lady cut the apron strings if you ask me. Anyway, beware. Don't get me wrong, they are lovely people and salt of the earth, but just don't tell Mrs West your secrets!' They both laughed. Jo knew exactly what she meant. There had been a few, more mature women she'd known in France like that. 'Apart from that,' Barbara continued, 'the best place for shopping is Oxford. All the major supermarkets are there, and you'll find some good shops in town too. I go in at least once a week if you need anything.'

Jo thanked her and decided to take a stroll into the village. Walking down the lane next to the house she could see the pub directly in front of her. A sign indicating that it was called the 'St George and the Dragon' swung from a post outside. She wondered if it was any good inside. The car park at the side had a few cars in it, not bad she supposed for the middle of the afternoon. To the right of the pub, set in a junction between two roads was a picture-perfect village church, gravestones like odd teeth poking up from grassy gums surrounding it. She would explore that another time she thought as she turned left, walked along the street, and found the Stores.

Jo entered to the sound of a bell jingling above the door and took a basket from the stack. She nodded a good afternoon to the two women who had stopped chatting behind the counter as she had come in. She wandered down the first aisle. It was well stocked, she thought, as she chose a few groceries, brands that were unavailable in France suddenly bringing back childhood memories. She selected everything she immediately needed and went to the counter.

'Find everything you want dear?' enquired the more senior of the two. She was a short, dumpy sort of woman with obviously dyed dark hair and glasses that perched on the end of her nose, from which swung a beaded gold chain. The other was younger, pretty with long fair hair tied up in a messy bun. She wore the expression of a girl with an overbearing mother.

'Thank you, yes, oh, apart from some stamps please.'

'Book of six or twelve, first or second class?'

'Twelve please, first class.'

'Ellen, love, pop out the back and fetch me some more first-class stamps, would you?' the dumpy woman asked.

This must be the infamous Mrs West, thought Jo as she watched Ellen scoot of down the back of the shop in obedience. The woman peered over her glasses at Jo in between scanning the things she had chosen.

'Haven't seen you in the village before dear. Just passing through or have you moved into that house the other side of the church that was up for sale recently? Ever so expensive it was, still that's what you get these days isn't it, being so close to Oxford? All those posh rich university people snapping up our houses, so village families are priced out of the market, it's a shame. I'm Mrs West by the way, pleased to meet you.'

Jo wondered when she was going to be allowed to answer the woman's initial question and whether if, in fact, she had been one of the posh rich university people, she would feel slightly offended by now.

'I'm Jo Stanton, Henri Arnaud's new gardener, pleased to meet you too. I've just moved in recently. I'm living in their cottage.' No secrets there.

'Oh, welcome to Oxbury then! I expect we'll be seeing a lot more of you. Of course, it was Mary who did the garden there when she was alive, God rest her soul, lovely woman, sang like an angel she did, like an angel, didn't she Ellen? Still, it's good that he's finally got someone in to sort it out, must be terribly overgrown in there by now. I'm surprised he left it so long.' She leaned across the counter as if imparting something confidential. 'He was a broken man, you know, when she died. Broken.' She leaned back and continued, 'Have you met the son? Some sort of writer he is, fiction, I think. I'm not a big reader myself. Quite a catch though, and those eyes! All the girls in the village have been after him at some time or another, haven't they, Ellen? This is my Ellen, by the way.'

Ellen had arrived back with the stamps, standing mutely besides her mother not even attempting, Jo noticed, to answer the questions that had been thrown her way. Jo smiled at the girl who looked about the same age as herself and she smiled meekly back.

'Lovely to meet you Ellen, well I must be off. Thanks for the welcome.' She picked up her bags of shopping and exited swiftly, before Mrs West could draw a breath again, leaving the shop bell jangling in her wake.

Chapter 7

A blackbird singing on the lawn outside woke Jo the next morning. As she ate her cereal in the cottage kitchen, she felt a tingle of excitement about seeing the garden properly for the first time. She would be in charge from now on, she would decide what needed doing and when. She hoped she had learnt enough in the last seven years and suddenly felt a little daunted. Dressing warmly, she went across to the main house to see if Henri was up and ready as he said he would be.

He was and together they went out the front door turning left to the garden beyond.

Before her stood two huge, ornate iron gates. By the flakes of peeling paint, she could see that they had once been black, and the scrolling gilded. Restored, these would make a magnificent entrance. Through them, along a wide grey flagstone path, Jo could see a rustic wooden archway and gate opening into a wood beyond.

'These gates are a little rusty, I have to admit,' Henri said, pushing each heavy iron gate open to its fullest, the rusted hinges screeching in protest. 'And they need oiling, but I'm assured that they are basically sound.'

Jo stepped in through the gates. The whole garden lay before her.

To the right of the path, lay an almost square area of unkempt lawn surrounded by weedy flagstone paths, on two sides of which, borders ran, choked by invading weeds. At the furthest end stood what looked like a fountain plucked straight from the streets of Ancient Rome. A wide, mossy-green, shell-like basin formed the pool above which stood a naked Adonis carrying a pitcher on his shoulder, his blind eyes gazing towards the house. She wondered how long it had been since it had worked.

To the left of the central path the ground fell away in a short slope punctuated by three sets of steps; two at either end of the path, which continued around a larger, rectangular lawn equally wretched with weeds, and one central set of steps which led down onto the lawn itself. The once beautiful borders draped with brambles and spent seed heads, broken under the weight of winter, continued around the garden which was enclosed by a high, red brick wall. The far right-hand corner of the garden wall extended into an area of wilderness, lying forlorn and forgotten. Here, Jo glimpsed at what she thought might be a shed roof. At the furthest end of the garden, opposite the naked Adonis, an enormous, arched double wooden door festooned with riotous honeysuckle invited investigation beyond.

'Well, what do you think?' Henri asked. 'Can you restore it?'

Jo stood for a moment to take it all in. This garden was a forgotten paradise, bewitched by the spell of neglect, just waiting to be awoken by a gardener's kiss. A Kipling poem that she had once learnt at school came to mind.

'*Our England is a garden that is full of stately views,*
Of borders, beds and shrubberies and lawns and avenues.
With statues on the terraces and peacocks strutting by;
But the Glory of the Garden lies in more than meets the eye.'

It would certainly take a lot of virtuous hard work to restore the glory to this garden, with or without any peacocks.

'I can do it, but it will take time,' she replied eventually.

'Good. Take all the time that you need,' said Henri, 'it's all yours.'

They spent the next hour or so walking around the garden. Jo had stopped mentally making a list of all the things that needed attention. Everything needed it. The mossy topped brick wall that enclosed the garden looked weathered but sound. There may be a little pointing that needed doing, as there was between the flagstones of the path, but it didn't look beyond repair. She could see that climbing roses had been planted at intervals, now left to scamper over the walls in wild abandon. On a balmy summer evening, their heady perfume must have once been truly intoxicating.

'What colour are the roses Henri? They look like climbers rather than ramblers.'

'The roses along this side,' he pointed to the wall nearest the house, 'were white and pink if I remember rightly. Mary planted those many years ago when we were first married. Don't ask me their names but I think I remember her labelling everything at some point. Some of the labels might still there as far as

I know, hidden in the undergrowth! We get a few flowers in the summer but not as many as years ago. They desperately need pruning. My hips are too bad for me to climb up ladders these days and Thomas is too busy writing to do any pruning. Do you know, they always remind me of when Thomas was very small, he would collect handfuls of the fallen petals and toddle on his chubby little legs to put them in whatever trug Mary was using? He liked to help her when she was out here.' He chuckled to himself and then a wistful look crossed his face as if yearning for the days when Mary was at his side and life was full and exciting. In his memory, he could see his young son toddling around on the lawn, childish laughter filling the garden with joy.

Jo felt for him. She knew what it was like to wish for times past, to want to hold on to happiness forever and never let it go. When loss and grief were far away strangers, not as now, her constant companions.

'Well, I will certainly give those some attention,' reassured Jo, 'and look out for any labels as I go. If the roses are too far gone to revive, I'm sure we would be able to replace them with the same or a similar variety. There are some excellent rose nurseries in Britain that have old as well as new species. It will be lovely to restore this garden to what it originally was.'

'Yes,' Henri said, turning to Jo, 'but you must feel free to put your stamp on it too. The past has good memories, but we cannot live in the past, can we? We cannot bring the past back to life however much we want to. We must look forward. Preserve, yes, but also improve, write new music on the pages of life. That way fresh memories will be made to treasure. After all, today is tomorrow's past.'

She was certainly here to make fresh memories and to write new music onto the pages of her life.

They walked on around the path and reached the wilderness part of the garden that stuck out at right angles from the main lawn and border area. Almost in the centre was a slightly shabby looking shed, behind which appeared to be an extremely ancient compost heap. To the right, up against the wall, a wood store. This would make an excellent kitchen garden, Jo thought to herself. She could see it now as it could be. A fabulous Victorian style lean to greenhouse against the opposite wall complete with a vine or a couple of peach trees. Raised beds with fresh vegetables and there, along the wall backing on to the wood, would be a bed of rhubarb and other soft fruit bushes. In the corner, a small area for a bonfire to burn up all the woody waste, the resulting ash to be added to the compost heap. But she was getting ahead of herself again.

'What would you like to be done in this area Henri?' She had better ask in case he had other ideas.

'Well, I think I will leave that up to you my dear. Do you see potential?'

'Oh yes, but I could let myself get too carried away. I mean there's endless potential here. What sort of budget do I have to work with?'

'The budget is open to discussion. Come up with some ideas and we will see what can be done,' a voice said behind them.

At this, they both turned to find that Thomas had joined them.

'It's quite cold out here Dad, you should come inside and warm up for a bit and Jo has only just recovered from the flu.' He turned to her. 'You ought to take it easy for a few days, I'm sure Dr Bob would agree. We don't want you passing out again in some forgotten corner of the garden. You might not be discovered for days!'

'I'm fine, really I am. I promise to be careful. Thank you for your concern, but I am stronger than I look and I'm feeling as fit as a fiddle.' She didn't want them thinking that they had employed some feeble weakling who wasn't up to the task in hand. She looked at Henri and felt guilty for keeping him out for so long. 'But yes, it is a little chilly when you're standing still. Perhaps we ought to go in and warm up.'

'Well, Barbara has the kettle on, and she's been baking again. I think it's time for elevenses.'

'Are you sure I'm not intruding?'

'Nonsense!' laughed Henri. 'You are part of our family now. It's not all work and no play you know! We are not slave drivers! Besides, I need a fellow conspirator to distract Barbara, so she doesn't know how many biscuits I've eaten. She encourages me to be healthy and then makes irresistible biscuits, I mean she can't have it both ways. Come on, I'll show you the shortcut to the kitchen.'

They made their way back across the neglected garden to the house, up some steps, through a small arched wooden door in the surrounding wall to a gravelled side area outside the kitchen. Here the spiral staircase from the balcony above touched the ground. Jo noticed at the back of the house, a much smaller walled garden, mostly paved but with a neatly laid out miniature parterre and a circular raised pond in the centre. This, in contrast to the main garden, had been beautifully kept. Once again, climbing roses adorned the walls, but these had been pruned and well looked after. The paths were neat and cleanly swept.

'Wow! This is a little hidden gem!' she exclaimed.

'Yes,' Henri replied. 'This was Mary's favourite part of the garden, her own private space, Barbara looks after it now. It's a suntrap even in the darkest days of winter. A good place for relaxation. You are welcome to sit out here any time you like.'

'Thank you, I'll bear that in mind,' Jo replied. She would take him up on that offer when the chaos of the main garden got too much, she suspected. There was nothing like order in a garden to bring calm to a troubled mind.

They continued into the house through a long, narrow room that ran along the side of the kitchen, presumably some sort of utility, as a washing machine and tumble dryer sat at one end. Here they divested themselves of their coats and boots and trooped into the kitchen. It felt wonderfully warm and homely. A large cafetiere almost full to the brim of sublimely smelling hot coffee sat on the table.

'Well, my dear, what do you make of the garden?' Barbara said, bustling about putting mugs and a jug of milk on the table. 'Do you take sugar in your coffee dear? Help yourself.'

Jo took the chair that was nearest her and sat down pouring herself some coffee.

'No, no sugar thanks. The garden is beautiful, it must have been truly breathtaking in its prime, and hopefully it will be again given time. There is certainly a lot to keep me busy over the next few months. I've been thinking. I've brought a few hand tools with me, but do you have a lawnmower and ladders tucked away somewhere?'

'Yes. They are kept in one of the stable blocks at the back. I'll show you after we've had our coffee,' Thomas said. 'And then I really must try to get some work done.'

As they sat around the kitchen table chatting and munching still warm ginger nut cookies, Jo felt the warmth seep into her bones. She could so easily sit here for the rest of the morning. However, she must get started. It was a bit cold outside, being February, but not freezing and once she got moving, she wouldn't feel it. Where to start though? The lawn needed weeding, she would make a start there, and the paths. Neat edges and paths instantly gave order to gardens and made everything else seem more manageable. It was not really done to be mowing the lawn in early February, but if it were dry enough and not frosty, she would give it a go. That was if the mower she had not yet seen was up to scratch. As if reading her mind, her thoughts were interrupted by Thomas.

'Let me show you the gardening equipment we have already,' he said, rising from the table and taking her empty mug to place in the dishwasher. 'We'll go out through the garden.'

Wrapping up warmly once more, they went back through the wooden door in the wall and down the steps onto the main garden path. Taking a left turn Thomas led her to the huge arched wooden doors that stood at the far end of the garden. He reached into an alcove in the wall that she had not noticed on her previous tour of the garden and brought out a large key.

'We always keep these doors locked, for security reasons,' he explained, 'but I guess if you are back and forth regularly, just make sure that they are locked at the end of the day. Ok?'

'Will do,' Jo replied.

On the other side of the doors lay what had obviously been a stable area at some point in time; not a horse in sight now though. To her right there were three stables in a row, perpendicular to the garden wall and another three at right angles to them opposite her. To her left, a large beech tree. The gravelled open area in the middle led out on to the road that ran down the side of the property. Jo followed Thomas into the first stable block on the right. As her eyes adjusted to the dim interior, she could make out a selection of gardening tools hung from which, the largest cobwebs she had ever seen in her life and a mower that looked as if it had not been used since last summer, encrusted with dry grass and dust. This would need a good clean out for sure.

'Sorry it's in a bit of a state. We have only been using the mower in recent years. These tools all belonged to my mother. She was the real gardener.'

'Do you mind if I have a good sort out in here? Then I can see what I have to work with and make a list of anything that needs replacing.' She hoped the spiders were not as big as those cobwebs suggested. Generally, she loved all creepy crawlies, and she was ok with small spiders, but large hairy-legged ones that seemed to move much faster than she ever could were another matter. A long-handled broom would be the answer to those. She would sweep them out and they could find a nice cosy home in one of the other stables that she did not have to go in!

'Sure, go for it. Mum used to have everything hanging in its place. She was a very organised person, the rest of us are…less so.' He paused. 'Well, I will leave you to it, books don't write themselves!' He handed her the key, his fingers brushing against hers, as he did so an unexpected tingle ran up her arm. She caught his gaze. 'Don't overdo it,' he said gently. He turned, and she heard him crunch his way across the gravel back to the house.

Jo started by taking everything out. That way she could see what was there and give the stable a jolly good sweep out. She found that the mower was a petrol one and although dusty and covered in last year's grass cuttings looked as though it would work well with a good clean up. The blades looked reasonably sharp. She checked the reserve. Just a little fuel left in it. She looked around, spying a couple of petrol cans. The first was empty but the second seemed fairly full by the weight of it. One by one tools emerged from the dust and cobwebs. Long handled grass shears, great, they might need a bit of a sharpen but were otherwise serviceable. Loppers for smaller branches, she would definitely need these. Rakes, hoes, brooms and even a dustpan and brush. Everything she needed was here; old but useable. Nothing that a sharpen and maybe an oiling wouldn't fix. After a final sweep round and expulsion of the ubiquitous spiders, Jo started putting tools back in. Helpfully, there were hooks along one side of the stable wall where most of the long-handled tools could be hung. Some wooden crates could be used to store smaller hand tools. The mower wheeled in easily, looking much more useful now she had given it a clean over, and there was quite a lot of room to spare.

Jo made her way back into the garden, the sun peering out from behind light clouds making her feel more positive. Now she knew she had everything she needed it was just a case of getting stuck in. She bent down to feel the grass. Yes, it was dry enough to cut. After lunch, she would give it a go.

The afternoon was spent coaxing the lawnmower to life and cutting the grass on both lawns. Thankfully, she found a grass collection box that fitted on the front of the mower. She would have to empty it onto the old compost heap for now and sort the new heaps later. Although still weedy, the neatness of the newly cut grass was pleasing to behold. Even stripes giving an air of formality. The weeds, Jo thought to herself, could be tackled gradually. She had an old fork amongst her tools that acted as an excellent daisy grubber, and when the weather was warmer, a good dose of weed and feed should help sort it out. By the time all the tools had been cleaned and safely stored again, it was beginning to get dark, and she was gasping for a hot cup of tea. She headed back the cottage where she removed her boots and coat and put the kettle on.

No sooner had she collapsed onto the sofa, steaming cup of tea in hand, than there was a knock on the door.

'Come in!' she called 'It's open!'

'Hello! I just thought I'd call in on my way home from surgery to see how you're feeling. Barbara told me you had moved in here now.' Dr Bob smiled as he came into the kitchen.

Jo jumped to her feet in surprise. 'I'm fine, thanks for coming round. You really needn't have gone out of your way, it's very kind of you,' she replied. It was kind she thought, the least she could do was offer the man a drink. 'Cup of tea?' she asked. 'I've just made a fresh pot.'

'Don't mind if I do. You know I usually get given tea by the little old ladies I meet on my house calls, either insipidly weak or so strong you can stand a spoon up in it!' He laughed as Jo found another mug and took the milk out of the fridge. He had a pleasant, easy laugh and eyes that crinkled at the corners each time he did so.

'Well, I'll pour, and you can add milk the way you like it. I'm afraid I'm of the insipid tea variety usually, probably comes of being too impatient to let it stew. I have biscuits if you're allowed to be slightly unhealthy at the end of the day.' She took the hobnobs out of the cupboard and put them on the bench with the tea.

'Just what the doctor ordered!' he said, eyeing them greedily. 'It's been a long day and my blood sugars need replenishing. Who am I kidding? Hobnobs, my favourite!'

Jo invited him to take a seat, which he did.

'So how are you settling in?' he asked. 'Met any of the locals yet?'

'I went to the stores yesterday,' she told him.

He laughed. 'You've met the village gossip then. I try not to go in there too often. You go in for a tin of soup and come out three hours later knowing everybody's business whether you wanted to or not if you're not careful. Ellen's lovely though. Quiet girl. Are they giving you days off here?' He sipped his tea.

'Yes, I have the weekends to myself but I'm sure Henri would be flexible if I wanted a weekday off instead. He's very nice.'

'I've been thinking, you ought to join one of the pub quiz teams, they are held every Friday evening and it's a good way to get to know a lot of people. Most of the villagers are very friendly. Gerry, the landlord, is the quizmaster. In fact, our team could do with a new member. We're a bit of a mixed bunch, but that's always good for a team. For example, I know zilch about football but one of my teammates, Tom, is all into sport, and his wife Anne knows everything there is to know about celebrities. I'm sure you'd fit right in and bring some gardening know-how to our little pool of knowledge.'

'Sounds like fun, although I'm not sure I'm very knowledgeable. I might be more of a liability.'

'Nonsense! Why don't you come along this Friday? How about we meet up for a bite to eat beforehand, the food is good. Six o'clock suit you? Quiz starts at 7:30.'

'Ok, yes, that would be lovely, thank you,' she replied.

'Excellent! It's a date!' He hesitated, realising how that had sounded. 'Well, not a date, date, you know what I mean.' He looked at her hopefully suddenly serious. 'Unless of course…you'd like to consider it that way?'

Was he asking her out? She thought about it for a minute, he was nice, good looking and they seemed to get on well, why not? He got up and put his mug on the kitchen counter. Jo rose to see him out.

'Let me think about the date thing,' she smiled at him. 'But I will see you Friday, thanks for inviting me.'

'Ok good, well, see you Friday then. Cheerio!' he smiled and with that and a quick wave he was gone.

Chapter 8

Jo started her work in the garden in earnest by pruning the roses and sorting out the well-rotted compost heaps. It was hard physical work and each evening she fell into bed, sleeping like the dead until morning. She had not mentioned to the others that she had a sort of date on the Friday evening, she wasn't sure why. She would have to tell Barbara soon she thought as she wouldn't need dinner, so she made up her mind to tell them that evening.

In the corner of the wilderness area, Jo had cleared a space for a bonfire, it looked from the scorched earth she found there that someone had previously had a similar idea. She piled up the woody stems from the roses and covered them over with a tarpaulin she had found in the shed to keep everything as dry as possible. The shed, Jo discovered, was actually in good repair. It was reasonably large and light inside with windows to the front and side. Usefully, under the windows inside, a bench ran around on two sides. The windows, currently encrusted with grime, needed a clean but it would make a good base for her when working. She would move the tools into here and imagined them hung neatly along the walls, a place for everything, and everything in its place. It could do with a lick of paint on the outside too, something colourful but not garish, to smarten it up a bit. She would ask Henri if he had any preference on colour.

She had also been thinking about how that area of the garden could be developed. Her initial idea of having a kitchen garden had grown and she had sat one evening and sketched out some possible plans. She had explored the cost of greenhouses online and had come up with several options from reasonably cheap to an amazing Victorian style lean to that would be the ultimate dream greenhouse for any gardener. She would start by pitching the idea of painting the shed she thought and then show them her plans for the kitchen garden at a later date.

At dinner that evening in the kitchen, a delicious curry that Barbara had made from scratch, Jo put forward her idea for smartening up the shed.

'My dear, I think painting the shed is a splendid idea, whatever colour you like, what did you have in mind?' Henri asked her.

'I was thinking maybe Celadon green, like the front door of the cottage. It will make it look a lot smarter but not stand out like a sore thumb when we've got plants growing there. I could take the bus into Oxford at the weekend to get paint, it shouldn't be too expensive.'

'Excellent,' said Henri. 'And you will not get the bus my dear, I'll take you. Have you thought about any plans for that area of the garden? No rush if you haven't, it's early days yet.'

'I was thinking that a kitchen garden would be a good idea. With the wall on three sides, it's sheltered and gets the sun most of the day. I have drawn up some sketches. I'll fetch them after dinner if you like.' She had not planned on mentioning the greenhouse yet but as they had started talking about developing the area, she thought she might as well throw it into the mix. 'I've also been wondering whether a greenhouse would look good there, it would certainly be useful for raising bedding plants, it's so much cheaper to grow your own from seed.' She suddenly pictured Maurice talking to his seedlings at the chateau and wondered if she would be the same. 'I've got some different options for you to think over, depending on the budget, of course.'

'Mum always wanted a greenhouse, didn't she, Dad? One of those fabulous Victorian looking ones,' Thomas said, joining the discussion.

'Yes, but by the time we got around to discussing it properly she was ill and then…' Henri trailed off. They were all silent for a moment.

'Well, I think it's a great idea, Jo, and I for one think a kitchen garden is a fabulous idea,' Barbara declared breaking the silence. 'Lots of fresh veggies and some herbs maybe?'

'Mm… and maybe some rhubarb and soft fruit bushes,' she added. 'If there was a greenhouse of any sort, I could grow tomatoes, cucumbers, all sorts of different things in the summer. I think it would definitely be an asset to the garden in general.'

They all agreed that it sounded like an excellent plan. A long discussion then ensued about what could be grown and which fruits everyone preferred, all agreeing that courgettes were tasty but marrows disgusting and could be left off the list. After dinner, they remained at the table whilst Jo fetched her sketches and then showed them how different greenhouse options might look from different angles and what money could buy in the way of greenhouses these days.

'What do you think Dad?' said Thomas after they had seen everything, 'I think we ought to honour Mum's memory and go for the Victorian lean to. I know it is the most expensive option, but my last book sold well. Jo, these sketches are amazing. Have you ever thought of going into garden design?'

'No, not really, been too busy and I think I'd probably need some sort of formal qualification to do that as a proper job.' They turned to look at Henri who, deep in thought, was still holding some of the sketches.

'Yes, Mary would love this. I can almost feel her approval. Jo, you and she seem to have similar tastes.' He looked at her, as if assessing her somehow. Oh, how she reminded him of Mary. 'Let's get this underway as soon as possible. I will leave it in your capable hands.'

Jo was slightly surprised that it had been so easy, but excited to have the opportunity to create a garden from scratch, be it only one area of a much larger one. The main house and garden had been around for a few hundred years she suspected and now she was adding her part to its history, something that would remain, she hoped, long after she had gone. It was both a thrilling and humbling thought at the same time. She would ring the greenhouse suppliers the next day to get the project started.

'And now my dear, I think it's time to stop work for the day,' Henri declared. 'We ought to tell you about Fridays, one of our other little weekly habits that you might like to join in with.'

'Oh, yes,' agreed Barbara, 'it's pub quiz night tomorrow. Jo you must come along. It's such good fun isn't it, Thomas? It's also my night off from cooking so we eat at the pub on Fridays and join in with the quiz after. You could join one of our teams.'

'Don't let them bully you into it Jo, you can make your own mind up, but it would be lovely if you'd like to join us,' Thomas said. 'The food is very good there, not as good as Barbara's cooking of course,' he added sending a winning grin in Barbara's direction.

'Flatterer, you!' she said getting up and giving him a squeeze around the shoulders.

'Well, actually,' Jo said awkwardly, 'I've already been invited, by Dr Bob. He also asked me to dinner beforehand as well.'

Did she imagine it or did a look flicker between Henri and Thomas?

'How lovely,' said Barbara, 'Well, he didn't hang around did he?'

'It's not a date…well I don't know. He kind of half asked me if I'd like it to be a date,' she explained.

'And would you?' said Thomas quietly.

It felt as if everyone was holding their breath waiting for her reply.

'I don't know. I don't want to rush into anything. But he seems nice, easy to talk to. I might think about it, see how we get along on Friday.'

'Hmm, well I've got some writing to attend to before bed. Goodnight, all.' Thomas rose from the table. He sounded a little annoyed, Jo thought. A slight frown creased his forehead as he left the kitchen and she heard him take the stairs to the studio. As she left the house that evening for the cottage, she could hear a particularly dramatic piece of Beethoven being thundered out on the piano.

The next day seemed to whizz by. Jo had arranged an appointment with the greenhouse company to come the following week so she got busy clearing away the tumultuous tangle of greenery from the site where it would eventually stand. Thomas did not turn up for elevenses, perhaps he was out.

By five o'clock, it was dark. She had time for a shower and clean up before meeting Bob at the pub. Standing with the scalding water running down her back in hot rivulets, she considered whether she wanted this to be a date or not. He was nice, she liked him and he seemed kind, which was a good starting point. She wondered what it would be like to be kissed by a man with a beard, perhaps it was time to find out. Now what should she wear? Jeans and a jumper, it would have to be, she did not have much else.

Bob was waiting at the bar when she arrived, looking more homely in a rugby shirt and jeans rather than his workday jacket and tie.

'What can I get you?' he asked as he greeted her with a slightly hesitant peck on the cheek and introduced her to Gerry the landlord, who was busy drying glasses behind the bar.

'Do you have any local ciders here?' she asked. 'Dry preferably.'

'Coming right up,' Gerry replied. 'Pint or half?'

'Just a half to start with thank you.'

The pub was quite spacious inside with a long, polished wooden bar opposite the main door. Behind it the ubiquitous bottles of spirit hung upside down and, in the fridges, bottled drinks stood to attention like miniature soldiers waiting to be sent on duty. At one end of the room, a large log fire crackled comfortingly in an enormous fireplace; the sap in the logs hissing as it was devoured by the flames. An old wooden settle sat one side of it with its back to the bar, and an assortment of comfortable chairs arranged around tables filled the rest of the space. A wonderful smell of beer and chips hung in the air and made Jo feel quite hungry. At the opposite side of the room, small booths lined the wall, cosy hideaways for intimate diners. It was to one of these that Bob showed Jo and they sat facing each other perusing the extensive menu. Jo chose the steak and kidney pudding, Bob the curry. It had been an awfully long time since she had been in a good old-fashioned British pub, and Jo was enjoying every minute of it.

They chatted amiably, as they ate, about their respective days, Jo telling him about the plans for the garden, he about the receptionist at the practice who had tripped over the bottom draw of an open filing cabinet that afternoon receiving a nasty gash on the shin in the process. They were just laughing about the words the receptionist had apparently used to describe said filing cabinet as she was being stitched up, when Henri, Barbara and Thomas arrived. Thomas looked over and nodded, she waved in acknowledgement. She noticed that they stood at the bar for a while and then found a table on the other side of the room to wait for their food. Soon more locals began arriving and by the time they had finished their meal there was a pleasant hum of conversation and laughter in the room.

'Better find our seats, we're over by the fire,' Bob said.

They wandered over and Jo found that most people seemed to be sitting in teams already. She noticed Ellen and another middle-aged couple had joined Thomas and Henri and that Barbara sat in the opposite corner with Mrs West, nodding while the other woman talked nineteen to the dozen. A few similarly aged ladies sat with them. Putting his hand possessively on her back, Bob introduced her to Tom, a tall, heavily built bald man in biker's leathers, and his wife Anne, petite, blond and similarly clad. Tom took her hand in a vice like grip.

'Pleased to meet you,' he nodded.

Jo hoped that none of the bones in her hand were broken as she turned to Anne to smile and say hello. They seemed friendly, even if Tom looked a little intimidating, she noticed the skull and crossbones tattoo on his forearm when he removed his jacket. They took their seats on the settle by the fire, apparently this was their team's spot, their team's name being 'The Settlers' as a result. Jo explained to Tom and Anne that she was Henri's new gardener and how she had come to know Bob. Anne, she discovered, was originally from Wales and had met Tom on holiday there fifteen years ago. He was a Chiropodist and she a

Beautician, Anne took a business card out of her handbag and handed it to Jo in case she ever needed their services at any time.

Answer sheets were passed around with an assorted tub of pens, in case people had not brought their own, and a hush descended as Gerry tapped on the side of a glass to start the quiz.

At the half-way interval, Jo went to the bar for a round of drinks. She had been pleased to be able to contribute a few answers, especially on the music round, and found she was surprisingly good at history too. Tom's encyclopaedic sports knowledge was impressive, and she discovered that he was a bit of a softy under his hard biker exterior. Anne was simply hilarious, making dry witty remarks about some of the questions that had their whole team in stitches. She had looked across the room at Mrs West, who seemed to talk the whole way through regardless and whispered to Jo in a strong Welsh accent. 'No competition there, thick as a pancake that one.' Jo had nearly spat her drink out laughing.

'Having a good time?' Thomas asked, nudging her elbow as she leant on the bar.

'Excellent thank you,' she replied cheerily. 'You?'

'Mm…Ok. Science and nature's up next, sure you don't want to swap teams, we could do with you over in our corner.'

'Sorry got to be loyal to my team,' she smiled, picking up two beers for Tom and Anne and leaving him standing.

'Pity,' he murmured, but she had gone and didn't hear him.

The quiz came to an end and after the totals had been added Jo was pleased to find that 'The Settlers' had come third. She did not think much of that was due to her contribution, but it was a satisfying feeling, nonetheless. Quite a few of the locals stayed afterwards, swapping places to chat to friends who were not in their teams. She noticed that Ellen seemed chattier when she was not with her mother. She caught her eye and smiled across the room. Ellen waved back. Jo saw Barbara sitting in the corner and went over to talk, leaving Bob deep in conversation with Tom, she was free now Mrs West had moved on to chew someone else's ear.

'Phew! I'm so glad she's moved on to talk to Mrs Preston now,' Barbara said quietly behind her hand. 'Barely got a word in all evening! We made sure Ellen's not in the same team as her mother, poor girl needs a break.'

'She seems different when she's not with her mother,' said Jo, glancing over at Ellen once more. 'I suppose it can't be easy living with a mother like that. Why doesn't she leave home?'

'I don't think she can afford to, poor lamb. Apparently, her dad ran away with another woman years ago and they've only got the shop between them to keep them going. Can't be much of a life for her stuck in the shop with her mother all day.'

'No,' mused Jo. She made a mental note to try and befriend Ellen next time she went to the stores.

'Anyway, how's your evening going?' Barbara enquired.

Jo told her about what Anne had said about Mrs West and they both had a good laugh. Henri came over find out what they were giggling about and to make arrangements with Jo for picking up paint the next morning. Eventually people drifted away, and Bob came over and offered to walk her home. She almost declined saying she would walk back with the others, but it was a sweet gesture, so she let him.

Standing in the moonlight outside the door of the cottage she turned to Bob to thank him for a lovely evening. He slid his arms around her waist and pulled her close.

'So, how about doing it again,' he suggested. 'But just the two of us, how about going on a proper date. I could check your pulse for you?' he grinned suggestively.

'I'm sure my pulse is just fine, thank you,' she laughed. 'But yes, a second date would be nice, what had you in mind?'

'I was thinking something along these lines,' he whispered and lowered his mouth to hers. The kiss was warm, sweet and gentle. He pulled back and looked into her eyes. 'I'm on call tomorrow. How about coming around to my house on Sunday for lunch, we could spend the afternoon together, you can meet Eunice.'

'I'd like that,' she smiled.

He let her go, promising to text her his address after they had swapped phone numbers and waved at the gate before disappearing down the lane. It was only when Jo turned to put her key in the door that she noticed Thomas silhouetted in the doorway of the main house, leaning against the frame, watching.

Chapter 9

Jo was up early the next morning despite that fact that it was Saturday and she was not going shopping with Henri until nine. It had been a restless night and she had woken cold to find herself spreadeagled across the bed, having completely kicked the duvet off onto the floor in the night. She thought about Bob and the kiss they had shared. It had been nice she remembered, romantic in the moonlight, but somehow, this morning, she felt slightly deflated. Perhaps it was the fact that Thomas had been watching them that had unsettled her.

She breakfasted and went out into the garden, cradling her mug of tea for warmth. Iridescent starlings that had been probing the ground with their spear-like beaks rose as one in a thrum of purple and green wings as she appeared, breaking the tranquillity of the morning. There had been a frost that night, its wintery breath coating the world in a layer of tiny diamonds which, with the sun's touch, became wisps of vapour that danced in the air. She loved moments like this, time suspended, while the world slumbered still. The garden seemed like a magical paradise that, for this moment at least, belonged only to her.

Jo wondered along the path and down to the wilderness area that was slowly being tamed by her touch. She froze. There, standing in the middle of the area she had cleared, was Thomas, his back to her, his hands on his hips, each warm breath sending an ephemeral misty plume into the still air. He was obviously inspecting the progress she had made. She was not sure she wanted to talk to him after last night and turned to go but her foot caught a twig on the path, and it snapped noisily. He turned at the sound and called her name. No escape now.

'Good morning,' she said as cheerily as she could muster. 'You're up early.'

'I usually am, best part of the day for thinking. It's quiet and peaceful, a time that's usually mine alone.'

Suddenly she felt guilty that she had intruded.

'I notice you're up early too though,' he continued, studying her. She looked tired. 'It is the weekend; you are allowed a lie in.'

'Mm, I know, bit of a restless night.' They stood for a while as if something unspoken hung in the air between them, a lonely robin's song the only sound. She looked towards the shed. 'I'm going to get paint this morning with your dad I might make a start on the shed this afternoon when it has warmed up a bit.'

'Jo, it's the weekend. Your time is your own. Don't spend it here working, go out and enjoy yourself.'

'I know, but I want to do it. Gardening jobs are sometimes like itches that have to be scratched, if there is something that needs doing, I feel I ought to be doing it. Today's itch is the shed, I'll have the materials to do it, no reason not to get on with it.'

'Want some help scratching then?' He grinned at her analogy. 'Dab hand with a paintbrush me.'

She forgot her annoyance with him, he had such a winning smile, and how could she refuse?

It was about one o'clock by the time Jo and Thomas started on the shed, each dressed scruffily in case of paint splashes. They had decided to start on diagonally opposite corners, so they had two sides to complete each.

'Race?' suggested Thomas cheekily 'Loser gets a forfeit?'

'That's not fair, I've got the door and two window frames that will take longer, and I have to go up and down on the stool to get the top bits you're tall enough to reach,' Jo protested.

'Yes, but you don't have to paint the space where the glass is, so that kind of equals it out don't you think?'

She pulled a face in disagreement.

'I'll help you with the top bits on the last side, how about that?' he grinned disappearing around the back of the shed to get started.

Henri had found a long garden bench on sale in the DIY store and declared that it would be perfect under the window outside the shed. He could sit and talk to her as she worked, he insisted, when the weather was kinder. As Thomas and Jo painted, Barbara helped Henri constructed the bench, collapsing onto it simultaneously when they had finished to watch the progress being made on the shed. They made a good pair thought Jo as she observed them. She wondered whether Henri had ever thought of remarrying. The way they sometimes sparked off each other, an outsider might think them an old married couple anyway.

'I'm getting chilly sitting still Barbara, how about we leave these young folks to the painting and find something to warm us up?' Henri suggested, rising from the bench and taking Barbara's hand to pull her up.

'Sounds like a good idea to me. Don't get cold you two,' she called as they picked their way through the remaining weeds to the path beyond.

Jo watched them walk back to the house together. Henry occasionally touching Barbara's back as they walked, heads bent together in conversation. She smiled. Love was not only for the young.

As predicted, Thomas finished his two sides of painting when Jo was halfway down her second side, having left the top bit for him to do anyway.

'I win, I think,' he declared coming around to fill in the gap at the top and reaching over her, paint brush in hand.

'Watch out, you're dripping on my head!' she squealed, reaching up to wipe the paint from her hair. 'Look!' she cried holding out her hand for him to see the paint on her fingers.

'Sorry,' he said laughing. He looked at her face. 'I think you've got a few new freckles as well, let me help you wipe those off.' He dabbed her on the nose with his brush.

She stood there for a moment in disbelief. 'Right,' she said, 'two can play at this game!' She flicked her brush at him. There was more paint on it than she had anticipated, and a great splatter of pale green paint landed across his shirt and face and dribbled down his chin. She bit her bottom lip. 'Oops,' she said covering her mouth with her hand and trying not to laugh. She backed off slowly as he came towards her menacingly.

'I think it's time you had a bath,' he growled dropping his paintbrush. And before she could turn to run, he scooped her over his shoulder fireman style and strode off up the garden towards the fountain, with her trying to wriggle free all the way.

'Thomas stop it!' she laughed. 'Put me down! I'm sorry!'

They reached the fountain and he held her over the cold pool of scummy green water.

'Thomas, no! Put me down!' she shrieked. They were both laughing now.

'Not until you agree to a forfeit.' He bent as if to drop her in the water.

'Arrgh! Ok, ok, I agree!' she wailed. Anything to avoid being dropped in that!

He slid her body down until her feet were touching the ground and they were standing face to face. He took her chin into his hands and tilted her face towards his.

'Play for me,' he said gently, suddenly serious. 'Like you did at the chateau.'

She looked into his eyes and saw a kind of sad longing that made her insides feel funny and tingly and her heartbeat suddenly too fast. A black bird swooped up on to the wall giving its raucous call and the moment was broken.

'Ok,' she said quietly stepping away from him. She turned and started walking away. 'We better finish the shed and tidy up first,' she called smiling over her shoulder at him. 'And I need a proper bath before going anywhere near your dad's piano.'

Jo sat at the piano that evening and stared at the keys under her fingers. It had been a while since she had played. She looked up. Thomas was leaning on the end waiting for her to start, his eyes fixed on her face. She felt the heat rise and breathed in slowly. Bach. Prelude and Fugue in C major. She shut her eyes and began to play, feeling the music lift her away. She knew it by heart. It spoke to her of summer, of longing and loss. It was such a simple piece really but conveyed so much emotion in the way it was played. It had been her grandmother's favourite and now was hers too. As the last note floated away into her ethereal dreams, she opened her eyes to find that tears had trickled down her face; it had that melancholic mood about it, and she couldn't help herself sometimes. She sat back holding her hands to her face to wipe the tears away as the ensuing silence was broken.

'My dear. That was simply beautiful,' Henri said, coming over to the piano.

'Sorry, can't help the tears,' she smiled. 'It always makes me feel sad even though I love it. It was Grand-mere's favourite,' she explained. She looked at Thomas whose eyes had never left her face. 'Forfeit paid?'

He nodded and whispered, 'For now.'

'How about a duet to cheer us up?' Henri suggested. 'I have that book I bought in Tours recently, do you remember?' He went over to an enormous pile of higgledy-piggledy music scores, rummaging through until he found what he wanted. Jo felt slightly daunted. She knew she was quite good but sure she was not up to Henri's standard of playing. He came and sat next to her on the piano stool putting the music on the rack.

'Thomas, will you turn the music for us? We'll start with Mozart and maybe try Chopin a little later. Ready?'

They played for what seemed like hours, Henri occasionally speeding up the tempo, which made her feel like they were in some sort of mad race, their fingers flying over the keys making them both laugh. It was hard laughing and trying to concentrate at the same time. By the end, she was exhausted but felt better than she had in a long time.

'Thank you, Henri,' she said. 'I'd forgotten how good it felt just to play. It feels like an age.'

'My dear it's been an absolute pleasure. We must do this more often and as I said before, you must come and use the piano whenever you want. Don't be shy.' He took both her hands in his. 'You have a talent Jo, and you must use it.' He looked across at Thomas and Barbara and then got up from the piano stool. 'Well, my dears, I think I will go up to bed, it's quite late you know. Bonne nuit, dors bien!' he called as he picked up the book he had been reading and shuffled from the room humming one of the tunes they had played earlier.

'Me too,' yawned Barbara getting up to follow Henri. 'See you in the morning dears.'

'Well, I suppose I'd better be going too,' Jo said closing the lid of the piano softly and putting the music on top of the pile. 'Thanks for helping with the shed this afternoon I really appreciated it, well, apart from the last bit,' she smiled and paused. 'Thomas, why were you watching me last night, you know, after the pub?'

He sighed and sat on the stool she had just vacated. He looked as if he was thinking about something faraway.

'Just looking out for you really. It is what friends do for each other. After what happened in France...' he trailed off.

'But Bob is nothing like Serge, Thomas. He's kind and gentle.'

'I know that and he's a good bloke really but, he...he has a bit of a reputation. Jo, I don't want to see you getting hurt.'

She didn't know quite what he meant by that. What sort of reputation? She looked puzzled.

He stood up and came towards her, rested his hands on her shoulders, and looked down into her face. 'I'm just trying to be a good friend. Jo you are the sort of person who loves deeply, gives their heart fully, and you need someone who will match the passion you hide in your heart. It is in your nature to give completely in everything you do…I'm just not sure it's in his.'

She was stunned into silence for a moment, at a loss for words to reply.

'Goodnight Thomas,' was all she could manage as she left, her face scarlet with embarrassment. He had no idea what she hid in her heart and what business was it of his anyway?

The heavens opened the following morning as Jo walked to Bob's house. A neat yellow-doored mid terrace a few streets away from the pub. She had popped in at the stores on the way to buy a bottle of wine and been given a thorough quizzing by Mrs West as to what it was for. Not being one to tell lies she had eventually admitted that she had been invited to lunch. It would be all over the village soon she thought. Still, they were adults, what business of anybody else's was it what they got up to? Not that she was intending to get up to anything.

Jo shook her umbrella out before she went in, and Bob took her coat. The front door opened straight into a small living room. A tiny Victorian fireplace with decorative tiles sat under a mantlepiece full of photos and a fluffy ginger cat lay on the sofa next to it looking for all the world as if it owned the place. Bookshelves filled the alcoves either side of the chimney breast, stuffed full of various weighty medical tomes. It had a homely feel.

'Hello, you must be Eunice,' she said going over to let the cat sniff her hand tentatively before bending over and scratching it behind the ears softly. The cat purred and rolled over revealing its belly for more fuss and adoration.

'Sometimes I think that cat gets more attention than I do,' Bob complained jokingly.

'Sorry,' Jo said. She straightened up and turned towards him. He wrapped his arms around her and kissed her urgently. 'I always wanted a cat when I was a child, but my father was allergic so we never could. They can be such affectionate creatures,' she managed between the kisses he was feathering down her neck. 'What's for lunch?' she asked wriggling free and going into the kitchen at the back of the house.

'Hmm? Oh, salmon fillets and apple crumble for pudding. Hope that's ok with you.'

He was a quite a good cook as it turned out. Jo sat and watched him make his own hollandaise sauce to go with the fish. They sat to eat at the small table one end of the kitchen. When she had finished, she sat back feeling thoroughly replete. The apple crumble had been delicious, it was a shame she couldn't manage a second helping. Outside the rain was coming down in stair rods. Jo offered to washup and as she looked out the kitchen window above the sink, she could see that the house owned a tiny garden. A circle of weed ridden grass the only greenery in an otherwise bleak landscape of bare paving. Two solemn dustbins sat by a faded wooden gate at the back which looked like it led out to a lane running behind the terraces.

'Not a gardener then?' Jo asked.

'No time,' he replied, picking up the tea towel to dry as she washed. 'Not my thing really either. I have two older sisters who are quite good though, but I always had my head in a book as a child and never learnt, I preferred the library to the garden.'

Jo remembered what she had been like as a child. They had not had an especially large garden she remembered but there had been a lawn and a sycamore tree with a homemade swing that hung from one of the branches. She remembered being out in the garden for hours at a time, especially in the summer. She had loved sitting on the swing feeling the lush grass tickle the bottom of her bare feet as she swung back and forth. Her mother had had a tiny aluminium greenhouse at the bottom of the garden where she would grow a few tomatoes and cucumbers. If she closed her eyes, she could still smell the wonderful pungency when the sliding door was opened on a hot day. She pictured her parents, Dad cutting the grass and Mum dead heading pelargoniums. And then she had gone and ruined it all.

'Penny for them?' he said, looking thoughtfully at her.

'Oh nothing, just thinking about gardens that's all.' It was a sort of half-truth. 'What are we doing this afternoon?'

'Well, I was thinking of doing some sunbathing,' he teased, looking out the window at the rain. The image of him sitting out on the grass in a pair of shorts and not much else at this time of the year made her giggle. 'But as the sun seems to be unavailable today how about a movie on the telly?'

'Sounds like a plan,' she agreed, pulling the plug from the sink and washing the bubbles away. It felt like a staying in kind of afternoon.

Collapsing on the sofa together he put his arm around her, and she snuggled into his shoulder comfortably. They flicked through Netflix trying to agree on something to watch. They settled on an action movie in the end, not her sort of choice for a peaceful, romantic afternoon. It did not really matter as by the end of the movie she had fallen asleep anyway, Eunice curled up on her lap.

'Wake up, film's over,' Bob called.

'Oh, sorry,' she mumbled and stretched, which made Eunice jump down. 'Dinner was so nice, and you are wonderfully comfortable to rest on, couldn't help it.' He switched off the telly.

'Let me show you around the rest of the house; you've already seen the downstairs. Come upstairs.'

Up the narrow stairs there was a small but perfectly adequate bathroom and two bedrooms, the smallest of which he used as a study, a desk with a computer taking up most of the space. He led her into the bigger of the bedrooms, a neatly made double bed sat in the centre. It was a very masculine room; grey sheets on the bed and stripey curtains hanging at the window that looked out over the sparse back garden. Walking over to the window, she could see the lane that ran behind the terraces more clearly now, wide enough for residents to park their cars along one side. She turned to ask him which car was his and found him standing closely behind her. He wrapped his arms around her, rested his head on her shoulder and kissed her neck again.

'You know you really do smell delicious,' he said, turning her to find her mouth, 'and taste delicious too.'

'Must be the apple crumble.'

'You know on a wet afternoon there's not much to do, we could always…'

'Go for a walk?' she interjected. 'I think the rain has stopped now. I could do with a breath of fresh air. Let me just use the bathroom before we go,' she said, smiling brightly at him. She knew exactly what he had in mind, and it was flattering in a way, but she was not ready for that yet and certainly not on their first official date. She looked at herself in the mirror on the bathroom wall, was she a bit old fashioned? Was that what was expected on first dates these days? She thought about the advice her grandmother had given her once as a late teenager. It had been good advice and she was sticking to it old fashioned or not.

They walked up to the church. The sun had come out briefly making everything look freshly washed and colour drenched, Bob did not feel like going inside so they strolled around the outside reading some of the gravestones. Some were fairly modern, others lichen encrusted with age. Jo noticed daffodils had poked their way up through the thick grass their nodding buds threatening to open at the first kiss of spring's warmth. It was on the way out that she spotted one of the newer graves next to the path. It had been immaculately kept unlike most of the others and a bunch of multicoloured freesias recently placed there. *Mary Anne Arnaud. Beloved wife of Henri and mother to Thomas. 'Vive l'amour'* and the dates of her life. Jo felt a sudden heaviness on her heart. Henri's wife, Thomas' mother, Barbara's friend. The person who had loved the garden before her, whose hands had planted, tended and cared for the place that was now her responsibility. Jo did not believe in ghosts, rather she liked to think that people in heaven were allowed to look down now and again to see how the loved ones they left behind were getting on. Silently she promised Mary that she would do her best to make the garden right once more and hoped that she would be pleased with the result she saw.

'Ready to go?' Bob said, coming up behind her and taking her hand. 'Oh, you're chilly, you know what they say about that though, *cold hands warm heart.'*

An image of Thomas from the night before flashed through her mind at the mention of hearts. 'Let's have a cup of tea and warm up then. My place is nearest,' she suggested.

Dodging the puddles, they arrived at the cottage as it started to spit with rain once more. Hot cups of tea in hand they stood at the French windows that looked out on the upper part of the garden.

'How long have you lived in the village Bob?' she asked him idly.

'It will be four years next month I think.'

So, he had not known Mary then. It must have been a predecessor who had helped with her care when she was ill.

'Do you think you'll always work here, or do you have big plans for the future?'

'I'm happy for the moment but the practise I'm attached to is quite small, I suppose one day I will want to move on and get experience in a different community. I like Oxford though. I've volunteered for a few shifts at the hospital next month. It's all good to have on your C.V. for the future. How about you? When you've restored the garden, are they going to keep you on?'

'I don't know. I'd like to even if it's part time by then.' She stared out the window lost in thought. 'Gardens are a bit like children, you tend them and watch them grow and they are very hard to say goodbye to. You pour so much of yourself into them they become a part of who you are.'

'Children,' he shuddered. 'Not sure I want any of those.'

Chapter 10

February passed into March and with it Spring arrived in earnest, awakening the world with kisses of golden sunshine and caressing plants to life once more with her soft breath. Jo had been working hard, the kitchen garden was no longer wild and untamed. The greenhouse foundation had been laid and awaited its main structure in the following weeks. She had marked out where the vegetable beds would go and ordered railway sleepers for the raised edges. Daffodils held their golden heads to the sky agreeing with the breeze that life was good.

Jo had started to put together a kind of journal for the garden, drawing up a detailed plan of each area, to mark the position of plants as she discovered them. Records were useful, she thought, for future generations to know what had been before. She wanted to record what Mary had planted and leave a record of her contribution to the garden she was slowly falling in love with.

The neglected orchard area that stood between her cottage and the outer wall of the garden, which ran down the side of the house, had been a particularly pleasing discovery. There were about twelve fruit trees in all, six espaliered against the outer wall and another six, free standing amongst the grass beneath, their now blossoming branches reaching as if in worship to the cloudless sky above. Apart from not having been tended for several years they looked healthy. She had pruned a few branches that were in the way or sticking out at the wrong angle, but the rest could be left to the autumn after they had fruited. Today the sun shone, and bees buzzed busily, stopping at each flower in the hope of a sweet reward. Jo had been excited to discover labels attached to the espaliered trees, presumably put there by Mary or her predecessor. Worcester Pearmain, Red Windsor, Bramley's, Ellison's Orange. Whoever had planted these had chosen excellent heritage varieties and she looked forward to autumn days of fruitfulness. The trees in the centre of the orchard she thought to be pears, from the shrivelled remains she had found from last autumn amongst the grass. She had not found any labels for these, so their names remained a mystery yet to be discovered. She was hopeful for a Williams Bon Chretien and Concorde at least. She thought about Alain and the heritage orchard he had created at the chateau. She expected blossom would be flowering there now too, its delightful aroma wafting to the garden beyond as it did every year.

Jo walked around, notebook and phone in hand. She had been trying to identify the different clumps of daffodils that had sprung up. Some were obvious like the miniature 'Jetfire' and multi headed 'Cheerfulness' which smelt so wonderful as she bent down to touch the silken petals, but there were so many varieties, and she was not an expert. She decided to photograph them to try and identify later online. As she strolled, Jo glanced up at the house. A whole section of the windows on the studio gaped open. Must be a sliding door out on to the balcony, she thought. She had never seen it open before and hadn't even considered how you would access it apart from the spiral staircase at the end. Suddenly, Thomas appeared from the doorway, running his fingers through his hair as he paced up and down the length of the balcony. He looked agitated, as if he were bothered by something important. He stopped, stretching his arms to lean against the railings and look out over the garden. He spotted her and waved. She waved back, trekking across the grass to speak to him.

'Are you alright?' she shouted up. 'You look worried.'

'Why don't you come up, then we won't have to shout at each other,' he yelled back.

She made her way through the kitchen doorway and up the spiral staircase, her boots sounding metallic notes on the treads. The view of the garden was almost breathtaking from the balcony, she had not seen it from this angle before. You could indeed see everything laid out before you as Henri had told her.

'Looks good from up here, doesn't it?' he said, noticing her take in the view. 'On days like this, I like to have the door open, fresh air helps me think. You haven't been up to the studio before, have you? Come in and have a look.' She followed him in after removing her boots and leaving them neatly on the balcony outside. 'That's not an invitation I extend to everyone you know,' he said, grinning, 'only particular friends.'

The studio was a large white airy space. Light flooded in from the long range of windows at the side and a pool of sunlight illuminated the floor at the front. It was a perfect place for an artist, she could understand why it had been built that way, with so many windows. Along the wall, opposite the windows, was a door that connected the studio to the main house via the galleried landing. The rest of the wall was filled with floor to ceiling bookshelves stuffed with hundreds upon hundreds of books and papers. An old three-seater sofa took its place against the far wall and an enormous mahogany desk sat under the window scattered untidily with dictionaries and an open thesaurus, books and papers almost engulfing the incongruous laptop in the centre. An old-fashioned desk lamp hung its dusty green shade over a chipped mug rammed full of pens and several other mugs containing various amounts of cold tea. To the right of the desk a worn leather armchair, cushions sagging, looked forlornly out towards the garden. In the air hung the comforting smell of books and Thomas.

'Wow, what an amazing space,' she said, turning around to take it all in. 'You have so many books!'

'Well, they say a room without books is like a body without a soul. Cicero, I think.'

She walked over to the desk. 'What a fantastic place to work from.' She realised that even sitting at his desk, he could still see most of the garden.

'Mm,' he agreed not sounding convinced, the worried look returning to his face as he rubbed the back of his neck.

'What's up? Tell me,' she demanded, sitting in the chair at the desk and swivelling to face him expectantly.

'Oh, I don't know. My brain seems to be all over the place at the moment. Writer's block maybe. I can't seem to settle on an idea for my next book. I need a new focus, a new character and a fresh idea and I've got an editor expecting a first draft soon.' He was pacing as he talked as if trying to mentally wrestle and idea from thin air.

She had read his first three books. They were good. A trilogy about a Scottish detective who worked for the French police after his girlfriend had been murdered in Paris. Each book had its own case to be solved but a dangerous sub plot wove through all three concluding in the final book where the girlfriend's killer was finally revealed.

She sighed not quite knowing how to help, but desperately wanting to, nonetheless.

'Why don't you take a break for a bit? Do something else for a couple of days,' she suggested. 'I know you are under pressure, but I always find that when I try too hard to find an answer to a problem it always eludes me somehow. If I focus on something completely different, I find my mind relaxes and an answer pops into my head later. As if my subconscious has been gently working away at it all the time.'

He stopped pacing for a moment and looked at her.

'What precisely did you have in mind, Miss Freud?' he said, coming to perch on the edge of the desk.

'Well…I have some jobs I need a bit of help with in the garden if you feel like some hard physical labour. No paint brushes involved at all,' she smiled holding up her hands innocently. 'It's a nice warm day out and you did say fresh air helps you think.'

He thought about it. Maybe she was right.

'Ok, you're on,' he agreed. 'What exactly do you mean by *hard* physical labour?'

'You're going to need scruffy clothes and pair of heavy-duty gardening gloves; I'll lend you a pair.' She looked at her watch. 'Come on it is nearly elevenses. Let's get some coffee first and I'll tell you about it afterwards.'

Thomas came down to the kitchen ten minutes later wearing the same paint-splattered shirt from when they had done the shed. Jo could not help but giggle when Henri came in, stopped in his tracks and gave him a surprised look.

'Jo's forcing me to do hard labour,' he explained, taking two biscuits from the plate in front of him. 'I think I'm going to need these.'

'I'm not forcing you. I merely suggested it might help,' she protested, 'and I could do with an extra pair of hands for this particular job.'

'Don't overdo things Jo, will you,' said Henri. 'And make sure you look after your hands? I thought we could try some more duets this evening after dinner what do you think?'

'Mm, that would be lovely. Thank you Henri.'

Thomas stared at Jo and then back at his dad looking as if somehow, he had been left out.

'Well, Thomas, if I thought you were going to play the piano with Jo this evening, I would be concerned about your hands too,' he said idly, sipping his coffee and looking at the newspaper in front of him.

'Oh, that would be nice,' said Barbara, 'I haven't heard you play for a long time Thomas. You used to be so good. Go on, you two would sound good together. Henri and I will be your audience.'

Thomas caught Jo's gaze and raised his eyebrow questioningly.

'I'm game if you are,' he said.

'Well, we'd both better be careful with our hands then,' she said, getting up and putting her mug in the dishwasher. 'Come on slave, time for some hard labour.'

'Coming master!' he grinned and mouthed at Henri behind Jo's back. 'Thanks Dad.'

Jo and Thomas spent the rest of the day, apart from a short break at lunchtime, moving the railway sleepers from where they had been delivered outside the stable blocks, to the kitchen garden. The sleepers were heavy, each one having to be sawn to the correct length before being carried across the main garden to the right plot. When they had finished edging the largest bed, they sat on the side of it drinking the cool lemonade that Barbara had brought out to them earlier.

'You really did mean hard physical labour, didn't you?' Thomas breathed, wiping the sweat from his face once again and lying down along the railway sleeper so his head was next to Jo's leg, and he was looking up at her.

'I always mean what I say,' she said sipping her drink. 'Gardening is not just sowing seeds and daisy grubbing you know. It's hard work and keeps you fit,' she said, rubbing her shoulder. 'Hmm…having said that, I think I've pulled a muscle.'

'Turn yourself sideways back towards me,' he instructed, sitting up.

She did, so that she was straddling the sleeper. She wondered how that would help. Gently, he laid his hands on her shoulder and moved his thumbs in small circles to ease the tightness in the muscle. She could feel the warmth of his fingers through her t-shirt and closed her eyes. It was heaven. He moved her hair out of the way, his fingers brushing her neck as he did so, and a thousand tiny fireworks exploded in her brain and travelled down her spine.

'Better?' he said after a while.

'Mm…much thanks. Where did you learn to do that?' she asked.

'Old girlfriend was a masseuse,' he admitted. 'When I was a student, she used to make money giving people massages in between her lectures, which was fine, until she preferred one of them to me,' he shrugged. 'Ce la vie.'

They finished their drinks and called it a day. There were still two more beds to finish, and although they had cut the sleepers already, it was too late and getting cold.

'How hard did you drive your slave this afternoon Jo?' Henri enquired during dinner. He glanced over at Thomas. 'Is he fit to play later?'

'Oh, I think he'll live. He didn't lose too many fingers doing the sawing, although he might find a few muscles tomorrow morning that he didn't know he had,' she joked.

'That's not fair, if I remember rightly, it was you that needed a massage,' Thomas protested.

A flicker of a glance passed between Henri and Barbara. Jo saw it and her face flamed.

'Let me help you load the dishwasher Barbara,' she said, rising from the table to hide her embarrassment.

By the time they had finished tidying the kitchen, music was already emanating from the living room next door.

'Beethoven,' said Barbara.

'Piano sonata number 8,' said Jo. 'Henri is so good. I would have loved to hear him in concert when he was in his prime.'

'I don't think that is Henri, Jo.'

The two women stole next door. It wasn't. Henri was sat in his armchair by the fireplace, eyes closed, fingertips together in contemplation as Thomas played, as if judging his performance. Thomas looked up and smiled at Jo as she came in, holding her gaze until the piece finished. They all clapped spontaneously, and he took a mock bow.

'I love that piece,' said Jo. 'Do you know the Billy Joel song where he uses the melody for the chorus, what's the song called?'

Thomas sat down at the piano and played the chorus of *This night*. He looked at Jo and began to sing.

It was the second time that day that Jo felt fireworks going off in her brain. She tried desperately to suppress them but couldn't. What was wrong with her? she thought to herself. She was going out with Bob, nice, kind, romantic Bob, about whom she hadn't thought all day. Jo felt suddenly guilty. Pleading a headache, she said she would get an early night and made her excuses, duets left unplayed. She hoped Thomas would get over his writer's block soon.

The following morning, Jo was up early; it was cloudier today and the door on the studio balcony was shut. She would make a start at moving the sleepers and hopefully get it all done before Thomas remembered that he was supposed to be helping her today as well. She wondered whether there might be any sort of wheeled trolley in one of the other stables she could use to help her. She thought the wheelbarrow would be a bit wobbly and the last thing she wanted to do was drop a sleeper off the side of it and make a big dent in the lawn, which was just starting to look healthier.

When she got to the door leading out to the stables, she felt in the alcove for the key and on finding it empty, saw that it was in the door already and that the door was slightly ajar. She pushed it open.

'Good morning, what time do you call this?' Thomas asked in mock surprise. He was sitting on the sleepers pulling on a pair of wellington boots, gardening gloves tucked under his arm.

'And I thought I'd got up early,' she replied.

'I knew you would. Which is why I got up even earlier. Jo, you cannot possibly lift these by yourself, I'm not sure I could. I am very happy to help you out. After all, it's supposed to be helping me too. I was so tired last night I got a better night's sleep than I have for the past week.'

Jo put her gloves on, and they picked up the first sleeper together.

'So, if you were a writer, how would you go about starting a new book?' he asked after they had dropped the sleeper into its final position.

She thought for a while as they walked back to get the next.

'I think I'd want to write about what I know most about, what was in my heart, something that mattered to me, if I were to be truly convincing. Which means I would probably write about a garden. I couldn't just invent a character from nowhere or talk about things I know nothing about, I would base them on people I know, draw on personal experience. I'm afraid that would make my characters very flawed.'

'But if you think about it, some of the best characters in books have a flawed element to them. It makes us relate to them more and want to engage with the story.'

She turned to him, remembering when he had told her about his letter to God. 'Think about what is important to you and just write from your heart, draw from your personal experience. Relax with an idea and start writing, see what comes out on the paper.' She felt she had got a bit serious and added, 'Maybe you could write a story about a young man jilted by his cheating masseuse lover.'

'Very funny,' he laughed. 'I will let my subconscious think about that.'

The construction of the greenhouse was completed in the first week of April. A small opening ceremony was held, with a red ribbon tied across one of the doors, which Henri duly cut with a pair of secateurs, declaring it open for growing. A peach tree, 'Charles Ingouf,' had been ordered and Jo had been busy preparing the bed inside the greenhouse for its arrival. There was also space for tomatoes, peppers and cucumbers. On rainy days, it was a welcome dry area for her to sow seeds she wanted for bedding plants and start off vegetables for the kitchen garden. A bark chip path had been laid around the vegetable beds, now newly dug over and topped up with fresh soil and compost from the old heaps. Jo felt Mary would approve of the use of the compost she must have created years ago. Everything was ready for seeds to burst into life once the warmer weather of summer truly arrived.

Jo had begun the herculean task of restoring some of the other flower beds too. At the far end of the garden, between the doors to the stables and the kitchen garden, was an area simply perfect for a lavender garden. Although there were climbing roses against the wall, their carmine shoots a promise of flowers after the heavy prune she had given them, the space in front had been sparsely planted with peonies. If she transplanted these to the beds along one of the other paths, the space would be hers to fill. After much thought, she had written to Alain to beg for any spare French lavenders he had going. She knew that Maurice had taken lots of cuttings the previous summer. She would create a garden that was a mixture of England and France, just like herself and the family she was creating it for.

She had not seen much of Thomas recently apart from mealtimes. He seemed happy enough though and on warm days he sometimes came out onto the balcony, cup of tea in hand, to wave at her across the garden. She hadn't been invited up to the studio again and didn't like to ask him how things were going. She spent the evenings either playing with Henri or at Bob's house if he was home.

It was at one evening meal that Thomas announced he had been invited to go on a book signing tour for a chain of well-known high street bookstores and would be away for the next three weeks travelling around the country.

'Can't you pop back between locations dear?' Barbara asked. 'Surely they can't be working you that hard.'

'I'm going to use the time in between for writing. It will do me good to concentrate, just sit and finish this off with no distractions. I can do a bit of editing and tweaking if I get it finished.'

'Do you have distractions, Thomas? I thought the studio was lovely and quiet. It's not my playing, is it?' Henri was concerned.

'No Dad. The studio is fine, but I have more distractions than you will ever know.'

Henri just smiled to himself knowingly.

Chapter 11

The Ashmolean Museum was the destination of Jo and Bob one fine Saturday morning when they made their way into Oxford via the park and ride bus. Jo was excited. She had heard so many things about its collections of art and architecture and had been eager to see the Alfred Jewel which they held there. Ever since she was a little girl and had learned about the Anglo-Saxons at school, she had wanted to see the real thing for herself. Seeing a picture of something in a textbook was a poor experience to seeing something for real with her own eyes, she felt. It was as different as holding the wide-open creamy petals of a rose in her hands, feeling its softness against her skin, and drinking in its delicate perfume, to seeing a picture of one in a catalogue.

The museum was vast. Even with a break for lunch, they had not competed it all before they were exhausted and thoroughly foot weary.

'It's no good, we will just have to come back another day,' Bob smiled as they left to find somewhere else to collapse for a while, his arm around her waist.

'It's all very interesting though, isn't it?' she enthused. 'I love the sense of history and culture that I get when I look at the exhibits. I try to imagine people from long ago making those things, I mean who made the Alfred jewel, who held it last and used it as it was meant to be used all those years ago? What did the people who stitched the Chinese clothes we saw actually think about when they were making them? And I don't suppose the Ancient Egyptians even considered for one moment that people thousands of years later would be looking at their personal things set out in little glass cases in a faraway country. It's quite mind blowing when you think deeply about it all.'

'Hm, I suppose you're right. You know there's also the Pitt Rivers Museum up the road,' Bob suggested over a cup of tea and cakes in the little café they had found. 'I think you'll find that really fascinating. They've even got some shrunken heads on display.'

'Well, you might find that particularly fascinating, but I might give that display case a miss. There's history and then there's just plain grisly.' She pulled a face in disgust which made him laugh. 'I think I'll stick to the history.'

The day had been a pleasant carefree one which Jo enjoyed immensely, despite being so tired afterwards. Bob was good company and fun to spend the day with. On the way home, they popped into a supermarket to pick up some ready meals for a quick dinner as neither of them felt like cooking. As Bob drove back to Oxbury, Jo looked out the window and wondered how Thomas was getting on with his book tour and whether he had finished writing his new novel. They hadn't heard much from him, although he had phoned Henri a couple of times to let him know he was ok.

After they had eaten and tidied up, they sat on the sofa, Jo snuggled into the crook of Bob's arm with her socked feet hanging over the arm at the end. Eunice had joined them as she usually did, paddling Jo's lap before settling down for a stroke and a snooze there. They watched the telly in silence until there was nothing interesting on any of the channels.

'Jo?' said Bob, bending her around so he could kiss her, which made Eunice jump off and prowl out to the kitchen in a huff. Cats certainly let you know when they are displeased, Jo thought.

'Mm?'

'I think it's high time we took this relationship to the next level, don't you?' he said insistently.

She knew what he meant and had tried avoiding the subject in the weeks they had been together. He had made a few suggestions before and increasingly put pressure on her recently. She didn't know what was holding her back, just that it didn't feel right. It wasn't that he was unkind or inattentive. They had fun together and she liked spending time with him. It was just that for her giving her body was the final act of commitment. It was all she had to give, and she only wanted to give it to the right man. She was not sure Bob was that man even though she couldn't put her finger on just why that was.

'Bob, I'm not sure.'

'You've been saying that for the past few weeks now darling, I think we're ready.'

'But this is about the two of us,' she said, sitting up and facing him. 'It's not just about what you think.' She felt slightly annoyed.

'I know that, but there's two of us in this relationship, what about what I want? Don't you want to make me happy too?'

'I do, but we have to both want this at the same time for it to be right.'

'I think you'll feel right about it. Come on.' He stood up taking her hand to pull her upstairs.

'Bob, this is not the right way to go about things. I think I ought to go home before we argue. We've had a really good day together; we are both tired and I don't want to spoil things.'

She was putting on her shoes now. She could tell by his silence that he was annoyed to but trying not to show it. She put her coat on and went over to the door.

'Are you sure you won't reconsider?' he murmured, coming over to her and looking into her eyes, a kind of puppy dog expression on his face. He kissed her hoping that she would change her mind.

'No Bob. Goodnight.' She kissed him back briefly and shut the door behind her.

Walking back to the cottage on her own she wondered what she ought to do. Other people had their mothers and girlfriends to ask advice from. Perhaps she could confide in Barbara. She would think about it for a while. She would not see Bob till next Friday's quiz anyway.

Feeling unsettled Jo spent the next day working in the garden. She needed nature around her to sooth her worries away. Plants rarely demanded anything, only gave of their beauty and tranquillity. She would dig the holes for trellising poles that would separate the now finished kitchen garden from the main garden beyond. She had already put a rustic wooden archway over the path that led into it and now wanted to complete its formal separation. A good work out digging holes with her trowel would do her good, and release some of her pent-up frustration. She started early and by lunchtime the holes were ready for the upright wooden poles to be cemented in. Having forgotten to put gloves on in her haste to take her mind off things, she found that her hands were a bit sore and blistered. She had the poles and cement but would need someone to hold the poles upright while she spaded the dry cement mixture round. Perhaps Barbara or Henri would help as Thomas was still away.

After lunch, she found Barbara in the small garden at the back of the house. She sat in a patch of sun with her eyes closed, a book face down next to her on the bench. She heard Jo approach and opened her eyes.

'Hello dear. Isn't it lovely out here? I came out to read really, but sometimes it's just nice to sit in the sunshine and think.'

'Thinking about anything in particular?'

'Oh, you know, this and that and what makes the world go round. Come and sit down.' She picked up the book and patted the seat beside her.

'This is a beautiful little garden,' Jo said, taking everything in around her. The waterlily in the central fishpond was just beginning to get going for the year, stretching its curled, waxy leaves to the surface for air. Here they would unfurl like miniature landing pads for the damselfly helicopters that darted overhead in summer.

'Yes, Mary and I often used to sit out here, we were best friends as well as nurse and patient. She could only manage to walk this far from the house in the last few weeks and then not at all towards the very end, poor love. Henri used to open the French doors from the living room and play to us. It was awfully hard on him you know, when she died.'

'I'm sure. It must have been hard for you too, losing a friend like that. Henri tells me that you look after this garden now. It looks perfect. Like a little hidden jewel at the back of the house.'

'Thank you dear. I vowed to Mary I would always keep it looking good for her. She made me promise I'd look after Henri and Thomas too, she knew they would be a bit lost without her, especially with Thomas being quite young still.' She looked around her at the garden 'There's only a few little bits to trim now and then, no grass, so it's not too arduous at all. Not like over there,' she nodded her head in the direction of the main garden. 'Henri couldn't bear to go there for a long while after she died. It was her place you see, her life apart from her music and every time he went out there, he felt her loss all over again. Thomas was not in a fit state either for a long time, felt he had let everyone down by not being there at the end. Henri was so worried about him.'

'Yes, he told me about that and the letter he wrote.'

'He's a fine young man, Thomas. Anyway, by the time we'd got ourselves sorted and on the mend, so to speak, the garden had already become overgrown, and it just got neglected, until Henri found you,' she said, smiling cheerfully. 'I'm so glad he did.' Barbara gave Jo a hug.

'I'm glad he did as well,' Jo said. 'By the way, I have a favour to ask, I wonder if you could give me a hand holding the trellis poles for me after lunch while I cement them in.'

Jo and Barbara worked through the afternoon. Jo shovelling dry concrete while Barbara held the poles and checked they were upright with the spirit level. They made a good team. When they had watered them in and left them to set, Barbara went back into the house to get dinner ready.

Jo went into the greenhouse. The tomatoes were now ready to plant into the grow bags she had bought. She loved the smell of the leaves as they brushed against her hand, it filled her mind with memories of long summer days of sunshine and happiness when she had been a child. If only she could go back in time and change what had happened. She sighed. What was done was done, no matter how much she wished it undone. Time always marched forward relentlessly wagging its finger at her in disapproval of her past mistakes. She only had herself to blame, it said. She wondered if she was making another mistake with Bob, but then again, they got on so well together and she liked him a lot. It was no good, her reasoning was just going around in circles and the more she thought about it the less she knew what she really wanted.

At last, her reverie was broken by a tap on the glass. It was Barbara.

'Coming in for dinner?' she called.

Roast dinners, especially cooked by Barbara, were delicious. Except that Jo hardly tasted hers, her mind preoccupied with Bob and what she should do. It was unfair to keep him hanging on. She reached across the table to her wine glass.

'What have you done to your hands, ma petite?' said Henri, noticing they were red and slightly blistered. He took hold of one of them, a look of horror on his face.

'It's ok, I just got a bit carried away digging the holes for the trellis this morning, forgot to put my gloves on. Had a lot on my mind this morning I guess.'

'What has got you so worried that you neglect yourself?' said Henri, still holding her hand. 'You know Barbara and I are very good listeners, my dear. Is it something in the garden?'

She shook her head. All of a sudden it became too much, and she put her hands over her face to hide her misery and confusion. Barbara got up and came around the table to hug her.

'Tell us what's going on my love. I knew you weren't right today when we were out in the garden, you looked at bit peaky.'

'Oh. I don't know, it's nothing and everything. I just don't know what to do,' she sighed.

'Is it Bob?' asked Barbara intuitively.

Jo nodded.

'He hasn't hurt you, has he?' she asked Jo gently, exchanging a worried glance with Henri.

'No, nothing like that. He's very kind.' She knew that she would have to tell them the whole of it. Perhaps they could help her make a decision. 'It's just that he wants to take our relationship up a peg, if you see what I mean.'

They nodded in understanding, silent for a while in contemplation.

'And you don't?' said Barbara.

'It's not that I'm against it,' said Jo, blushing slightly. 'It's just that I'm not sure he is the right person. I keep thinking back to the advice my grandmother gave me when I was younger.'

'And what was that dear?'

'She told me that true love was like a fairy cake that best friends make together. The cherry on the top was sex, the icing romance, and friendship was the cake underneath. If you only eat the cherry and the icing, in the end it will leave you feeling unfulfilled and ultimately empty. To make a good lasting relationship you really need to start with the cake of friendship and gradually add the icing and last of all the cherry. The trouble is I think that Bob wants to start with the cherry, and I don't think we have nearly enough cake going on. We want different things in life.'

'Are you in love with him Jo?' asked Henri, gently taking her hand once more and looking into her eyes.

She shook her head. 'No. I don't think I am.'

'Does he love you do you think?'

'That's just it, he's never actually said he loves me at all. What does love mean anyway?'

'For me,' Henri began, sitting back in his chair, 'true love is a longing to be with a person every moment of your day. They make your heart flip over and fill you with joy each time you see them. It is the feeling that you are incomplete without them because you are so deeply connected. It is the knowledge you want to be with them through good times and bad no matter what and knowing that even when life gets tough you have the solidity of friendship to face the world together because you share the same outlook on life.'

Jo noticed that he looked at Barbara as he spoke, and that the older woman blushed slightly.

'Oh, Henri that's so beautiful,' said Jo, 'I so want that out of life. I don't think Bob and I share the same outlook on life ultimately.'

Henri sighed and looked back at her. 'Then I think you should follow your grandmother's advice. She sounds like she was a very wise woman.'

'She was.'

'Jo, you are the sort of young lady that loves deeply and passionately with all her soul, and I think, can give her heart perhaps only once. I know that, you see, because I have seen you play the piano my dear, and when you play, I see more than just fingers moving over a keyboard. Make sure you give your heart to the right person. You will know, in here,' he pointed to her heart, 'when the time is right.' He squeezed her hand.

'Thank you. Thank you for helping me see things more clearly. I'd got myself in such a tizzy about it. I suppose I will have to pluck up the courage and put Bob out of his misery now. I hate upsetting people.'

'He will live,' was all that Henri had to say on that subject.

Jo and Barbara cleared the plates between them, the tinkling notes of a Mozart sonata coming from the other room.

The following Friday was quiz night once again and Jo did not think she could spend the whole evening with Bob pretending that everything was okay between them. She wanted to explain how she felt first, hoping that he would understand. Rather than do that over dinner at the pub she said she would cook for them both at the cottage. At least they would be private with no wagging ears, especially those as large as Mrs West's, to overhear. She had spent the entire week thinking about how to let him down gently but come the time she still had no firm plan in her head.

At five to six Bob arrived, a bunch of carnations in hand, looking apologetic as he stood in the doorway.

'Jo I'm so sorry,' were the first words out of his mouth and suddenly she felt guilty for what she knew must come next.

'Bob, don't apologise.' This was going to be an exceedingly difficult 'it's not you but me,' talk, she thought. 'We do need to talk though.'

'I was afraid you were going to say that,' he said, coming over to kiss her, but she turned her head and ended up with a peck on the cheek instead. 'Oh dear, I fear this is not going to be my day. Hear me out Jo before you begin.'

They went through to the tiny living room area and sat on the sofa.

'Jo, I really, really like you, I think we make a great couple, we get on well together and have fun, don't we? I will try not to mention the 's' word again. I will try my best to back off from that subject, but it is hard, I still think that we would be great together.'

If he said he loved her, he might have been in with the teeniest of chances Jo thought. But he had not and being *really, really liked* was not good enough. She knew she needed more. Henri was right.

'Bob, I really like you too and yes, we have fun together, but that is not enough for me. I need something deeper. We don't really have any interests in common and ultimately want different things from life, I'm thinking of long-term stuff. Eventually I want children and I'm not sure you do.'

He looked at her silently.

'Basically, the things that make us tick are too different for this to work long term, and I'm just not into this short-term fun stuff, it's just not who I am,' she continued.

'There's nothing wrong with short term fun, as long as you're careful,' he added.

'Maybe not for you, but I want someone who knows me inside and out, who shares my passions in life, who understands me. Someone who loves me for who I am, and until I find that person I can't commit. Bob, I'm so sorry. It's better that we break up now before we end up breaking each other because we are pulling at life in different directions rather than pulling together.'

He sat looking at her for a long time, obviously thinking about what she had said.

'Perhaps you're right,' he sighed eventually. 'Do you think we can we still be friends?'

She hugged him then.

'Bob I would love to be friends with you,' she hesitated. 'Do you still want to stay for dinner?'

'A man can't quiz on an empty stomach. What is it anyway?' he said brightening.

'Pizza.' She was glad that she did not seem to have broken his heart too badly.

'Better get the oven on then.'

The evening seemed to pass in a blur for her after that. She could sense Henri and Barbara watching her across the pub, but here and now with so many people around was not the time to tell them what had happened. She walked home with them afterwards and they sat in the kitchen together, drinking tea.

'So how are you feeling after all that, ma petite?' Henri said.

'Kind of sad but strangely relieved at the same time. He took it well. I think we both knew we were on a road to nowhere.'

'It's nice that you can still be friends, so many relationships end acrimoniously these days,' said Barbara. 'You did the right thing love.'

Henri twinkled at her. 'Mm…so, you are a free agent now Miss Stanton, I must ring Marie and get her back on the case.'

'Please don't!' she laughed. 'I think I am able to make my own decisions, I'll just be a lot more careful in future.'

Just then they heard the front door open, and the bustling sound of a suitcase and bags being brought in.

'Hello everyone. Did you miss me?' Thomas called, coming into the kitchen. He was swiftly followed by a blond woman in high heels and far too much make up who glanced at him somewhat adoringly. 'This is Elaine, she'll be staying for a few days.'

Chapter 12

'Hello nice to meet you, thanks for putting me up. Thomas said you wouldn't mind,' Elaine said, stroking Thomas' arm before reaching out to shake hands with Henri and Barbara, her bangled arm jangling each time. Jo just got a nod and a 'Hi.'

Henri looked a little puzzled. Clearly to Jo he knew nothing of this arrangement but hid it well under the circumstances she thought. Barbara was her usual welcoming self.

'Well. I'll put the kettle on, you must have had a long journey today, Come and sit down both of you. Do you drink tea Elaine?'

Jo made her excuses, said goodnight, and went back to the cottage. It had seemed like a long day all in all. As she lay in bed she thought through her day. She wondered about Elaine and her relationship to Thomas. Clearly from her behaviour and the two minutes she had spent in her company there was something going on there. Perhaps they were an item. From the way she dressed, she did not seem like the sort of woman Thomas would go for but then what did she know? And, she told herself firmly, it was none of her business.

At elevenses, the next morning there was no sign of Thomas or Elaine. She thought Thomas was in because she had seen the balcony door open when she had been in the garden earlier, checking on the poles she and Barbara had cemented in yesterday. Maybe they were busy.

After lunch, Jo made herself busy cutting long half rounds of timber which would sit across the top of the new poles and link up with the rustic archway to complete the trellising. She had some half height open diamond panels that would fit between the poles at the bottom and hoped to plant a clematis at the base of each one when it was complete. It would look charming when fully established in a couple of years' time. She could imagine it now, large silken bloomed flowers scrambling over the archway and trellis in different hues of purple and lilac. It was difficult to decide just which clematis to choose. She had looked online at some mail order companies that seemed to have a lot more choice than the nurseries nearby. 'Victor Hugo' with its spear-like velvet petals of deep royal purple was an absolute must, especially being her all-time favourite, as was the newer 'Wisley'. She would need some paler ones too, maybe a white 'Hyde Hall' would set off them off nicely. Mentally contemplating different combinations of clematis while she worked, Jo glanced across the garden and saw Thomas descend the spiral stairs from the balcony. She watched as he strode across the garden towards her.

'Hello Jo,' he said and engulfed her in a hug. He smelt clean and comforting and she remembered the very first hug he had given her when her grandmother had just died. 'I missed you.'

Her heart gave a little flip and mentally she told it to stop misbehaving.

'Did you?' she asked. 'How did the tour go?'

'Of course, I did. The tour was good, I had a brilliant time actually. The books sold well, and I finished the new one in record time. It's been edited already. I didn't have to make many changes at all. Can't believe it's gone through so quickly. My editor, Rosemary, loved it.'

'That is fantastic news. What is it about?'

'Wait and see,' was all he said. He looked around him. 'So, looks like everything is progressing well in the garden.'

'Yes. You know, it keeps me busy and employed,' she smiled. 'I'm just working on the trellising here as you can see. I might get it finished by the end of tomorrow.'

'Need a hand?'

'You're not too busy?'

'Elaine has gone shopping, there's a few things she needed. She'll be back later.'

'Well, if you'd like you can hold the other end of the poles in position while I screw them in place that would be very useful, thank you.'

They set to work, Jo up the ladder screwing the half round timbers down while Thomas held them in place from below. She was becoming a bit of a dab hand with a drill and screwdriver now. Seeing a project like this come together was very satisfying. It did help when you had another pair of hands to hold things steady though.

'Is she an old friend of yours?' Jo ventured eventually, curiosity getting the better of her.

'Sort of,' he replied instantly knowing to whom she referred. 'Part of the book tour was in Edinburgh; I had a few days free up there, so I visited the university to see if any of my old professors were still teaching. Turned out the head of faculty was still the same, so I knocked on his door to see if he remembered me. He did, which was lovely. We chatted a bit about old times, and he said he had read my books and really enjoyed them. The next evening, he invited me to dinner, where I met Elaine, she is his daughter. Amazingly, she works at the University of Oxford on the English team and happened to be visiting at the same time.'

'How lovely,' Jo said trying to sound enthusiastic.

'Yes, she's between houses at the moment. Had to move out of a flat she was renting because the landlord sold it and she hasn't found a new place yet, so I said she could come and stay for a bit while she gets sorted. She's had to put most of her stuff in storage.'

'That's a shame,' murmured Jo, pushing a screw in firmly with the electric screwdriver.

'Anyway, turns out she's part of the team that plans the modules for the students and asked me to be a guest lecturer for half a term next academic year.'

'Wow! That sounds a bit daunting, I'm not sure I'd want to stand up in front of a load of students.'

'I think it will be quite interesting. Inspiring the next generation of writers.'

'Hardly the next generation, you're not that old. How long ago did you leave university?'

'Seven years. Feels like longer sometimes. We are going to do some planning while she's here, you know, go over the things that need to be taught, make sure I'm up to scratch.'

'I expect you will be quite busy then,' she said, moving the ladder to screw down the other end of the timber.

'Mm…we'll see.'

About an hour later Thomas was just helping Jo off the ladder, not that she really needed it, when Elaine arrived. Jo could hear her bangles jingling as she got nearer.

'Ooh, I'm not coming in there,' she wailed looking at the bark chipping path of the kitchen garden. 'My heels will sink in. Tommy, we really need to have a look at the outline for the new modules. I think we've just got time to make a start before dinner.'

Tommy?

'I'd better go,' said Thomas quietly to Jo. 'Will you be ok to carry on?'

'Of course…*Tommy*,' she said even more quietly. He smiled.

'See you at dinner,' he called back to Jo as he joined Elaine on the path.

As they walked along towards the house, Jo distinctly heard Elaine ask, 'Do you often come and work with the staff Tommy?' but then they turned the corner, and she didn't catch Thomas' reply.

Dinner that evening was an interesting affair. They sat around the table in the kitchen as usual, Jo observing Elaine and Thomas. *If she sits any closer to him, she will be on his lap,* she thought, and then chided herself for being too judgemental. Henri seemed to be in a slight state of shock, and it was left to Barbara to make conversation. Not that she needed to make too much of an effort as Elaine seemed to be able to eat and talk about herself at the same time quite happily. Jo was glad when the meal was over and stayed in the kitchen to help Barbara tidy up afterwards.

'Do you think she's related to Mrs West?' Barbara whispered after the others moved into the living room.

'Lord help us if she is!' Jo said and they tried not to make any noise as they giggled together.

Mentioning Mrs West made Jo think about Ellen. She had not been at the last quiz night and Jo hoped she was ok. She decided that she would call into the shop sometime that week to see if she was and do something about rescuing the girl from her mother.

As the bell jangled, Mrs West appeared from the back of the shop, cardboard box in hand looking slightly flustered.

'Hello Jo, dear,' she said, 'haven't seen you for a while. Mind you, I expect you have been busy working now the weather is better. I love this time of year, don't you? Makes you feel as if summer is on its way again. How is that handsome doctor of yours? Has he checked your vitals lately?'

Jo ignored her suggestive remark and refused to be drawn on the status of her private relationships. Even if they were no longer together it was none of her business and Jo did not like the idea of being gossiped about to every other customer who came in the shop.

'I was wondering if Ellen was about actually.'

'Ellen?' Mrs West seemed slightly taken aback.

'Yes,' persisted Jo, waiting.

'She's out the back...Ellen!' she yelled.

Ellen appeared holding another cardboard box. It must be delivery day, thought Jo.

'Hello Ellen, I was wondering if you could do me a favour,' said Jo drawing the girl to the front of the shop away from her mother who was busy now stocking the shelves. 'I need to do some clothes shopping in Oxford, and I've only been there once, to the museum. I was wondering if you would like to come with me, show me the best places. We could have lunch out together, my treat. What do you think?'

Ellen looked for all the world as if she had just been invited to Buckingham Palace to have tea with the Queen. Her face lit up but then fell again.

'I'd better check with Mum first, when did you have in mind?'

'How about this Saturday?'

Mrs West was so surprised that someone had invited Ellen out for the day that she agreed without protest. As the older woman disappeared through to the back of the shop once more, Ellen surprised Jo with a hug.

'Thank you so much,' she squealed. 'I can't wait!'

Waiting at the bus stop the following Saturday Ellen could barely contain her excitement.

'I love shopping,' she said, jumping up and down.

'Calm down, it's only for jeans and tops, nothing exciting,' Jo said, laughing.

'Yes, but it's a day out, away from the shop,' Ellen continued excitedly.

The bus arrived and they got on, finding seats at the back behind two elderly ladies.

'Don't you like the shop?' Jo asked her, already half knowing the answer.

Ellen shook her head violently. 'I hate it.'

'Why don't you find a job somewhere else then?'

'I can't afford to.' She was calm now and an air of melancholy seemed to descend around her. 'Mum doesn't want me to leave her. I'm all she's got since Dad walked out. It's difficult you know?'

Jo did know. It was hard to leave people when they needed you, when you were all they had. It had been a slightly similar situation for her and her grandmother after the first stroke.

By the time they reached the city centre, Ellen had told Jo all about her dad who had run off with another woman from the village, he had taken all their savings and gone to live in Spain apparently, leaving Ellen and her mum pretty much penniless running the shop and post office. She hadn't seen him since and, as technically her parents weren't divorced, there was nothing her mum could do about the situation, nothing she had tried to do anyway.

Jo spent the morning trying to cheer her up by letting herself be led around the shops, Ellen talking nineteen to the dozen about the latest fashions she had seen in the magazines in the Stores and how good she thought Jo would look in them. Jo had never been into fashion in her entire life, but it was fun, nonetheless. They stopped for lunch in a pizza restaurant on the high street.

'My treat,' insisted Jo, 'as a thank you for coming with me today.'

'Was Bob busy today then?' Ellen asked as they waited for their food to arrive.

'Actually, we are not together anymore,' Jo confessed, 'I think we were too different for it to have lasted. We're still friends though, which I suppose is the best outcome for both of us.'

'Oh,' said Ellen, 'I didn't know.'

'Well, we didn't shout it from the rooftops, it's kind of personal, nobody else's business really.'

'You mean you didn't want my mother to know. Don't worry, I understand completely. She's the biggest gossip in the world. I try not to tell her things myself.' She smiled sadly at Jo. 'I don't think she sees me at all really, thinks I'll be ok staying in a dead-end job all my life and that I'll just take over when she retires.'

'What would your dream job be if you had the chance?'

Ellen brightened suddenly.

'I want to be a nurse or maybe a midwife. I have always wanted to, ever since I was little. I saved up and bought a nursing textbook a few years ago. Mum doesn't know I've got it. I read it at night when she's gone to bed. Fat lot of good it will do me though. I can't afford to do a nursing degree.'

'There must be grants available.'

'Yes, but even with that it still takes a lot of money, and I would be away from Mum.'

'I'm sure she'd get used to it, find someone else to take your place.'

'Not going to happen though, is it?' She shrugged and bit into her garlic bread. 'Mm...this is good.'

After lunch, they strolled through the city some more, Jo in a thoughtful mood. Ellen stopped suddenly outside an expensive looking shop that had posh evening dresses in the window.

'Let's go in and try some on.'

'Ellen, I don't need an evening dress, I'm a gardener. I can't wear one of those while I'm digging potatoes, it would get terribly muddy at the bottom.'

Ellen giggled at the thought of Jo gardening in a posh dress.

'Oh, go on, just for fun. I will if you will,' Ellen goaded.

As the day was supposed to be about cheering Ellen up, Jo reluctantly agreed, and they went in. Ellen made up a fantastic story about them both being invited to a film premier, which, to Jo's amazement, the woman in the shop seemed to swallow, and so the fun began. First, it was Ellen's turn to try on dresses. With her fair hair spinning out behind her, she twirled around on the little podium in the middle of the changing room, like a small child at a party, her reflection twirling simultaneously in the mirrors that surrounded it. She tried on different styles and pretended to the assistant that she couldn't make her mind up about each one. Jo had trouble keeping a straight face and then it was her turn.

'What would madame like to try on? Have you any styles in mind?' enquired the assistant.

Jo could hardly believe she was going along with this, but they were both in too deep to back out now.'

'I'm not sure, something simple and elegant maybe,' she replied. Was that the right thing to say? She really had no idea.

The assistant looked her up and down as if appraising her figure.

'Do you know, I think I have just the thing,' she said.

Ten minutes later Jo emerged from behind the curtain and stood on the podium in front of the mirrors. She had never worn such a dress before. She looked at her reflection, her dark hair hastily arranged in a messy bun. Forest green velvet fell from a sweetheart neckline and tiny off the shoulder sleeves, hugging her waist and hips to swirl around her feet. A daring slash in the skirt revealing one of her slim legs to mid-thigh when she walked.

Everyone was silent for a moment.

'Oh, my goodness! Jo, you *have* to get that dress!' Ellen shrieked, 'You look like a million dollars.' Ellen came up closer to inspect her new friend. 'Makes your eyes look really green! Jo I am not leaving here till you buy it. I'll save up the money myself and buy it for you if you don't.'

Jo looked back at her reflection. It did make her eyes look green. But what would she do with a dress like this? It was a ridiculous suggestion, but she could not say that to Ellen after the charade they were putting on in front of the shop assistant.

'We have a pair of matching shoes for that dress. Would you like to try a pair?' enquired the assistant, hopeful of an extra sale.

'Yes, she would,' Ellen piped up before Jo could reply.

Half an hour, and to Jo an exorbitant amount of money later, they left the shop. The dress in a zipped-up cover, and shoes and a wrap the assistant had found all carefully parcelled in tissue paper and boxed, hanging from Jo's shoulder.

'I can't believe that just happened,' Jo was almost hyperventilating. 'I'm never going to wear it you know, it's far too racy for a start. I am *never* coming shopping with you again.'

Ellen laughed.

'You'll have an occasion to wear it at some time in your life I'm sure, and if you don't, you can get it out your wardrobe every so often and wear it while you do the housework.'

'I'm more likely to wear it in my coffin when I die an old maid because I never went out anywhere in it in the first place,' Jo joked.

On the bus on the way home, they were still laughing about the dress. It had been a really good day out and Jo felt she had made a new and true friend in Ellen. As they got closer to Oxbury and their stop, Ellen became noticeably quieter and less bubbly.

'Ellen, we must do this again, but maybe not the dress bit. Come round for tea one evening.'

'I'd like that, I'll have to check with Mum though.'

'Ellen, how old are you?'

'Twenty-three.'

'Then I think it's time you politely but firmly told your mum you were going out when you wanted and stopped asking her permission all the time. You have got to stand up for yourself a bit more. Be confident, like you were in the shop earlier. Honestly, it's like you were a different person in there.'

'I know,' she said, 'but it's not easy when you have a mother like mine.'

After dinner, when Thomas and Elaine had retired to the studio, Jo told Barbara and Henri about her day with Ellen and how different she had been away from her overbearing mother. She did not tell them about the dress though or how much it had cost. She had hung it up in her wardrobe at the cottage after having another look at it and wondered whether she should take it back and get a refund.

'She's a sweet girl really. I think she felt the brunt of her mother's anger when her dad left. Life is so unfair to some,' Barbara said.

'Yes, she told me all about that. But I have an inkling of an idea how we could maybe help her. Barbara, I need to pick your brain about it.'

'Don't want to pick my brain?' Henri said, pretending to look mildly offended and getting up from the table.

'Not this time Henri, strictly girl stuff I'm afraid.'

'Hmm…I shall go and play my piano then…just a lonely old man…on his own.'

Barbara threw a tea towel at him as he left. He caught it and winked at her cheekily, whistling his way into the living room.

Chapter 13

'Where are Barbara and Jo tonight, Dad?' Thomas asked, coming down to the kitchen for dinner a few weeks later. Normally Barbara would be bustling about putting food on the table by now.

It was a rare occasion that Elaine was not with them, her ability to find somewhere to live was sadly lacking in Henri's opinion. However, for once she had decided to meet up with some of her other friends on the faculty and although she had invited Thomas, he had declined pleading that he should be writing up some notes for the coming term's lectures.

Henri was sat at the table with a newspaper spread out before him.

'Having a *girl's night* at the cottage with Ellen apparently. They are having a Chinese take away too, which I think is grossly unfair of them.'

'Why is that?'

'Because they haven't ordered any for us. Barbara told me I was old enough to get my own dinner for once and waltzed off to Jo's without a by your leave. How do you like that? They are up to something those three.'

'Well, have you asked them what?'

'I did. Jo just said it was "girl stuff",' Henri made an inverted comma sign with his fingers, 'and wouldn't say any more.' He shrugged his shoulders in despair.

'I'm sure Jo knows what she's doing, Dad. I wouldn't worry too much; I'll talk to her later and see if I can find out what is going on. Now what are we going to have for dinner tonight?' He went over to the fridge and looked inside. 'Well, it looks like there are two options on the menu tonight, I can rustle up some scrambled eggs or we can go to the pub.'

They looked at each other for a few seconds.

'Pub,' they both said at once.

Barbara, Ellen and Jo were just emerging from the cottage, all three women still chatting excitedly when Henri and Thomas ambled back home from the pub. Ellen gave both the women a hug and went out the gate greeting the two men cheerily as she passed them. Barbara wandered over to Henri sliding her arm through his.

'I don't know Henri, I really am going to have to give you cooking lessons, aren't I? You are completely hopeless.'

'But at least I'm alive,' said Henri as they walked towards the house. 'The alternative was Thomas' scrambled eggs.'

'Oh dear! Are you really that bad a cook?' Jo looked at Thomas.

'Shocking!' Thomas grinned. 'Got time for a chat?'

'Sure, come in. Tea?'

'Please,' he replied, and they went into the cottage.

Jo put the kettle on, the remains of the Chinese and a pile of dirty plates, mugs and glasses sat by the sink alongside a couple of empty wine bottles.

'Looks like you had quite a party in here.'

'Mm, we girls know how to have a good time you know. I'll have to wash a couple of mugs for the tea, hold on.'

'Let me do that,' he said, coming to the sink and taking the mugs out of her hands. 'I'll wash, you wipe.'

She didn't argue and busied herself binning the leftovers before drying the mugs and everything else which he also washed.

'So, what's all this "girl stuff" about then?' he asked finally.

'I'm sorry, that is classified information I am not at liberty to divulge,' she said primly, putting the tea towel down. 'If I told you, I'd have to kill you afterwards and I'm not sure your dad would let me stay on if I did that,' she laughed.

'Oh really?' he said, coming towards her with two handfuls of washing up bubbles. 'I may just have to torture you then Miss Stanton, to extract the information we require.'

She started backing away and giggled.

'I will never tell you; you can't make me,' she squealed.

She was up against the front door now and had nowhere left to go. He continued advancing until he was no more than an inch away from her, virtually pinning her in place with his body, his two hands slowly dripping bubbles on the floor. Neither of them were giggling now, they just stood looking at each other, breathing, for what seemed like an eternity.

'Tommy are you there?'

A rap sounded on the door behind, making Jo jump. Thomas closed his eyes and turned to wipe his hands on the towel.

'Coming!' he called and turned to Jo smiling. 'I will find out you know.'

He left, swiftly escorting Elaine back to the house and Jo shut the door behind her, silently sending up a prayer of thanks for being saved from what could have been a very awkward situation.

Endless summer days kept Jo busy for a long time after the incident in the cottage. The trees had opened their canopy of dark green leaves, reaching skywards to the radiant warmth of the sun. Flowers, that had been freed from their prison of weeds, wafted their perfumes on the zephyrs of balmy air that played gently around the garden and the roses bloomed. Their silken petals once spent, drifting to their eternal rest on the ground beneath. Swallows swooped their dare devil acrobatic flights over the lawn and velvet winged butterflies danced across the grass to a tune that only they could hear. But Jo felt strangely melancholic throughout it all.

Elaine was still with them, and she occupied Thomas' time as much as she could, demanding that they fill their weekends with days out and socialising with other university staff. Much to Henri's relief, she had eventually found new place to live but could not move into it for another few days yet.

The afternoon before Jo's birthday, a large, exciting, parcel arrived for her, post marked 'France.'

'Open it then,' said Barbara excitedly. She and Henri had brought it across the garden to Jo who sat on the bench outside the shed. They sat down next to her, one on each side.

Jo could smell the perfume before she opened the lid. Ten beautifully bushy lavender plants sat in the box, their already purpled heads beginning to flower. There was a note inside from Maurice about the varieties and a card from Alain and Marie with 'Bon anniversaire' written on the envelope in Marie's typically looped handwriting.

'Oh, how lovely!' Jo exclaimed. 'I had forgotten I had written to Alain earlier in the year. I must plant these out and get them watered in as soon as possible. They must be quite thirsty poor things.'

'I thought lavenders liked it quite dry,' Henri said, pinching one of the flowers and inhaling the aroma.

'They do,' she replied, 'but they've had a long journey and are about to have their roots disturbed a bit when they are planted. I want to make sure they are not stressed any more than that.'

'We will leave you to it then my dear,' said Henri, rising from the bench. 'Don't overdo it will you, it's a hot day today.'

Jo's phone pinged just then, and she reached into the shed where she always left it, to check the message. Her face lit up in a broad smile.

'Barbara look, it's a message from Ellen!' she said excitedly, showing the older woman the screen.

Barbara held it at length to focus on what it said.

'Oh, thank goodness for that!' she smiled and the two of them exchanged a hug.

Henri looked on completely baffled.

'Women!' he muttered, shaking his head and starting off down the path to the house.

Despite the good news that Jo and Barbara received that day, planting the lavenders made Jo think about her life in France, the soothing favourite fragrance of her grandmother and how much she missed her. She thought about the summer holidays she had spent with her as a child, long hot days of bliss. Jo closed her eyes. She could see Grand-mere now, cooking up something delicious in her tiny kitchen, the back door wide open to let the summer breeze waft in laden with the scent from the few lavender bushes growing in the tiny courtyard beyond. Halcyon days, before it all went wrong. Stricken with a sudden desperate loneliness and yearning for times past, Jo decided to take a walk up to the church. She didn't know why, it seemed maybe a good place for her to be alone for a while. She couldn't work out what had got into her recently, maybe she was tired and the gift from Alain had made her just a little homesick for France.

Seeking solace in the cool interior of the church, Jo wandered aimlessly around drinking in the peace and quiet. The stained-glass windows radiated Bible stories and left periodic rainbow-coloured pools of light on the tombstone strewn floor. At the top of the nave to the right, a burnished brass eagle with outstretched wings and open beak perched on a tall wooden stand as if frozen mid take off, on its back an open gospel. Between the choir stalls Jo could see a baby grand piano, identical to Henri's, the keyboard left open as if in invitation. She walked over and sat down in front of it looking at the music left on the stand. 'Ave Maria.' Why not she thought, there was no one to hear. Jo began to play, the lilting notes filling the silent church with golden waves of music. As she sang, tears prickled at the backs of her eyes and blurred her vision.

Hearing the music from outside, Thomas silently crept into the back of the church and sat in one of the pews. He watched her for a while, her eyes shutting now and then as she felt the music, putting her heart and soul into her singing. He closed his eyes to listen. He had never heard anything so utterly perfect and captivating in his entire life. As the final note died away, he tiptoed out not wanting to intrude on her solitude. His news could wait a while.

Jo sat at the piano for a few moments, this was no good she thought, wallowing in the past, making herself feel lonelier than she already was. She must look forward, get on with her life, keep herself busy. She closed the lid of the piano, the stark sound echoing off the walls. Time to get back into the sunshine and her work in the garden. Jo strolled out the church and along the path to the gate. It was odd, she thought, she hadn't noticed the fresh roses on Mary's grave on her way in.

'Did you find her earlier, Thomas?' asked Henri as he helped Barbara lay the table for dinner.

'I think she must have gone out for a while,' he replied vaguely.

'Go and tell her dinner's ready, we are a bit earlier today and you can tell her your news at the same time, I think she'd like to hear it from you directly,' Barbara said.

Thomas found Jo cleaning, sweeping out the shed in the kitchen garden, billows of soft brown dust emanating from the door. He called out to her not wanting to get too close.

'Hello Thomas,' she said peering around the door, broom in hand. She had wrapped a scarf around her hair and looked a bit like a young Mrs Mop. He laughed when he saw her.

'What on earth have you got on your head?'

Embarrassed, she quickly snatched the scarf off and stuffed it in her pocket.

'It keeps the dust out of my hair,' she explained. 'How can I help you?'

'I've got a bit of news I thought you might be interested to know.' He handed her an official looking letter.

Putting the broom to one side and quickly wiping her hands down the front of her trousers, she took it from him and began to read, her face slowly lighting up from the inside.

'You've been nominated for the Malling Book Prize for Fiction? Thomas, that is wonderful!' Spontaneously, she hugged him tightly. 'You've been working so hard. Oh, well done! Clever, clever you!' She hugged him again and he kept his arms around her as she leant back. 'But you still haven't told me what the book is about.'

'I'll let you read it soon. I wanted to thank you for your help, Jo.' He leant forward and kissed her on the forehead. 'I couldn't have written it without you, you see.'

She stepped back and looked away over the beds of sprouting vegetables feeling slightly confused.

'Well, I don't see how I helped at all. I'm only the gardener.' She handed back the letter and picked up the broom turning to hang it in the shed.

'You are so much more than that, Jo,' he sighed. 'Come on dinner is ready. I think Dad is planning to crack open the champagne.'

Everyone one was in a celebratory mood over dinner. Secretly, the fact that Elaine was moving out the next day had cheered Henri and Barbara no end, but they were also bursting with pride about Thomas' nomination.

'When do you find out if you've won?' asked Barbara as the five of them sat down to eat.

Henri poured champagne into tall flutes he had got out especially.

'Oh, not for ages yet, late November, I think. They have some sort of presentation up in London that all the nominees in the different categories are supposed to attend. The letter says they will send more details nearer the time.'

'My Tommy is so clever,' said Elaine, leaning herself up against him. 'I knew he had it in him as soon as we met. I said to myself: Elaine, there is a prize-winning man if ever I saw one.'

Thomas looked at Elaine and smiled.

Her Tommy? Was there something she had missed? Jo looked between the two of them. She reminded herself again that it was none of her business. Henri passed around the glasses of champagne and, holding up his own, proposed a toast.

'To Thomas, to inspiration and to love! Well done, my boy, your mother would be so proud of you.'

'To Thomas!' they all chorus together.

Elaine put her glass down after taking a sip and took hold of Thomas' face pulling him close, she kissed him on the lips passionately. Henri and Barbara looked at each other eyebrows raised. Jo did not know where to look. She made her excuses after dinner saying she had a lot to get done the next day and left them to it. She was so thrilled for Thomas but something in her felt flat and unsettled.

Dawn broke fine and sunny, although Jo's night had been dark and full of storm-tossed nightmares. She stood in her towelling dressing gown in the kitchen of the cottage drinking strong black coffee, trying to bring herself to life a bit more. Gazing out of the window she could see lipstick pink peonies on the far side of the lawn nodding their heavy heads in the gentle breeze. She must cut the grass today, she though absently. A knock on the front door woke her out of her reverie. She wondered who on earth it was at that time of the morning. Opening the door, she saw Thomas, he looked anxious.

'I need you in the kitchen straight away, there's an emergency,' he said and dashed off towards the house.

Panicking, Jo dropped her coffee in the sink, slipped her feet into her gardening boots by the door and followed him. Please God, don't let it be Henri or Barbara she thought as she ran.

Breathless with fear, she dashed into the kitchen and stopped in puzzlement as three lots of party poppers went off around her.

'Happy Birthday!' they all chimed together.

Henri came up and gave her a kiss on the cheek.

'Joyeux Anniversaire ma petite,' he said smiling. 'No emergency, we just wanted to surprise you.'

'Happy birthday dear,' Barbara said, giving her a hug.

'Sorry about that earlier, didn't mean to scare you,' Thomas said, coming over and enveloping her in a hug. 'Happy birthday, darling girl.'

'Well, you certainly surprised me,' Jo laughed, picking the multi coloured strings of paper off herself. 'My imagination went into panic overdrive for a moment there. I'm not even dressed yet,' she said looking at her strange ensemble.

'I hear that dressing gowns and gardening boots are the height of fashion this season,' Thomas looked her over, 'and unbrushed hair too!'

'Oh gosh, do I look a right sight?' She ran her fingers through her long dark hair to try and make herself look a little more presentable.

'You look lovely as always dear, come and sit down and open your presents.' Barbara sent a withering look in Thomas' direction.

Jo sat at the table and Henri pushed his present towards her. It was small and rectangular. She opened it and gasped to see a beautiful silver bracelet. She picked it up and noticed that hanging from it was a tiny silver grand piano.

'Oh, Henri it's beautiful! Thank you!' she exclaimed and leant over to give him a kiss.

Barbara insisted that she go next, hers was bigger and quite lumpy. Inside was a beautiful summer dress, navy blue with small cream polka dots and a pair of summery slip-on shoes that matched. Jo stood and held the dress up against herself. The material was soft and silky.

'Gosh Barbara, it's lovely and shoes too, how did you know my size?' She gave Barbara a kiss and another hug.

'I have to confess. I took a quick sneak peak in your wardrobe when we had our girl's night. I saw the dress in Oxford ages ago and thought it would look good on you with your dark hair, and you're so slim my dear. I hope you like them.'

'I do like them, very much, thank you Barbara.'

'Mine now,' said Thomas as he pushed a flat square box across the table towards her. She opened it carefully. Inside was a rose gold chain necklace with a tiny gold heart sliding along it and a small, folded piece of paper. She took the piece of paper out and opened it, on it were written the words 'For Friendship.' She didn't know what to say. She looked at him slightly open mouthed. He sat opposite her, eyebrows raised as if in question.

'Thomas…I don't know what to say…It's so pretty! Thank you.'

'Do I get a kiss and a hug as well?' he said, getting up and coming around the table to her. She stood as he wrapped his arms around her and kissed her cheek. His skin felt warm as his face pressed against the side of hers, his unshaven beard slightly bristly.

'Sit down,' he instructed and picked up the box, taking the necklace out of it. She sat as he stood behind her and put the necklace around her neck, its tiny heart reflecting the light as it swung back and forth. Having done the clasp up, very gently he lifted her hair out from underneath the chain. She could feel his fingers against the skin of her neck and closed her eyes. Once again, her brain exploded in a sensation of lights, and she shivered involuntarily. He rested his hands on her shoulders momentarily and gave a slight squeeze.

'How does it look?' he asked the others.

'Beautiful,' said Barbara.

'Jo, you should never take it off, it's perfect,' Henri said turning to her. 'Now, today young lady, you will not be doing any gardening. We are taking you out to lunch somewhere very special and then you are going to put your feet up for the rest of the day, I insist. Hopefully, we will fit in a little music too, eh?'

'But…' Jo began, but the look on Henri's face stopped her.

Just then a sleepy looking Elaine wandered into the kitchen, dressed in a skimpy satin nightdress and matching cover up that was not doing its job.

'What's going on?' she said, eyeing up Jo in her dressing gown. Then she noticed the wrapping paper on the table. 'Somebody's birthday?'

Thomas looked like he was about to answer her, but Henri got in first.

'Yes. It is Jo's birthday and we've got a very special day planned for her. I am sorry none of us will be available to help you move out. You see we've had this all planned and booked up for ages and we can't change our plans I'm afraid. Oh, and Thomas, don't forget that we have to go into Oxford briefly this morning, remember?'

Thomas did not look like he remembered at all to Jo, but he seemed to cotton on quite quickly.

'Ah, yes. I'm sorry Elaine, I had completely forgotten about that. I'll help you load your car in a minute and then I must be off with Dad, I'm afraid.'

Elaine looked like she was silently preparing to implode.

'Well, I'm going to have a long hot soak in the bath,' Jo said, 'and then get dressed for lunch.' She smiled and picked up her other birthday presents. 'I hope the move goes well for you Elaine. Good Luck in your new house.' And diplomatically she left. She really didn't want to witness the fallout from Henri's statement.

Jo looked at herself in the long mirror of the wardrobe in her bedroom and was surprisingly pleased with what she saw. The dress that Barbara had given her fitted perfectly and made her feel feminine and pretty, she hadn't worn a dress for ages, apart from the green evening one that she had purchased with Ellen and that didn't count she told herself. She wore her hair down, clipping it back from her face each side and just a little make up to make herself feel extra special. She still had on the necklace Thomas had given her, having not taken it off, even in the bath. Henri's bracelet completed the look. She checked the time. Still a little early for lunch, she would just go and water the tomatoes in the greenhouse.

Chapter 14

The greenhouse was a little hotter than Jo expected when she opened the door. Glancing up to the roof she was disappointed to see that only one of the three automatically opening window vents were working. She would have to ring the greenhouse company to get someone out to fix them. At least, they had a good long guarantee on them. Having watered the plants and picked a few of the ripe tomatoes she checked the peach tree. Plenty of leaves, but it might take a few seasons to get fruit. Still, it looked as it were thriving and that was the main thing. She looked up to see Thomas coming across the garden.

'Ready to go?' Thomas asked as he came into the greenhouse.

'Just coming,' she smiled.

He looked her up and down appraisingly and did a cheeky wolf whistle.

'Never seen you in a dress before. You have legs!'

'Of course, I have legs!' she giggled, blushing that he had been looking at her legs. 'Here, take some of these tomatoes in for me.'

They walked back to the house together and in through the kitchen. Barbara was just popping a comb into her handbag and clicked it shut when she saw them.

'Well, don't you two look lovely together, looks like you coordinated your outfits?'

Jo looked at Thomas. He was wearing a navy open neck shirt and dark cream chinos, smart but casual. The navy of his shirt made her notice his eyes, liquid pools of summer skies that stared back into hers and smiled. Her heart missed a beat.

'Are we all ready? Oh, Jo you look lovely. You have legs!' Henri said, coming into the kitchen and bending sideways slightly to look at her.

'What is it with you two and my legs today?' she said, putting the tomatoes on the table and looking between Henri and Thomas.

'Sorry Dad, got there before you I'm afraid.'

'Now stop trying to embarrass Jo you two and behave. Otherwise, *I* will take Jo to lunch and you two can stay home and eat scrambled eggs!' Barbara said, trying to be stern.

The two men tried to look contrite but failed miserably and everyone ended up laughing on the way out to the car.

Lunch was superb and probably the best meal Jo had ever eaten in her life. They had taken her to a very up market hotel and restaurant the other side of Oxford, set in its own grounds and gardens that patrons were allowed to wander around and enjoy after their meals. The dining room was large but still had an intimate atmosphere about it. Crisp white linen tablecloths, sparkling cut glass goblets and silver cutlery spoke of elegance, sophistication, and quality. It was a thoroughly luxurious treat. Jo was very thankful that Barbara had bought her the dress as they sat in the sunshine on the terrace at the back of the hotel drinking their coffee afterwards. Jeans and a tea shirt would be totally inappropriate here.

'Fancy a wander around the garden?' Henri suggested to them all after a while. 'I think my lunch has gone down sufficiently.'

They all agreed that to be a lovely idea and set off down the stone steps from the terrace that lead onto a wide green velvety lawn. Barbara and Jo walked ahead, the two men following behind.

'You know we are going to have to talk to Mrs West soon,' whispered Barbara, checking behind to make sure she wasn't overheard.

'How do think she will take it? Do you think she will be very cross?'

'I don't think so. After all, what can she do? Ellen is an adult and free to make her own choices in life. She'll only be cutting off her own nose to spite her face if she kicks up a fuss and at the end of the day it's in her own interests to go along with it. She'll probably end up with a better relationship with her daughter as a result.'

'Mm…I just hope we're doing the right thing,' Jo mused.

'I'm sure we are,' she said, putting a hand on Jo's arm. 'We will have to take Ellen shopping soon too, there will be quite a few bits and pieces she'll need.'

'Why don't we arrange a girl's day out, we should be able to get most of it done in one go.'

'Well, if we don't, we will just have to have another day out to finish it won't we? More scrambled eggs for the boys I fear.' They laughed and simultaneously turned to look at Henri and Thomas.

'What are you up to, you two? Dad, I think they are talking about us.' Thomas eyed the two women suspiciously.

'Just girl stuff,' they chimed together and giggled some more.

'Seriously?' Henri sighed.

'Oh! Not that again!' groaned Thomas. 'I think we should split them up, don't you agree, Dad? Jo, let me show you the vegetable garden here, it will make you green with envy.'

Jo was literally led off down the garden path and through a gap in a tall beech hedge, leaving Barbara and Henri to wonder off on their own. Before her stood a wrought iron gate set in a tall surrounding brick wall. Thomas opened the gate, and they went in. Eight equally sized large plots of rich brown earth, sown with a profusion of vegetables and fruits at various stages of harvest opened up before them. Wigwams of runner beans stood to attention in orderly lines and courgettes splayed their frilled leaves to the sun. A veritable feast of colours on display. At the far side, an enormous greenhouse suggested more delightful culinary ingredients being cultivated. Four gardeners, in a uniform of shorts and polo shirts toiled, some picking, others digging and sowing.

'Wow!' breathed Jo. 'You were right, I am green with envy, puts our little kitchen garden to shame, doesn't it?'

'Our kitchen garden is just perfect for us. There's only four of us to feed, here they are catering for a whole restaurant!'

'I wonder whether we are allowed in the greenhouse. I might get some inspiration for growing some more unusual things in ours,' she wondered aloud.

They strolled in a leisurely fashion towards the greenhouse, Jo stopping to look at what was growing in each plot as they passed. She peered through one of the windows hoping to see what was inside.

'Would your wife like to come in and have a look?' a cheery voice said from behind them. 'She'd be most welcome.'

Before Jo could say anything, Thomas piped up.

'I'm sure she would love that, wouldn't you dear?' He looked at Jo, the corners of his mouth twitching into a smile.

The man led the way around to the side door. Behind his back a scarlet faced Jo pulled a 'what did you say that for' expression at Thomas, who couldn't help but laugh.

'You are incorrigible,' she hissed at him before following the gardener in.

A dense jungle of vegetation filled the greenhouse. Vibrant chillies in fiery oranges and molten reds, golden yellow tomatoes and rich purple aubergines were all waiting to be picked at their peak of perfection and flavour for customers' plates. Thomas came up behind Jo and put his arm around her waist in a husband-like gesture. She tried to peel his fingers away surreptitiously as their host explained the different varieties of tomatoes they grew. Jo was trying to think of interesting questions to ask, all the while the silent battle ensued behind her back. They eventually came out the other end of the greenhouse and the man wished them a pleasant day and wondered off to talk to one of the other gardeners. 'Lovely couple must be on their honeymoon,' he was overheard saying as they walked off. Thomas kept his arm around her waist as they strolled back down the garden, Jo at a much faster pace than she had come in.

'Oh, my goodness Thomas! How could you do that? I was so embarrassed,' she exploded when they reached the gap in the hedge.

'I wasn't,' he said, still smirking slightly. 'It was his mistake; I merely took advantage of it.'

'And of me,' she said crossly.

'No,' he said seriously. 'This would be taking advantage of you.'

And he pulled her close, bringing his mouth down on hers in the most passionate kiss she had ever had in her entire twenty-five years. All her senses became heightened at once and then exploded in a million tiny shards of light from the top of her head to the tips of her toes. He put her down and they stood breathlessly staring at each other. Jo put her hands up to her face. Tears already welling in her eyes.

'Jo…I…' he began.

But she had already turned and run off in the direction of the hotel.

Half an hour later, she had composed herself and sat on the terrace looking out towards the garden, a cool glass of iced water chinking in her hand. Henri and Barbara wandered across the lawn, arm in arm.

'What have you done with Thomas?' Barbara asked, looking around.

'Must have lost him somewhere,' she said squinting against the sun and shading her eyes with her hand, hoping that they would not notice any strain in her voice. 'A bit careless of me really.'

'More like a bit careless of him,' muttered Henri, seeing his son come out of the hotel and look in their direction. His face spoke a thousand words of regret that Henri read perfectly. He patted Barbara's hand.

'Why don't you two ladies enjoy sitting in the sun for a little, while we go and sort out the bill?' And a few other things as well, he thought to himself.

'Did you have a lovely stroll?' Jo asked Barbara a bit too brightly.

Barbara looked at her for a second, whatever had happened, and something had she was sure, was not for this moment.

'Splendid, dear. It is a lovely spot for a hotel here isn't it? Last time I came, there was a wedding on. Super gardens for the photos, of course.'

'Mm…'

'Henri and I have been talking about taking a holiday soon.'

'Oh? That's nice. Where were you thinking of going, home or abroad?' Jo enquired.

'France actually. He'd like me to meet Alain and Marie and see the area where he grew up.'

'Oh Barbara, you'll love it, and them! Such lovely welcoming people. I am very jealous already.' She looked across at her friend. Was she blushing? 'Barbara, is there something you're not telling me? You're blushing!' she smiled.

'He's such a dear man,' she said, smiling and twinkling at Jo at the same time. 'Mum's the word though, for the moment.'

'My lips are sealed,' said Jo, pretending to zip her lips across. Her day had suddenly got better.

'Well, my dears, I think we are all ready to go, Thomas is just bringing the car around to the front door,' Henri announced.

The ladies stood and all three of them walked through the hotel. Before they reached the front door where Thomas was waiting with the car, Jo stopped and turned to them.

'Thank you for this,' she said. 'You've both been so kind, I've had a lovely birthday.'

'It's not over yet, my dear,' Henri laughed.

Barbara and Henri monopolised the conversation on the journey home discussing which places to visit on their holiday. Henri promising to book everything that week. Thomas was almost completely silent, concentrating on driving. When they pulled into the house, an old green Land Rover Defender sat on the driveway.

'Looks like you've got a visitor,' said Jo. Although she could not see anyone sitting in it. Perhaps they were waiting in the garden.

Henri unlocked the front door and picked up an envelope from the mat, he handed it to her.

'I think this is for you Jo.'

She took it, puzzled. It was lumpy. Opening it she found 2 car keys. She Looked at Henri who nodded towards the car on the drive.

'Jo it's for you,' smiled Barbara. 'You can drive, can't you?'

'Yes, but…I can't accept this, it's way too much and I haven't driven in this country since I was eighteen!' She was completely overwhelmed.

'Think of it as a perk of your job, my dear,' said Henri kindly. 'It will be useful when you need to buy materials and plants for the garden, and you can use it when you go out other places as well. It was Thomas' idea originally and a jolly good one too, no more having to get the bus. Thomas, go with Jo now for a little spin, will you? Boost her confidence a bit while Barbara and I have a little rest.' He winked at Barbara and they both disappeared inside, shutting the door behind them.

Jo unlocked the car and they got in in silence.

'Jo, about earlier,' Thomas began, turning to her and putting his hand over hers on the gear stick.

She pulled hers away and turned to listen to what he had to say. She could do that now she'd had time to get herself under control. She had not been able to even look him in the eye before. She noticed he looked worried, and suddenly felt guilty for having run off and not spent time sorting this out when it happened.

'I'm so incredibly sorry. I really did not mean to upset you. I've been a complete idiot. Your friendship means everything to me, and I would hate to think that I had lost that. Forgive me? Please?'

He looked so remorseful that her heart went out to him.

'I value our friendship too, so you are forgiven.' She had to lighten this situation somehow otherwise it would be unbearable for both of them. 'But I think you owe me a forfeit now Thomas Arnaud,' she smiled.

'Oh dear,' he smiled back 'What had you in mind?'

'I need some time to think about that, but I will come up with something.'

'As long as it doesn't involve "girl stuff".'

'Oh! Now there's an idea!' she laughed.

He groaned and put his head in his hands, shaking it as she drove out the gate.

The tension between them eased during their little trip around in Jo's new car and by the time they got back they were enjoying a friendly argument about whether men or women were the best drivers. He let her win, of course.

By the time Jo got back to the cottage that night, she was exhausted. She sat on the edge of the bed and touched the little gold heart still hanging around her neck. For friendship. She was beginning to wonder what that actually meant.

The following quiz night, instead of all of them eating at the pub as usual, Barbara had shooed the men out of the house early. Mrs West and Ellen had been invited to dinner. Jo was nervous, this could go either way.

In the event, Mrs West had been amazingly quiet, even listening to her daughter's point of view. She agreed to Barbara and Jo's terms and conditions not to say anything without a fuss, and hugged them both whilst dabbing her watery eyes on the way to the pub to join everyone else. Jo, Barbara and Ellen sat in different corners of the room all looking like cats that had most definitely got the cream. Thomas sat watching Jo wondering what on earth she was up to.

'You are looking very chipper Jo,' Bob said as he came and sat next to her on the settle.

'Am I? Can't imagine why, must be the weather,' she smiled. How are things with you?'

'Oh, you know, so-so.'

He looked a little down in the dumps, unusual for Bob she thought. She invited him up to the bar to get drinks for Tom and Anne who had texted her to say they would be a few minutes late and could she get the first round in so they could start the quiz straight away when they got there.

'Come on, out with it, we are still friends you know.'

'Well, it's not easy sometimes, when you've only got Eunice for company in the evenings,' he whispered, leaning on the bar.

She looked him in the eye. Such lovely brown eyes she thought, it was a shame they hadn't worked out. Still, she didn't feel any regret and knew the right outcome had been achieved between them. However, she could see that he was lonely and wondered what she could do about it.

'I know,' she sighed and hugged him around the shoulders. 'Have you ever tried online dating?'

'Bit nervous of that, I mean it seems a bit like a 'crisps' situation to me.'

'What on earth do you mean by that?' she asked, slightly confused.

'Well, you know,' he said awkwardly. 'They look like salt and vinegar on the screen and when you meet them, they turn out to be pickled onion and it's all a bit disappointing.'

She couldn't help laughing out loud, which made him laugh too. At least, she had cheered him up even if she didn't have the answer to his problems. Just then she caught Ellen's eye across the room, and they smiled at each other. A fabulous idea popped into her brain.

'Excuse me, Bob, I need to have a word with Ellen.'

She walked across the room to where Ellen was sitting next to Thomas and Henri. She whispered something in the girl's ear that made her smile and nod in agreement. Ellen got up and went across the room where she began an avid conversation with Bob.

'What are you up to Jo?' Thomas asked as she sat down next to him.

'Not much, just swapping teams with Ellen for a bit. Thought I'd come and see if your general knowledge is up to scratch,' she said as innocently as possible. It was clear he did not believe her.

'Ok, let's go head-to-head this evening, loser pays a forfeit,' he challenged. She shook his hand.

'You're on! Can I remind you, Mr Arnaud, that you already owe me one forfeit? I am going to have some serious fun thinking of something else for you to do as well.'

Henri leaned across the front of Thomas to speak to her.

'I can give you some ideas Jo, if you need them.'

'Thanks for that vote of confidence Dad,' Thomas replied sarcastically.

Just then Gerry tapped on the side of his glass to start the quiz and everyone went silent, apart from Mrs West who was busy chatting to her neighbour as usual. The entire room heard the end of her conversation.

'…and she's only gone and got herself a place on a nursing degree course for September.'

Barbara looked at Jo and rolled her eyes. Henri looked at Barbara, eyes wide open in surprise and Thomas looked at Jo and whispered in her ear.

'I *knew* you were up to something.'

Throughout the evening the knowledge gradually became more widespread, as people talked at the halfway interval and afterwards, that Ellen would soon be leaving the shop and moving to Nottingham where she had a place at the university there. Ellen sat deep in conversation with Bob most of the time, talking about the nursing books she had read and he to her about medicine in general. Mrs West had broken her assurance of silence at the first opportunity it had seemed.

Jo won the head-to-head challenge with Thomas but the light atmosphere between them seemed to have disappeared, so she made nothing of it. As the four of them walked home together they were all still thinking about Ellen's news, Jo hoping that they had just about got away with it. Thomas was the first to speak.

'I know Mrs West can be a bit of a gossip, but at heart she is a good woman, she is really going to Miss Ellen.'

'Yes,' Henri agreed, 'but it is time Ellen had a life of her own. She should have done this a long time ago.'

'The shop still needs two people to run it, Mrs West can't manage it all by herself,' he said.

'We know dear,' soothed Barbara, 'that's why we put an advert in the local paper a few weeks ago and Ellen's got some younger cousins nearby who she said would love to come and help out at the weekends. They cover odd days already. We did think everything through carefully Thomas.'

'How on earth is the poor woman going to afford it though? She will have to pay any new staff probably more than she pays Ellen and University is not a cheap thing to do these days. Did you think of that Jo,' he said accusingly turning to her, 'on all your "girl stuff" evenings?'

Barbara opened her mouth about to answer him, but Jo looked at her and imperceptibly shook her head to warn her not to say anything. If she did, there would be a whole lot of explaining to do and she was not ready for that yet.

'I'm sorry you don't agree with us helping Ellen,' was all she could think of saying.

'It's not that I don't agree, I'm sure Ellen will make a superb nurse. It's the consequences for her only parent I'm disappointed you didn't think about.'

'Thomas, I don't think you are being fair on Jo,' Barbara put in.

Jo shot her another warning look. If Thomas wanted to be disappointed in her, then let him. She could not explain right now. They reached the house and Jo walked off to the cottage. Shutting the door behind her she burst into tears. How could he think that she would behave like that and be so thoughtless after all she had given up in her life?

As she lay in bed that night thinking it through, she wondered whether she had better start looking for another job, away from here and a pair of blue eyes that thought her so uncaring. She felt as if their friendship was breaking and her heart with it.

Chapter 15

Jo tried hard to avoid Thomas after that evening. She spent the following Saturday in Oxford wandering aimlessly around the shops until she was so tired, she had to go home having already told Barbara that she would not be back for dinner. Sunday afternoon she wandered up to the church again just to get out. It was empty, all the parishioners having left after the morning service. She sat at the piano but could not bring herself to play anything, she just felt too forlorn. She ended up back at the cottage, curled up on her bed for the rest of the afternoon.

She was roused by a knock at the door. It was Henri.

'I've got some new duet arrangements that I'd like to try, will you come and practice them with me?' he asked as she invited him in. 'Are you alright Jo, you look a little…under the weather.'

'I'm fine, it's probably just a summer cold coming on or something. I'm sorry Henri, I just don't feel like playing today, why don't you ask Thomas?'

'I can't, he's gone to see Elaine. He is helping her throw a housewarming party and won't be back until very late. Come on, it will cheer you up, do you good.'

Knowing that Thomas was out, she reluctantly agreed. Perhaps it would do her good. She sat with Henri at the piano but knew that her playing was not up to scratch as she made several mistakes. He was too polite to comment.

After dinner that evening, she sat with Barbara at the kitchen table while Henri continued to play the piano in the living room.

'You are going to have to tell them, you know,' Barbara said. 'Henri is quite worried about the two of you.'

'You haven't told him, have you?'

'No, not yet, but I don't like having to keep secrets from him, love.'

'I'm sorry you have ended up in the middle of all this, but I can't explain everything yet it's too complicated.'

'There's more to this than you've said isn't there?' Barbara said.

Jo nodded.

'I suspected as much. Jo dear, you know we love you very much, you can tell us anything.'

She had grown to love them too she realised, but they would not love her very much at all she suspected, if they knew the whole truth. She would not be able to bear the disappointment on all their faces and Thomas was already cross with her.

Thomas did not come back that evening and at elevenses the next morning Henri said that he had texted to let them know he was staying over with Elaine. Well, that was that, thought Jo. The passionate kiss Elaine had given him must have been for real. It was obvious that she had been attracted to him all along, perhaps that was why she had put off buying a house for so long.

The week went by slowly for Jo who tried to spend as much of it as possible in the garden, her mind on the job she was here to do. It was late summer now and everything was at its peak. Tall plants like leucanthemum with their friendly daisy faces needed staking to stop them flopping sideways, vegetables needed harvesting and the greenhouse was bursting with produce. She had chosen her favourite tomato varieties back in the spring, Alicante, Gardener's Delight and Moneymaker as well as a few new to her, including a couple of yellow ones and an orange one called Big Orange Stripe. They had all flourished under her care and produced a bumper crop.

Occasionally, she had looked in the direction of the house and seen Thomas on the balcony watching her. She did not wave, just carried on, pretending she hadn't seen him. She had tried to avoid the evening dinners, making the excuse of inviting Ellen over to help her make lists of things she would need to take with her to university and spending evenings with her and Mrs West, looking at the C.V.s of people who had already applied for Ellen's job.

Friday elevenses came round, and Jo made her way up to the house. The others were already sitting around the table, Henri reading the newspaper and the others chatting quietly together. She avoided all eye contact with Thomas who looked up as she arrived.

'The greenhouse company rang,' Barbara announced as she came through the door, 'said they would send someone out as soon as possible to fix the vents. Taken their time about it though, haven't they?'

'Yes, I rang them ages ago,' Jo replied. 'It's been so hot in there this week I've had to leave to doors open to cool it down. The heat is probably what's made the tomatoes all ripen at once.'

'I've found a good recipe for tomato soup, which I thought I'd try, but we will still have too many for us to eat.' Barbara sat with a couple of recipe books spread open on the table before her.

'Why don't we take the surplus to the quiz this evening, it being the last one before they stop for the summer holidays? I'm sure people will take them off our hands. I know Tom and Anne haven't got a very big garden, they might like a handful,' Jo suggested. 'I'll do a thorough pick this afternoon before we go and offer them around as people come in.'

'Good thinking,' agreed Barbara. 'I've got a lovely wicker basket somewhere you can put them in, I'll look it out and bring it over to the greenhouse later.'

Henri put down the paper he had been reading.

'Dad and I have got an appointment this evening for dinner. In fact, we will be busy this afternoon too, won't we?' Thomas said mysteriously, looking at Henri who nodded at his son. Thomas glanced at Jo crossly. 'So, we will see you two ladies for the quiz.'

'Oh!' Barbara exclaimed, 'That reminds me, I said I'd call in to see Euphemia Chance before the quiz.'

'Great name!' Jo and Thomas said together, catching each other's eye. Jo looked away first.

'Yes, isn't it? She is trying to recruit me for the church choir. I said I wanted to find out what it involved first, before I commit to anything. She works you see and could only manage that time. Jo, are you okay to get your own dinner tonight?'

'Absolutely. Don't worry about me, I'll see you all at the quiz then, with lots of tomatoes. I'll try and get there early,' she said, getting up from the table to take her coffee outside with her.

It was a long hot afternoon. Jo trimmed the lawns with the old mower. The grass was slightly dry and going brown in places, but she just wanted to nip off the straggly bits and tidy the edges. She liked a tidy lawn whether it was going brown or not.

She got herself a quick sandwich at the cottage for her dinner and then went out to the greenhouse to pick the tomatoes. Looking up briefly she saw Barbara coming across the lawn with the basket and a man who was dressed in navy blue and wearing a cap. Must be the man from the greenhouse company, come to fix the vents, Jo thought idly to herself. She hoped he would not take very long, or she would be late for the quiz. Barbara gave the man the basket when they reached the archway into the kitchen garden and pointed towards the greenhouse before making her way back across the lawn to the house. Jo watched through the glass as the man made his way to the greenhouse, she couldn't see his face as he had his head down looking where he was walking between the vegetable beds. There was something oddly familiar about him. As he opened the door, he looked up.

'Bonjour Cherie!' he smiled, 'I've missed you.'

Jo felt all the blood in her face drain away her hands and feet go numb. Serge!

She looked at him, open mouthed, unable to speak. He put the basket down and came towards her, casually leaning on the bench next to where she stood frozen to the spot in fear. Her eyes flicked across the garden towards the house, but Barbara had gone, she was all alone. Even if she cried out for help, this time there was no one to hear her.

'You left the chateau Cherie and didn't tell me,' he drawled slowly, at last looking towards her. 'That made me very sad.' He pouted dramatically. 'I've been looking for you everywhere, Cherie, but nobody would tell me where you had gone. Why is that do you think?'

She knew full well why it was, but she was not going to tell him she'd asked the few people who knew not to say anything, it would only make him angrier. Her heart was beating nineteen to the dozen, she had to get away from him. Perhaps she could talk him out of the greenhouse at least then she would have a chance to run.

'W…Well, this job came up very suddenly,' she stammered nervously. 'I…I didn't have time to tell everyone, you know how things are, here one day gone the next.' She shrugged trying to make light of the situation. As she gradually backed away from him towards the far door of the greenhouse, he followed her.

'I asked *everybody,*' he said menacingly. He was close to her now, she could see the muscles of his neck twitching and smell his foul alcohol-laden breath.

'How did you find me then?' she asked, her voice barely a whisper.

'Ha! It was so easy in the end.' He threw his head back and laughed. 'I believe you had a delivery a few weeks ago?'

The lavender?

'How did you know about that?' she said, puzzled. 'It was from Alain.'

'That old fool Maurice left the box in the nursery, didn't he? I saw it one afternoon as I went to pick up some plants. It was such a gift!' he smiled, raising his eyes as if it had been a blessing sent by heaven itself. 'Just as I was beginning to think I had lost you for good. There you were, on the address label, ready for me to find.' He fixed her with a hot stare.

She had reached the opposite door now and, with her hands behind her back, clung on to the door frame for support. She would have to take her chance soon.

'Do you remember what I said when I had you all to myself last time, Cherie?'

She closed her eyes and nodded. How could she ever forget?

'I love you, Cherie. Let me take you back to France, where you belong, where we belong together. You belong to me,' he declared insistently.

'But I don't love you, Serge, and I will never belong to you,' she said as calmly as she could manage. He shut his eyes, obviously summoning up what to say next, and she took her chance. She turned and fled out the door as fast as her legs could carry her.

As she ran, she could hear the heavy thudding of his boots behind her. He was faster than her, his long legs making up the ground she had gained. Suddenly, she felt him push her from behind. Losing her balance she tripped, catching her foot on the heavy wooden sleeper of one of the vegetable beds. The pain that ripped through her ankle and leg was agonising. She struggled upright still trying to get away, but he was upon her now. Roughly, he pushed one hand through her long hair, gripping it to hold her head still, the other held her upper arm in a tight grip. He pushed his face close to hers.

'You will love me!' he growled into her face. She felt small drops of his spittle hit her skin as he spoke, he looked truly wild, almost insane now. 'I will make you!' he shouted.

'You will have to kill me first!' she screamed as he dragged her headfirst into the shed and let go of her, shoving her over to the far side away from the door.

Jo could hear her heart thundering and the blood whooshing in her ears. She knew she couldn't run now. It was obvious she had seriously damaged her ankle in the fall, besides he was blocking the only way out. In her terror, she looked around for something, anything she could use as a weapon against him, but all the tools had been tidied away for the day and there were only a few plastic plant pots that she had left out ready to wash the next day. Her eyes landed on her phone she had left on the bench. Perhaps if she could just reach it and press the emergency button. They both lunged for it at the same time, he reading her eyes and thoughts.

Unfortunately for her, he reached it first and quickly flung the phone against the far wall, where she heard it shatter as it hit a shovel hanging up there. He came towards her, put one of his large hands around her throat and pushed her back against the far bench. He pinned her there with his body and scratched at her neck, tearing the top of her t-shirt with his other hand. She felt it rip. Her hands were flailing at his arms trying to pull them off her, but she was finding it difficult to breathe and could not grip him in her panicked state.

'Stop! Serge, please stop!' she tried shouting, her voice only coming out as a hoarse whisper.

She had to get him off her. She brought one of her knees up, wincing as she took the weight of her body on her injured leg, and thrust it into his groin has hard as she could, momentarily pushing him away. He swore violently, cursing her to hell and back. Then, in the dim light of the shed, he noticed the little heart hanging from the necklace around her neck, glinting as it caught the light from the window as she gasped for breath.

'What is this?' he demanded, coming back towards her and picking up the heart in his fingers, suddenly, extraordinarily calm.

'Nothing. It's nothing. We're just friends.' She closed her eyes in despair, knowing she had just said the wrong thing.

'The English man?' He looked between her face and the necklace and drew his own conclusions.

Slowly, his face contorted grotesquely. He snatched at the necklace, and she felt the chain snap as he tore it from her neck. He looked at it twinkling in his hand for a second and then flung it to the floor. Lifting his fists to cover his face, he gave an anguished cry of pure rage that Jo felt convulse right through her.

'You whore!' he screamed. 'I will kill you!'

He hit her then, losing all control, punching at her face and body with his fists like a madman. She tried to push him away, but she had no strength left and he was too powerful for her. She knew this was it and she was going to die. Jo had never felt such pain and as everything began to spin around her, she fell, hitting her head against the corner of the bench on the way down. Lying on the floor of the shed, blood oozing from a gash on her forehead, the last thing she remembered before her world went black and her eyes closed, was the sight of his booted foot swinging towards her body.

'You are going to have to apologise to Jo when she gets here, you know, after all we've been told today,' Henri said.

He turned to his son who was sat bent over in their usual corner of the pub, his head buried in his hands.

'I'm not sure she'll want to listen,' Thomas said, rubbing his face and then running his hands through his hair. He sat back and sighed heavily. 'I think I've really mucked up this time.'

'Then you must find a way to make her listen, nicely of course. She is too…important to lose.'

'What do you mean by that Dad?'

'Thomas. I know,' he said, looking at his son seriously.

'What?' said Thomas, trying to feign that he didn't know what his father was talking about.

'That you love her, of course.'

Thomas closed his eyes and put his hands behind his head. He took a deep breath in.

'What use is love when she doesn't even want to be my friend anymore? She's avoided and ignored me all week and if I tell her that we went behind her back she will never trust me again.'

'Then you must start again, regain her trust and then you can explain things. These things take time Thomas.'

They sat in silence and watched as the pub began to fill with people. Thomas noticed that Ellen went to join Bob's team, she looked up and smiled at him shyly and then turned to Bob to start a conversation. Barbara came in looking flustered. She quickly ordered a drink at the bar and then came over to the two men.

'You two look about as happy as a wet weekend.'

Henri just harrumphed and did a sideways nod towards Thomas.

'Jo not here yet?' she said, looking around as she sat.

'Not yet,' said Thomas. 'I thought she was going to bring the tomatoes to offer around before we started.'

'Mm, she's probably busy chatting, she'll be along soon I expect.'

'Chatting to whom?' Henri asked.

'Oh, she had a visitor, just before I left to see Mrs Chance.'

'What kind of visitor?'

'A French one,' said Barbara.

'What kind of French one?' Thomas asked, sitting up. 'Male or female?'

'Male. He said he was a good friend and they used to work at the chateau together. Very polite. He said he was on holiday in the UK and thought he would look her up while he was in the area. That's nice for her, isn't it, that her friends want to come and see her? I took him over to the greenhouse. I expect she'll bring him along in a bit.'

Alarm bells began sounding in Thomas' brain.

'Was he tall, dark hair, gangly looking?' Thomas asked urgently.

'Yes,' Barbara said. 'I forget what he said his name was now.' She looked puzzled as if trying to remember.

'Serge?' Thomas exploded from his seat, knocking his drink over in the process.

'Yes, that's it! Thomas, whatever is the matter?' She looked at him with concern as he pushed his way passed her.

'Bob, I need you, Jo's in trouble!' he shouted across the room.

Thomas was already running for the door; he had never felt so much fear and panic. If Serge was here, then Jo was not only in trouble, she was also in danger. Bob dashed out of the pub after him. It was the look on Thomas' face as well as the urgency in his voice that told him this was serious.

Thomas sped towards the kitchen garden, checking the greenhouse to his right as he passed it. The shed door stood open. He could see her feet and dashed in. The sight he saw shocked him to the core. Jo was lying on her side, across the width of the shed, her head in a pool of blood, hair covering her face. Her t-shirt had been ripped almost to the waist and her neck and upper chest were covered in long red scratches as if some wild animal had attacked her. Her arms and legs lay at unnatural angles, her face looking for all the world as if she had gone ten rounds with a prize fighter. Bob skidded in behind him and took one look at the situation.

'Don't move her, I'm calling an ambulance.' He took out his phone. 'See if she is breathing, talk to her!' he shouted.

Thomas knelt down beside her to look for any signs of life. 'Oh God please let her be alive,' he prayed. He could see she was breathing. He felt for a pulse, it didn't feel very strong, and it was quite fast.

'Jo! Jo, can you hear me? It's Thomas, my love, we are getting you some help. Hold on for me please. Just hold on. I love you, Jo. I need you to hang in there.'

Gently, he stroked the hair away from her eyes. He could see the gash on her head but had nothing to stem the flow of blood with. A trickle of blood ran from the corner of her mouth onto the floor of the shed, and he wiped it gently with his fingers. Bob came in and knelt down beside Jo. He was on the phone and put his finger behind her ear to feel for a pulse. Thomas stood back to give him space.

'Yes, she is breathing but not conscious,' he said down the phone.

Bob continued the conversation with the emergency call operator, calmly giving the address and details of Jo's condition as he carefully examined her prone body.

Thomas stood in the doorway, staring at Jo in shock and disbelief. Outside the shed, Henri, Barbara and Ellen ran up, breathless after rushing from the pub. He turned to look at them, his face stricken with grief.

'What's happened?' Barbara asked.

'It's Jo, she's…' He could not get the words out.

Henri came across and pulled Thomas out of the doorway gently as Barbara went in to help Bob. He saw the blood on his son's fingers and intuitively knew it was bad. He put his arms around his son.

'She's in the best hands,' he said, looking into his face. 'Let them do their job. What do you need me to do? I take it an ambulance has been called?'

Thomas couldn't think straight and just nodded. All he could see was Jo lying in a pool of blood.

'I'll get people organised to wave the ambulance in then,' Ellen piped up, 'so they know exactly where to bring the stretcher.'

'Thank you,' said Henri. 'That's good of you.'

It was all a bit of a blur to Thomas after that. Paramedics arrived with bags of equipment, and he wasn't allowed in the shed while Bob took charge and talked to them about her condition. The police arrived next, and Thomas sat with them to give them a statement. Barbara added her bit with a description of what Serge had been wearing and what he had told her about being a friend from the chateau.

The next time he saw Jo she was on a wheeled stretcher, eyes shut and oxygen mask over her face, her neck in a brace. One of her arms and one leg had been wrapped in large orange padded splints. One of the paramedics had his hand on a dressing on her forehead, but the blood was seeping through his fingers. When the dressing had been changed, Jo was loaded into the back of the ambulance. Bob went with her as an attending doctor.

Thomas stood on the drive and watched the ambulance leave. Making its way carefully to the junction opposite the pub, it signalled left and the blue lights came on as it sped off in the direction of the hospital. It was only then he realised that tears had been streaming down his face the whole time.

Chapter 16

When Jo came to, she did not know where she was momentarily. There was whiteness and bright lights and voices. Was she dead? Was this heaven or hell? From the pain she felt she decided it must be the latter. A kindly female face bent over her. Maybe this was not hell then.

'Hello Jo,' it smiled. 'You been a bit in the wars, haven't you? Do you know where you are? Don't shake your head love, just speak if you can.'

Jo tried focusing on things around her, she did not seem to be able to see anything much out of her left eye. It was a hospital. She was in hospital. Why was that? And then she remembered. It had been Serge. Serge trying to kill her. She could see his contorted features and his fists coming at her and she cried out.

'It's ok. You're in hospital Jo. We are looking after you now, nothing to be scared about. You are quite safe. I'm Becky, one of the nurses here.'

Jo tried to move but found she couldn't, her head seemed to be strapped down, her left arm was in something rigid and padded that she could just feel with her fingertips, but it hurt. Everything hurt, the pain made her moan, and she felt her eyes watering.

'I think we need more morphine. How much has she had already?'

Jo could hear voices around her and hands touching her, a sudden coldness in her arm and then she slept.

The next time she woke she was on a ward, propped up in bed. On opening her eyes, the first thing she saw was the grey-haired woman in the bed opposite who seemed to be lying in a similar position to herself. Her head lay back on the pillows, her toothless mouth wide open in sleep. She was snoring loudly.

Jo surveyed the wreck of her own body. Her right ankle was enclosed in a plaster cast, she could feel the hot throbbing of her foot inside. Her left arm, also encased in plaster, lay in a sling around her neck and she had a drip in the back of her right arm. She followed the line of the drip tube with her eyes, it was attached to a stand at the side of the bed that carried a transparent bag of liquid which was slowly being fed into her body. As she moved her neck, she could feel an intense soreness in her muscles and reached up with her hand. She had some sort of dressing on her neck and one on her head too which made her wince in pain when she touched it. Jo took a deep breath in then. The pain in her side was truly awful and her chest did not feel right. She craned her head down and saw a tube coming from under her hospital gown. She lay her head back on the pillows and closed her eyes, trying hard not to cry.

'Ah, Miss Stanton,' said a male voice.

Jo opened her eyes again to see a group of people staring at her from the bottom of the bed. Doctors she assumed.

'I'm Doctor Taylor. I've got some medical students with me today. Do you mind if they listen in?'

Jo gently shook her head and looked at his name badge. A nurse drew blue curtains around the bed to give them some privacy.

'Good.' Dr Taylor smiled at her. 'How are you feeling today?'

'A bit rough.' Her voice sounded funny to her. Like she hadn't used it for a while.

The doctor laughed.

'I expect you are,' he said. 'But actually, I think you've been quite lucky. Your injuries could have been a lot worse.'

Jo looked down the length of her body. She did not feel lucky at all. The doctor continued, half talking to her and half to the medical students who stood, some of them with clipboards, making notes as he spoke.

'Let's start at the top,' he said cheerily. 'Miss Stanton, you have a nasty cut on your forehead that we have stitched up for you. Don't panic, the scar should fade to almost nothing in time,' he added, seeing her worried face. 'The dressings on your neck we can remove this afternoon, they are just superficial grazes that will heal completely.' He looked at the nurse who nodded and then smiled at Jo. 'You have a broken radius, that's one of the bones in your forearm, that should take about six weeks to heal completely. You sustained 3 broken ribs and a slight pneumothorax on your left side, which we have drained with a needle, it has been in for a couple of days so it can come out later. The ribs should heal up by themselves. We will give you some breathing exercises to do, I'm afraid they will be quite painful for a while. Moving down, your right ankle is broken, I'm afraid that may also take about six weeks to heal. We will take another x ray then to check, before we take the cast off. You may need some physiotherapy afterwards to help you get full movement back. The bruising elsewhere will heal on its own. I'm afraid you will be turning all colours of the rainbow during the next few weeks. But overall, I think you are quite fortunate.'

'How so?' she asked. She felt like he had just looked her over like one would do a shopping list, ticking off the things already in the trolley.

'Well, you've no brain injury that we can see on any of the scans for a start, and the fractures were straight forward to set, no surgery needed. When the chest drain has been removed, I expect it will only be a couple of days before we can send you home. We will give you some lovely strong painkillers to take with you. You will need plenty of rest though, for a few weeks. Do you work?'

'Yes, I'm a gardener.'

'Hmm, well, it will be a good few weeks before you can take that up again. Do you have someone at home who can look after you for a while?'

She thought about it. Maybe Barbara could give her a hand in the cottage from time to time, she would manage somehow.

'Probably.'

'Right, I will leave you to it then. We will be back to take the drain out later, good to see you, Miss Stanton.'

He swept his way on to the next patient, the little crowd of students following in his wake.

Had she really been here two days already? She had completely lost track of time and did not know what day it was. Just that it was daylight, and she was in hospital feeling alone and in pain with an old lady who snored loudly in the bed opposite her.

It was later that day that her bed was wheeled into a small side room by a couple of cheerful hospital orderlies and two policewomen came to see her. They needed to take a statement about the attack. They were both kind and patient, one of them holding her hand when she wept in distress from having to relive it all again. They left, assuring her that they would do everything in their power to find Serge and arrest him. She slept after that, the painkillers being fed into her arm making her feel heavy as if they were trying to drag her down into a dark pit of despair and oblivion.

At some point in the evening, she became aware of someone holding her hand, stroking her fingertips gently. She opened her eyes. There, sitting on a chair next to the bed, was Henri.

'Hello Henri.' She managed a weak smile as he raised his head, he looked weary she noticed.

'Ah, ma petite, I didn't mean to wake you. How are you feeling?'

'Oh, you know, not so good at the moment. I'll mend though.'

'Mm...in time'

'How are things with you? Is Barbara with you?' She looked around as if to see her and noticed that some of the other patients had visitors too, sitting by their beds chatting busily. The lady opposite her had no visitors and Jo suddenly felt deeply sorry for her.

'She is just getting some coffee downstairs, she will be back in a minute.'

As if on cue Barbara arrived carrying two cardboard cups, little wisps of steam emanating from their plastic lids.

'Hello love, you're awake today,' she smiled, looking at Jo. 'How are you feeling?'

'I'm ok, a little sore. It is so good to see you. What day is it?'

'Monday, dear. Do you remember what happened?'

She sat for a while telling them what she could remember and how the police had been to take a statement. She couldn't help the tears. Barbara dabbed at her face gently with a tissue from the box by her bed. They told her in return how Thomas had found her, and Bob had rung the ambulance, and everyone had come over from the pub to see how they could help in any way. Jo felt truly humbled at the thought of everyone trying to help. She couldn't remember anything from the time she had passed out in the shed to the time she came to in the hospital.

'I expect this will keep Mrs West in full gossip mode for a long time,' concluded Barbara.

'Mm...They say I'll be good to go home in a few days, when the drain is out, I thought they were doing that today, maybe they were all busy. It might be a few weeks until I can manage the garden properly Henri, I'm so sorry. I seem to have caused so much trouble since I came, haven't I?' Fresh tears ran down her face.

Henri looked at her with astonishment.

'My dear,' he said gently, 'you have been nothing but a joy to me and Barbara since you arrived. The garden can wait, we will take care of that for a while. You will rest until you are completely better. You are not to worry about a thing.'

Bob arrived then and Barbara and Henri kissed her goodbye and said they would come back the next day.

'I hear I owe you a very big thank you,' she said as he sat down and took her hand. 'I'm sorry I can't remember your heroic actions. I must have been out of it completely.'

'You certainly gave us all a fright,' he smiled. 'You look awful. How are you feeling now?'

'Well, thank you for the positive bedside manner.' She tried to laugh but winced in pain. 'You know, so-so.' She remembered him using that phrase awhile back. 'You?'

He picked up the chart hanging on the end of the bed and perused the attached sheets. 'Um…getting better, early days yet though.'

'Tell me,' she demanded, but he refused to say any more on the subject.

'Looks like they will be discharging you sometime this week. It's all a bit patch and dispatch these days,' he said, sitting down again. 'You are going to need a lot of help Jo. You know you've got about six weeks in plaster apart from the ribs. You might be able to hobble around with one crutch I suppose but it's a bit awkward with both an arm and a leg out of action, isn't it?'

'I'll manage, stiff upper lip and all that,' she said stoically. 'Not quite sure how I'm going to shower though.'

'Cling film,' he said suddenly. 'Or a plastic bag to cover over the plaster. Barbara can help you.'

They chatted for a while about inconsequential things and then visiting time was up. Bob assured her that he would look in on her again as soon as she was home.

Over the next few days, the chest drain was removed and the dressings taken off her neck. One of the hospital physios, a forbidding German woman called Lina, came to get her up on her one good foot, which was excruciating on her ribs. However, trying her best she found that she could hobble with one crutch, which seemed to tick some magical box for allowing her to go home. She was made to practise a set of breathing exercises and told to stay off alcohol because, for a while at least, she would be on some pretty strong painkillers.

Henri and Barbara had come in every day and even Ellen and Mrs West had popped by, but she had not seen Thomas since she had been there. Maybe he was still cross with her she thought sadly.

Discharge day arrived. The previous evening, Barbara had brought her a loose sleeveless nighty and extra-large dressing gown to come home in, which the nurses had helped her into. There had been a lot of laughter while she tried to balance on one leg and negotiate her broken arm through the armhole at the same time. Now she sat in a wheelchair exhausted, half-dressed, and half wrapped in the dressing gown, waiting to be collected and feeling like an abandoned parcel at the post office. She looked in her lap at the leaflets about exercise and the big box of painkillers that she had been given to take with her.

'Hello Jo. I've come to take you home.'

Looking up she saw that Thomas stood at the end of the bed. He looked about as good as she felt. His bristly unshaven face gaunt, hair somewhat unkempt and dark shadows under his eyes which were full of remorse.

'Hello Thomas.' As she looked at him her eyes filled with tears which spilled over and ran down her face unchecked. 'Thank you for finding me last Friday,' she sobbed.

Instantly he pulled up a chair next to her and very gently put his arms around her. She rested her head on his shoulder.

'Shh, it's ok,' he whispered. 'I'm so sorry.'

'I'm making you all wet again,' she sniffed and lifted her head.

'You seem to have a habit of doing that.' He smiled but she noticed it didn't reach his eyes. 'Come on, let's get you out of here.'

The journey home was uncomfortable for Jo, to say the least. Even moving from the wheelchair into the car had seemed like an almost impossible assault course of pain and the seatbelt yet another encumbrance. Despite Thomas' car having excellent suspension, she felt every bump and crater in the road as if it had been magnified tenfold. They drove in silence, Jo hanging on with her good arm to try and minimise her movement. She looked out the window and thought how weird it was to be driving along in broad daylight dressed in a nighty and dressing gown.

Henri and Barbara helped her slowly out the car when they arrived home and she turned to go over to the cottage.

'Where do you think you are going, young lady?' Henri said in surprise.

'Home,' said Jo.

'No darling, you are going to stay in the main house with us until you're better,' Barbara explained kindly. 'You need a lot of care still and we need to keep an eye on you. You didn't think you were going to be on your own over there, did you?' She tutted as if it had been a totally preposterous idea. 'Come on, you can rest on the sofa in the living room while I make a cup of tea. Thomas, help her, will you? I've made some fresh cookies too, feed you up a bit.' She bustled back into the house to put the kettle on.

'It's ok. I can do this,' Jo said as Thomas came over. She could see that he didn't really know how to help her apart from carry the medication and leaflets as she hobbled slowly through the house and into the living room at the back. He hovered at her elbow all the way. Very gingerly, she lowered her bottom down onto the sofa.

'Can you swivel?' he asked, picking both her legs up and turning with her slowly, so she was lying length ways. 'Do you want a cushion under this leg?' he said, gently resting his fingers on her toes poking out the end of the cast which tickled and made her toes wriggle. 'Ticklish?' There was a hint of a smile.

'Yes, to both. Please,' she said, indicating the cushion.

'Now then, what time are you due any more tablets?' Barbara came in with a tray of tea and biscuits.

'Three o'clock, I think. What time is it now?' She glanced over to the mantelpiece and the clock that stood there. A quarter past three already. 'Better take some now then.'

She was a bit slumped down for swallowing tablets with her tea, so Thomas lifted her carefully under the arms and she shuffled back into a more upright position, extra cushions wedged behind to support her. Within half an hour, they and the journey home had taken effect. She nodded off, empty teacup still held in her good hand, head resting sideways on the back of the sofa. The others crept out of the room and let her sleep.

Barbara woke her later with some delicious homemade tomato soup. It tasted so good after a week of hospital food, and she realised she was actually quite hungry. Eating was a tricky business, and she felt a bit like a small child again, with a tea towel draped over her sling her to catch any spills whilst she balanced the tray of soup on her outstretched legs and carefully spooned it into her mouth.

Henri played the piano after dinner, soft, gentle lullaby music that made her close her eyes and imagine herself somewhere beautiful and pain free, like a bluebell wood in spring with dappled sunlight rippling over her up turned face and birds hopping from branch to branch in the canopy above. Despite the fact she had done little except sleep and eat since she had been back in the house, she felt weary to the bone and was ready for bed when Barbara suggested she go up. Painfully, she hobbled to the stairs and looked up towards the landing.

'Need some help?' Thomas said as he came out the kitchen and across the hall to where she stood, one hand on the banister.

'I might be ok if I hop.'

'Don't be ridiculous. Come on, put your good arm around my neck and I'll carry you up. Where is it least painful for me to put my hands?'

After some slightly awkward adjustments, as everything seemed sore and painful to Jo, he lifted her very carefully and ascended the stairs. He kicked open the guest bedroom door as he had done once before.

'I seem to be making a habit of this as well,' he said. He sounded tired all of a sudden.

'I'm sorry to be a nuisance,' she replied. 'Honestly, I'm sure I would be fine over at the cottage. It would be easier on everyone.'

'Stop being so damn independent, Jo, and just accept help for a change, will you?'

'I'm sorry.' She had never heard him sound so angry before.

'And for goodness' sake, stop apologising, none of this is your fault.'

He carried her over to the stool by the dressing table and gently put her down. She sat and watched him as he prepared the bed, stacking the pillows at the headboard end so that she would be comfortable sleeping sitting up slightly. He opened the adjoining door into his room and disappeared into it. A few second later he came back with an extra pillow. Pushing the duvet aside, he put the pillow where her broken ankle would rest.

'Ready for bed?'

'I need to use the bathroom first.'

'Do you need help?'

She felt the heat rise in her face and must have looked a little awkward as he added rapidly, 'I can whizz down and ask Barbara to come up.'

'I think I can manage.'

'I'll just wait here and make sure you get into bed safely then.' And he sat on the edge of the bed with a sigh and watched her hobble into the ensuite.

It was only when she stood in front of the mirror above the sink and saw her reflection, that she realised she had not actually seen her own face since the attack. Looking back at her was a face she hardly recognised. Great black and purple bruises covered most of the sides of her face which was still swollen, and she had two black eyes. Her hair looked like she had been dragged through a hedge backwards and in places was still matted with crusty dried blood. She couldn't see the gash on her forehead under the dressing, but she knew it wouldn't be pretty. More bruises covered her neck, and three, great, angry looking red scratches ran from under her chin to the top of her breasts. She slipped the dressing gown off her shoulders to see that the tops of her arms were equally covered in large ugly bruises. Serge had really gone to town.

She couldn't stop the cry that escaped her lips and the shock made her shake violently, she looked truly horrific.

'Jo are you alright in there? Jo?'

She couldn't speak. She just stood there staring at herself in the mirror in disbelief.

'I'm coming in.'

Fortunately, she had not locked the door. The handle slowly turned, and Thomas cautiously came in. He realised at once that she had not known the extent of the bruising.

'Jo look at me,' he commanded, trying to avert her eyes from the mirror. 'Jo!' more softly now.

She turned then and saw the look of pity on his face. Somehow, he got her out of the bathroom and sat her on the bed. Quickly running to the landing, he shouted over the banister for Barbara to come up. He returned and sat next to her, holding her good hand, and adjusting the dressing gown to cover her shoulders once more.

Barbara rushed in and looked at Jo.

'She's just looked in the mirror,' Thomas explained.

'Help me get her into bed, it's the shock probably,' she said, 'I'll give Bob a call.'

Carefully they manoeuvred the still silent and shaking Jo into bed. Thomas sat at her side talking softly to her and holding her hand while they waited anxiously for Bob to arrive.

After a quick examination, Bob delivered his verdict to Barbara, Henri, and Thomas as they came back in the room and stood around the foot of the bed. Jo was already nodding off, her eyes closed, and her head laid back on the pillows.

'She's physically ok, apart from the existing injuries of course. I have spoken with her and reassured her that the bruising will go in time but she's understandably very low at the moment. I think we need to keep a close eye on her over the next few days especially. Try to make her feel positive. Can someone stay with her tonight, just to keep an eye on things?'

Henri and Barbara both looked at Thomas.

'Good,' Bob said. He looked at Jo nodding off and whispered. 'Don't hesitate to call me anytime if you think something more might be going on. I've got a day off tomorrow, so I'll call in sometime, just as a friend, try and cheer her up a bit.'

After seeing Bob out, Thomas came back upstairs. He kicked off his shoes silently and slowly lay down next to her on the bed. He did not sleep. He just lay in the darkness next to her, listening to her breathe, remembering the last time they had shared a bed and how he had let her down after that as well.

Chapter 17

When Jo opened her eyes, she could see that it was beginning to get light outside. A small gap in the curtains showed a tiny square of pale blue sky and the thin golden light of dawn on a day that was sure to be hot later. The top window had been left open in the night and through it came a soft cooling breeze laden with the sound of the dawn chorus. Jo closed her eyes again and listened. It was such a pure magical sound.

And then the mattress wobbled slightly under her. Turning her head in the opposite direction she saw Thomas, lying on his back, one arm tucked behind his head, the other across his chest. He was watching her.

'Good morning,' he said softly. 'You're awake early.'

She studied him more carefully now, still wearing yesterday's clothes, still unshaven, looking like he had not slept in a week.

'Have you been there all night?'

'Pretty much.'

'Have you had any sleep?'

He didn't answer.

'Oh, Thomas, I'm sorry. Honestly, I will be fine on my own, I will manage. I've caused enough trouble already. I can't let you do this and not get any sleep, it's not good for you.'

'I think I will be the judge of what is good for me,' he said tersely.

'Well, how about me being the judge of what is good for me then?' She felt slightly annoyed. 'What if I don't want you here watching me all night?' She regretted saying it as soon as the words left her lips.

'You have no idea about what is good for you at the moment Jo,' he snapped. 'Dammed independent woman! But if you don't want me here that's just fine.' He slid off the bed and stormed into his room, slamming the adjoining door behind him. She heard him stomp across his room, along the corridor outside and down the stairs.

Jo sat stunned for a while and then the tears flowed. She didn't know why she kept crying, she didn't seem to be able to help it at the moment. There was a soft knock on the outer door of the bedroom.

'Come in,' she sniffed.

It was Henri. Dressed in his pyjamas and an old-fashioned maroon dressing gown tied about the waist.

'Everything ok ma petite? I heard voices.'

'I'm sorry Henri, I didn't mean to wake you.' She burst into tears again.

Henri passed her a handful of tissues from the box on the dressing table.

'Mind if I sit down?' he said.

She shook her head. He picked up the stool, put it down next to the side of the bed closest to her and sat down.

'Tell me about it,' he said calmly.

She took her time, trying to get all the jumbled thoughts in her head straight whilst wiping her tears away.

'I think I've just been very ungrateful to Thomas,' she sniffed. 'Henri, he stayed here all night and I don't think he slept at all. We argued about it, and he stormed out. Henri I'm worried about him. He doesn't look like he's slept for a whole week. What's going on?'

Henri looked at her kindly, he looked like he was weighing up what to say and how much to tell her.

'Jo, you need to know that when Thomas found you, after the attack, it was a huge shock to him. Initially he thought you might be dead. He was almost out of his mind with…grief I suppose.' He sat back and sighed. 'He felt it was his fault.'

'But how can that be? None of this is his fault.'

'Jo, he told us about Serge, about what he witnessed when you were in France, the evening he picked you up.'

'But he wasn't to know that Serge would come here. Neither of us could have predicted that and I was so careful about not telling people where I was going. I had no idea that he would actually hunt me down like that.'

'I know, ma petite. But you see on the evening of the attack Barbara, Thomas and I were out and that is something he regrets. It's a little more complicated and I will let him tell you in his own time, but he feels that if we hadn't been, he would have been there to recognise Serge when he came to the house and he could have protected you, stopped it all from happening in the first place. He blames himself, Jo.'

Henri sat back and let her take in what he had said.

'I have to put this right Henri. He has to stop blaming himself, I can't bear to see him like this.'

Barbara popped her head in the door then, she was carrying a tray of tea.

'Everything alright? Thought I would make us all a cup since we are up early today. Looks like you could do with something stronger Jo. I'll put a bit of sugar in yours.'

'Thank you. Barbara, have you seen Thomas this morning, I need to talk to him?'

'Oh, darling he's just gone out. Face like thunder.' She looked at Henri and then Jo. 'Ah.' She paused. 'I'm sure he'll be back, what's happened?'

Jo explained about the argument.

'Give him time Jo, then you can talk it through between you. I am sure you can work it out. He has never been one to hold a grudge for long, has he Henri?'

Thomas did not come back all that morning. Jo spent her time in bed trying to read a book, but the painkillers made her drowsy and she kept nodding off. Eventually the book slid to the floor. It was too painful to try and reach it, so she sat and stared out the window at the sky, watching the swallows swoop by in their aerial manoeuvres.

After lunch, Bob arrived. He looked cheerful in a Hawaiian style shirt and Bermuda shorts.

'Gosh, don't you look jazzy!' Jo remarked as he came in holding a bunch of flowers for her. 'Thanks for those,' she added. 'You'll have to ask Barbara to put them in a vase.'

'Been shopping, time I updated my wardrobe,' he smiled and sat at the end of the bed. 'Feeling better than yesterday?'

'Are you asking as a friend or a doctor?'

'Friend today.'

'So-so,' she replied.

'That good huh? Tell me about it.'

She told him then about the argument with Thomas and what Henri had said about him blaming himself.

'I know,' he said, 'at the hospital they had to force him to go home eventually. He was in such a state.'

'What do you mean at the hospital? I didn't see Thomas the whole week, not until he came to take me home.'

Bob looked at her in surprise. 'You know he was there almost constantly for the first couple of days?'

She shook her head.

'Refused to leave you. You must have been really out of it then,' Bob continued. 'After I went with you in the ambulance, Henri and Thomas turned up at the emergency department. I was still there, and we sat together in the relatives' room for hours while they did all the tests and scans. When you went up onto the ward Henri offered me a lift home, but Thomas refused to come back with us, kept going on about how he should have seen this coming and should have been there for you. He insisted on sitting by your bed. I don't know whether he was worried Serge might try coming back and get to you somehow.'

She looked at him, shocked. Why had nobody told her this?

'Eventually one of the doctors had to insist that he go home.'

She thought about the argument that morning and what she had said to him. Now she felt truly guilty and ungrateful.

'I had no idea! Oh, Bob, what am I going to do? How can I fix this?'

Taking her good hand, he looked at her and sighed.

'Let him help you, Jo. You need help and he wants to provide that. Don't push him away. He is angry with himself and hurting inside. We both know this is not his fault, or anybody's apart from Serge's. He needs to realise that. You need to support each other.'

She nodded. 'You're a good man Bob Everton, did you know that?' She winced as she tried to lean towards him. 'I'm so glad we're friends.'

'You have lots of friends Jo. Let us all help you out for a bit, hm?'

Afternoon dragged into evening. Barbara had come and sat with her for a while and told her about her life as a young nurse. She had many interesting and amusing stories, but Jo's mind was elsewhere wondering where Thomas had gone and whether he was alright.

It wasn't until after dinner that evening, she heard the front door slam and the eventual creak of the floorboards in his room next door told her he was back.

Gingerly and extremely slowly, she got out of bed. She hobbled with her one crutch to the adjoining door and, leaning the crutch against the side of the bed, knocked with her good hand.

'Can I come in?'

162

She did not wait for a reply, instead turned the handle and pulled the door towards her. Suddenly finding that hobbling backwards was not as easy as she first thought without a crutch to support her or spare hand to steady herself, she over balanced and ended up in an extremely painful and ungainly position on the floor, her good leg folded underneath her and broken ankle sticking through the doorway. The pain in her side was excruciating. Thomas was there in an instant.

'Jo are you badly hurt? You are a complete idiot sometimes,' he said standing over her and surveying the wreckage.

'I know, that's what I was coming to tell you,' she winced. 'Give me a hand up, please.' She looked at him imploringly.

It was exceedingly difficult trying to pick her up when she was positioned right through the doorway and although he'd got her arm around his neck, she couldn't push up with her good foot as it was tucked underneath her. In the effort to lift her and due to their awkward positions, his foot slipped, and he landed half on top of her with his arm still around her, one of his legs wedged between hers. They froze for a few seconds both surprised by what had just happened.

'Jo, I'm so sorry,' he gasped into her hair. 'Have I hurt you?'

'No, it's ok. You landed on my good side,' she squeaked through gritted teeth. She turned her head to see his face. 'I'm sorry, this is all my fault I…'

Before she could finish, the bedroom door was flung open, and they both looked up. A breathless Barbara came rushing in followed by an equally breathless Mrs West. They stood for a moment taking in the scene before them, a slightly puzzled look on their faces.

'We heard a thump,' said Barbara weakly.

'Oh Lord!' sighed Thomas. He looked at Jo who bit her lip and rested her head back down to the floor before breaking out in a fit of painful giggles, which made him laugh too.

'It's fine Barbara, I was just helping Jo up, she slipped and…' he began.

'We'll wait downstairs,' Barbara whispered, virtually pushing Mrs West back into the corridor and rapidly shutting the door behind her.

Jo and Thomas looked at each other and broke out laughing.

'Oh…ow…stop!' she gasped, trying to breathe between bouts of laughter, 'It hurts!'

'It had to be Mrs West didn't it, of all people and of all moments. That is going to be all around the village in no time. Come on let me get you up, carefully now.'

Eventually, Jo was lying back in the bed, her foot up on the pillow. Their giggles had subsided, and they sat looking at each other.

'Thomas I'm really sorry for this morning, I was totally ungrateful.'

'No, it's ok, it's me that needs to apologise,' he said shaking his head.

'I don't think so,' she said. 'Bob came around this afternoon and told me how long you were at the hospital when I was taken in. I'm sorry, I honestly had no idea you were there.'

'You were pretty out of it on painkillers, I think.'

'Henri told me you blame yourself for what happened. I wish you wouldn't. I don't. It wasn't your fault in any way. How could you have possibly foreseen any of what happened? None of us could.'

'But if I'd been there and we'd all gone to the quiz together instead of…' he trailed off.

'Thomas, listen to me. Serge would probably have waited and found an opportunity at another time. Please, I can't bear the fact that you feel guilty over this.'

He looked thoughtful for a while.

'Let me help you Jo,' he said quietly. 'Let me in, let me be your friend again, I feel as if I've lost you in the past few weeks.'

'Thomas, you will always be my friend.' She wondered what he meant by losing her, it was an odd thing to say but she didn't question him further. 'Where did you go today? I was worried about you.'

'Oh, you know, I just drove around for bit, until I'd calmed down and then I went onto Oxford to collect something.'

He got up and went next door into his room. He returned and held out his closed fist in front of her. She put her open palm underneath in puzzlement until she looked at what he had dropped into her hand. A little rose gold heart winked back at her. The necklace he had given her for her birthday.

'For friendship?' he asked.

'For friendship,' she replied.

'I found it on the floor of the shed when I went to tidy up. The chain was broken, so I've had it put on a stronger one.'

'Thank you, Thomas, that's so thoughtful of you.' Fleetingly a picture of Serge's contorted face flickered across her mind as he had pulled it from her. 'Help me put it on will you, please?'

'It won't hurt your neck? The scratches…' He didn't quite know what to say.

'I'll live. Bob reassured me they will heal completely. I don't think this is going to get in the way.' She smiled up at him.

He took the necklace and kneeling down beside the bed, slipped it around her neck. He kissed her cheek ever so softly when he'd finished. The same tingling sensation she felt the first time he had done that repeated itself down her spine.

'You need a shave,' she said, putting a hand up to his rough cheek. 'And a good night's sleep.'

'I will sleep better if I know you are ok.'

'How about you leave the door ajar then?' she suggested. 'Pass me the painkillers, will you; I think I need a couple.'

The medication helped Jo sleep solidly through the night, in fact it was mid-morning before she woke and hobbled stiffly over to the bathroom. Bravely, she looked in the mirror. Everything still looked pretty horrendous, but the swelling seemed to have gone down considerably. A step in the right direction at least. She looked at the nightie and dressing gown. She really needed a shower and change of clothes and her hair felt disgusting. When she came out of the bathroom, Thomas poked his head around the door.

'Heard you were up.'

'You look better,' she said.

He had shaved and obviously slept well too.

'Is Barbara around? I really need to have a shower and my hair needs washing. I look like Stig of the Dump,' she complained.

'Um...no. She's gone into Oxford with Dad. Last minute holiday shopping.'

She had forgotten all about the holiday Henri and Barbara had planned.

'When are they going?'

'The day after tomorrow. Can I help? I mean there must be a way to do this somehow and still give you privacy.'

'Cling film, and plastic bags it is then. If you can find me a bucket or something to sit on it might be a bit easier than having to stand on one leg.'

'I'll see what I can find.'

A little while later he was back, armed with on old metal stool he had found in the garage, a box of clingfilm and some tape. He put the stool in the shower and wrapped her foot and arm in cling film, securing it with the tape.

'There,' he said stepping back and admiring his efforts.

'I feel like I'm ready to pop in the microwave!' she said hobbling to the bathroom.

'Are you ok undressing? I mean, I can close my eyes.'

'I will manage thank you,' she said giving him a not-on-your-nelly look and shut the door behind her.

The shower felt so good. However, it was painful trying to bend or reach up and she found it impossible to do her hair. There was just too much of it to manage with one hand and she didn't want to get the stitches on her forehead wet. She squeezed the water out of the ends. It would have to wait until Barbara came back. Towelling herself dry she realised she had no fresh clothes and had to ask Thomas to go over to the cottage to find something that would fit over the leg cast. She knew she had a pair of loose shorts somewhere. It was slightly embarrassing, knowing that he would have to rummage through her underwear drawer and wardrobe. He handed the clothes around the door on his return. Dressing on her own was difficult. She managed everything except doing up her bra, which was simply impossible, she would have to ask for help. She put the tee shirt on over the top and was as dressed as she could be before she went back into the bedroom.

'That took a while. Better?' He was lounging on the bed looking at the book she had been reading.

'Much, thank you, although I have one small problem.' She could feel herself blushing already. She turned around with her back to him. Perhaps it would be less embarrassing if she didn't look at him while she asked, 'Could you do my bra up please?'

His hands were warm and gentle reaching up under her t-shirt to find the two ends to pull carefully together. She couldn't help shivering at the feel of his fingers on her skin. Once done, he pulled her shirt back down and ran his hands down her back as if smoothing the material.

'Your hair is very wet still,' he said, feeling it.

'Yes, the ends got wet, but I couldn't manage the shampoo. It will have to stay a bit manky until Barbara gets back.'

'I can wash it for you.'

'How are we going to do that? I am not supposed to get the stitches wet and bending over a sink is too painful.'

He thought for a moment and then disappeared downstairs calling to her that he would be back shortly.

Fifteen minutes later he carried her downstairs and into the kitchen.

'It's a bit Heath-Robinson but I think we can manage, what do you think?'

The kitchen table had been dragged over to the sink, each leg raised on a pile of old hardbacked books to make it the right height, the intention being that she could lie on her back with her head over the sink. A plastic measuring jug and bottle of shampoo sat on the draining board. Jo looked at it, impressed. It might just work, and she wouldn't have to bend over.

'I'm game if you are,' she said. 'Are you sure you don't mind?'

'Come on, what's the worst that can happen?'

'We both get very wet and flood the kitchen?'

'It's fine!' he said smirking. 'We can clear it up before the grown-ups return.'

Slowly, without trying to cause her any pain he lifted her onto the table and made sure that she was in the least uncomfortable position possible. Gently he ran his fingers through her hair wetting it thoroughly before adding shampoo. Jo could not remember the last time anyone had washed her hair for her, probably her mother when she had been a little girl. It certainly had not felt anything like this. It was almost sinfully blissful.

'I might need to get a comb or something, you've got a fair bit of dried blood matted in this bit,' he said, frowning and holding a bit of her hair up.

'Just get out what you can.'

He reached over to one of the kitchen drawers and pulled out a big pink comb. Showing it to her he explained.

'It was my mother's, she always kept one in this draw. She liked to make sure my hair was smart before school when I was little. I used to get a tap on the side of the head with it if I didn't stand still. I always used to mess my hair up when I got to school mind you. Let's see if it helps.'

Patiently, he worked away until her hair was clean and then rinsed it though. With the towel wrapped around her head, Thomas lifted Jo on to one of the kitchen chairs which is where Barbara and Henri found them on their return. He standing behind her in the kitchen, very gently towel drying her hair.

Chapter 18

'What's been going on here then?' Barbara said in mock horror, looking at the kitchen table still by the sink and on its stilts of books.

Jo looked up through her tangle of semi-dried hair.

'Thomas has washed my hair for me.'

'Go careful around those stitches won't you Thomas,' she said, watching him rub Jo's head with the towel and putting down her shopping.

'He is,' she reassured her. 'He's been very helpful.'

'They should be coming out soon, shouldn't they?' Barbara queried.

'Yes, the hospital said to make an appointment with my GP, but I haven't actually got around to registering with one yet. Do you think I can ask Bob?'

'Probably, although you still ought to register. Have you had lunch? We ate out, didn't we Henri?'

'Mm, nice little café off the High Street, not too busy,' said Henri as he started removing the books under the table legs.

Jo had lost all track of time and apologised profusely to Thomas on finding out that it was nearly three o'clock. He didn't appear that bothered. After combing her hair, he walked with her as she hobbled into the living room and then returned to the kitchen, promising to come back with food.

They sat for a while in companionable silence on the sofa, munching their way through a plate of sandwiches that Barbara had hurriedly put together, Jo with one leg resting on a pile of cushions at the end of the sofa, her back slightly towards Thomas. He sat the other side of her, holding the plate between them and passing her cup of tea and tablets as required into her one good hand. Henri joined them, sitting in his chair by the unlit fire with his newspaper. After they had finished, she leant back to look at Thomas.

'Thank you for helping me with everything this morning. I feel a bit worn out now, how about you?'

'Why don't you have a snooze? Rest yourself back against me for a bit, I don't mind. Here, let me move my arm out the way.'

When Henri looked up from his paper next, he was not surprised to find them both asleep. Thomas with his head rested back on the sofa and one arm half around Jo who was asleep in the crook of his arm. He put a finger to his lips as Barbara came in and nodded in their direction. She bent around the side of the sofa, took one look at them, smiled and left them to it.

Bob came to visit the following evening with Ellen, who was fascinated to watch Jo's stitches being removed.

'It looks a bit pink at the moment,' he said, looking at the scar. 'But they've done a very good job and it will fade. You may not even be able to see it in time unless you look very carefully.'

'And you can always use a bit of make up in the meantime,' added Ellen, trying to be helpful.

Jo looked in the hand mirror she was holding. She supposed they were right. She noticed today that some of the bruising on her face and body was starting to turn a yellowy green colour as it healed.

They sat and chatted for a while. Ellen told them that she had started packing already to go off to university. It seemed to be a day for packing. Henri and Barbara had been bustling about with suitcases and various bits all day. They had loaded the car ready to be off at the crack of dawn to catch the early ferry. Barbara had helped Jo dress that morning and suggested that she get Ellen to take her shopping some time to find some underwear that she could slip on over her head, rather than having to ask Thomas to help her, which seemed like a very sensible idea to Jo. She would miss Barbara and Henri. Three weeks seemed a long time to be without their company. Whilst Bob and Thomas were busy chatting in the kitchen, Jo and Ellen went to the living room where she explained her underwear predicament.

'I'd love to help, but I can't until next Saturday. I'm sure Thomas doesn't mind helping out till then,' she said cheekily and laughed.

Jo blushed; it had been embarrassing enough the first time let alone having to ask him for the next few days.

'Jo, you look a bit pink, everything alright?' Thomas said coming in with Bob.

'Yes, she was just telling me about how you have to…'

'Shhhhh!' broke in Jo to stop her, 'Everything is fine, nothing going on here. Ellen and I were just planning a shopping trip to get some…er…essential items.'

'Do you think that's wise? It's early days yet Jo. I know you are still in a lot of pain. Hobbling around a busy shopping centre is not going to be easy, I mean you are only just managing around the house at the moment.' Thomas looked concerned.

'How about you borrow a wheelchair?' Bob suggested. 'I know a lady who volunteers for the Red Cross, they lend them out. I'll contact her, shall I? It will be much easier than you trying to hobble around Marks and Sparks on one crutch.'

'Good idea Bob, and I'll take you both in, absolutely no going on the bus,' Thomas insisted.

'You can come with us Thomas, help Jo choose some pretty underwear,' Ellen blurted out before Jo could stop her. She wished the sofa would open and swallow her up. Really the girl was more like her mother than she realised.

'I'd love to,' he said smirking in Jo's direction at her horrified expression. 'But I have other things to do so I will leave you two ladies to it and pick you up when you're finished.'

Henri and Barbara left early the next morning. Barbara had been in two minds whether to go but Henri had insisted. Having packed the fridge with food, Barbara told Jo that she would have to teach Thomas how to cook or she would be surviving on scrambled eggs for two of the next three weeks at least. They had hugged and laughed about it and Jo had wished them a safe trip as she and Thomas waved them off.

The rest of the day was quiet. Thomas went up to the studio while Jo lounged on the sofa downstairs trying to read between bouts of sleepiness caused by the painkillers. She was a bit fed up feeling sleepy all the time and decided she would try to manage without them if she could. By the afternoon, Jo was feeling bored. She decided it was time to go back out into the garden, plants would need attention in the greenhouse by now even though she knew that Barbara had been keeping an eye on things and had given everything a thorough soaking the day before last.

Carefully, Jo hobbled her way out through the kitchen door. The steps were a little problematic, but sitting down, she slowly shuffled on her bottom and reached the last one. Making her way around on the path she saw the garden with the fresh eyes of one who has been away for some time. Flowers were in their last bloom of summer, begging autumn to stay its hand for a while longer, and green leaves were outstretched, lifted skywards. The grass was desiccated and straw-like, thirsty for soft drops of long-awaited rain. Pausing by the lavender she pinched one of the now dried heads and breathed in. The aroma was like cool water on her parched senses, reviving her love for it instantly. She had so missed just being out here.

She was halfway to the kitchen garden when she heard the studio door slide open and saw Thomas descend the stairs. She noticed he did not look very pleased as he came towards her.

'You shouldn't be out here on your own, what if you had an accident or…You should have asked me, and I would have carried you out. How did you manage the steps?'

'Calm down! I'm fine. Do stop worrying about me, please. I was just bored and needed to get out the house. I'm going to water the tomatoes, what's left of them.'

'I'm coming with you then.'

'As you wish,' she sighed and continued on her way slowly.

Thomas opened the greenhouse door and she went in, hobbling over to the bench to lean against it. She turned to speak to him but instead of seeing Thomas framed in the doorway, she saw Serge as he had been that evening, his menacing eyes looking up at her from under his cap. She could hear his voice calling her 'Cherie' and felt suddenly faint and sick as the blood drained from her head.

'I thought this might happen,' Thomas said coming over to her and holding her while she recovered.

'I'm sorry, bit of a flashback. I'm alright now.'

'Sure?'

'Mm…let me go, I need to see what needs doing.'

Between them they watered plants and picked the ripe fruit. Jo perched on an upturned bucket telling Thomas what to do. She felt so useless with one arm and one leg out of action.

'I need to go over to the shed.'

'Jo, I don't think that is a good idea, you've done enough for one day. Let's take the tomatoes back to the house.'

'No, Thomas I need to do this,' she insisted.

Opening the door of the shed, Jo went inside. It was silent and still apart from tiny motes of dust which danced in the soft shaft of bright sunlight coming in the window. Everything looked how it always did, tools hung tidily along the walls, plant pots on the bench, until she looked down. A large ugly brown stain of dried blood blotted the floorboards by her feet. It was obvious that someone had tried to clean it at some point, but the stain remained, staring back at her and bringing memories freshly into her mind. She closed her eyes to try and shut them out. Taking some deep breaths, she looked across at Thomas who was standing in the doorway.

'I should have been here for you. If only I hadn't been so busy…' He didn't finish. Just shook his head and looked away in regret. She could see he was blaming himself again.

'Stop it, Thomas. Let's not go there again.'

'Yes, but I was so busy doing something I shouldn't have done, instead of trusting you and being there for you. Jo, I'm so sorry.'

'What do you mean Thomas? You are not making a whole lot of sense.'

'Let's go back to the house. You need to sit down for a while. I have a confession to make, and you are not going to like it.'

She didn't know what he was talking about, but he seemed genuinely in turmoil over something, so she agreed, letting him carry her back across the garden and into the kitchen. She sat at the kitchen table as he made them both coffee. It was strong and hot and by the look on his face she felt she felt she was going to need it. She waited for him to begin.

'Do you remember the afternoon of the attack…no, I need to go back further than that.' He rubbed his hands over his face and leaned back. 'I suppose it all started the day you went shopping with Ellen. Do you remember?'

Jo nodded thinking about the expensive dress still hanging in her wardrobe.

'It was when all the secret "girl stuff" began. I knew you were up to something and then Mrs West let the cat out of the bag at the quiz, and we all discovered what it was. I was glad initially that something had been done to help Ellen and then I felt a bit annoyed that it had taken a complete newcomer to the village to actually do something about that situation, when we'd all been sitting around for ages saying "poor Ellen" but not doing anything to help her. I was annoyed with myself really. And then I began to mull over the practicalities of what it would mean for Mrs West. I know how much it cost to put me through university, and I knew that Mrs West in her situation couldn't afford it. I thought you had been a bit thoughtless, even though you intended well, but instead of talking to you I just snapped at you. I'm sorry Jo.'

She sat in silence waiting for him to continue.

'I'm afraid it gets worse,' he continued. 'The afternoon of the attack I persuaded Dad to come with me to the bank. I thought I had to do something about it all you see. My books are selling ridiculously well, I thought I might as well do something good with the money. I don't need it all. We discussed with the manager about setting up a fund for Ellen to help pay all her expenses and fees, then in the evening we went to see Mrs West and Ellen to put it to them. We didn't want it to sound like charity or anything, just helping a neighbour out. I couldn't believe it when they turned the offer down. Ellen wouldn't say why, I could tell she was hiding something. Mrs West buckled under a little bit of pressure and eventually confessed that you had already done something very similar, and she wasn't having to pay a penny thanks to you. Ellen tried to stop her telling me, but you know Mrs West, can't keep a secret for more than two minutes. I felt so bad. I had been so rude to you. I know Barbara tried to warn me. I went completely behind your back and stuck my nose in where it wasn't needed because I hadn't trusted that you'd thought it through properly. I didn't even occur to me for one moment that you might have had enough money of your own to be able to do that sort of thing. Jo, you have been truly good and unbelievably kind and generous, and I've been a grumpy, rude, idiot. I felt so bad about it and then the attack happened, and I didn't get the chance to apologise. Then we argued and you've been in so much pain, I didn't want to add to that. I'm so sorry Jo. When you went out to the garden, it all came flooding back I just had to tell you. Can you forgive me?'

She thought for a moment before replying. It had not been his place to get involved in something that was nothing to do with him, but his motives had been good ultimately.

'Thomas you were only trying to do what you thought was right. I can't say I wasn't a bit upset when you got cross with me, but you didn't know the whole story and I didn't tell you. It was between me and Ellen. She wanted to make the most of her life and I could help her with that. We don't all get that chance in life. I needed Barbara's input because she was a nurse and she helped Ellen with the application process. I thought she was the best person to confide in. She didn't really get involved in the financial side of it. I arranged that with the bank. It's not something I'd ever done before and it's not something you really go around telling people about. Thinking about it, I suppose there is not a lot to forgive in the scheme of things really. Maybe you should have talked to me, maybe I should have told you. We are probably both a bit at fault here. But we are friends at the end of the day, I don't want to spoil that by arguing over this.'

'Jo Stanton you are the kindest person I've ever met,' he said. 'But there is one thing I want to ask you, just to set my mind at rest.'

She knew what it was before he asked her. It was what she had been afraid of all along, this one question that could lead to so many others.

'I know what you sold your grandmother's house for Jo, and it wasn't that much, and Alain told us you were paying the bills by taking on the music job at the chateau to earn a bit extra. Can I ask how did you come by so much money that you could afford to do this for Ellen? Gardeners don't earn that kind of money.'

'Please don't ask me that.' She got up from the table to indicate that the discussion was over.

'Jo what are you not telling me, you're not in any trouble are you?'

'No, nothing like that and it's nothing you need to worry about, please don't ask me anymore. I don't want to talk about it.'

'I'm sorry,' he said coming around the table and hugging her. 'I didn't mean to upset you.'

'You haven't.'

'You know you can talk to me about anything. I worry about you sometimes Jo, you're so…'

'Dammed independent?' she finished for him.

He laughed. 'Yes, I was trying to put that more tactfully though.'

After a dinner of chicken casserole that Barbara had left, Jo lounged on the sofa with her book, while Thomas tidied up.

'Do you need your tablets?' he asked, coming into the living room with the box.

'I'm trying not to take them. I hate how they make me feel woozy and sleepy all the time. Do you know, I think I've read the same chapter in this book about four times now and not taken any of it in? I might get an early night if that's ok?'

'Of course. I'll take you up.'

'It's ok, I can hobble to the bottom of the stairs,' she said as he came over to lift her. 'And then you can give me a lift. Thomas, I'm very grateful but you don't need to carry me everywhere. You've done enough today as it is,' she said hobbling across the hallway.

'But what if I want to?'

She stopped at the bottom of the stairs and looked at him for a moment not knowing quite how to answer. Carefully he lifted her, and they started making their way up.

'You can put me down now, thank you,' she said as they got to the top of the stairs.

He carried on, kicking the door open as usual with his foot and then put her down in the bedroom, near the bathroom door.

'Turn around,' he instructed.

She did so. Gently he slid his hands up the back of her t-shirt and undid her bra, pulling the shirt down again after he had finished. It was a beautiful caring gesture. He left her then and went into his own room leaving the door ajar in case she needed him further. She heard the floorboards creak as he walked across the room, and she hobbled red faced into the bathroom to change for bed.

Chapter 19

In her ears she could hear the terrifying roar of the approaching danger which she knew would ultimately overwhelm her as it always did. Panicking, she ran as fast as she could, but she wasn't getting anywhere. She had made it happen and as she tried to fight it off, she cried out, 'I'm sorry, I shouldn't have done it.' But it was too late, and the whiteness took her. Somewhere someone was calling her name, far, far away.

'Jo! Jo! Are you alright? Wake up. Jo open your eyes for me.'

Thomas? He didn't belong here, in this.

'Jo!'

She felt something cold on her face and opened her eyes. The bedside light was on, and it was dark outside.

'What happened?' she said groggily, suddenly aware that she was drenched in sweat as usually happened on these occasions. Her good foot had pushed the duvet back and her leg with the cast on was hanging over the side of the bed. She lifted it back onto the mattress.

'Want to tell me that? I think you were having a nightmare.'

'I'm sorry I didn't mean to wake you,' she said suddenly feeling the pain sear through her ribs as she took a deep breath in. Turning her head, she saw Thomas sitting on the bed with her, wearing just a pair of pyjama bottoms and holding a flannel, concern written all over his face.

'I'm sorry, I had to wake you. You looked as though you might flail your way off the bed any second.'

'Thank you.'

'Want to talk about it?'

She shook her head.

'Really? Jo, it might help.'

'I think a glass of water and maybe a couple of paracetamols might help.' And you putting a dressing gown on, she thought but could not say. 'Sorry to be a bother.'

He went into her bathroom to fetch the glass of water and then into his own for some paracetamol.

'Want some company?'

'No, I'll be fine, thank you,' she said, swallowing the pills and putting the glass by the bed. 'Goodnight' she tried to say as kindly as possible as she turned out the light.

She saw him stand in the doorway for a few moments, half lit by the light from his room. Elaine was a very lucky woman she thought as she closed her eyes. She wondered why he had not mentioned her in the last week or so.

A knock on the outer bedroom door woke Jo the next morning. It was Thomas, fully dressed this time and looking urgent.

'Jo, you need to get up quickly, the police are downstairs.'

He came over to the bed and helped her upright.

'Do you want to dress or go down like this?'

'I'd like to dress. Is it about Serge? Have they arrested him?'

'They wouldn't say, I think they would rather talk to you. I'll go and make them a cup of tea while you dress and then I'll come back to help you with...er...you know. Ok?'

She dressed in the bathroom and ran a brush through her hair so that she was presentable. What if they had not found him and he was still on the loose? Maybe that was why Thomas had been cross with her for going out in the garden yesterday on her own. But if they never captured him, she could not live her life locked up in the house, could she?

Thomas was waiting for her as she came out the bathroom.

'You're shaking,' he observed as he did her up.

'Will you stay with me, while I'm with the police?' She looked at him imploringly and laid one hand on his arm. 'Please?'

'Always.'

He picked her up and, descending the stairs went into the living room. There sat the two female officers who had taken her statement in the hospital, one was carrying a blue file. Thomas put her down and then sat on the arm of the sofa next to her.

'Hello again Miss Stanton, you are looking much better than the last time we met. Do you remember us? I'm PC Harper and this is my colleague PC Patel.'

'Yes, I remember,' she said, shaking hands with both of them.

'We potentially have some news regarding your attacker,' PC Harper said gently. She flicked a look at Thomas. 'Are you happy for Mr Arnaud to be present?'

'Yes, absolutely, he was the one who found me in the first place.' She turned and smiled weakly at Thomas who rubbed her back with his hand. 'What do you mean by potentially?'

'Yesterday, a man's body was pulled out of the River Thames, downstream from Oxford. We have reason to believe that it might be Serge.'

Jo's face went ashen under her fading bruises.

'You don't know for certain?' she said.

'The body had been in the water for a few days and there were no documents on it to help us identify it. However, all the descriptions given of Serge fit the man recovered and the clothes are French in origin, so it is highly likely that it is.'

'We are not going to ask you to come down to the station to formally identify the body,' said PC Patel. 'But we do have some photographs. It would be useful if you could look at them to confirm our suspicions. If you are up to it.'

Jo nodded. 'Yes, ok.'

'I'm afraid they are not pretty,' warned PC Harper as she withdrew a couple of photos from the blue file on her lap and passed them to Jo. 'But at least they are in black and white.'

The bloated face of a man, his dark eyes staring in death and mouth slightly open, looked back at Jo from the pictures. Clearly some decomposition had already begun to take place, his nose being more distorted than the rest of his features. The face had dark hair that had been swept back and lay in straggly wet rat tails around it. The second picture had been taken in profile. It was undoubtedly Serge.

'It's him,' Jo said handing back the photos and swallowing the bile that had risen in her throat.

'Thank you. Well done,' said PC Harper.

'Do you know how he died?'

'We think he most likely drowned as there was water in his lungs, but we don't know how he got in the water in the first place. There is no evidence of foul play, however, the level of alcohol in his blood was very high. We suspect that he might have been drinking somewhere local after he attacked you,' she shrugged. 'He may have been extremely drunk, fallen in and just not been able to get himself out again. He had no wallet or ID on him, that may have fallen out of his pocket in the water or been stolen. We will probably never know for sure.'

'So, what happens next?'

'We will be in touch with the French police who will then contact any family. There is nothing more you need to do. We can put you in touch with a counselling service if you feel you need it?'

'No, I'll be alright. Thank you for all you've done,' Jo said. She was still in shock. Despite all that Serge had done to her, she felt sorry for him to have died in such a way. She did not know what family he had back in France, but this would be an awful time for them, and she felt for their future pain.

'Right, we'll be on our way then,' said PC Harper as both the officers rose. 'Take care of yourself Miss Stanton, looks like you've got yourself a good one here,' she glanced over at Thomas.

'We're just good friends,' Thomas corrected her quickly.

Jo hobbled to the front door and out on to the drive with Thomas where the two officers had left the police car. As they drove off down the lane, Jo promptly doubled over painfully and retched.

Bob called in briefly at lunchtime to deliver the wheelchair and Jo told him what had happened as the three of them sat around the kitchen table. It was cathartic to talk about it all and afterwards she felt a sense of release.

Later, Thomas suggested that they give the wheelchair a spin and go up to the church for some fresh air. He had not left her side for a moment apart from to pick a few dahlias from the garden to put on his mother's grave.

'I feel like a little old lady,' Jo said as he pushed her along. 'All I need is a rug over my knees and the look would be complete.'

'That could be arranged,' he quipped. 'I can easily pop back and fetch you one.' He stopped the chair as if to go back.

'Don't you dare,' she laughed. 'It's too hot today anyway.'

It was one of those late summer days whose heavy closeness held the possibility of a thunderstorm later, large cumulonimbus clouds already bubbled overhead. She hoped they would get back to the house before the rain came.

On reaching the church, Thomas stopped on the path and refreshed the graveside flowers and then pushed her inside where it felt cooler and fresher.

'My parents were married here,' he told her, parking her in the nave and sitting in the pew besides her.

'It's a beautiful church, I came up here a while back to have a look around. I noticed they have a piano identical to your father's.'

'Yes, he donated it after Mum died. She used to sing in the choir here, and the piano they had was never very good. This church was quite a big part of her life really.'

'Do you miss her terribly?' Jo said, turning to him.

'I do. I will always miss her, but I know she wouldn't want me to live the rest of my life being sad, so I try to think of her in happier times. In the garden or here, singing.'

He turned to look at her and she suddenly had that feeling again that he could see right into her soul. He got up and pushed her towards the piano, wheeling her close so that she could see him while he sat on the stool in front of the keyboard. Stretching out his fingers, he began to play. The music filled the church with its beauty and longing. As he played, she noticed that he watched her, never taking his eyes from hers until she closed them to listen. She knew the piece, 'Mariage d'Amour.'

'Appropriate don't you think?' he asked when he had finished.

'For a church? Yes. You play very well. The acoustics give everything a slightly other-worldly feel, don't you think?'

'Want to join me at the keyboard? You could do the right hand, I'll do the left.' He rifled through the pieces of music that had been left on the stand and selected one, not waiting for her reply. 'Do you want to share the stool? We can probably both fit on. Possibly easier than trying this from the wheelchair.'

Once in position on the stool, she found they were sitting extremely close. He with his right arm around her, holding her to stop her sliding off the stool, her with her broken arm resting in her lap. She could feel the warmth of him down the left side of her body. She looked at the music he had chosen. 'Air' from Handel's Water Music. He counted them in slowly and they started to play together, their bodies moving as one with the music. When the last chord died away, they sat in silence for just a moment neither of them wanting to break the spell just woven around them.

'That was beautiful,' he whispered at last.

Jo didn't turn around, she knew he was looking at her and deep down inside she felt something that she knew she shouldn't. Instead, she got up from the stool and hobbled over to the wheelchair. As she sat down, she heard the thunder rumble overhead.

'I think we ought to get back before it rains, don't you?' she said, not meeting his gaze.

He got up and pushed her down the aisle. As they exited the church the first heavy drops of summer rain splashed into her lap and the wonderful smell of thirsty earth being quenched filled her senses. By the time they got home, the heavens had truly opened and they were both laughing about being soaked to the skin.

The following Saturday Jo and Thomas picked up Ellen on their way into Oxford for the long-awaited shopping trip.

'What are you going to be doing while we're shopping Thomas?' Ellen asked after they had pulled into a layby and Jo had loaded herself into the wheelchair.

'I'm meeting up with Elaine,' he smiled. 'I haven't seen her for a while, things to catch up on. Have a good shop ladies, text me when you're done.'

And with that he got back in the car and pulled out into the traffic.

'Where shall we go first?' Ellen asked, taking up her position as Jo's driver 'I know a lovely shop along here somewhere that does evening dresses.'

'No! Absolutely not, I need underwear,' Jo shrieked. They both giggled as they made their way to Marks and Spencer. Jo noticed that her ribs were a little less painful when she laughed now. Her bruises were also beginning to disappear, although her skin had still looked a bit of a funny colour in places when she had checked herself over in the mirror that morning.

Being a Saturday, it was fairly busy in the shop. It was surprising, Jo thought to herself, people's attitude to wheelchairs. Most people held doors for them and were very helpful. Others, usually people walking along chatting in groups, did not seem to see them at all and Ellen had to pull in amongst the clothes while they passed, completely unaware in their selfishness.

They located the underwear section, Jo finding what she needed quite quickly. Ellen wanted to browse so they wandered around back and forth until they came to a lacy selection that Jo mentally labelled as definitely *sexy* underwear. They would not leave much to the imagination once on she thought. Ellen rummaged through finding a set in her own size.

'What do you think?' She held them up for Jo to admire. 'I think I might treat myself.'

'They are very pretty. Not very practical for everyday though are they, under a nurses' uniform?' She looked at Ellen who had raised her eyebrows. Suddenly she felt a little dense. 'Oh…these are not for going under a nurses' uniform, are they?'

'Not at university anyway,' she giggled.

'That's far too much information already!' Jo laughed. 'Dare I ask?'

'Let's just say I will be coming home for as many weekends as possible,'

Jo hesitated, waiting for her to continue.

'A certain pair of very nice brown eyes?'

'Bob?'

Ellen nodded.

'You don't mind, do you?' Ellen looked suddenly concerned.

'Not at all,' Jo replied, she actually thought it rather sweet. 'I think you will make a lovely couple. I'm very happy for you. I knew swapping quiz teams was a good idea.'

They purchased their respective items and found a cafe for lunch where Ellen talked almost nonstop about Bob the entire time. Telling Jo lots of information that she already knew, but it didn't matter, it was good to see her friend happy.

'How does your mum feel about it?' Jo asked, sipping her coffee.

'Surprisingly, she's good. Thinks she will see more of me if I'm coming home all the time. Everybody likes Bob, don't they? I mean he's just an amazing doctor.'

'He's a good friend. He certainly helped me out when I needed him most.'

'Yes, but it was Thomas who was your real knight in shining armour that evening. Jo you should have seen his face when he ran out of the pub, he was absolutely beside himself. And after, when they'd taken you off in the ambulance, well, I've never seen anyone look so…lost. You know he's always been considered quite a catch in the village.'

'Mm…but he's already been caught, by Elaine,' Jo explained, 'so all those single women in the village will have to look elsewhere.'

'Oh, I've met Elaine, she came in the shop a few times. Funny, doesn't seem quite like his type to me. Still, you never can tell these days, can you?'

They pottered around a bit more after lunch and then Jo felt she ought to give poor Ellen a break, so they texted Thomas and arranged a pickup point.

'Successful trip?' he enquired when they were underway.

'Yes. We got everything we needed, you could say…it was most revealing.' Jo looked at Ellen who giggled.

'I'm not even going to begin to ask what that means,' Thomas said, looking in the rear-view mirror at Jo.

'How was Elaine?'

'Fine,' he replied perfunctorily.

Obviously, he did not want to share any details of his day, so she didn't enquire further.

After dinner that evening, Jo raised a subject that had been sitting at the back of her mind for a couple of days now.

'Thomas, now I'm on the mend a bit, I don't want to be a bother to you. You must have things you want to go and do, people to see and so forth. I don't mind being left on my own for a bit.'

'I think we've covered this before Jo, I like helping you and you still need help getting around. You are not, nor ever will be, a bother to me. Unless you are trying to get rid of me?'

'No, not at all, but I feel as if I've completely monopolised your time recently.'

'I like being completely monopolised by you,' he said, smiling. 'I'm happy if you are.'

She wondered how Elaine felt about that but did not feel it her business to ask.

'What about your writing Thomas? I'm not holding you up in any way.'

'No, I'm kind of between books really,' he said, getting up and clearing the table. 'The last one was a one off. I'm still looking for inspiration for the next one. Got any ideas? What have you recently seen that really made you feel something inside?'

Jo thought for a minute. A picture of him playing the piano in the church popped into her mind and she banished it quickly. Apart from that, the last thing that had really pulled at her heart strings had been her grandparents love letters.

'Over in the cottage, I have a collection of my grandparent's letters to each other that they wrote when they were courting. I remember reading them when I was sorting the house out. They were quite moving. I could go over and dig them out if you'd like to have a look. I'm not sure they will help much.'

'I'd like that. People don't do that anymore, do they? Write to each other, put their feelings down on paper. They should.'

'You'll have to start a campaign,' she laughed.

'I might just do that. Do you want to go and fetch them now? I'll take you across.'

'I'll hobble but you can come. There are a few things I need anyway so you can carry them back for me.'

On lifting the lid of the trunk in the bedroom of the cottage, a waft of lavender and the smell of her grandmother's house engulfed Jo. She closed her eyes and breathed it in. She could see the house in her mind as if she were still there, sitting in the front room on the sofa rather than here on the cottage bedroom floor, far away.

'They are in here somewhere,' she said, taking things out and piling them up on the floor next to the trunk. Maybe they were under the photographs. She lifted out a pile of photographs in frames which toppled as she put them down and slithered across the floor untidily.

'Take your time, there's no rush,' Thomas said, sitting on the side of the bed next to her.

He picked up one of the photographs to look at. It was of a young couple and a dark-haired girl of about seven.

'Your parents?' he asked holding up the picture for her to see.

Jo took it from him and put it face down on the floor besides the others without answering. Looking back in the trunk she found what she was looking for.

'Here,' she said, handing him the letters and carefully fitting everything else back in. 'I'll just grab a few bits and pieces and then we can go.'

'You didn't answer my question,' he said as he helped her off the floor.

'Yes,' she said. 'My parents.'

'Tell me about them. You look a lot like your mother.'

Jo hobbled over to the drawer pretending to be busy looking for something. 'Not much to say really, they're dead. Please don't ask any more.'

This was the second time she had closed down any conversation about her parents. Thomas looked at her thoughtfully and sighed.

'As you wish.'

They locked up and made their way back to the main house. Jo could not face any more questions and she feared they would be forthcoming so she asked Thomas to take her up to bed so that she could get an early night. He didn't argue.

He put the pile of letters and the spare clothes in the kitchen and came back to the bottom of the stairs to pick her up.

'Do you need any help?' he asked her when he had deposited her next to the bathroom door.

She turned her back and waited for him to undo her before she hobbled into the bathroom and shut the door. At least, that was one thing he would not have to do for her tomorrow.

Chapter 20

Jo knew that her nightmares had become more frequent since being back in England, but at least she had not managed to wake Thomas last night. With any luck she thought, she could move back to the cottage as soon as her casts were removed and then it would not matter so much.

Managing to dress completely by herself the next morning made Jo feel better. It had been a little bit painful getting into the new underwear but certainly less embarrassing. Thomas had not knocked on her door or appeared as he usually did on hearing her up and about and she wondered whether he was waiting next door. Having learnt her lesson the hard way, she knocked and carefully opened the adjoining door peeping in to see if he was there. He wasn't.

She had never actually been in his room before and saw instantly that it was a mirror image of hers but slightly larger. However, whereas hers was pink wallpapered and slightly outdated, in this room the original beams of the building had been revealed between whitewashed walls. An enormous four poster bed stood head-to-head with hers on the other side of the partition wall, its dark barley twist posts winding nearly to the ceiling. An old oak wardrobe and two chests of drawers stood on the opposite wall, an ensuite bathroom in the corner the only indication of modernisation. It smelt slightly of cologne and Thomas. Carefully she crept back out and pushed the door to.

Making her way out onto the landing she saw that the studio door was open at the end of the corridor, and she could feel a breeze coming through it. The balcony door must be open too. She hobbled along to see if he was there.

'Can I come in?' she called, opening the door.

On pushing the door wider, she could see him out on the balcony, arms splayed on the railing, looking out across the garden. She made her way across the studio to the outer door, her movement catching his field of vision. He turned and smiled.

'Good morning. Looks like rain today,' he said, looking up at the leaden sky and then back at her. He looked slightly worried as if he had something on his mind. 'Ready to go downstairs?'

'Please,' she replied, turning to make her way back across the studio.

He scooped her up then without a word and proceeded towards the stairs. She knew better than to argue.

After they had both breakfasted. Jo hobbled to the fridge and took a look inside. Just about enough eggs to make an omelette, and a packet of ham.

'I think we need to do a bit of food shopping. We've probably got enough for today but tomorrow we will run out of a lot of things.'

'We could always go to the pub,' he suggested.

'Well, why don't we do that tomorrow and use up the eggs and ham today. I'll teach you how to make an omelette.'

'You are a brave woman if you think you can teach me to cook,' he laughed. 'Barbara keeps threatening to teach Dad, I think even she has accepted that I'm a lost cause.'

'Challenge accepted,' she smiled back. 'What are you doing today?'

'I thought I'd read your grandparents letters if that's ok with you? I've got some reading for you to do as well. I've got the first copies of my book from the printers. Want to read it?'

She nodded, 'Can't wait!'

'I'd like you to read it all the way through before you tell me what you think. Is that ok? Why don't you come up to the studio? You can lounge on the sofa or take the comfy chair, whichever you prefer. We could have a reading morning.'

'I'd like that, thank you,' she replied.

Once settled on the sofa in the studio, Thomas passed her the book. On the cover was a picture of a large wrought iron garden gate set in an archway. Over the arch scrambled a white climbing rose. Emblazoned in gold lettering at the top, the title 'Restoration' and at the bottom the author's name, T Arnaud.

'Happy reading,' he said and then settled himself at the large desk taking out the first letter from the pile to read.

The first chapter opened in a semi lit bedroom where a woman lay dying, her husband by her side. She was young and beautiful and he, grief stricken. The language used to describe the feelings behind their last conversation was heart wrenching. Jo shut her eyes for a while to imagine the scene, what it looked like and how each of the characters felt. The writing was so beautifully descriptive, she could see herself there, standing at the end of the bed watching the scene like some ghostly time traveller from another world. As the woman died a tear slipped from the corner of Jo's eye. It was profoundly moving.

She closed the book for a moment and looked across at Thomas. He was sat in the swivel chair, his socked feet up on the desk. One hand held a letter, and the other arm was propped between his forehead and the arm of the chair, his hand rubbing his forehead slowly as he read. Occasionally he would shift his position slightly when he turned a letter over to read the other side. It was so quiet she could hear him breathing and sigh softly every now and then.

Jo returned to the book.

Following his wife's death, the young man who was a writer, struggled his way through funeral arrangements and finally the funeral itself. The graveside scene reminded her of her grandmothers' funeral and how she had stood under the umbrella with Marie, the cold rain streaming down around them. She sympathised with the grief-stricken man in the story and felt for his loss.

By lunch time, she had to stop. Her emotions were in turmoil, and she had used all the tissues she had in her pocket. Thomas swivelled around hearing her blow her nose. He smiled.

'Don't say anything,' he said, looking at her slightly tear stained face. 'Not until you get to the very end. Ok?'

'Ok,' she sniffed. 'How are the letters going?'

'They are beautiful, aren't they?' he said, picking one of them up. 'I can tell they loved each other very much. What did your grandfather do, it sounds like it was something horticultural from the hints in the letters?'

'I believe he had a small nursery at some point. At least, he did when he was first married to my grandmother, probably where I get my green fingers from. Sadly, he died when I was quite young, and I think the nursery fell into disrepair then the land was sold off for housing. I wish, in a way, I had asked my grandmother more about him. You don't think about that when you're young though do you? And then people die and it's all too late to find out.'

'Mm…I suppose you're right. I must ask Dad about our family history, get him to record any stories about relatives from long ago. You never know, our French ancestors might have even known each other.'

'That is quite a strange thought. Makes me feel all goose bumpy.' She shivered.

'Let's go down for some lunch,' he suggested. 'And then I was thinking we could spend a bit of time out in the garden this afternoon. The rain never materialised, did it? Maybe I could cut the grass, it seems to have come back to life after the last lot we had.'

'I don't know Mr Arnaud,' she said as he carried her downstairs, 'you'll be after my job soon.'

'I don't think so, you haven't seen me use a mower yet!'

They passed the afternoon in the garden. Jo sat on the steps in the middle watching and directing as necessary as Thomas pushed the mower back and forth creating neat stripes. He was a bit cack-handed with the edging shears but eventually he finished and came over to join her on the steps. The sun had come out and she lay back on the path, knees bent, feet on the top step, looking at the sky above.

'Phew. I'm exhausted!' he said, lying down on the path next to her. 'How do you manage to do this all day?'

She laughed.

'I suppose I'm used to it, besides I enjoy it. Jobs are always easier when you enjoy them. A garden is always changing so no two days are ever the same. I never get bored.' She breathed in and closed her eyes. She felt the warmth of the sun on her skin and a slight breeze ruffle her hair splayed out on the path around her head. When she opened her eyes, it was to see Thomas propped up on one elbow studying her. She turned her face to him and caught his gaze. Gently he ran one finger down the side of her face.

'Your bruises have almost disappeared now,' he said softly.

She put up her good hand to brush his fingers away and he took hold of it, raising it to his lips where he placed a kiss on the back of her hand. She felt a tingle travel all the way down her arm and quickly pulled her hand away. Really, he had no business do that when he was attached to someone else. She tried sitting up and found that it was not as easy as she had anticipated, making her ribs ache again. Thomas gave her a gentle lift from behind and eventually she was up.

'I'm going in,' she announced. 'I'll put the kettle on if you put the mower and tools away.'

'Do you need help up and down the steps?'

'No,' she called behind her. 'I'll go in the front door.'

That evening Jo sat at the table in the kitchen instructing Thomas step by step how to make an omelette. The result wasn't too bad in the end, although he seemed to use nearly all the utensils in the drawer in the process.

'We've got quite a few apples ready to pick in the orchard. Maybe I should get you to try making an apple tart next time,' she suggested. 'My grandmother used to make the best apple tart ever. I'm sure the recipe is in her book in the trunk. I must look it out.'

'Sounds a bit ambitious to me,' he replied.

'It's quite straight forward really. Just a case of following the instructions in order. You can do it if I help you, we can't go and eat at the pub every night. I'll end up as fat as a pudding by the time your dad and Barbara get home. Have you heard from them?'

'Yes, Dad phoned last night; I forgot to say, they send their love. Wanted to make sure I was looking after you properly. Am I?' He looked at her across the table.

'Just about,' she smiled, teasing him. 'I don't know how I'm going to repay you actually. You've all been so kind.'

'I'll think of something. How about we try a bit more music before bed?'

The next few days were spent in a similar fashion. They would spend their mornings in the studio, Jo reading her way through the book and Thomas reading the letters and scribbling ideas down on paper every now and then. In the afternoons, they would garden, Jo doing as much as she was able with one hand and Thomas helping her. Sometimes Thomas would wheel Jo down to the church or shop, picking up ingredients for the next cooking lesson.

On one visit to the shop, Ellen gave them an invite to her 'leaving do' at the pub the following Saturday.

'I know I'll be back lots,' she said, 'but I thought it would be nice to have a small get together, just the four of us and Mum.'

Pushing Jo back to the house in the wheelchair, Thomas was suddenly puzzled.

'What did Ellen mean, the *four* of us and her mum?'

'You, me, her mum, Ellen herself and Bob,' said Jo.

'Why Bob?'

'They are an item now. Didn't you know?' she said, leaning her head back in the chair to look at him.

'Ah, the old doctor, nurse romance thing,' he laughed and then twigged. 'So that's what all the giggling was about in the car on the way home from Oxford the other day.'

'Well, yes, amongst other things,' she replied. 'I'm happy for them, they make a very sweet couple. Swapping quiz teams was a good idea.'

'Yes, in more ways than one,' he agreed. 'I get you on my team now.'

'I think you might live to regret that.'

'I think not,' he said cheerfully as they arrived back at the house.

Lounging in the studio, the comfy leather chair was a very lovely place to read a good book. When she wanted to take in what she had read, she could just lean back and close her eyes or stare out across the garden, seeing only the pictures the beautiful words had painted in her mind.

The young man in the story had been struggling with his grief. The house he had once shared with his now dead wife had become like a tomb of memories too hard for him to live in. He had sold up and gone to live in the country, buying an old cottage in a small village with a large derelict garden in which he was determined to bury himself and his grief for the rest of his days.

The advent of a young dark-haired gardener to the house that stood opposite his in the village began to change his solitary world however, when she had volunteered to tidy the garden for him and he had reluctantly agreed.

Jo looked up and noticed that Thomas had been watching her as she read. He had a puzzled expression on his face as if he were trying to work out what she was thinking. She smiled at him but said nothing and carried on reading. Over the next few mornings, she read on, hardly wanting to put the book down. Parallels were beginning to dawn on her between the characters in the book and the reality she was living.

Captivated by the gradual restoration of the garden outside his window, the solitary young man gradually spent more time there himself. Entranced not only by the wonders of nature being restored, but by the gardener who got him to talk to her about his wife. She drew metaphors for him between the healing of a soul broken with grief and the healing of a garden being restored to new life.

Saturday came around and Jo and Thomas made their way to the pub for Ellen's leaving celebration. She would be gone in a week, just before Henri and Barbara were due to return. Mrs West hogged much of the conversation as she always did. Jo thought Bob looked a little downcast again.

'Cheer up,' she said to him when Mrs West and Ellen had gone to the ladies' room. 'She'll be back for weekends as often as she can.'

'I know,' he sighed. 'I'm going to miss her though. It will be back to just me and Eunice for a while.'

'Well, you know what they say about absence,' Thomas chipped in. 'Makes the heart grow fonder. Besides, you've got us around and the quizzes will start up again soon. I'm sure the time will fly by.'

'I suppose you are right. How much longer have you got in your casts, Jo? Must be about two weeks?'

'Yes, they said they would x-ray again just to check and then I should be good to go. I can't wait. My skin feels horribly itchy underneath sometimes.'

'No knitting needles now!' Bob warned. 'It causes so many problems when people try to poke things underneath their casts.'

'I'll be a good girl, Doctor,' she said, batting her eyes at him in jest.

Hugs and promises of keeping in touch were exchanged at the end of the evening as the two companies parted ways outside the pub and Thomas pushed Jo back home.

'You're right, they do make a very sweet couple,' Thomas agreed as he took her up to bed.

The following days were spent as before. Jo reading while Thomas worked. He had finished the letters now and begun writing. Clearly, he had found something inspirational to write about. Jo didn't ask him what, or whether the letters had been useful as she did not want to intrude into his creative mood. She continued to read 'Restoration.'

The young writer was now spending as much time as he could in his garden and had begun to keep a journal of how it changed through the seasons and what projects he and the beautiful dark-haired gardener had been working on. The relationship between the two characters had changed over time from wariness on his part to a strong friendship between them. Now he looked forward to being with her and missed her when she wasn't there. The grief in his heart had begun to heal. In the undergrowth, they had discovered an old fountain which together they cleaned and restored. It was seeing the crystal-clear droplets of water splashing into the bowl beneath that he had first realised he was falling in love with his now best friend.

Jo put the book down on the sofa and hobbled out onto the balcony. She looked towards the far end of the garden and the naked Adonis fountain. The water in the bowl had mostly evaporated over the summer, but it was still quite green. It would be a good idea to clean it out and see if it could be restored. There must be pipework somewhere and a valve to turn the water supply on. Maybe they could look at it that afternoon. Thomas joined her on the balcony.

'Do you want to take a look at the fountain later?' he asked as if he had been reading her mind.

She smiled, maybe he knew where she'd got to in the book.

'It's going to need a lot of scrubbing to get it clean. Is it broken in anyway do you know?' she asked, turning to face him.

'Not that I know of. Dad switched it off a few years ago, the summer Mum died, and we just never turned it back on. I suppose it got a bit neglected like everything else in the garden. There is a valve under one of the paving slabs where all the pipe work is connected. I think the key is somewhere in one of the stables. I'll find it after lunch.'

'Do you think he would mind us turning it back on to see if it works, or will it remind him of your mum too much? I don't want him to come back tomorrow morning and be upset or anything.'

'I don't think he will be upset at all. I hope when he gets back, he will have more than a fountain to keep his thoughts occupied. Shall we get lunch? I guess we will need to find some scrubbing brushes afterwards.'

Cleaning out the fountain proved to be a filthy job. Thomas scrubbed the bits Jo could not reach from where she sat in the wheelchair working her way around the edge. She had covered her arm cast in cling film to try and keep it clean, but even with that and a glove wedged over the top, the rest of her was bespattered in green gunk by the time they were done, as was Thomas. They rinsed the basin out, syphoned off as much of the dirty water as possible and then refilled it before they stood back to admire their handiwork. It had taken them the entire afternoon apart from a few short breaks for drinks. Thomas located the valve under one of the nearby slabs and stood ready to turn it on.

'Are you ready?' he called, turning the valve with the long-handled key.

For a while, nothing happened and then there was a prolonged gurgling and bubbling sound before a spurt of water emerged from the vase on the shoulder of the Adonis. As the water splashed into the bowl below, they both gave a spontaneous cheer.

'I think you need a bath.' Thomas eyed her up wickedly and looked at the fountain.

'You can't. I'll dissolve,' she laughed knowing what he was thinking and waving her cast at him. 'But you're right, I think we both do. Time to stop for the day, it's getting late.'

'How about a shower then the pub, I'm too tired to cook,' Thomas suggested, wheeling her into the house.

'Sounds good to me,' she said.

Jo collapsed into bed that night, full after a good meal at the pub and tired after their efforts cleaning the fountain that afternoon. She fell asleep thinking about Thomas' book and sparkling fountains and wondered if the man in the story had blue eyes too.

Jo didn't know which way to run. Wherever she looked whiteness surrounded her, filling her eyes and mouth until she couldn't see or breathe. She tried to push it away, she had to find them. She was sobbing now in despair, why couldn't she ever get to them? Why was there no one to help her? Please God let her find them just this once. 'I'm sorry' she shouted out into the void. 'I'm sorry!' she sobbed.

'Jo, wake up!'

Startled, she opened her eyes to see Thomas sat on the side of the bed. He was holding her arms still. The pictures of her nightmare still swirled around her brain and she burst into tears unable to control herself. Thomas gently put his arms around her and held her close smoothing her hair until she was calm.

'Alright now?' he asked, holding her away from him.

She nodded. 'I'm sorry.' She didn't know what else to say.

'Jo what is all this about? You have to tell me. I can't bear seeing you like this night after night.'

'I'm sorry, I get nightmares occasionally. It's nothing to worry about really. I'm probably tired after all the work on the fountain.'

'Jo, you do this every night.'

She looked at him not quite understanding what he had said. She knew she had nightmares sometimes, but not every night, surely.

Thomas sighed and ran his fingers through his already untidy hair. He looked tired.

'You have had a nightmare of some degree or other every night you have been in this house since you came out of hospital. When you had the flu, you had one, and on the way back from France. Usually, you just talk in your sleep, sometimes I've had to wake you up when it looks like you're about to do yourself another injury. I am not moving off this bed until you start talking and tell me what is going on. This is to do with your parents, isn't it?'

'I can't tell you,' she said, shaking her head at him. 'Please don't ask me.'

'Jo, whatever it is you can trust me. I can help you.'

'You can't, no one can,' she said sadly.

'Why is that?'

'Because I killed them,' she whispered.

Chapter 21

It was out now. It was almost a relief. Jo looked at Thomas' stunned face staring back at her. She didn't know how long they sat there; it seemed like an age. Then, he got up and paced over to the bathroom and back. Without saying a word, he scooped her up and took her downstairs, depositing her on one of the chairs at the kitchen table. She sat feeling wretched and miserable and not knowing what to say while he made them both mugs of tea. Once seated he turned to her.

'Tell me everything, from the beginning,' he said gently.

She hesitated for a few minutes, staring at the wobbly reflection of the kitchen light on the surface of her tea. This was it she thought, looking up at Thomas who was waiting for her to say something. When he heard her story, she would lose a friendship that she suddenly realised she valued very highly and inside her heart began to break.

'I was fourteen at the time,' she began. 'Just at that awkward age when you think you are more grown up than you are, when you think you don't need your parents so much, but actually you need them more than ever. I suppose I was very fortunate as a child. My parents both had good jobs. Dad was an architect and Mum a teacher and I was their only child. I think they spoilt me a bit really, to make up for not having any brothers or sisters, but I had lots of friends at school who often came around to our house. I was never lonely or anything, it was a very happy childhood. Then we went on a family holiday to Switzerland. Skiing in Verbier. We had been a couple of times before as a family. Both my parents were good skiers having learnt before I was born, but I never really enjoyed it. I just didn't feel very confident. I used to pretend that I was enjoying myself because I knew Mum and Dad loved it so much.' She breathed in deeply and blew out through her mouth trying to remain calm. This was not going to be easy. She had tried to forget the events of that holiday for the last eleven years.

Thomas reached across the table and took her hand.

'Take your time, I'm listening.'

'It snowed hard for the first couple of days when we arrived and most of the guests sat around getting to know each other, joking about how we were going to be snowed in for the whole holiday. There was another English middle-aged couple, a Mr and Mrs Bradshaw, who had kind of attached themselves to us. They were quite well spoken, "posh" my father would have said. They liked to show off about how many resorts they had skied at all over the world and tell people how expert they were about the mountains. The second afternoon when it was snowing, I remember Mrs Bradshaw telling me all about avalanches and how they were caused by loud noises.' Jo shut her eyes. 'I can hear her voice in my head now.' A tear slipped down her cheek and she let go of Thomas' hand to brush it away. 'The third day we were there, it had stopped snowing overnight, it was a beautiful sunny morning. Everyone was eager to get out on the slopes, make the most of the remaining week. Mum and Dad wanted to try one of the more challenging runs and I said I would too because I wanted to make them happy. It wasn't going to be a fun week for them, stuck on the baby slopes, which is where I belonged really. Anyway, off we went up the ski lift, Mum and Dad all excited and me pretending that I was. When we got to the top, they started skiing and I kind of slithered in a very ungainly fashion off to one side out of their way. I fell halfway down, I just seemed to go headfirst into the snow. I don't know why though, I thought I was going quite slowly and carefully. Anyway, when I lifted my head off the snow, there was a whole patch of blood on it and more blood dripping from my nose. Of course, the first thing I did was to open my mouth and yell for my mother.'

Jo had to stop for a minute. Closing her eyes again, she could hear the roaring in her ears, feel the panic rising in her.

'The next thing I remember was this awful rushing sound.' Jo began to sob as she continued. 'I…I looked up and there was just a wall of whiteness coming towards me. Bits of ice and snow pelting me, swirling around me, pushing me over and over. I couldn't see anything. And then it seemed to stop almost as if it had passed me by and for a while there was no noise at all. It was eerie. I was semi-buried but ok, apart from a pain in my leg.'

'Your parents?' said Thomas quietly.

Jo shook her head.

'They didn't find them until the next day,' she sobbed. 'They must have caught the main force of it. I knew it was my fault. I had shouted for help and made the avalanche happen, just like Mrs Bradshaw had said.'

'What happened to you, Jo?' He encouraged her to go on.

'I was rescued quite quickly and taken to the nearest hospital, where they found I had fractured a bone in my leg. I kept asking the nurses about my parents, but no one would tell me anything. My grandmother arrived the next day and told me about Mum and Dad. I think I must have gone into complete shock. I couldn't speak for about two weeks afterwards. It was the realisation of what I had done, I think.'

'Did you ever tell anyone that you thought you had caused it?'

Jo shook her head.

'I couldn't. Imagine what it would have done to Grand-mere if I told her I had caused the accident. That her daughter was dead because I had shouted and caused the avalanche. I just couldn't break her heart like that. So, I buried it inside myself.'

Thomas shut his eyes, trying to imagine what it must have been like for her. 'What happened after that, Jo?'

'My grandmother took me home with her. She took care of all the legal stuff and left me with her neighbours while she travelled to England and dealt with the funerals. Mum and Dad were cremated and buried in the churchyard up the road from our house. The house and its contents were sold and then Grand-mere came home. I could see what a strain it had been on her. She seemed to have aged almost overnight. It's understandable really, parents aren't supposed to bury their children, are they?' Jo stopped, remembering her grandmother's face when she had come to collect her from the neighbours who, although kind enough, were complete strangers to her. 'We never really talked about my parents much after that. I didn't want to upset her further and it was just too painful for me. I was sent back to England to boarding school, away from everyone I had ever known. I spent my holidays in France with Grand-mere and term time in England. That's when I took up the piano in earnest. Music became something I could express my emotions through, it was both my release and my sanctuary. Nobody knew what was going through my head but me, it became my own inner therapy if you like, and a way of dealing with the world and what I had done.'

'Why didn't you continue with it?'

'I wanted to, I applied to the Royal College of Music and got a scholarship place. Then Grand-mere had her first stroke. I had to go back to look after her, she had done everything she could for me, and I loved her so much and had caused her such pain. Giving up my dreams seemed a small price to pay.'

'So where did the gardening come in?'

'My piano teacher at boarding school used to run the gardening club. She knew I had lost my parents. She suggested one day I come along, she thought it might help me and she was right. That was the beginning of it really. I learnt so much from her, Mrs Wiggins her name was. She was exceptionally kind. She gave me the set of gardening journals I've got on the shelf in the cottage. I used to read them at night. I'm sure all the other girls thought I was a bit weird, but I didn't really care, I wasn't much into fashion and make up like they were. The school had a small vegetable plot and some flower borders, and after our music lessons, she and I used to sit and plan what we could grow and what colours we could plant in the borders. It helped me come out of myself a little. Anyway, that's about all there is to it. Now you know why I don't talk about my parents.'

Jo picked up her tea to drink, but it had gone cold now, so she sat just staring at it in front of her. She didn't want to look at Thomas and see the disappointment on his face.

'And the nightmares? When did they begin?'

'I'm not entirely sure, probably from the very beginning. Sometimes I don't remember having them and just wake up with the duvet in a tangle or on the floor. Sometimes I do remember or wake up sweating as if I've been running hard, even though I haven't left the bed.'

'Do you always see the same things in them?'

'Pretty much, yes. There's always snow and a whiteness that I can't see though. I'm always looking for my parents, trying to find them, trying to run to them to say I'm sorry, but it's like I can never move. The whiteness fills my eyes and nose until I can't breathe, and I feel like I'm suffocating. I try to fight back but it always wins in the end.' Jo wiped the tears that had been running down her face with the back of her hand.

Thomas picked up the tea towel and took her chin his hand, turning her face towards him. Gently he wiped away the remaining tears.

'I'm so sorry,' Jo continued, 'to have been such a nuisance. I will pack my bags in the morning and leave before your dad and Barbara get here. I don't think I could face them and go through all this—'

She was silenced by his lips on hers. A soft gentle kiss that tasted of tears and sadness. Shocked for a second, she pulled back and looked at him in surprise as he sat back down in his chair.

'You will do no such thing, Josephine Stanton. I do not believe for one second that you were responsible for your parents' deaths. Of all the people I know in the world, you are the most thoughtful and caring and the least likely to cause anybody any harm,' he said firmly.

'But I shouted and caused the avalanche. I know it was my fault.'

'Avalanches can happen for lots of reasons. I cannot believe that a girl of fourteen shouting for her mother would cause one.' He got up and took her mug, tipping the cold tea down the sink.

'Well, I was there. I saw it happen.'

'Hm…Did you ever read anything about it afterwards, in the newspaper or the results of an inquest? I suppose there must have been one?'

'No.' She shook her head. 'I wasn't in a fit state afterwards and I knew it was my fault anyway. What was the point?'

He glanced at the clock, and she followed his gaze. Four o'clock in the morning.

'I think that you've talked enough for one night,' he said leaning back against the sink. 'You are not going to leave tomorrow or at any other time Jo, over this. I cannot believe the thought of doing so even crossed your mind. We are going to go back to bed now to get some rest before we welcome Dad and Barbara home tomorrow.'

'Are you going to tell them about this?'

'No. I think we can keep this to ourselves for the moment,' he sighed. 'Come on.'

Once upstairs, he rested her gently on the bed and tucked the duvet around her as if she was a small child. Then he got on the bed next to her and rolled over on his side to face her.

'You don't have to, I'll be alright,' she said, turning to face him.

'I know that,' he smiled, 'but I think you need the company tonight and I want to be here for you. Just in case.'

'Thank you,' she whispered before closing her eyes. 'That means a lot.'

The sound of a vacuum cleaner woke Jo the following morning. She hobbled out onto the landing and looked down. Thomas was hoovering the hallway, tidying up before Henri and Barbara got home like a naughty teenager who'd had a party while his parents were away. She smiled to herself and went to get dressed, then sat on the top step of the stairs and watched as he picked up a feather duster and flicked it around over the furniture. It was only when he began on the stairs that he noticed her watching him.

'Wow!' she said, impressed. 'Confidante and domestic god. Your talents are endless, Mr Arnaud.'

He smiled and came up the stairs to where she sat, feather duster still in hand and waved it at her.

'Sit there for too long and you'll get dusted too,' he joked. 'How are you feeling this morning?' He came and sat down next to her.

'Better, I think. I'm sorry about last night.'

'No need to apologise. I had suspected for quite some time there was something worrying you. Then when we went to the cottage and you wouldn't talk about your parents, I kind of put two and two together.'

'I've never told anyone before. I felt too ashamed really, and guilty,' she confessed.

'Do you feel better for talking about it?'

'I suppose I do, but it doesn't change anything does it? I still have to live with the fact that I caused my parents deaths for the rest of my life,' she sighed and changed the subject. 'Anything I can do to help with the cleaning?'

'No, I'm all done really. How about you help me make a cake this morning to welcome home the travellers later?'

'You know we'll have to change your name to Mary Berry soon,' she said looking at him in amazement. 'I will willingly help you, but I need coffee first, ok?'

Just as they had finished the cake and the last sprinkling of icing sugar had been wiped away, they heard the turn of a key in the front door.

'Hello all, we're home!' Barbara called as she came through the front door.

Thomas went out to help them with the luggage, and everybody came into the kitchen together to greet Jo.

'Oh! You look so much better!' Barbara exclaimed, giving Jo a hug.

'Yes, you do,' agreed Henri coming across to kiss her on the cheek. 'Maybe we should go away more often, eh?' he said, winking at Barbara.

'How was the holiday?' Jo asked in return. 'Did you have a fabulous time? Come and sit down and tell me all about it.'

'Tea?' said Thomas.

It was while they were sat at the table that Jo noticed Barbara's left hand as she cupped her mug of tea. On her fourth finger sat the most beautiful diamond and ruby ring.

'What is this?' Jo smiled as she picked up the older woman's hand to look at the ring and then at Henri and Barbara who were busy grinning at each other across the table like a pair of besotted young lovers.

'Barbara has done me the honour of agreeing to become my wife,' Henri said. 'About time we made things official, I think.'

There were more hugs and congratulations all around then. Thomas, Jo noticed, was not all that surprised.

'Did you know about this?' she asked him when they had all sat down again.

Thomas looked across at his father.

'He asked my permission actually,' he smiled. 'Don't know why, bit of a no brainer if you ask me. Welcome to the family again Barbara or would you like me to call you step-mother?'

'Oh no! Makes me sound like something out of Cinderella! Barbara will do just fine dear,' she laughed. 'Actually, we've got something we'd like to ask you both haven't we Henri?'

'Mm…Yes. Thomas, would you be my best man?' Henri turned to his son, who promptly shook him by the hand in willing agreement.

'And, Jo dear,' said Barbara, 'I would love it if you would be my bridesmaid. Would you?'

Jo was overwhelmed.

'Oh, Barbara I'd love that!' she exclaimed and went to hug her again. 'Have you set a date yet?'

'Yes, actually we have,' Henri replied. 'We oldies haven't got time to hang around you know. I rang up and booked the church as soon as Barbara said yes. We thought a Christmas wedding would be nice, not too long to wait but time to get everything organised. We've booked it for 27th December.'

'And the reception is going to be at that lovely hotel we took you to for your birthday. I'm so excited!' Barbara squealed and clapped her hands together which made them all laugh.

'Well, I think we could all do with a piece of celebratory cake after that,' Thomas declared, reaching out behind him to bring the cake to the table.

'Jo, have you been cooking?' Barbara asked.

'No, Thomas has. I just helped by reading the recipe. He's quite good, when he puts his mind to it. He can now make omelette, casserole and apple tart amongst other things. I haven't had to eat scrambled egg once since you left.'

'Good gracious Jo, you're a miracle worker,' Henri said, tucking into a generous slice. 'Barbara we must definitely go away more often.'

'Well, you know what this really means don't you Henri?' Barbara sat back in her seat.

'What's that dear?'

'It means that Jo and I can have nights out together to talk about weddings and girl stuff, and you and Thomas have no excuse to go to the pub!' she glanced across at Jo triumphantly.

Henri and Thomas looked at each other in shock while Barbara and Jo gave each other a high five and laughed.

Chapter 22

The next week became a bit of a whirl for Jo. Barbara and Henri were full of things they had done on their holiday including visiting Alain and Marie who had been shocked to hear about Serge. As far as they knew he had taken his annual leave and gone to visit his family and had no inkling at all that he meant to go to England and track her down. Henri had not elaborated about Maurice and the address label on the box. What was done was done and Serge had now paid the ultimate price.

Barbara told Jo and Thomas at elevenses one day how Henri had proposed. They had been at the chateau walking in the parterre garden. She had sat down on one of the benches and Henri had gone down on one knee there and then. Jo could imagine the scene so clearly and her thoughts drifted to what would have been planted in the beds at that time. Apparently, Barbara had had to help Henri up afterwards, which everyone except Henri found amusing, but still, it had been very romantic. She was so thrilled for them both.

There only seemed to be one morning that week when Henri and Barbara had gone out, that she found herself upstairs with nothing to do. She was keen to finish reading Thomas' book and knew she had left it in the studio. Knocking on the door she turned the handle and went in. Thomas was on his laptop, he quickly shut down the page he had been looking at and swivelled around to greet her.

'Mind if I come in?' she said. 'I need to fetch the book.'

'Let me get it for you.' He dashed over to the sofa picked up the book and came over with it in his hand. 'Jo, do you mind if you read downstairs this morning? I've got something I really need to concentrate on and a couple of phone calls to make. Would that be ok?'

'No problem at all. In fact, I might sit out in the garden and read. It's still warm out.'

Settling herself down on the bench, outside the shed, Jo picked up where she had left off in 'Restoration.'

Having realised he had fallen in love with the gardener, the man in the story had wrestled with his conflicting emotions. He loved the gardener who had brought both him and the garden back to life but worried he was betraying the memory of his dead wife. Uncertain of what to do, the man sat down and emptied out his feelings the only way he knew how. In a letter to his late wife.

It was such a beautiful letter Jo kept welling up, which blurred the words as she was trying to read. It took her four attempts before she could get through the whole thing in one piece.

The man poured his heart and soul out through his pen, recalling the good times he had enjoyed with her and how much they had loved each other but also how much he loved and admired the young gardener. She had given him a new life that he now looked forward to living each day. It was when he had finished writing and tried to imagine how his wife would reply to him if she could, that he finally found his answer. He was not betraying her at all. They had been loving and faithful to each other whilst together, but their time had now passed, their story was finished and closed. A new book was opening for him, full of hope and love. Finally, the man in the story plucked up courage and explained to the gardener how her friendship had helped him heal and that although he would never forget his wife, he was ready to love again if she would have him. Which, of course, she did.

Jo shut the book and lay down along the bench. Closing her eyes, she thought about what Thomas had written. It was a uniquely beautiful piece of work exploring loss, grief and ultimately healing through friendship and eventually love. She could see why it had been nominated for the Malling prize. The words he had chosen spoke to the very depths of her soul and pulled at her emotions. The characters, a mixture of realities of the family she found herself in.

She must have nodded off eventually as she was woken by Barbara standing over her waving a wedding magazine.

'I see Thomas gave you his book to read,' she said, sitting down as Jo sat up and swivelled her legs off the bench.

'Yes, I've just finished it in fact. Have you read it?'

'Yes, Henri and I took a copy away with us. It's beautiful, isn't it? But more to the point have you read the dedication?'

Jo hadn't, she usually didn't bother with the front pages, just dived straight into the start of the story. She picked up the book and found the dedication page.

'*To the woman who has been my inspiration since the day I met her,*' Jo read aloud. 'Gosh, Elaine must love that.'

Jo was still looking at the book when Barbara gave her a funny look and shook her head.

'Anyway, the reason I came to find you is, I need your help.' Barbara flipped open the wedding magazine which showed pictures of elfin featured brides with legs that were preposterously long for their tiny waisted bodies. 'I have no idea where to start finding a dress. They don't seem to do dresses in here for us slightly mature ladies who love their food a bit too much. Will you come with me to the bridal shop and help me find something that will not make me look like mutton dressed as lamb?'

'I would be delighted,' Jo said. 'When shall we go?'

'How about after you have your casts off tomorrow? You might feel more like trying on some bridesmaid's dresses then as well.'

'Let's get you sorted first,' Jo insisted. 'Then we can think about me. Did you have a colour theme in mind?' She was trying to think about how Ellen might approach this, after all, what did she know about fashion?

'Well, for me, probably ivory? I think I'm a bit too old for white, and it's not appropriate anyway,' she blushed. 'I was thinking maybe red for you, something that ties in with Christmas anyway.'

'This is going to be such fun, Barbara!'

The two women spent the next half an hour sitting on the bench flipping through the magazine talking about styles and materials. Jo felt a bit out of her depth, but Barbara was so understandably excited, it was contagious and hard not to get carried away with it all. Jo looked up at the house and saw that Thomas was out on the balcony on his phone. She waved and he waved back. At least, men only had to pop on a suit and wear the right coloured tie, it was so much easier for them she thought.

After x-rays had been taken and confirmed all was well, being cut out of the arm and leg casts was a huge relief to Jo, although finding she now had one disgustingly hairy and slightly paler leg compared to her other one was not so pleasant. Fortunately, Barbara, who had come with her, had warned her that this might be the case and she had brought a pair of long trousers to change into afterwards. Her ankle was still slightly swollen, but she was reassured that it would go down in time and with physiotherapy. The crutch was replaced with a walking stick and a physio appointment made for the following week. Then she was free to go for the day, dress shopping with Barbara after an early lunch of packet sandwiches at the hospital.

After trying on dresses in many styles and fabrics, Barbara found a full-length empire waisted dress in ivory crepe de chine that had a long-sleeved lace top and straight skirt which had a slit up the back. They both knew it was the one as soon as she came out of the changing room.

'Oh, Barbara you look like a Hollywood movie star from times gone by,' exclaimed Jo. 'It's truly beautiful.'

'It is rather nice, isn't it?' she said twirling around to each side to see how she looked. 'I think this is the one.'

'Are you going to have a veil?' Jo asked. She got up from the armchair she had been sitting in to look at some of the veils hanging on a rack nearby.

The assistant in the shop helped Barbara try on different lengths and styles but she settled in the end for a stylish fascinator which had just a short piece of netting over her face. It was perfect. Beaded ivory shoes and a faux fur wrap were also selected, and Barbara's look was complete.

'Now for you, young lady,' Barbara declared. 'Let's go upstairs to the bridesmaid section and have a look, shall we?'

It was surprising how many shades of red there were when it came to dresses. Bright crimson through to dark maroon. It seemed that nearly all the styles were available to be made up in any of the fabrics, the choice seemed almost endless. The assistant who had helped them downstairs brought up Barbara's dress so that they could find something that coordinated style wise.

Jo felt like she had been trying on dresses for hours before Barbara finally settled on the design and fabric she wanted. Figure hugging cherry red crepe de chine with a lace top and long sleeves, it had a lower neckline than Barbara's but the two went together perfectly. Satin shoes were chosen to be dyed a matching colour.

By the time the two women exited the shop, it was nearly closing time and they were both exhausted but still full of excitement. Jo didn't know how Barbara was going to contain herself for the next three months, however there was a lot still to organise which she guessed would keep her busy. Jo thought about what she would be doing in the next three months. Now she was cast free she could get back to the garden in earnest. She had been warned to take it slowly to start with and not to do too much heavy lifting but there was so much she needed to catch up on.

When they arrived home, it was to find that Thomas had made a casserole, even getting Henri to prepare some of the vegetables.

'We thought you might be a bit tired after your busy day,' he explained. 'Did you find a dress?' he asked Barbara.

'Yes, I did,' she replied, 'and we found a lovely bridesmaid's dress for Jo too.'

'What's it like?' Henri asked, coming over and giving his fiancé a kiss, potato and kitchen knife still in hand.

'Not for you to know until the day, cheeky, and don't go asking Jo either; I've sworn her to secrecy.'

'Girl stuff, I suppose,' Henri mumbled, going back to the sink.

Jo exchanged a smile with Thomas behind Henri's back.

'So how does it feel to be cast free now?' Thomas asked her.

'Amazing!' she said, sitting down at the table. 'Although I currently have one smooth brown leg and one pale hairy leg, which looks a bit weird.'

'That I have got to see,' Thomas said, coming over intending to lift the bottom of her trouser legs.

'Get off!' She pushed him away both laughing as she swivelled her legs under the table out of his reach. 'It also means I can move back to the cottage and get on with the garden properly again.'

'No more carrying you up and down the stairs then,' he said pulling a sad face.

'Stay for tonight and we'll help you move back tomorrow,' Barbara said. 'I think we are all a bit tired this evening and it's been a busy day.'

By the end of September, Thomas had started his job as guest lecturer at the university which took up a lot of his time, preparing lecture materials and even marking essays. Some days he didn't make it back for dinner in the evening. The rest of the time he squirrelled himself away in the studio, writing. Henri and Barbara were busy organising bits of the wedding and Jo kept herself out the way in the garden, weeding, storing the ripe apples in crates and tending the kitchen garden which was still producing crops in abundance. Jo thought that this was the most golden time of the year in the garden. An Indian summer sun hung in the sky making the tips of already turning leaves glow as if they were being set aflame. Michaelmas Daisies in purple hues glowed in mellow sunsets and the swallows finally departed for warmer African climes.

It was one Saturday morning that Thomas found her in the greenhouse.

'I've got something that I think you will want to read,' he said, passing her a large, brown envelope.

'What is it?'

'I'll leave it with you. See what you think. Come and find me in the studio if you want to talk about it.' He looked serious.

Well, that was as clear as mud, thought Jo as she took the envelope and watched Thomas as he walked back across the garden, hands in pockets.

Opening the envelope, she tipped the contents out onto the bench in front of her. Several sheets of paper fell out. The top one was a photocopy of a French newspaper article. The date at the top was familiar to Jo, burned into her memory eleven years ago. *Anglo-French couple tragically killed in avalanche.* The headline read. She felt her legs go wobbly. Gathering up the sheets, she went and sat on the bench outside the shed and noticed that her hands were already shaking as she held the paper to read further:

An English man and his French wife were tragically killed in an avalanche at the alpine resort of Verbier, east of Geneva, on Wednesday morning. The couple, who died at the scene are thought to be Mr Michael Stanton and his wife Amelie. It is believed one other person was taken to hospital as a result.

A police spokesman said, 'The avalanche occurred at 10:20 in the morning. It is thought that the heavy snow from previous days became loose and swept the couple away. I'm surprised that the ski run was open, and no avalanche warnings had been given.'

An investigation has been launched.

The deaths come after several days of heavy snowfall across Switzerland, which led to the loss of another skier in an avalanche in Gstaad.

Underneath the article was a picture of mountain rescuers digging in the snow. Jo closed her eyes and wondered what it must have been like for her parents. To be buried under the snow, not being able to get out. Taking a deep breath to stop herself crying, Jo looked at the next sheet of paper which was the findings of an inquest into their deaths. Scanning all the waffle at the beginning, which just seemed to reiterate the facts she already knew, Jo found the conclusions section:

A verdict of accidental death has therefore been reached. It is concluded that Michael and Amelie Stanton died as a result of asphyxiation due to carbon dioxide build up around their bodies, which were found fifteen feet under the surface; it is probable that they were unconscious by the time the avalanche came to a halt.

The cause of the avalanche is thought to be a combination of minor seismic activity in the area at the time and unstable snow conditions.

Seismic activity; that meant earthquakes, didn't it? Confused, Jo turned to the final sheets of paper. It was a report from the Swiss Geological Survey.

It was initially quite hard to understand and talked a lot about snowpack stratigraphy and vibration parameters. Then there was a list of minor earthquakes that had occurred near Verbier. One had been highlighted across the page. 10:19 am, Magnitude 3 on the day her parents had died.

Jo sat stunned for a moment. What did this mean? That she hadn't caused the avalanche after all, that it had been caused by an earthquake? That all these years she had blamed herself unnecessarily? She had to find Thomas.

Clutching the papers in her hand, she ran across the garden. Barbara was just coming out of the kitchen.

'Elevenses!' she called.

'Got to see Thomas!' Jo called back and dashed up the spiral staircase arriving breathless in the open doorway of the studio.

He had obviously watched her sprint across the garden and was waiting with outstretched arms, into which she flung herself, wrapping her arms around him in return.

'How did you...? What does this mean?' she began, breathless now not only from her run but from the almighty squeeze he was giving her.

'Come and sit down,' he said, releasing her at last.

They sat on the sofa together and he took the now slightly crumpled papers from her hand.

'It means, dear girl, that you are in no way to blame for the deaths of your parents. It was an accident.'

'How did you find all this stuff?' she said, looking at the papers in his hand.

'Ah, the internet is a wonderful thing,' he smiled. 'After digging out the newspaper report in the archives of the paper and knowing that further investigations happened at the time, it was just a case of making a few phone calls and waiting for people to email me the relevant documents. After I received the inquest findings, I contacted the Swiss Geological Survey, spoke to a very nice lady who looked out the data for the time the accident happened. There it was, plain for all to see. The most likely reason you fell over on the slope was the earthquake shifting the snow under you. By the time you called to your mother, the avalanche would have already been happening.'

She could see what he was saying, everything began to fall into place and make sense now.

Thomas continued, 'I also spoke to a colleague in the Geology Department at Oxford, pretending I was doing some research for a book. He said it was extremely unlikely that a young girl shouting would cause an avalanche. It would have to be a louder more strident sound, like an explosion or gunshot.'

Jo sat letting everything sink in again.

'So, it wasn't my fault at all,' she said, wiping a tear away. 'Oh, here I go again.'

'Yes, but happy tears this time?' he said, handing her a clean hanky from his pocket.

She nodded.

'It's weird, I've spent the last eleven years of my life blaming myself, avoiding thinking of my parents because it hurt too much, and I felt so guilty all the time. And now suddenly, I'm free from that, it's not hanging over me anymore and I have you to thank. You really are the best friend a girl could have. Thank you, Thomas.' She leant over and kissed him on the cheek.

He got up, walked over to the window, and looked out across the garden.

'Jo, how about visiting your parents' grave one day? Lay the past to rest once and for all. I think you might find it quite a healing process. I'd be happy to take you,' he said, turning to face her once more.

She thought for a while. She had never been back. Maybe now was the right time.

'Yes. That would be good. Maybe in a couple of weeks? Let me get my head around this first, it's all so new. I want to let it sink in properly.'

'Let me know when you are ready.' He looked at his watch, 'Let's go down for some coffee, shall we? I'm surprised Barbara hasn't come and poked her head around the door.'

'I saw her on my way up here. She must be wondering what's going on.'

'Do you want to tell them?'

'Not yet, if that's ok with you. Do I look as if I've been crying?' she asked as they made their way out via the balcony.

He put his arm around her shoulder and gave her a sideways hug.

'You look as beautiful as always Jo. Come on.'

On arrival in the kitchen, Barbara took one look at her and asked her if she was ok.

'Yes, fine,' she said brightly. 'Just a touch of late hay fever probably.' She caught Thomas' eye and she could see a smile play around the corners of his lips. She hated lying and knew she wasn't very convincing.

'You are a terrible liar,' he mouthed at her smiling and shaking his head when he thought Barbara and Henri were not looking. She only just managed not to spit her coffee out laughing and turned it into a cough instead.

'What's going on between you two?' said Henri looking up from the newspaper on the table.

'Nothing Dad, just *girl stuff,*' quipped Thomas, shrugging innocently, which only made her laugh and cough even more.

That evening when she returned to the cottage Jo sat by the trunk in the bedroom and took out the photograph of her parents and herself that Thomas had picked up before. She remembered her grandmother taking it on one of the rare occasions she had visited them in England, they had been so happy then. Jo made up her mind that she would always remember her parents like that from now on, happy and smiling. She stood the photograph up on top of her shelf of books.

Chapter 23

Two weeks later, Thomas and Jo set off for the town of Timsbridge in Hampshire where Jo had lived until the accident that killed her parents. Thomas had told Barbara and Henri that they were shopping for the wedding. He wasn't a very convincing liar either thought Jo, but maybe that was a good thing. She sat as he drove, looking out the window wondering how strange it felt to be visiting her parents grave for the first time. She had packed plenty of tissues in her bag as well as sneaking a bag of gardening tools into the boot of the car. She didn't know how well the graveyard had been kept or even whereabouts in it the grave was situated, only that it was in the churchyard up the road from their old house. It might be completely overgrown by now and she imagined having to hack her way through brambles in some dingy corner of the churchyard. She had picked a few late roses and some greenery which she popped in an old jam jar and wedged upright behind her seat.

'Are you okay?' Thomas asked, looking across at her quickly. 'You're very quiet.'

'Lots to think about, you know. It's weird, the last time I was in Timsbridge was the day we went on holiday. I had no idea that I wouldn't be back for eleven years.'

'I'm surprised you were never allowed to go back to your house to collect anything. It seems a bit cruel.'

'I know. I suppose my grandmother thought that was the best way to deal with everything. I was only fourteen, pretty traumatised by it all, broken leg and not talking, etcetera. I guess she thought it would cause more harm than good for me to go back home so she just sold everything. It must have been heart breaking for her to do, clearing out her daughter's stuff. The only things I've got from Mum and Dad are their wedding rings, a bit of Mum's jewellery and a couple of photo albums of me growing up that Grand-mere brought back with her.'

'Did you benefit from the sale of the house? I suppose strictly speaking that inheritance was yours.'

'Yes, I did, but I only found out about it when Grand-mere died. She didn't have much in the way of savings at all, as you know I had to scrimp together the money to pay for her care and all the bills. I think she may have used her savings from the sale of the nursery land to pay for my school fees. When I visited the notaire after she died, I found that I had inherited everything my parents had left. It had just been put away for me. If only I had known about the money before, life might have been a bit easier both for her and me. I don't know why she never told me.'

'Is that how you funded Ellen's university fees then?'

'Yes, I had this huge amount of money, that I didn't feel I deserved at all, sitting in the bank doing nothing. Ellen wanted a career but couldn't afford the training. It seemed like a perfect solution for both of us. I'm still glad to have helped her, I don't regret it, even now I know the accident wasn't my fault. I also have the money from the sale of Grand-mere's house. I so wished I hadn't had to sell it, but it was in the will, and I had no choice. I still have plenty if I wanted to buy a house somewhere or set myself up a little gardening business in the future.'

'Not planning on leaving us, are you?' Thomas asked her, a frown creasing his forehead.

'Not right away, but you never know what the future holds do you? You might not need me in a few years.'

He didn't answer her, she noticed. Maybe things were more serious between Elaine and Thomas than she realised. If they got married, she didn't think she could bear being treated as 'staff' by Elaine for the rest of her life even if it meant her having to leave Henri and Barbara too. Also, she was starting to think that her heart couldn't bear the thought of seeing Thomas and Elaine being all loved up. It was hard enough just thinking about the two of them together even if Elaine didn't seem to come to the house anymore.

Eventually, they reached the church and pulled into the small gravel car park next to it. 'St Michael and All Angels,' the sign said. Getting out the car and walking along the pavement to the entrance brought a whole load of memories flooding back. She had walked along this road so many times as a child; with friends, with her parents, on the way to and from school, it was so familiar and yet strangely alien at the same time.

'Feeling alright?' Thomas asked as they entered the churchyard.

'Mm,' was all she could manage as they started looking around the graves.

The church yard looked to be well kept, the grass neatly trimmed even around the oldest graves. Wooden benches, most of them with inscriptions for lost loved ones were dotted around for visitors to sit and enjoy the tranquil atmosphere. Following the main path around to the back of the church, Jo and Thomas discovered a section of newer, smaller headstones, many with urns of real or artificial flowers on them. Jo scanned the dates, working backwards until at last she found them. It was a simple grey granite headstone with their names and dates and 'Rest in Peace' engraved at the bottom.

Quietly, she knelt next to it and traced the letters of their names with her fingers, as if somehow, they would feel it and know that she had come at last. Thomas stood back and gave her space to grieve, her tears falling silently and unchecked. She suddenly felt all the loss of the last eleven years, the pain of separation between parent and child that she had almost forbidden herself to feel out of misplaced guilt. She turned to him and he came and wrapped his arms around her. They stood for a long while just being sad together.

Jo heard Thomas sniff and saw him reach into his pocket for a hanky, she looked up to find tears running down his face too.

'Look at the pair of us,' she sniffed. 'You're as bad as I am!'

'Can't help it,' he said wiping his eyes and then hers. 'It's all so sad. Besides, it's my turn to make you soggy.'

They both laughed at that.

I'll go and fetch the flowers, shall I?' he suggested, giving her a squeeze. 'You stay as long as you need.'

When he returned, Jo arranged the flowers as best she could. She stood up, took a deep breath and breathed out slowly.

'Enough,' she said after a while. 'Enough tears. I don't think they would want me to be sad anymore. We were always so happy as a family, Mum, Dad and me. I think they would want me to continue that. I know where they are and I can come and visit if I need to, but I need to move on. Can we go?'

'Whenever you like.'

They walked back around the church. Jo would have gone in to look around, but the door was locked. Maybe next time, she thought. She knew there would be one at some point in the future. On exiting the church yard, she turned to Thomas.

'Would it be ok to walk up the road a bit? I'd like to see our old house I expect it looks a bit different after all this time.'

'Sure. You're not going to find it a bit...upsetting?'

'I don't know, I just feel I have to. Part of the closure if you like.'

The two of them walked along the pavement in silence until they reached a tall beech hedge which opened into a small, gravelled driveway and a nineteen sixties style house. A balding middle-aged man was busy cutting the grass to the right of the driveway and looked up as they stopped to look at the house. He turned the mower off and came across to talk to Jo.

'Can I help you?' he asked.

'Sorry. I didn't mean to interrupt your mowing, it's just that I used to live in this house as a child. I'm just visiting today and thought I'd see how it had changed. I didn't mean to be nosey or anything. It's just that I had a lot of happy memories here.'

'Come in, come in,' the man smiled. 'I'm Derek Masters.'

They introduced themselves and shook hands.

'The wife and I have lived here for the last eleven years. Lovely house for bringing the kids up in. They're both at university now though. When did you live here then?'

'Um...eleven years ago,' replied Jo slightly awkwardly.

'Oh, then you must be the daughter of...Terrible tragedy that, terrible,' he said shaking his head. 'Read all about it in the local paper at the time. You must be the girl that was sent to France to live with the old lady that was selling the house then.'

'Yes, that was my grandmother. I was unwell at the time and never came back.' Jo didn't feel she wanted to tell him the whole story.

'Well, well, well. Come and have a look around. I bet it's changed a bit since you were here.' He went to open the front door.

'Do you mind if I don't come into the house, but I'd love to see the back garden if that's ok?' she said.

Jo didn't want to see the inside of the house, it wouldn't be the same anyway and she wanted to remember it as it had always been, not see the changes somebody else had made. But the garden was different. Perhaps her mother's greenhouse would still be there or her old swing. Following Derek down the side path, the back garden suddenly opened in front of her, she gave a little start of surprise.

'Oh! The tree's gone!' she exclaimed, unable to stop herself. 'Sorry I didn't mean that to sound like an accusation, I was just a bit surprised.'

'Ah yes, the old sycamore. Yes, that came down in a gale about…now let me see…would be about 5 years ago now, took the old greenhouse with it too. Lucky it didn't fall the other way onto the house really,' Derek said.

Jo looked down the garden to where the greenhouse had stood. Now there was an area of wooden decking with a set of modern patio furniture arranged on it. In fact, looking around, it didn't feel like the garden she had known at all. None of her mother's roses and pelargoniums were left. She suddenly didn't want to be there anymore. Time had moved on and it was time she did too.

She thanked Derek profusely for letting her be an intruder for a short while and wished him many more happy years in the house she had grown up in. With Thomas following, she walked back down the street to where they had left the car next to the church.

'Time to go home,' Jo said when they reached the car.

'Are you sure? Do you want to look around anywhere else while we are here?'

'No. It's funny, although everything is familiar and there are lots of memories, I don't belong here anymore. It's not my home, it's just part of my past. I think it's time to start looking forward, enjoy the life I have now. Leave the past in the past once and for all.'

'Excellent idea. Let's make a start by finding some lunch, shall we? My stomach is beginning to think my throat's been cut.'

They drove away from Timsbridge and found a small pub by the side of the road where they stopped and had lunch. The food was not as good as at The St George and Dragon in Oxbury, nevertheless it was warming and sufficient.

'What are you getting your dad and Barbara as a wedding present?' she asked Thomas as she ate her soup.

'I've been thinking about that. Dad says they don't want anything, just to have a nice day with friends and family and it's not as if they're setting up home for the first time. I was trying to think of something a little more outside the box. Have you thought of anything? We could get together and do a joint present if you like.'

'Mm…that would be nice. I was trying to think along the music line for your dad, but what do you give someone who already has everything? I thought maybe some nice pearl earrings for Barbara, as an extra "something new" on the day, to go with her dress.'

'We could find some cufflinks for Dad, possibly with a musical theme. How about we nip into Oxford this afternoon, do a bit of shopping then think about what we could add to those ideas?'

'Sounds like a plan,' she agreed.

The pearl earrings and silver musical note cufflinks were surprisingly easy to find. A small family-owned jeweller away from the main bustle of the High Street were able to supply both. It was one of those slightly old-fashioned shops where customer service was obviously important. Thomas had only to tell the proprietor what they were looking for and he replied with a 'I have just the thing out the back, one moment sir.' Items purchased, they wandered back to the main shopping thoroughfare to buy some wrapping paper and cards. Outside the card shop, a couple of students Thomas recognised from the University were busy busking on guitars. They were quite good. He stopped to put a few coins in the open case at their feet.

'Thanks Mr Arnaud!' they both called and carried on playing.

Watching them gave Jo an idea. She wondered how it would go down with Thomas and turned to speak to him.

'I've just had an idea about a sort of wedding present,' she said.

'I know what you're about to say, I think I've just had the same idea,' he replied grinning.

'Duet?' they both said at once and laughed.

A long discussion then ensued between them about what could be played and when, both deciding that it would be great as part of the service but that they would probably have to run it past Henri and Barbara first and see what music they would want after all, it was their wedding.

'That is a truly lovely idea,' said Barbara over dinner that evening. 'Isn't it, Henri dear?'

'Yes, did you have a piece of music in mind Jo?'

'Well, not specifically, we had a long talk but ended up agreeing it would be up to you two to choose. I don't know whether you've already chosen music and hymns yet for the service or whether you have a favourite piece you'd like played. Even if it's a piece that's not a duet to start with, I could probably arrange it so that it becomes one.'

'We haven't fixed anything in concrete yet,' Henri said, 'but I think Barbara has a favourite piece she would like to include.'

'Pachelbel canon in D,' Barbara said. 'My all-time favourite piece of music. Is it possible, do you think?'

'I'm sure it is.' Thomas looked at Jo and raised his eyebrows in question.

'I'll give it a go,' she answered.

'Want some help?' he said. 'We could play around with it after dinner, do a little improvising. Dad has the music I think.'

'Yes. It's in the pile somewhere.' Henri, waved vaguely in the direction of the living room.

So, after dinner Thomas looked out the music and they sat at the piano, Thomas taking the bottom section and Jo the top. Jo made pencil notes on the score every so often about how it would need to be adapted for four hands rather than two. Henri gave her some sheet music paper so that she could write it out properly when they had finished.

'This may take some time, leave it with me and I'll let you know when I'm ready for a proper run through,' she said to Thomas when she left for the cottage that evening. He had seen her to the front door to lock up after she'd gone, Barbara and Henri already having gone up to bed. 'Thanks for taking me to Timsbridge today, you were right, it was a very healing process and I'm so grateful that you were with me.'

'No more nightmares?' he asked.

'I don't think so, I've certainly felt better in the mornings the last two weeks anyway. Goodnight Thomas.'

It took Jo a couple of weeks to write out the music until she was fully satisfied that it would work as a duet. She had wandered down to the church occasionally to practise, not wanting Henri and Barbara to hear it until their big day. Thomas had been busy at the university, and she had hardly seen him since their day out. The garden had kept her busy at other times. Leaves from the woodland trees whirled their way to earth forming never ending drifts that Jo was constantly raking up. Dried oriental poppyheads scattered their gunpowder grey seeds each time the wind blew, and Jo knew that come the spring she would have a million tiny seedlings to deal with. The summer greenhouse crops were now at an end finally, and the compost heaps bulging with old plant material that would break down to produce rich, dark compost she could use around the garden next year.

Tidying the shed one afternoon Jo found Thomas' book that she had left in there the day she had finished it. She remembered that she had been distracted by Barbara and all the talk of wedding dresses, and then the revelation about her parents, and had never actually told Thomas that she had finished it. She picked it up and made her way up to the studio via the spiral staircase. She looked through the window to see if he was there, but he wasn't, so she made her way back down and into the house through the kitchen. Barbara was busy looking at wedding cake recipes and Henri reading through the proofs of the wedding service newly arrived from the printers.

'Is Thomas around?' she asked. 'I need to return his book, with all the wedding excitement I never told him I had finished. He wouldn't let me talk about it until I had read the whole thing, you see.'

'He's gone up to London for the week,' Henri said. 'It's to do with the Malling nomination, he won't be back till Friday, but he left this for you.' He handed her a white envelope.

'Sit down dear, I'll pour you a cup of tea,' Barbara said, exchanging looks with Henri.

Clearly to Jo they both knew what was in the envelope. She sat as instructed, opened the envelope carefully and drew out a gilt-edged invitation card reading it aloud:

Mr Thomas Arnaud kindly requests the pleasure of your company at the Malling Prize Book Awards evening on Friday 30th November at the Burton Hotel London. Black Tie, it said at the bottom.

Jo looked at Henri and Barbara who were grinning like Cheshire cats.

'Looks like you are going to have to go dress shopping again,' Barbara said excitedly. She looked at Jo's slightly puzzled face. 'You do want to go, don't you?'

'Yes, I'm honoured that he's asked me. Are you coming too?'

'No dear, just you. He's asking you to be his "plus one",' she explained as if it was perfectly obvious.

Jo was even more puzzled.

'Why hasn't he asked Elaine if he's only allowed to take one guest? After all, he dedicated the book to her, and they are an item. Aren't they?' Jo hesitated and looked between Henri and Barbara, she suddenly felt as if she was missing something that everyone else understood.

Henri rolled his eyes and looked at Barbara as if to say, 'will you explain, or shall I?' Taking Jo's hand, he looked into her eyes sincerely.

'No, ma petite. He dedicated the book to *you*. As for Elaine, you can ask him about her yourself when he comes back on Friday.'

Jo was speechless. She picked up the book and looked at the dedication page again. *To the woman who has been my inspiration since the day I met her.* Then she looked at Henri and Barbara and back at the book again. She went all floaty and lightheaded as if coming down in a lift too quickly.

'Holy Moly!' was all that came out of her mouth. Nobody had ever said anything so beautiful about her in her entire life.

'You haven't got long to find a dress, dear. The thirtieth is the week after next. We had better go shopping tomorrow. There's a good shop in Oxford that does evening dresses.'

'Actually Barbara, no need. I already have just the thing,' said Jo, still undecided as to whether she should accept. She then spent a good while explaining how she had come to buy an evening dress, much to the mirth of Henri and Barbara.

Chapter 24

Thomas arrived home late on Friday night, long after Jo had gone to bed. So, it was not until early Saturday morning that she made her way, book and invitation in hand, up to the studio. She knew he was in there; the light was on, and she had seen him sitting at his desk from the garden below.

'Good morning, you're up early, a bit dark still for gardening, isn't it?' he said as he slid the balcony door open to let her in.

'No, it's fine. It always looks darker outside when you're inside with the light on anyway. I've come to return your book and say thank you for the invitation.'

'What did you think of it?'

'Book or invitation?' she asked.

'Book first. Come and sit down.'

She sat in the leather armchair which had been turned to face the desk. Thomas sat in the swivel chair waiting for her reply.'

'I loved it, Thomas. It was so beautifully written. The words you used were so poignant and painted such meaningful and clear pictures in my mind. I felt for the young man losing his wife and then burying himself in the country like that. You know it made me cry. I'm glad it had a happy ending though. I'm not surprised you were nominated.' She didn't feel she could ask him about the parallels she saw between fiction and real life that would be for him to explain.

'All good stories should have a happy ending, especially that one.' He was looking at her carefully as if trying to read her thoughts. 'Did you read the dedication page?'

'Yes, eventually, after Barbara pointed it out to me. About that, your dad said…' she trailed off, it was just too awkward, and she couldn't bring herself to say it. She looked out the window not wanting to look at him.

'That I dedicated it to you?' he finished for her.

'Did you?' she whispered looking back at him.

He sighed.

'What do you think?' he said softly, smiling at her as if the answer was obvious.

She didn't know what to think any more.

'When I first read it, I assumed you had written it for Elaine.'

He looked puzzled and a little surprised.

'Why would I dedicate it to Elaine?'

'Because…she is your other half…isn't, she?' This conversation was getting way too awkward, Jo thought as Thomas laughed out loud.

'Goodness Jo, what on earth made you think that?'

'I don't know, maybe it was the passionate kiss she gave you in the kitchen that day or the fact that you stayed over with her after the housewarming party. I don't know, it's none of my business anyway. Look, here's your book back.' She stood, flustered, put the book on the desk and made to walk over to the balcony door. She had to get out of there.

He caught hold of her arm and waylaid her.

'Jo, wait! Let me explain.'

'There's really no need.'

'Well, I need to know whether you are coming as my date next Friday at the very least.'

'Do you really want me to?'

'Jo,' he said standing up and enveloping her in one of his all-encompassing hugs and virtually pinning her to the spot whether she wanted to be or not. 'I want you to come more than anything in the world. You are…my best friend and the person I most want to share this with whether I win or not, as long as you are there, with me, that's all that matters.'

'Really?' she squeaked into the front of his jumper.

'Josephine Stanton, you are a complete goose sometimes. What am I going to do with you?' He let her go and held her face in his hands. 'Please say you'll come.'

'Ok. Yes, then. I'll come with you. Thank you for the invitation.'

'Good.' He kissed her on the forehead and let her go. Walking over to the desk he picked up his diary and looked inside. 'I have to be up in London again this week. So, I will see you on Friday evening in the lobby of the Burton Hotel at six-thirty sharp. I've booked a room for you so you can change when you get there. I'm not sure when all the shenanigans finish afterwards but you might get some sleep before breakfast,' he smiled. 'Make sure you wear a posh frock, there might be a few members of the press around.'

Thomas left for London again the following day and the week seemed to drag by endlessly for Jo without him. She kept mulling over his reaction when she had said she thought Elaine was his other half. His surprise had been genuine she was sure but thinking about it, he had never actually denied it. She knew what she felt for him now was more than friendship, but she was an old-fashioned girl at heart and not about to possibly embarrass or humiliate herself by making the first move in case she had read this all wrong.

Barbara had insisted on taking Jo to the hairdressers in the week so that she could be taught how to put her hair up nicely and then invited Anne around on the Thursday evening to do her nails. It was all a bit overwhelming and new to Jo, but she had to admit the results did make her look and feel good. She hadn't shown anyone the dress but secretly tried it on again one evening just to make sure that it still fitted and then zipped it up in the cover again ready for Friday.

As it happened, Henri and Barbara drove her to London on the Friday afternoon. They had got last minute tickets to see a West End show that evening and although not booked into the Burton, had promised to meet them in the lobby at six thirty to see them off to the ceremony.

'We're too nervous to sit around and wait for news at home,' explained Henri. 'Better to go out and enjoy ourselves. Thomas will let us know any results by text, I'm sure.'

They dropped Jo, her dress and suitcase at the entrance promising to see her later. She walked in through the door of the hotel, held open by a liveried doorman who immediately called to a bellboy to come and help. Her baggage was promptly taken off her hands like she was the most important guest they had ever had. Standing just inside the door she realised that this was a very grand hotel indeed. Everywhere polished surfaces gleamed, glittering chandeliers hung from the ceiling and a beautiful curved wooden staircase filled one end of the vast lobby area. To her right, an expensively dressed couple lounged in armchairs next to a lavish flower arrangement. The whole place reeked of opulence and luxury. She had worn a casual pair of trousers and jacket to travel in and felt distinctly out of place and underdressed. The bellboy, on seeing her hesitation, pointed her in the direction of the main desk which stood to her left. Jo thought about the dingy motel in St Malo which was the last place she had stayed with Thomas, there really was no comparison.

'May I help you, Miss?' asked a cheerful concierge, dressed likewise in a smart uniform bearing the hotel name and logo on the breast pocket. Jo noticed her name badge, 'Janet Carter.'

'Yes, thank you. I have a reservation. It might be in my name, Jo Stanton, or it might be in the name of Mr Thomas Arnaud.'

'Ah yes, room 112 on the first floor.' She turned around and picked a key off the hook handing it to Jo. 'Mr Arnaud says he will see you in the lobby at six-thirty. Jamie here will see you up.' She smiled at Jo and indicated the bell boy who was still hovering behind her with the luggage.

'Thank you, Janet,' she smiled back and followed the bell boy up the staircase.

On reaching her room, he took the key and opened the door for her carrying her case in and hanging up the covered dress on the outside of the wardrobe. She tipped him, not sure whether that was the one thing or not. He didn't object and thanked her, closing the door behind him.

The room was sumptuous. A huge double bed with the crispest, whitest sheets Jo had ever seen stood against one wall. The rest of the furniture was grand and slightly antique looking with gold metal scrolling along the tops of the doors and around the handles. Two comfortable looking armchairs sat either side of a small table in front of the window and a dressing table stood against the wall opposite the bed. On it was the most beautiful bouquet of red roses. There was a card attached to them. Jo picked it up and read it. *Thank you. Thomas x.* How lovely! she thought. Then she noticed another envelope propped up against the bottom of the vase. 'Jo' it had written on it in Thomas' handwriting. She picked it up and, kicking off her shoes, flopped onto the bed to read what was inside. There were two sheets of paper. The top one read:

Jo,

Before I see you tonight, I wanted to set the record straight and explain a few things that I feel were left unsaid last week. You need to know the truth about my relationship to Elaine. There never was or has been at any time a romance between us. I believe she wished there to be at one point, the kiss you witnessed in the kitchen was, believe me, all on her part and I set her straight about my feelings afterwards. The night of the housewarming she got so drunk that she passed out. I could not with a clear conscience leave her on her own, so I put her to bed and dozed in the chair all night. She is quite a lonely woman who needs friends. But that is all I will ever be to her.

Well, that cleared that up. She turned to the second sheet.

Darling Jo,

Yes, the book is dedicated to you. It is all about you Jo, you are my inspiration and have been since the day I met you. You are the beautiful dark-haired gardener who restores not only gardens but lives as well, bringing hope and joy. From the first moment I saw you, I knew I loved you. I wanted to be your friend, heal your hurts, make you laugh, have my arms around you every moment of the day. It has always been you, Jo, always and only. The question is will you, Jo, like my gardener in the book, take on me and restore the hopes of this lonely writer?

I love you, Jo Stanton. Please say yes.

Thomas x

He loved her? She closed her eyes and thought back over the last ten months. He had never said it in words but saw now that he had told her in a thousand different ways, through friendship, constantly being by her side, helping her, in the way he made her laugh and the little gestures that had made her think, in the way he played music to her and with her, in the way he had found out about her parents and healed her from years of guilt and misery. She had seen it in his eyes so often and just not recognised it. Oh, how blind she had been! Yes, of course he loved her, and she suddenly realised that she loved him too.

Jo lay back on the bed and hugged the letter to herself. She glanced at her watch, time to get her skates on. Whatever happened this evening, she wanted to look her best for him.

At six twenty-eight precisely, Jo took a last look in the mirror. She hardly recognised herself. She had done her hair in a low chignon and woven a few pieces of ivy through it as the hairdresser had suggested, quite fitting for a gardener she thought. Barbara had lent her a pair of dangly greenstone earrings, and she wore the necklace Thomas had given her for her birthday. The green velvet dress swirled deliciously around her ankles. A touch of makeup and dab of her favourite perfume later and she was ready. She had never felt so elegant. Carrying the wrap and her small clutch bag in one hand she made her way along the corridor and down the staircase to the lobby.

She saw Thomas with Barbara and Henri standing at the bottom of the stairs. Henri saw her first and nudged his son who turned to watch her come down the stairs. Thomas was dressed in a dinner jacket and bow tie and looked incredibly handsome. Wanting to savour the moment and the look on his face, which was priceless, she took her time descending the stairs.

'Hello Thomas,' she said when he didn't say anything and just stared at her.

'Jo, you look…stunning!' he said at last dropping a kiss on her cheek. The look he gave her made her insides melt.

'Well, don't you make the perfect couple,' said Barbara taking her phone out and getting them to stand together for a few photos.

'Jo, you look ravishing, make sure my son looks after you tonight, eh?' Henri said as he gave her a kiss and shook hands with Thomas. 'Let me know what happens as soon as you've got any news.'

Henri and Barbara took their leave, and Jo and Thomas were left staring at each other. Suddenly, he hugged her to him.

'I missed you so much this week,' he whispered. 'Did you read the letters?'

'Yes,' she was not able to hold back a smile.

'And?' he said, holding her away and searching her face for an answer,

'Ah! Mr Arnaud. I wonder whether you've got time to give us a short interview,' said a female voice, followed by a microphone waved fairly close to his face. 'Frances Button, YBC News.'

Jo made a 'well go on' face at him. She could give him her answer later.

For at least the next hour, Jo stood by while Thomas answered questions from various reporters. Some armed with Dictaphones, others with microphones of various sizes and colours and even a few with camera and sound crews. As more nominees and their guests filled the lobby, they were shepherded into a large reception room towards the back of the hotel where drinks were brought around by waiters dressed smartly in black and white. In a short gap between interviews, Thomas introduced Jo to his editor Rosemary and her husband Lawrence. Rosemary was about fifty and dressed in a royal blue floaty affair, her husband looked decidedly older and had a slightly henpecked expression. He was obviously uncomfortable in black tie as he had the habit of running a finger around his collar every so often.

'It's lovely to meet you at last Jo. Thomas has told me so much about you,' Rosemary smiled.

'He has?' Jo managed to say, glancing over at Thomas who was busily chatting to yet more reporters.

'Never stops! And then there's the book of course,' she continued. 'He's told me all about how he came to write it.'

'Oh, yes.' Jo wasn't sure what to say. It didn't matter, Rosemary was in full flow.

'About how you helped him when he had writers block and told him to write from the heart about things he cares about? And him watching you working in the garden restoring it back to life. So clever of you. His last three books were good but darling, this is in a different league altogether. You are obviously good for him, stick around, won't you?' She spied someone over the other side of the room and waved at them. 'Got to go, see you later Jo.' And she wafted off with her husband in tow who merely raised his eyebrows at Jo and smiled.

Seeing Jo on her own Thomas reached out his hand and drew her to his side. The reporter looked at her for a second and then held out the microphone towards her, while her photographer took pictures of them.

'And you are?' she demanded.

'Jo Stanton,'

'And what's your relationship to Mr Arnaud?'

Thomas looked at her with eyebrows raised and a slightly amused expression on his face.

'I'm his gardener,' Jo replied, smiling back at him.

'Oh,' the reporter said, not very impressed, and then the penny dropped, and she looked at Jo's dark hair. 'Oh!' She looked between the two of them. 'Tell me more then, Mr Arnaud, is Miss Stanton here your muse for the gardener in your book? Is this work slightly autobiographical?'

'I couldn't possibly comment on that at the present time,' he said laughing.

'Miss Stanton? Anything to say about that?'

'No comment,' she said, blushing.

The photographer snapped away with his camera, the flashbulbs were almost blinding. They were saved any more questions by an announcement asking the members of the press to retreat so that the nominees and their guests could go into dinner. Thomas grabbed her hand and led her towards an open double doorway on the on the other side of the room which people were beginning to filter through.

'Cheeky beggars, reporters,' he said, leaning towards Jo. 'They'll want to know my inside leg measurement next.'

She couldn't resist.

'What *is* your inside leg measurement, Mr Arnaud?'

'I am shocked at you, Miss Stanton! Shocked!' he teased as they went through into the other room. 'But if you are very good, I'll tell you later,' he whispered which made her blush and laugh at the same time.

The room was vast and as opulent as the rest of the hotel. Jo didn't think she had been in so huge a room in her life or seen so many people all in one space dressed up in their finery. At the far end of the room, there was a stage with a rostrum in the middle and a large screen to one side ready for the awards to be announced later. In front of that, an open wooden dance floor. Thomas hadn't said there was dancing later, perhaps, that was what he meant by 'shenanigans.'

They were seated at an enormous round table, one of about forty. Jo was sat in between Thomas and Lawrence, with Rosemary and about eight other people she didn't know. Everybody around the table introduced themselves. Most were in the publishing business or were writers. Thomas seemed to know all of them. When Jo explained that she was a gardener, she could see their eyes flick between her and Thomas, making the same assumptions as the reporter earlier. However, to her relief, they were too polite to ask any further questions.

Dinner was served, once everyone was seated. She chatted happily throughout the meal with Lawrence, who she discovered had a love of gardening himself and had travelled extensively in France. He had many stories to tell and turned out to be a surprisingly good dinner companion. Thomas was busy talking to the couple seated next to him and it was not until the coffee was served that they got to talk to each other. Jo looked at the programme of awards, several copies of which had been left on each table. Fiction was last out of eight categories; it would be a long and nervous wait for Thomas. Finally, the stage lit up, the screen came on and a hush descended as the chairman of the Malling Book Awards Committee introduced himself and gave a brief speech on the history of the prestigious award.

Each category was introduced by the author who had won the previous year, who then gave a short speech about the importance of their genre to the world of literature. Different celebrities who were themselves authors, then announced the four finalists in each category, their pictures and the covers of their books coming up on the screen each time. Sometimes a short piece of their work was read out or a pre-recorded interview with each author played on the screen. The previously winning author then drew a card from a golden envelope and announced the winner who went up on stage to collect their award amid a round of cheers and applause. The new recipient finally made a short speech of thanks.

Everything seemed to go on for ages and Jo could feel Thomas getting more nervous the nearer they got to his category.

'Are you ok?' she whispered to him.

He nodded and took hold of her hand under the table not letting it go as the final category was announced. The Malling Prize for Fiction. This was it.

Jo watched as each of the finalists was introduced. It was strange seeing Thomas' picture up on the screen, hearing his voice come through the sound system as he talked about how he had written the book, drawing on his life experiences of grief and writing from his heart about the garden restoration. She squeezed his hand and he returned it, neither of them looking at the other, both with nerves on edge. At last, the golden envelope was held up and opened. She could feel her heartbeat pounding in her chest and held her breath in anticipation.

'And the winner of this year's Malling Prize for Fiction goes to…Mr Thomas Arnaud for *Restoration*.'

Chapter 25

Jo squealed in delight and turned to Thomas who was almost frozen in shock. He looked at her in disbelief for a second then they were both on their feet, arms around each other.

'I'm so proud of you. Well done, Thomas,' she gasped. 'Go! Go and get your award!' she said, pushing him towards the stage, while the entire room rose to their feet in a standing ovation. The clapping seemed to last forever as Thomas made his way through the tables and up onto the stage, many friends or acquaintances shaking his hand or giving him a slap on the back on the way.

Jo watched as he shook hands with the chairman of the Malling Book awards Committee who handed him the award. Thomas stood at the rostrum then, removing a note card from the inner pocket of his jacket. The room hushed and people sat waiting to hear his acceptance speech.

'Mr Chairman, members of the committee, ladies and gentlemen, thank you. I am truly honoured to have been chosen amongst such a great line up of finalists, all worthy winners themselves. There are several people to whom I owe thanks for this award. First of all, my editor Rosemary, for her endless patience and all at the publishing house, for taking me on in the first place, thank you. To my father Henri and his fiancé Barbara, who have given me endless love and encouragement to fulfil my dreams of becoming a writer over the years, I am truly grateful. But there is one person without whom this book would never have been written. She is my inspiration, my best friend and the person who makes me want to be the best version of myself on a daily basis. Jo, this is for you.'

It felt to Jo as if the entire room swivelled their eyes in her direction before once more erupting in a standing ovation. She watched through blurred vision as Thomas made his way back towards her. Putting the award down on the table he swept her up in a hug and spun her around before putting her down and kissing her in front of everyone. The onlookers cheered and clapped even more wildly as a result. She was sure her face was completely scarlet by the time he finished but she didn't care. She was just so thrilled for him. The clapping gradually subsided as Thomas hugged Rosemary and shook hands with the other people around their table. The Chairman announced the end the awards proceedings and the beginning of the after awards party.

Thomas came back around to Jo, took her hand, and pulled her towards the dance floor.

'Come on,' he smiled, 'winners have to start the dancing, it's tradition.'

'You never told me about that!' she hissed at him through smiling teeth.

The music started and he put his arm around her waist and pulled her close.

'Didn't I? How remiss of me,' he whispered into her hair as they stood together with the other award recipients and their partners in the middle of the dance floor, the music swirling around them. Gradually more couples joined in until eventually after two or three pieces of music, it was quite crowded.

'As much as I would like to stand here all night, dancing with you, I think we have an unfinished conversation that I would dearly like to conclude right now Jo. How about we find somewhere quiet for a few moments and catch our breath?'

'Good idea,' she agreed.

He led her out through one of the side doors that had been opened to let some cooler air in, and she found that they were on a terrace overlooking a small but neatly laid out garden at the very back of the hotel. There were steps that led down onto a path that ran around a square of grass, with raised concrete flower beds around the edge. A tiny oasis in the middle of the metropolis. Tucking her arm through the crook of his, he led her down the path towards the back of the garden, away from the hubbub of the party inside. It was surprisingly quiet and peaceful.

'So, you read the letters then?' He turned to face her.

'Yes Thomas,' she said looking into his eyes, still blue in the dim light of the garden.

'Will you go out with me Jo, let me date you, be my better half with a view to a more permanent arrangement in the future?'

'Yes, Thomas I will,' she smiled up at him.

He kissed her then, like he had done before on her birthday. It was sweet and passionate, making her insides tingle and stars explode in her brain.

'I love you Jo Stanton,' he murmured. 'I have loved you for so long, my dearest, sweetest friend.'

'And I love you, Thomas Arnaud. I think I have for a while now and just didn't want to admit it,' she sighed and rested her head against him.

Their tranquillity was short lived however, interrupted by the appearance of Rosemary on the terrace, who was clearly looking for Thomas. She came down the path where they were still standing, arms wrapped around each other.

'Sorry to intrude on this romantic moment you two, but I need to steal Thomas away for a few more interviews and photos with the Chairman and all the other winners. You can come too, Jo, and watch if you'd like. It's in the room we were in before dinner.'

'It's ok. I'll sit with Lawrence inside and let you have your moment of glory,' she said to Thomas.

'You will not,' he insisted. 'You are coming with me every step of the way in this.'

'It's your book!' Jo retorted. 'You wrote it and fully deserve all the credit and attention.'

'Oh dear,' Rosemary laughed. 'I haven't started your first argument, have I?'

'No. Jo will be coming with me,' Thomas replied. 'Dammed independent woman,' he growled at Jo softly and she laughed as he took her hand and they followed Rosemary in.

As it happened, Jo was required for a few of the photos, as was Lawrence, but the rest of the time they sat together at the side of the room, chatting about life in general and drinking coffee which a very kind hotel employee had brought around for them. Jo texted Henri and Barbara, she knew they would still be up waiting for news. They replied with 'Congratulations! See you both tomorrow.' It was well after one in the morning when Thomas was at last free and came, award all boxed up under his arm, to collect her. The party was still going on the dance floor although by now a lot of people had drifted away.

'Want to stay and party?' she asked him.

'No, I think I'd like to find somewhere quiet for a while and let this all sink in. It's been a bit of a crazy night one way or another,' he said, undoing his bow tie and top button. 'Your room or mine?'

'Yours?'

They walked, arms around each other up the staircase and along to Thomas' room which was the other side of the corridor to Jo's. Thomas unlocked the door to let them both in. It was a remarkably similar room to her own.

'So, what's next for you?' she asked and flopped back onto the bed after kicking off her shoes.

'Spending a bit of quiet quality time with you for a start.' He kicked off his shoes too and joined her on the bed. He rolled onto his side propping his head up with one arm and then leant over to kiss her, gently pulling her close with his other arm. He stopped and looked down the length of her body. 'That dress is very…er…revealing,' he said at last, grinning at her. 'I like it.'

She looked down to see what he meant and immediately went to sit up, intending to adjust the skirt to cover her legs, but he stopped her and looked at her legs more closely. 'Jo Stanton, are you wearing stockings?' He put his hand on her knee slowly sliding it up her thigh, watching her reaction as he reached the top of her stocking.

'Stop!' she giggled putting her hand on his to stop him going any further. 'What is it with men and…and…women's legs…and stockings?' She felt all flustered, but nicely so.

'It's not any woman's legs and stockings, just you and yours, Jo. You know you'll have to get used to it. I can't help the way seeing your legs make me feel.' He shrugged and kissed her then flopped back on the bed with his arms behind his head.

'The next few days are going to be so busy, and I just want to spend them with you.' He sighed. 'The publishers have a whole host of radio programmes and even a couple of TV slots they want me to do interviews for. It's all good publicity and I can't turn it down.'

'When does that all kick off then?' she asked, turning to him.

'Tomorrow afternoon at one. There's a car picking me up for a Radio Four interview.'

'Then I think you had better get some sleep Mr Arnaud and I will see you for breakfast,' she said, sliding off the bed and slipping her shoes back on.

'I'll walk you home then.'

Jo laughed.

'I'm only across the corridor.'

'Well, you can't be too careful, can you? Besides, I need to give you a goodnight kiss.'

Although the bed was soft and comfortable Jo only managed to get a couple of hours sleep, she kept thinking over the previous evening and how exciting everything had been. She woke early to shower and wash her hair. At eight-thirty, there was a soft tap on her door, she opened it to find Thomas, looking like he had had less sleep than she'd had.

'Good morning beautiful.' He greeted her with a lingering kiss. 'Ready for breakfast?'

'Did you get any sleep?' she asked him on their way downstairs.

'About an hour probably, too many things to be excited about. You?'

'About two, I definitely need coffee this morning.'

Many of the staff who had heard about Thomas' Book Prize congratulated him as they made their way to the breakfast room, where they were seated at a table for two and their order taken. Jo only felt like coffee and toast, but Thomas went for the full English.

'Got to keep my strength up, busy week ahead,' he explained. He reached into his pocket and brought out a small box which he pushed across the table towards her. 'This is for you.'

Jo took the box and opened it slowly. Inside was a small, folded piece of paper and a pair of rose gold heart shaped earrings that matched her necklace. Putting the earrings down, she opened the paper. 'For Romance', it said.

'Thomas that is very romantic, thank you.' She squeezed his hand across the table. 'Just as well I said yes last night.' She put the earrings on straight away. 'What would you have done if I'd said no?'

'Waited, tried to persuade you, I don't know. I didn't think you would say no. I think we both know how we have felt about each other for a while, I just needed the right opportunity to ask you out properly.'

'Well, as first dates go, last night would be extremely hard to beat. I suppose I won't see much of you this week at all will I?'

'No, I should be done with all the immediate stuff by Thursday at a pinch, possibly Friday. I spoke to Dad this morning. He suggested they pick you up on their way home. I haven't told him about "us" yet.'

They paused their conversation as the food was delivered and Jo poured herself a coffee.

'Thomas, would you mind if we didn't tell them about us until after the wedding?'

'Why is that?' he said through a mouthful of bacon and egg.

'It's just that there's less than a month to go and I want Barbara and Henri to be the centre of attention and enjoy all the build up to their big day. I don't want to steal their thunder in any way. It should be a special time just about them, not about whether their best man and bridesmaid are a couple.'

'You mean I can't come and ravish you in the kitchen at elevenses?' He pulled a face which made her laugh.

'No, I'm not sure that would be appropriate in front of your dad anyway. It just means we would have to be a bit careful, that's all. It's only for a short while. We can tell them when they come back from their honeymoon.'

'I hear what you are saying. Josephine Stanton you are a hard woman, but a kind-hearted and thoughtful one. I will do my best.'

'Thank you. What time are they picking me up?'

'Eleven.' He looked at his watch. 'In two hours' time. Better make the most of you while I can then.' And he fixed her with a stare that made her insides do somersaults.

Just as Henri, Barbara and Jo were leaving for the pub Friday evening, Thomas arrived home, looking tired but still buoyant. It was hard for Jo not to rush into his arms immediately and carry-on walking with the others to the pub, where he said he would meet up with them after a quick change. She had spent the week trying to listen to every radio broadcast that he had done, and they had all sat together and watched him on The One Show on the television. Henri's pride in his son was palpable. He had collected every newspaper cutting and picture about the award ceremony itself, including one of her and Thomas dancing together afterwards. She had not even been aware that the picture had been taken.

As the four of them sat in the pub together and ate their meal, she could feel Thomas' eyes on her and tried as best she could to treat him as she always had, as a friend, so as not to give the game away to Henri and Barbara. She asked him questions about his week as if he had not texted her about ten times every day to tell her what he was doing and how much he missed her already.

As people arrived for the quiz there were lots of hugs, handshakes and congratulations for Thomas who bought everyone their drinks for the evening. He had brought his award with him, and it was passed around for everyone to have a look at. Jo went and sat with Bob on the settle before the quiz began.

'When is Ellen home for Christmas?' she asked him.

His face lit up.

'End of next week. I feel like I haven't seen her for ages. I think even Eunice is missing her.'

Jo laughed, 'Dear old Eunice.'

Bob turned to her and spoke in a low voice.

'I've read the book you know, as has nearly everyone in the village. It doesn't take a lot of imagination to put two and two together, writer plus dark-haired gardener plus dedication page.'

'And?' she said as innocently as possible.

'As one of your best friends I have to warn you that speculation is rife Jo. Mrs West has not stopped on the gossip mill since she read the last page. Anything you want to tell me?'

'Not right now.' She couldn't keep the grin from her face and knew by his expression that he'd guessed.

'About time too, is all I can say. Jo I've known for a long time how he felt about you.' He lowered his voice to a whisper as Mrs West arrived through the door.

'How?' she asked surprised, she had not fully realised until last week.

'The night of the attack, while I was on the phone, I overheard him telling you he loved you. Of course, you were completely out of it, and it didn't register with you.'

She looked at him in surprise and he nodded and smiled.

'Bob, you have to keep this to yourself, at least until after the wedding. Promise me, please?'

'My lips are sealed. Want to join my team for the evening?'

'I think I better had. I will tell Henri you're lonely or something and I'm trying to cheer you up. Oh, I hate lying.'

'But I am lonely, and you do cheer me up, so you won't be,' he said as she made her way over to talk with Henri. Thomas was still at the bar chatting.

After everyone had taken their places and Gerry had tapped his glass to start the quiz, from the settle, Jo watched as Henri told Thomas that she wasn't going to be in their team that evening. Thomas mouthed the word 'later' at her across the room and then grinned at her which she tried hard to ignore.

Tom and Anne arrived slightly late, as usual, and during the interval wanted to hear all about the award ceremony, so she was kept busy all evening after that.

As they arrived back at the house afterwards, Thomas made the excuse of wanting to talk to Jo about the wedding music and followed her into the cottage. Henri and Barbara returned to the main house.

Before she had even closed the door behind them his arms were around her waist. He pushed her back against the wall and kissed her passionately and deeply almost taking her breath away.

'I missed you,' he said, pulling her jacket off her and dropping it on the floor and then doing the same with his own. He found the bottom of her shirt, gently pushed his hands up underneath it and ran them over her bare skin which made all sorts of sparks fly about in her brain. 'Do you mind?' he asked, kissing her neck. 'Or is this too much too soon, do you want me to stop?'

She put her hands up to his face and made him look at her.

'It's not too much too soon, and I don't want you to stop, because I love you and I trust you. I'm not sure I'm quite ready to go all the way though. Is that ok with you?'

'Of course,' he said. 'After all this is only our third date, and I need to seduce you properly first before I have my wicked way with you.'

She couldn't help giggling.

'Third date?'

'Yes, the award ceremony, breakfast in the hotel and now,' he said and continued kissing her.

'I'm not sure I would class this or breakfast a date,' she laughed. 'We haven't been anywhere or done anything as a couple tonight.'

He stopped finally and let her go.

'Well, why don't you put the kettle on, and make us both a cup of tea and then we can say that I came to your house for tea, and we can call it a date. I'll sit over on the sofa and ogle you while you do all the hard work.'

He kissed her on the forehead and then went over to the sofa, kicking off his shoes and swinging his legs up until he was reclining comfortably watching her. By the time she had made the tea and brought it over to him, he was fast asleep, head resting back against the cushion. Jo sat on the other sofa and watched him, letting him sleep until she had finished her tea. She thought how utterly lucky she was to have met someone like him and wondered what the future held for them both. Finally, she went over and woke him gently.

'Some date you are, Mr Arnaud. Come on, time you went home to bed,' she said and pulled him up off the sofa handing him his coat after he had put his shoes back on. He was very apologetic, and after a quick goodnight kiss, vowed he would take her somewhere nice for their fourth date.

Chapter 26

Barbara came over to the cottage the following morning, and asked Jo whether she would like to help decorate the house ready for Christmas, which was an invitation she could not refuse. Henri sat at the piano and played his way through a selection of Christmassy music while the two women put together a large artificial tree. They spread the branches to make it look bushy and sang along to a few carols that they could remember the words to. Thomas did not appear until ten, coming downstairs in his dressing gown looking deliciously tousled and still a bit sleepy.

'Sorry, did we wake you?' asked Henri tongue in cheek, knowing full well that they had.

'Kind of, but it was a nice sound to be woken up by. I think the past week has caught up with me at last.' He yawned and wandered into the kitchen returning with a cup of tea and a mince pie.

'Those were for elevenses,' Barbara scolded him.

He came over and kissed the older woman on the cheek.

'I know, but they are too nice to wait for, Barbara, and this is breakfast for me.' He sat on the sofa and watched as Jo and Barbara trailed some lights around the tree and switched them on to check they were working properly. 'Jo, I think we ought to spend some time practising today, don't you?'

For a split second, she wondered what he was referring to and then she saw the wicked smile that played around his lips, and she understood his meaning perfectly.

'Yes,' she said confidently, not talking the bait, 'We could wander up to the church later if you like, when you are dressed. Barbara is there any other help you need with the wedding?'

'Well, I'm making the wedding cake this afternoon, but I haven't made the Christmas cake yet. Normally I make it in November, but I seem to have got a bit behind this year. Can't think why,' she said looking over the top of her glasses

240

at Henri who shrugged innocently and then winked at Jo. 'Would you give me a hand with that tomorrow dear?'

'Why don't Jo and I do that, Barbara?' Thomas suggested. 'She's quite a good teacher in the kitchen you know. I'm sure we can manage a Christmas cake between us.'

Barbara looked between the two of them. 'It's a deal, if you don't mind Jo. Henri and I can go up to the church then and finalise all the details with the vicar's wife about flowers and so forth. Thank you, Thomas. Oh, and don't forget that you need to write your speech for the reception, so do you Henri.'

'It's on my to-do list this week,' said Thomas getting up to go and get dressed. 'I'm getting quite good at speeches, aren't I, Jo?' he called back as he left the room.

'He's in a funny mood today,' Barbara shook her head.

'Must be the fame gone to his head,' Henri said, looking at Jo quizzically.

She made herself busy hanging decorations on the tree and did not answer.

Thomas and Jo sat side by side at the piano in the church with the music of Pachelbel's Canon in D propped up on the stand in front of them. Jo had already learnt her part, so it was just a case of bringing Thomas up to speed. She counted them in, and he began to play. The first eight bars were his alone and then she joined in with the top half of the music, their fingers moving swiftly over the keys, touching occasionally when they played notes close together. It was a strangely intimate experience, their combined efforts making a single piece of music. Jo closed her eyes and listened, feeling Thomas move with her, it was even as if they breathed in time with each other. When last chord sounded, it seemed to hang in the air around them.

'What do you think of the arrangement?' she said, turning to him at last.

'It's perfect, but I think we need *lots* of practise before the wedding.'

'Do you? I thought we were rather good for a first time through,' she said ignoring his double meaning deliberately. 'Do you want to go through it again a couple of times now and then we could come back in the week and give it another go?' Jo tried to focus on the music sheets in front of her.

He swivelled himself around on the stool, so he was straddling it and put his arms around her pulling her close.

'You know what I mean,' he said turning her face to his and looking into her eyes.

'Thomas Arnaud please remember where you are, and that anyone could walk in at any moment.'

He kissed her anyway.

'We are in a church, and God is love so they say, and I love you. People kiss at weddings, nothing wrong with kissing in a church.'

She pulled a face.

'There is if we are seen, I'm afraid Bob has guessed already. He said he's known for a long time, since the attack. Apparently, the village is rife with gossip as everyone has now read or is busy reading the book and putting two and two together to make 64. I have sworn him to secrecy, I think he's trustworthy.'

'Actually, they would be putting two and two together and making 4,' Thomas corrected her. 'But I suppose you are right, we ought to be careful if we are to keep this under wraps until the wedding.' He swivelled back around ready to play the piano again. 'But after the wedding, Jo, I am going to take you down to the Stores and kiss you in front of Mrs West and then everybody will know for certain. Shall we go through this again then?' and he began to play.

The following afternoon, having soaked the fruit overnight, Jo talked Thomas through Barbara's Christmas cake recipe and helped out by zesting an orange and weighing out ingredients ready for him to add to the mixture. They worked well as a team and sat at the table while it was cooking in the oven discussing whether they would be able to manage cooking Christmas lunch together to give Barbara an easier few days before the wedding. When Barbara and Henri returned, they put the idea to them. Barbara was delighted and readily agreed.

The next couple of weeks passed in a blur of activity. Ellen returned from university and Jo managed to arrange a day out shopping to catch up on how things were going for her. Jo had some shopping to do that she knew her fashionista friend would be able to help with plus she needed to find Thomas a Christmas present. Ellen guessed straight away that things had changed between her and Thomas but gave her solemn word of honour not to breathe a word, especially to her mother.

Jo and Thomas had managed to get out for a couple of surreptitious dates, going to Oxford or just driving anywhere to be able to spend some quality time together with the excuse of Christmas shopping or practising the music at the church. But it was more usual for him to come and find her in the garden and just help her in whatever she was doing. If she were in the shed or greenhouse, he would wrap his arms around her from behind and kiss the back of her neck while she was busy which sent delicious tingles down her spine every time. Sometimes if Jo knew he had been writing all morning she would make a cup of tea and take it up to the studio just so she had the excuse to be with him for a few minutes. Thomas in return would pull her down onto his lap and kiss her while his hands explored her body. It was becoming increasingly hard to keep everything a secret.

In the week before Christmas, Barbara and Jo went together to collect their dresses for the wedding while Thomas and Henri collected their suits. All the plans for the wedding were in place and during the last few days there was nothing to do but enjoy Christmas itself and await the big day on the twenty-seventh.

Christmas morning arrived and Jo was up early. Dispensing with her usual t-shirt and jeans she put on a dress that Ellen had helped her choose, red and fitted with a scooped neck and three-quarter length sleeves, the straight skirt finished just above her knees. Walking into the kitchen of the main house, she reached for an apron ready to get started on the preparations for lunch. Thomas arrived in the kitchen at the same time and, taking the apron off her, made her twirl around.

'Are you trying to drive me crazy?' he said. 'I can't believe you are going to wear that dress all day and make me pretend that we are just friends still. Honestly, Jo, it's a bit unfair.'

'I could go and change if you prefer,' she teased putting the apron on again. He stood behind to do it up for her. 'Besides, the apron covers nearly all of it.'

'Not from behind it doesn't,' he said wickedly running his hands over her bottom.

The sound of someone coming down the stairs made them jump apart and Thomas made himself look busy by picking up the kettle to fill it while Jo scooted over to the fridge to take the turkey out, both of them trying to hide their giggles as Henri and Barbara came into the kitchen together and wished them a Happy Christmas.

The day passed in a busy whirl of cooking, eating, swapping gifts and playing music and by the time Jo and Thomas had cleared up after tea they were both tired. Jo had given Thomas a posh fountain pen for his next book signing, and he had given her tickets to the RHS Chelsea Flower Show in May, an event she had always wanted to go to.

Entering the living room, they found that Henri and Barbara had nodded off on the sofa together.

'Let's leave them for a bit, shall we?' Thomas suggested and drew her back into the kitchen. 'Fancy a late-night stroll around the garden, just you and me?'

'Sounds lovely,' she agreed.

After putting on coats, they slipped quietly out of the kitchen door and on through into the moonlit garden beyond. The air was cool, and a slight breeze swayed the silvered silhouettes of the plants lit by the star tossed sky above. They strolled arms around each other down the partly illuminated path.

'Do you really believe in love at first sight?' Jo asked after a while.

'Absolutely. I knew the first time I set eyes on you. It was the same with Dad and Mum. He knew straight away; she took a little persuading. We Arnaud men know what we want when we see it.'

'And then I went and spoilt it all by going out with Bob.'

'I have to say you had me worried there for a bit, Bob had a bit of a reputation as a lady's man back then. I thought I might have lost you for good, and then Dad told me about the conversation you had with him and Barbara.'

'He did?'

'Jo, there's something you should know,' he hesitated.

'Go on,' she encouraged him. 'Sounds like a confession.'

'Dad and I kind of plotted this whole thing together. He saw the look on my face when I heard you sing, at the chateau, he knew straight away how I felt about you. That's why he offered you the job.'

'What? But I couldn't have accepted it if Grand-mere hadn't died. What would you have done then?'

'Stayed with Alain for a bit, got in your way a lot. Generally made a nuisance of myself until I won you over with my charms. I would have found a way.' He smiled and hugged her close.

Jo laughed.

'But Grand-mere might have lived to ninety.'

'Then I would have bought a house in France, and we would have looked after her together. Jo I'm serious, I will prove to you one day that love at first sight exists.'

'I can't imagine how you are going to do that.'

'You'll see.' They had reached the fountain at the top of the garden now and Thomas swung Jo up into his arms suddenly. 'Fancy a dip?'

'Don't you dare!' she laughed knowing that he wouldn't really go through with it. 'This dress was expensive, and I don't want to snag my…'

'Stockings?' he finished for her. Putting her down gently he bent down and ran his fingers from her feet up her legs and then over the top of her dress until they were entwined in her hair. He pulled her close for a kiss. 'I think we had better go in before I get carried away, don't you? Besides, your legs are cold and it's getting late.'

The morning of the wedding Jo was up early as usual. She knew as soon as the others were up it would be all systems go and she wanted to take a few moments to herself in the garden, just enjoying the calm it always gave her. Wrapping up warmly she slipped through the gates and wandered down the path to the kitchen garden. She sat for a moment on the bench with her eyes closed drinking in the early rays of winter sunshine on her face and listening to a robin singing his heart out from the top of the trellis. When she opened her eyes again, she noticed that Thomas was out on the balcony. He waved so she walked across to greet him.

'Barbara's up,' he said. 'I'm making Dad stay in his room until she's finished her breakfast. Bad luck to see the bride before the ceremony. Do you want to come up?'

Jo made her way up the spiral staircase on to the balcony and was greeted with a kiss and a quick hug.

'I'll go down, shall I? We've got the hairdressers first thing anyway and then she's changing at the cottage so it should be fairly easy to keep them apart,' she smiled. 'I guess I'll see you later then, Mr Arnaud.' She gave him a quick peck on the cheek and then descended the staircase for the kitchen below.

'Save me the first dance,' he called to her.

'Always,' she smiled back and left him to deal with his father.

Barbara was a bundle of nerves when Jo found her in the kitchen.

'I don't think I can eat anything,' she said pacing backward and forwards across the kitchen. 'I'm so nervous, I'm shaking.'

Jo went over and took both her hands in hers and spoke softly to her.

'Barbara, you love Henri, don't you?'

'Yes, more than anything.'

'And we've been through all the planning for the day, and everything is booked and in place and ready to go, yes?'

'Yes.'

'Good, let's have some breakfast together, then I'll drive us to the hairdressers because you are going to relax and enjoy your day. Ok?'

'I'm so glad you are here Jo, Thank you.'

'Now, I'll put the kettle on, while you sit down and tell me what you love most about Henri.' Jo said.

By the time the two women were dressed and ready to leave for the church, Barbara was more excited than nervous. They had decided to walk the short distance as it was dry, so arm in arm they carried their bouquets down the lane by the house and turned right towards the church gate. Jo could see the vicar waiting for them at the main door. At the gate, Jo checked Barbara's veil and gave her a kiss for luck.

'I'm so happy for you both,' Jo said. 'You are positively glowing Barbara.'

'Well, my dear, it will be your turn next. Don't look at me like that Jo, Henri and I noticed ages ago!' She laughed at Jo's surprised face. 'Come on, I think our men are waiting for us.'

Barbara went through the gate and stopped by Mary's grave. She pulled out a rose from her bouquet.

'I promise I will take great care of him, Mary,' she said, kissing the rose and laying it down on the grave. Then she followed the vicar through the main door, Jo bringing up the rear as the organ began to play.

The church had been beautifully decorated inside with Christmas greenery tied to the ends of every pew down the main isle. As she walked behind Barbara, Jo could see Henri and Thomas standing at the top of the nave both looking dapper in morning suits and red waistcoats that matched the flowers and her dress. Henri only had eyes for Barbara and dabbed at them with a hanky as she approached. Thomas, it seemed, only had eyes for Jo and they both stood grinning across the happy couple at each other when everyone rose for the exchange of vows.

After the signing of the register in the vestry, Henri and Barbara sat together at the top of the nave holding hands. Jo and Thomas sat together at the piano between the choir stalls and Thomas began to play. Jo could feel them watching and hoped that they enjoyed listening to the music as much as she enjoyed playing it. When she looked up at the end, the happy couple were both dabbing their eyes, and everyone broke out in a spontaneous round of applause. Thomas put his arm around Jo's back and whispered 'I love you' very quietly in her ear. She just turned to him and smiled.

After photographs inside the church had been taken and confetti and rice thrown outside, mostly by Ellen and Mrs West, the newlyweds were bundled into a shiny beribboned classic Rolls Royce and swept away to the reception. Thomas took Jo in his car, both glad for the peace of the journey after a hectic morning.

'Didn't Barbara look beautiful today?' sighed Jo.

'I don't know,' Thomas replied, 'I only noticed the bridesmaid. She looked pretty hot.'

'You are impossible, Thomas!' Jo laughed. 'You know she told me, before we entered the church, that they've both known about 'us' for a while.'

'Yes, Dad said a similar thing to me this morning too. I guess the cat is out of the bag then.' He glanced across at her. 'Do you still want to try and keep it quiet till after the reception?'

'I suppose we ought to, it's their wedding day. Let's not tell anyone until tomorrow. Let the gossip mill grind for one more day.'

'I'm still claiming the first dance though, it's tradition for the best man to dance with the bridesmaid anyway. Ah, here we are,' he said, turning into the hotel.

The reception was a joyous occasion, it was good to see friends old and new celebrate the marriage of two such lovely people. Alain and Marie had come over from France and Jo sat with them for a while after the speeches to catch up while the tables were cleared for the first dance.

'We have missed you this year at the chateau,' Alain said. 'The parterre is not the same without you, neither Miles tells me, are the concerts. Any chance of stealing you back?'

'Not at the moment,' she smiled. 'I think I have my hands full here currently. You will have to come around and see the garden.'

'Henri showed us lots of pictures when they visited, he couldn't stop singing your praises,' Marie said. 'Looks like you've worked hard. We have to travel back tomorrow but I'm going to persuade Alain to come and visit in the summer when everything will be at its best.'

They watched as Henri and Barbara took their places on the dance floor. The lights dimmed and the music started. Thomas came to sit next to Jo. They all clapped when they finished and then the music started again, and Thomas whirled Jo onto the floor. They had only been dancing for about thirty seconds before Henri and Barbara cut in and suggested swapping partners. Jo discovered that Henri was quite nimble on his feet.

'Thank you for everything you have done to help out with the wedding Jo,' he began. 'There is one thing that I would like to ask though, if you would indulge on old man on his wedding day.'

'What is it, Henri?'

'I know my son loves you, but do you love him, ma petite?' he said, looking her in the eyes.

'Heart and soul, Henri.'

'Good,' he sighed. 'Then I know that you will both be very happy together.'

'I hear that you had something to do with that all along,' she teased him. 'Thomas told me.'

'Well, I knew, you see, when he saw you. How could I not help my son secure the love of his life? I promised Mary, that I would help him find a love like we'd had and now I have kept that promise. You know there is so much about you that reminds me of her.'

'Thank you, Henri, I'm honoured that you feel that way. I think she would be happy about today too, don't you?'

'I know she is, I can feel her smiling,' he said.

They danced for a little while longer and then Henri and Barbara decided it was time to leave. Thomas had just had time to tie a few cans to the back of the car and stick a 'just married' sign in the back window before everybody bundled outside to wave them off, throwing more confetti and rice.

'Look after each other!' Barbara called out the car window as they drove away into the night.

It took a while for people to gradually leave after that.

'We will see you in the summer,' Marie said as she hugged Jo goodbye. 'Perhaps for another wedding?' she whispered.

'Stop matchmaking, Marie. I don't think she needs your services anymore,' Alain said, giving Jo a kiss on both cheeks.

Jo smiled but didn't say anything as she and Thomas waved them off.

When everyone had gone, Thomas and Jo loaded the car with wedding presents people had brought and headed home themselves.

Chapter 27

'Come in for a while, I feel I've hardly had you to myself for one minute today,' Thomas said, opening the front door of the main house. As soon as it was shut behind them and he had removed his jacket, tie and waistcoat and Jo her wrap, he put his arms around her. Jo undid the top two buttons of his shirt.

'Better?' she asked.

'Mm, much, thank you. We never did get our dance properly, did we? I have an idea though.'

Thomas took Jo by the hand and led her up to the studio. It was dark, but instead of switching on the main light, he led her over to the window where the moonlight made shadows of the window frames across the floor. Picking up a remote, he switched some music on. The first few notes of Handel's Air from the water music floated through the darkness. She remembered back to the summer when they had played it together in the church as a duet.

'Dance with me?' he whispered and held out his hand to her.

They danced without talking, just listening to the music and letting it speak for itself and them. Jo thought it was wonderful dancing in the dark, just moving together holding each other, knowing she was loved and being able to love in return. She had never felt like this in her entire life and knew that whatever happened next, she wanted it to be with Thomas.

'I love you Thomas,' she whispered and rested her head against him.

He held her close and kissed her hair.

'I love you too, darling girl.'

'I'm quite tired after today, do you think, perhaps, we could retire for the night? Your place or mine?'

He stopped and held her away from him to make sure that he had just heard her correctly.

She smiled shyly. 'I...er...might need some help with my... um... stockings?'

Bringing his mouth down on hers he kissed her softly at first and then more passionately. Without saying a word, he scooped her up into his arms, walked down the corridor of the landing and kicked his bedroom door open. After depositing her on the bed, he shut the door quietly behind them both.

It was blissful, having the house to themselves for a while. Thomas did not get any writing done that week, nor Jo gardening. It was only on New Year's Eve that Jo was finally persuaded out of the house by Ellen who was desperate to go shopping before returning to Nottingham the following week.

'It's fine,' Thomas assured her. 'I'll cook tonight, go and enjoy yourself for the day.'

'Trying to get rid of me already?' she joked, over a late breakfast.

'Actually, I have some important work to get done today, it might help if I'm not quite so…distracted.' He grinned wickedly at her. 'Although you are quite the loveliest distraction, and I hope to be completely distracted by you later. Shall we say dinner at six? Since it is New Year's Eve, why don't you wear your little red dress, and we'll make it a proper date?'

'What a lovely idea. Ok, six o'clock it is then,' she agreed, getting up from the table to answer the front door to Ellen.

'Do I get a goodbye kiss?' he said through a mouthful of toast after following her to the front door.

She kissed him on the cheek, and he looked thoroughly disappointed.

'Not with a mouthful of toast! See you at six,' she said and closed the door behind her.

Ellen seemed to want to go into every shop in Oxford that day, not that she bought much, Jo noted. Still, it was nice to catch up again and just talk.

'Where have Henri and Barbara gone on their honeymoon?' she asked Jo over lunch. 'If it were me, I'd go somewhere tropical like Bali or St Lucia.'

'Italy, I believe. Sienna, Rome, Sorrento. Travelling around a bit, I think. Henri asked Barbara where she would like to go so, they sat and planned out a kind of road trip of major places they wanted to see and then just booked hotels along the way. I'm sure they will have a lovely time even if it is a bit chilly.'

'Bob and I are thinking of planning a holiday next summer, if he can get the time off.'

'Things are going well between you then?'

'We seem to have a lot in common. I met his sisters before Christmas. They are very like him. Same eyes but no beards,' she said, and they both laughed. 'Thomas has got nice eyes hasn't he, I noticed he couldn't keep them off you at the wedding. Mum noticed too. In fact, I think everyone noticed.'

'Well, I suppose it had to come out at some point.'

'Did he really write that book and dedicate it to you?' Ellen asked. Jo nodded. 'That is so romantic, Jo. I would love it if Bob wrote a book for me. Sadly, I think I'm more likely to get a medical diagram.'

'Well, that could be romantic,' Jo suggested and both of them laughed so much at the thought of just what it would be a diagram of, that they had to finish their lunch quickly and leave because other customers were beginning to stare.

It was twenty-to-six by the time Ellen had finished dragging Jo around the shops and she got back to the cottage. Just enough time for a quick shower and change.

At six o'clock precisely, she let herself in to the main house. It was quiet and dark inside, no lights on at all apart from a faint glow coming from the open kitchen door.

'Thomas?' she called. There was no reply.

Jo went into the kitchen. On the table were five lit candles around a folded piece of paper. She picked it up. *Follow the lights*, was all it had written on it in Thomas' handwriting. Slightly confused, she looked around and noticed another, smaller tea light on the floor by the outside kitchen door. Cautiously, opening the door wide, she could see a trail of candles flickering gently in the evening breeze. They led to the gate that went into the garden. Making her way outside, she stood at the gate and looked across the main garden. A thousand tiny lights danced their way around the path. It was breathtakingly beautiful against the velvet softness of the dark night. Feeling that she was stepping into some enchanted paradise, Jo followed the lights on the path and found that they wove themselves into the kitchen garden, around the vegetable beds and into the greenhouse. She could see a collection of candles had been lit on the bench and made her way inside. Here there was an envelope with her name on the front. She picked it up and carefully opened it, removing the letter inside.

Darling Jo

You may be amazed to know that for a writer, I find myself at a surprising loss for words when it comes to describing all that you mean to me. They say that a soulmate is a person with whom you have an immediate connection the second you meet them and for me that person is you. From the first moment I looked into your eyes, I was lost and have only fallen in love with you more each day.

I love and adore you, heart and soul Jo. You are the life and breath in my body, my reason to rise each day and the fulfilment of my dreams at night. You have become my strength and my inspiration, and I hope to be that for you too.

Jo, I want to spend the rest of my life with you. I want to make you happy, help you fulfil your dreams. I want to bring up a family with you, watch our children grow up together, grow old together, enjoy our first grandchild together, and go through good times and bad with you by my side. Whatever happens in life, I want to be in it with you.

I love you Jo, which is why I have something especially important to ask you. Take as long as you need to think it over.

Jo, darling, will you marry me?

Forever yours
Thomas. x

It was the most beautiful letter. She had to find him. Looking around she saw that under the envelope had been another smaller piece of paper that she hadn't noticed at first. *Try the living room. T x*, it said.

Racing back around the path, oblivious to the beauty of the night, she entered the house. She could hear Thomas playing the piano. Mariage d'Amour. Catching her breath, she tiptoed to the living room door and watched him, his features illuminated by the light of a single candle on the piano. He saw her in the doorway, smiled and continued to play. She walked over to the piano and leant against it waiting for him to finish, never taking her eyes from him.

'This is for you,' he said when he had played the last note, reaching into his pocket, and taking out a small velvet box which he put on the top of the piano.

Jo picked it up and opened it. Inside was a small, folded piece of paper. She unfolded it and read the word he had written. 'Forever?'

She was in his arms in an instant then.

'Yes, absolutely, one hundred percent, yes!' she said before she kissed him.

'You might like this then,' he grinned, reaching into his pocket again and bringing out the most beautiful diamond ring Jo had ever seen. He slipped it on her finger and, bringing her hand to his lips, he kissed it and then her.

'So, this was your important work you had to get done today,' she said as she sat on his lap on the piano stool.

'Yes, although I did have a little help,' he confessed. 'Bob helped me with the candles, and I had to ask Ellen to take you shopping for the day to get you out the house and keep you out until it was nearly six.'

'I wondered why we went into every shop in town,' she laughed. 'Did they know that you were going to propose?'

'No, just that I was planning a surprise. Did you like the letter?'

'It was the most beautiful thing I've ever read. I'm going to frame it and put it on the wall in our bedroom so I can read it every day. I suppose we will have to start planning another wedding now.'

'Let's not wait too long,' he said. 'How about early summer?'

'Sounds perfect,' she said and kissed him again.

The marriage of Josephine Stanton and Thomas Arnaud took place in June the following year at the church in the village of Oxbury. Jo had asked Henri to give her away and, as they waited at the door of the church for the music to start, he turned to her.

'Welcome to the family again, ma petite. I couldn't have wished for a better wife for my son than you. You have made both Barbara and me very happy.'

She lifted her veil and kissed him on the cheek.

'Nor could I have wished for a better father-in-law, thank you Henri, for helping to bring us together in the first place, I promise to love him always.'

'I know you will. Shall we?' he said as the organ began.

The happy couple walked to their reception venue after the service. A marquee on the lawn in the middle of the garden Jo had restored to life. It seemed fitting to them both to celebrate here with friends and family; it was a place where their love for each other had grown and blossomed. This time of the year the garden was at its best, Jo had worked hard that spring to make sure it would be. Roses bloomed along the high wall around the garden, the lavender was a haze of purple and the clematis had reached its winding stems to the top of the trellis, its star-like flowers open to face the sun.

After the speeches, Thomas took Jo in his arms for their first dance.

'I love you Mrs Arnaud,' he whispered into her ear as they danced together.

'And I love you, Mr Arnaud, with all my heart. Are you going to tell me where we are going on our honeymoon now?'

'Well, I know a lovely little motel in St Malo…' he began but couldn't help laughing when she pulled a face.

'Don't you dare! Seriously, where are we going?'

'Wait and see,' was all he said and refused to be drawn further.

As more people joined in the dancing and the reception progressed into the evening hours, Thomas drew Jo aside and took her up to the studio via the balcony.

'I thought we might grab a minute to ourselves, I've something I want to give you. It's not quite finished, and it still needs editing.'

He handed her a large brown envelope. Jo slipped out the contents. It was a manuscript. 'A letter from France by T. Arnaud' the front page declared. She looked up at him amazed, and then sat down in the swivel chair at the desk and opened the first page. There was a dedication: '*To my wife Jo, with all my love.*'

'Oh, Thomas, thank you. I didn't know you had finished another book. What is it about?'

'I'll let you read it for yourself, but let's just say it's generally about a man who owns a small nursery in France and writes the most beautiful letters to the girl he intends to marry.' He looked at her lovingly.

'You used my grandparents' letters? I can't wait to read it.' She was out of the chair now and putting the manuscript carefully on the desk, wrapped her arms around her husband. 'I will bring it with me on our honeymoon.'

'You can bring it with you on our honeymoon if you like, but I don't intend on giving you much reading time, Mrs Arnaud,' he said, kissing her thoroughly.

It was with some trepidation that Jo found herself arriving at the Dover ferry terminal early the next day. Thomas handed her a small box.

'You might need these. Sorry,' he said, looking apologetically at her. 'It was the shortest crossing I could find.'

She looked at the box. Travel sickness pills. This was not going to be the best start to her honeymoon.

However, the crossing was short, and the sea calm. Jo managed to keep her breakfast down, even though she spent the entire sailing out on the deck just in case. Thomas never left her side for a moment.

'I'm so glad that bit of the journey is over,' she sighed as they headed south in the car. 'Are you going to tell me our final destination, now I know which country we are in?'

'Not yet, in fact, I need you to wear this from now on.' He tossed her a blindfold across the car.

'Seriously?'

'Seriously. I want to surprise you. Trust me?' he grinned.

'I suppose I shall have to, seeing as I have only just vowed that I would,' she said, putting the blind fold on. 'I might have a little sleep then since I can't do much else. Wake me up when we get there.' Jo rested her head back and closed her eyes under the blindfold.

She was woken a few hours later by Thomas rubbing her leg.

'Wake up sleepy, we're here,' he said. 'Don't take the blindfold off yet. I'm going to help you out the car first. Ok?'

Swinging her legs round, he helped her out the car and shut the door after her.

'Just a few steps more,' he said, leading her gently by the hand. 'Now hold out your hand.'

She did as instructed, and he dropped something into it. It felt like a key. He lifted the blindfold from her eyes. Momentarily, the bright afternoon sun blinded her. Then she looked at the key in her hand and the door in front of her. She knew it instantly. She had lived here on and off nearly all of her life.

'You rented Grand-mere's house for our honeymoon?' she gasped.

'Not quite,' he said, grinning.

She looked confused. He wrapped his arms around her from behind and they both stood looking at the house in front of them. It hadn't changed a bit.

'You know I said I would prove to you that love at first sight exists?'

'Mm?'

'Well, I have a little confession to make. I bought the house from you when you had to sell it. I'm afraid I coerced the estate agent into telling you a fib about it being bought by a property developer. It was me. I knew you loved it here, and I thought one day I would give it back to you, as a wedding present.'

Jo stood utterly speechless for a few moments taking in what he had said. He took the key from her hand and opened the front door.

'Alain and Marie have been looking after it for us. I haven't changed the inside at all. Everything is as you left it. You can redecorate in time, or not, as you like.'

She went to go in, but he held up his hand and stopped her. Picking her up, he carried her over the threshold and into the front room. It smelt of lavender and of a time long ago when she had been happy.

'Welcome home, Mrs Arnaud,' he said and kissed her.

'You are the best husband a girl could ever have Thomas Arnaud,' she said as the tears began to flow. 'I believe you; love at first sight really does exist.'

Ingram Content Group UK Ltd.
Milton Keynes UK
UKHW020354210623
423772UK00005B/80